THE G FILE

Håkan Nesser is one of Sweden's most popular
crime writers, receiving numerous awards for his novels
featuring Inspector Van Veeteren, including the European
Crime Fiction Star Award (Ripper Award) 2010/11, the
Swedish Crime Writers' Academy Prize (three times)
and Scandinavia's Glass Key Award. The Van Veeteren
series is published in over 25 countries and has sold
over 10 million copies worldwide. Håkan Nesser
lives in Gotland with his wife, and spends
part of each year in the UK.

HÅKAN NESSER

THE G FILE

A VAN VEETEREN MYSTERY

Translated from the Swedish by
Laurie Thompson

MANTLE

First published in Great Britain 2014 by Mantle
an imprint of Pan Macmillan, a division of Macmillan Publishers Limited
Pan Macmillan, 20 New Wharf Road, London N1 9RR
Basingstoke and Oxford
Associated companies throughout the world
www.panmacmillan.com

ISBN 978-1-4472-5934-3

Originally published in 2003 as *Fallet G* by
Albert Bonniers förlag, Stockholm.

1 3 5 7 9 8 6 4 2

A CIP catalogue record for this book is available from the British Library.

Typeset by Ellipsis Digital Limited, Glasgow
Printed and bound by CPI Group (UK) Ltd, Croydon, CR0 4YY

Visit **www.panmacmillan.com** to read more about all our books
and to buy them. You will also find features, author interviews and
news of any author events, and you can sign up for e-newsletters
so that you're always first to hear about our new releases.

Anyone walking along a beach
sooner or later meets somebody else.

Unknown

1987

She knew that she would wet the bed during the night, and she knew Auntie Peggy would be angry.

It was always the same. Whenever she had to sleep at Auntie Peggy's instead of with her own mother, that's what happened.

Mami. She wanted to be with Mami. To sleep in her own bed in her own room with her doll Trudi under the duvet and her doll Bamba under her pillow. That's what ought to happen; and when it did happen and she fell asleep with the lovely smell of Mami in her nostrils, her bed was never wet when she woke up. Well, hardly ever.

Auntie Peggy didn't smell anything like Mami. She didn't want Auntie Peggy to touch her – and thank goodness, she didn't do. But they slept in the same room, separated by a big blue curtain with splashes of red and some sort of dragon pattern, or maybe it was snakes; and sometimes other people slept there as well. She didn't like it.

Neither did Trudi and Bamba. When they slept at Auntie Peggy's, Trudi had to sleep under the pillow as well, so she didn't get any pee on her. It was cramped and awkward – but obviously she couldn't leave her dolls at home as Mami had suggested. Sometimes Mami could come out with the most ridiculous things.

One week, for instance, she had said: You can stay with Auntie

Peggy for a week – I have to be away in order to earn lots of money. When I get back you'll have a new dress and as much ice cream and goodies as you can eat.

A week was a lot of days. She didn't know how many, but it was more than three and all that time she would have to sleep in that awful room with cars and buses driving past in the street all night long, hooting and braking and rattling non-stop. She would wet the bed, and Auntie Peggy wouldn't bother to change the sheets, just hang them over the back of a chair to dry during the day – and Trudi and Bamba would be so sad, so very sad, that it simply wasn't possible to console them, no matter how hard she tried.

I don't want to be with that awful Auntie Peggy, she thought. *I wish Auntie Peggy was dead. If I pray to God and ask Him to take her away and if He does that, I promise not to pee a single drop all night long: and when Mami comes to collect me next morning and takes me home, I won't need to be here ever again. Never ever.*

Do you hear me, God? Please send Mami back to me, and take away all the pee and Auntie Peggy. Kill her, or put her on an aeroplane to Never-Never Land.

She clasped her hands so tightly that her fingers hurt; and Trudi and Bamba prayed along with her as ardently as they possibly could. Perhaps things would turn out as she wished, despite everything.

1

On his way to work on Wednesday, 3 June, Private Detective Maarten Verlangen bought six cans of beer and six new vacuum-cleaner bags.

The first-named purchase was routine, but the second was exceptional. Not since Martha left him five years ago had his cleaning ambitions soared to such heights, and it was with a slightly unfamiliar feeling of a good conscience that he unlocked the steel door, treated with anti-corrosive paint, and occupied his office.

It was easily done. The room measured four by four by four metres, and no architect the world over would have dreamt of writing the word 'office space' on the plans. It was in one of the filthy old tenement houses at the far end of Armastenstraat, next to the railway line, and half a flight of stairs lower than the entrance to the building. It had presumably been intended from the start to be a sort of storeroom for the caretaker – a space where odds and ends needed by the tenants could be kept: spare lavatory furniture, shower hoses, hotplates and other utensils that frequently need replacing.

But now it was an office. Albeit scarcely a fashionable one.

The walls had been covered from the start in dirty, earth-coloured plaster, the floor had been painted dark blue some twenty or thirty years ago, and the only source of natural light was a small sort of porthole at street level, i.e. just below the ceiling. The furniture was simple and functional: a desk and a desk chair. A grey filing cabinet made of sheet steel, a low bookcase, a buzzing 1950s refrigerator, a kettle and a threadbare visitor chair. Hanging on one wall was a calendar advertising a petrol station, and on another a repro-duction of a gloomy Piranesi lithograph. The other two walls were bare.

Apart from the calendar, which Verlangen changed with the precision of a sleepwalker every year at the end of January or the beginning of February, the office looked exactly the same as it had done for the last four years. Ever since he had moved in, in other words. One should never underestimate the ability of one's surroundings to provide one with stability and security, he used to tell himself. One should not despise the dust that the years deposit on our shoulders.

He switched on the ceiling light as the desk lamp was broken, hung up his light windcheater on a hook on the back of the door, and put the beers into the refrigerator.

He sat down on the desk chair and put the vacuum-cleaner bags in the top right-hand drawer of his desk. He had no intention of using them in the office, certainly not. The Melfi vacuum-cleaner he owned – one of the very few items he had retained after the divorce, possibly because it worked about as badly as his marriage had done – was in his flat in Heer-banerstraat. That was where he intended doing the vacuum-cleaning. That was where the limit had been reached. He wondered whether he ought to leave the bags out on the desk: if he put them away there was a risk that they would be forgotten and left in the drawer when he went home after work, but he decided to take that risk. Vacuum-cleaner bags were not among the items a client expected to see in the office of a private detective of repute.

Verlangen's Detective Agency. That is what it said on a simple but neat and tidy plate on the office door. He had made it himself and enclosed it in a plastic cover: it had taken him a whole morning, but the result didn't look too bad at all.

He consulted his timetable for the day. He was due to attend a meeting at the insurance company in the afternoon, but that was all. He checked to make sure that there were no messages on the telephone answering machine, then took out a beer from the refrigerator and lit a cigarette.

He checked the clock: ten minutes past ten.

If I don't have a client before noon, I'll treat myself to a slap-up lunch at Oldener Maas, then shoot myself in the head, he thought and smiled grimly to himself.

It was a thought that came to him every morning, and one of these days he might actually do it. He was forty-seven years old, and the number of people who would miss him could be counted on the thumb of one hand.

She was called Belle, and was his daughter. Seventeen, almost eighteen. He contemplated her laughing face in the photograph next to the telephone directory, and took another swig of beer. Blinked away the tears that the bitter taste had brought to his eyes, and belched loudly.

How come that a swine like me could have a daughter like her? he wondered.

That was also a frequently recurring thought. Quite a lot of things kept coming back into Maarten Verlangen's brain. Especially old, complicated questions that were impossible to answer. In occasional moments of clarity, this was a fact that could scare the life out of him.

But there was a remedy for fears that struck in moments of clarity. Luckily. He took another swig of beer and inhaled deeply on his cigarette. Stood up and opened the window. And sat down.

It was now thirteen minutes past ten.

She rang shortly before eleven o'clock, and turned up half an hour later.

Quite a tall woman aged about thirty-five. Auburn, shoulder-length hair. A narrow face with high cheekbones and delicate features. Slim and shapely, with strikingly prominent breasts. She was wearing well-fitting black trousers and a wine-red blouse with very short sleeves. Neatly plucked eyebrows. He thought she was beautiful.

She glanced quickly around the room. Paused for a moment when she registered the Piranesi print before finally focusing on Verlangen's melancholy physiognomy.

'Do you mind if we speak English?'

Verlangen explained that he hadn't forgotten the language during the thirty minutes that had passed since they spoke on the telephone. There was a trace of a smile on her face as she settled down on the visitor chair. She crossed her legs and cleared her throat. Verlangen offered her a cigarette, but she shook her head and instead produced a packet of Gauloises from her red handbag and lit one with an elegant little gold lighter.

'So you are a private detective, are you?'

Verlangen nodded.

'There are not so many of those about nowadays, I gather?'

'There are a few.'

'Only five here in Maardam.'

'How do you know that?'

'I checked the telephone directory.'

'I don't suppose they're all in there.'

'Really? That's where I found you anyhow.'

Verlangen shrugged. Noted that she had a small tattoo at the top of her left arm, just underneath the edge of her blouse sleeve. It looked like a swallow. Some kind of bird, at least.

He also noted that she was a little sunburnt. She must have been soaking up quite a lot of sun already, he thought, despite the fact that it's only the beginning of June. Her skin had a pleasant tone reminiscent of café au lait: he wondered what it would be like stroking it with the tips of his fingers.

But then again, perhaps she was just one of those solarium chicks?

'What would you like me to help you with?' he asked.

'I'd like you to keep an eye on somebody.'

'Keep an eye on somebody?'

'Or whatever you call it. I take it that's one of the things you do?'

'Of course. And who is it you'd like me to keep an eye on?'

'My husband.'

'Your husband?'

'Yes. I want you to keep an eye on him for me, for a few days.'

'I see.'

He turned to a new page in his notebook and clicked his ballpoint pen a couple of times.

'So what's your name, if I might ask?'

She had declined to give her name over the telephone, and hadn't introduced herself when she came to his office. She seemed to hesitate for a moment now as well, as she took a drag of her cigarette.

'Barbara Hennan.'

Verlangen noted it down.

'I'm American. My maiden name is Delgado. I'm married to Jaan G. Hennan.'

He had written as far as the middle initial before pausing.

Jaan G.? he thought. Good Lord! *Jaan G. Hennan.*

'We've only been living in this country for a couple of months – although my husband comes from Maardam originally. We're renting a house out at Linden . . . Thirty kilometres from here – I take it you know where it is?'

'Yes, of course.'

Could there be several people called Jaan G. Hennan? Maybe. But what were the odds against this being one of the others? And how? . . .

'How much do you charge?'

'That depends.'

'Depends on what?'

'The kind of work involved. The time it takes. The costs incurred . . .'

'I want you to keep an eye on my husband for a few days. From morning till night. You won't have time to undertake any other work.'

'Why do you want him kept under observation?'

'I'm not going to go into that. All I want is for you to check what he gets up to, and then report back to me. Okay?'

She raised an eyebrow and looked even more beautiful.

Classic, he thought. I'll be damned if this isn't a classic case. It wasn't often that he felt like Philip Marlowe – not while he was sober, at least. Perhaps he ought to suck away at this sweetie for as long as it lasted . . .

'It's not exactly an unusual commission,' he said. 'But I do have a number of questions.'

'Let's hear them.'

'Distance and discretion, for instance.'

'Distance and what . . . ?'

'How much detail do you want? If he goes to a restaurant, for instance, do you want to know what he eats, who he talks to, what they say . . . ?'

She interrupted him by raising her left hand a few centimetres over the table. The swallow wiggled rather sensually.

'I understand what you're saying. It will be sufficient if you tell me what happens in broad outline. If I think any particular circumstances seem to be especially interesting, perhaps I can let you know?'

'Of course. You are the one who makes the rules. And I assume he is not to know that I'm keeping an eye on him?'

She hesitated again.

'Preferably not.'

'Might I ask what your husband does for a living?'

'Business. He runs an import company. Only just started, of course . . . But he did something similar in Denver.'

'Importing what?'

She shrugged.

'All kinds of things. Computer components, for instance. What does it matter what my husband does for a living? All I want is for you to keep an eye on what he's up to.'

Verlangen clasped his hands on the table in front of him, and paused briefly.

'Fru Hennan,' he said in a tone of voice that he hoped would be interpreted as incorporating masculine firmness, 'might I draw your attention to the fact that I haven't yet accepted your commission. You want me to keep your husband under observation, and if I agree to do that I must know exactly what I'm letting myself in for. I'm not in the habit of jumping into whatever comes along with my eyes closed – you wouldn't last long in my profession if you did that.'

She frowned. He could see that the possibility of him turning her down had never occurred to her.

'I understand,' she said. 'Forgive me. But I assume you are used to acting with a certain degree of . . . discretion?'

'Of course. Within reasonable limits. But without a knowledge of certain facts I simply can't do what you want me to do in a satisfactory way. I have to know a little about your husband's habits. What he does in a normal working day. The places he goes to, the people he meets. And so on. Most of all, of course, I would like to know what is behind all this – why you want to have him kept under observation: but I suppose I could do without that information.'

She made a vague movement of her head from right to left, and looked again at the Piranesi print for a few seconds.

'Okay, obviously I respect your professional code of practice. As far as his routines are concerned, they are not exactly complicated. As I said, we live in that house out at Linden. He has his office in the centre of Maardam, and he spends six or seven hours there every day. We sometimes have lunch together, if I happen to be in town for some reason or other. I usually prepare the evening meal for seven o'clock, but occasionally he has dinner with business contacts . . . We don't have many social contacts – we've only been living here for a couple of months, after all. Anyway, that's about it in broad outline. Weekends are obviously rather different – we're usually together all the time, and so I won't need your services then.'

Verlangen had been making copious notes as she spoke, but now he scratched the back of his neck as he looked up.

'What social contacts do you have, in fact?'

She dug out another cigarette.

'None at all, really. Obviously my husband meets various people in connection with his work, but I only ever come into contact with the Trottas, if you can call it that . . . They are our nearest neighbours – a pair of utter bores, to be honest, but we have at least had dinner together in both our houses. He's a pilot, she's a housewife. They have a couple of insufferable children as well.'

'Trotta?'

'Yes.'

Verlangen made a note of the name.

'Photo?' he asked. 'I must have a photograph of your husband.'

She produced a white envelope from her handbag and handed it over. He took out two photographs, both of them 10x15 centimetres.

Jaan G. Hennan stared him in the eye.

Ten years later, but still the same Jaan G., no doubt about that. The photographs seemed to have been taken very recently, probably on the same reel, and both of them in profile – one from the right, the other from the left. The same deep-set eyes. The same austere lips and firm jaw. The same close-cropped dark hair. He put the photographs back into the envelope.

'All right,' he said. 'I'll do it. Assuming that we can agree on details, of course.'

'What details?'

'Time. Method. Payment.'

She nodded.

'Just for a few days, as I said. No more than a couple of weeks in any case. If you could start tomorrow, I'd be grateful . . . What do you mean by "method"?'

'Twenty-four hours a day or just twelve? The degree of

discretion or intrusion – the kind of thing I mentioned earlier.'

She inhaled and blew out a thin stream of smoke as she pondered. Just for a moment he had the feeling that she didn't normally smoke at all, and had just bought a packet of Gauloises to make an impression on him. Some sort of impression.

'Whenever he's not at home,' she decided. 'That will be sufficient. From the moment he sets off in the morning until he comes back home – either early or late in the evening.'

'And you don't want him to notice me.'

There was another brief pause, and he registered that she still hadn't quite made up her mind on that point.

'No,' she said. 'Don't let him see you. If I change my mind about that I'll let you know. How much do I have to pay?'

He pretended to think about that, and wrote down a few figures in his notebook.

'Three hundred guilders per day, plus any expenses.'

That did not seem to worry her.

'Payment for three days in advance. I might have to rent a room in Linden as well . . . When do you want me to report to you?'

'Once a day,' she said without hesitation. 'I'd like you to ring me every day at some time during the morning. I'm always at home in the mornings. If I think it seems necessary, we can meet – but I hope it won't come to that.'

Verlangen had another 'why?' on the tip of his tongue, but he managed to swallow it.

'Okay,' he said instead, leaning back on his chair. 'I take it that we are in agreement. If you can give me your address and telephone number, I can start tomorrow morning . . . And I need the advance, of course.'

She took out a dark-red purse and produced two five-hundred-guilder notes. And a business card.

'A thousand,' she said. 'Let's round it up to a thousand for the time being.'

He took the money and the card. She stood up and reached out her hand over his desk.

'Thank you, herr Verlangen. I'm very grateful that you could take on this job. It will . . . It will make my life easier.'

Will it really? he thought as he shook her hand. How? She was looking him straight in the eye for a long fraction of a second, and he wondered once again what it would feel like to touch some other part of her body than the firm and pleasantly cool palm of her hand.

'I shall do my best,' he promised.

She smiled, turned on her heel and left his office.

He remained standing, listening to her footsteps as she walked up the stairs. It almost felt as if he were waiting for some sort of curtain to fall.

Then he opened the refrigerator and took out a beer.

2

The moment he opened the door of his cramped little flat in Heerbanerstraat he realized that the vacuum-cleaner bags were still in the drawer of his desk in the office.

On the other hand, not a single one of the beer cans was left in the refrigerator. You win some and you lose some . . .

So his cleaning intentions would have to be put on ice: but one lost day was neither here nor there, of course. The smell of old, stuffy dirt and the stench of something stale which was presumably the mould underneath the bathtub, struck him as a sort of 'welcome home' greeting. One shouldn't simply shrug off old habits and sell off the things that make you feel safe and secure just for the sake of it. Dust and dirt should not be held in contempt . . .

There was a pile of advertising leaflets and two bills on the floor underneath the letter slot. He picked it all up and threw it onto the basket chair, which was full of similar stuff. My home is my castle, he thought as he opened the balcony door, then turned back to observe the devastation. He contemplated the unmade bed, the unwashed dirty crockery and the rest of the chaotic mess. Switched off the stereo equipment, which must have been on for at least twenty-four hours.

Noted that the right-hand loudspeaker was broken, and that he ought to do something about it.

Then he went into the bathroom, glanced at the filthy mirror and confirmed that he looked about ten years older than he had looked that morning.

Why do I bother to go on living? he wondered as he stepped into the shower and switched on the water.

And why do I keep on asking myself these optimistic questions, day in and day out?

An hour later it was eight o'clock and he had washed up three days' worth of dirty dishes. He flopped down in front of the television and watched the first ten minutes of the news. The murder of a policeman in Groenstadt and a ministerial meeting in Berlin in connection with unrest in the financial markets. A mad swan that had caused a pile-up on the motorway outside Saaren. He switched off and telephoned his daughter.

She was not at home, and so he was obliged to exchange a few pleasantries with his ex-wife's new boyfriend instead. It took half a minute, and afterwards he was able to congratulate himself on not having sworn a single time. Two cheers.

There were four beers in the fridge and a bottle of mineral water. He made a sandwich with salami, cheese and cucumber – but with no butter as he had forgotten to buy any – and after a brief inner struggle he selected the water. Sat down on the sofa again, took out his notepad and read what he had written.

Barbara Hennan. The beautiful American woman.

Maiden name Delgado, but now Hennan – thanks to having married that bastard Jaan G. Hennan. For some damned reason.

G, he thought. Why on earth pick G when there was a whole world of men to choose from?

And why the hell should he, Maarten Baudewijn Verlangen, have to spend what little time he had on something so bloody stupid as shadowing Jaan G. Hennan? The man he – more or less on his own – had made sure was placed under lock and key some . . . yes, it was almost exactly twelve years ago, he decided after some rapid mental calculations. The end of May 1975. While he was still working as a respectable police officer.

While he still had a proper job, a family, and a right to look at himself in the mirror without averting his gaze.

While he still had a future.

It was at the beginning of the 1980s that it all went to pot. 1981–2. Buying that house out at Dikken. All the arguments with Martha. Their love life simply shrivelling up like . . . like a worn-out condom.

The bribes. The sudden opportunity of earning a bit extra on the side by turning a blind eye to things. Not just a bit extra, in fact. Without the extra income they would never have been able to afford the interest and mortgage payments on the house. He had tried to explain that to Martha afterwards, after he had been caught out and his world had collapsed. But she had just shaken her head and snorted.

What about that lady? she had wondered. In what way had

it been necessary for the preservation of their marriage for him to spend so many nights with her? Could he kindly explain that to her?

No, he couldn't.

Five years, he thought. It's five years since the world collapsed, and I'm still alive.

Just occasionally there were now moments when that didn't surprise him any more.

He gulped down the rest of the water and went to fetch a beer. Moved over to the armchair with the reading lamp, and leaned back.

Barbara Hennan, he thought, and closed his eyes.

How the hell could such a beautiful woman become involved with an arsehole like G?

It was a riddle, to be sure, but not a new one. Women's judgement when it came to men had backfired before in the history of the world. Gone astray when confronted by rampant stags in rut amidst the superficial values of everyday life. He dug out the photographs and studied them for a while with a degree of distaste.

Why? he wondered. Why does she want me to keep an eye on him?

Was there more than one answer? More than one possibility?

He didn't think so. It was the same old story, of course. The unfaithful husband and the jealous wife. Who wanted proof. Evidence of his betrayal in black and white.

Maarten Verlangen had spent four years playing this game by now, and he reckoned that about two-thirds of his work was of this nature.

If he excluded the work he did for the insurance company, that is: but that aspect of his work was not really a part of his sleuthing activities. It was rather different. The insurance company Trustor had wanted a sort of detective who could investigate irregularities using somewhat unorthodox methods – and what could possibly be more appropriate in the circumstances than a police officer who had been sacked – or rather, *had chosen to leave the force rather than be hanged in a public place*. A gentleman's agreement. There had been no question of a formal appointment; but as time went by there had been a commission here and another commission there – usually resolved to the advantage of the company – and so their cooperation had continued. When Verlangen occasionally checked his somewhat less than prodigious income, he concluded that it was about fifty–fifty: roughly half came from the insurance company, and half from his sleuthing activities.

He lit a cigarette – the day's fortieth or thereabouts – and tried once again to conjure up the American woman in his mind's eye. Fru Barbara Hennan. Thirty-seven or thirty-eight? She could hardly be any older than that. At least ten years younger than her husband, in other words.

And ten times more desirable. No, not ten times. Ten thousand times. Why on earth would anybody want to be unfaithful if they had a woman like Barbara? Incomprehensible.

He inhaled a few times, and thought the matter over. Was it really all that likely that it was the same old story, the same old motive? Had Barbara Hennan née Delgado come to him because she suspected her husband was having an affair with another woman? After only a few months in the new country?

Or was there some other reason? – In which case, what?

He would have liked to ask her straight out – he had been on the point of doing so several times during their conversation, and he didn't usually beat about the bush in such circumstances. But something had held him back.

Perhaps he hadn't wanted to embarrass her. But perhaps there were other reasons as well.

Just what they might be was something he couldn't be sure about. Not then, when she had been sitting on the other side of the table; and not now, as he sat there in his cramped and stuffy lair, trying to think things over and work out a strategy.

A strategy? he thought. Rubbish. I don't need a strategy. I'll drive there tomorrow morning. Sit in my car outside his office all day, staring at him. Smoking myself to death. Given the extent to which I've grown older, there's no chance of him recognizing me.

This is an easy job. A classic. If it was a film, the building would no doubt blow up at about half past four.

He drank the rest of the beer, and wondered if he should allow himself another one before going to bed. During the course of the day he had drunk eight. That was close to the maximum – which was ten – but why not allow himself the luxury of a clear conscience for once?

Two still to go? Somewhere deep down inside him, of course, a voice was whispering somewhat pitifully that ten beers a day wasn't a deal that was beyond discussion. But what the hell, he thought. Everything is relative apart from death and the anger of a fat woman. So what?

He had read that last thought somewhere. Quite a long time ago, in the days when he could remember what he had read in books.

He belched, and stubbed out the last cigarette of the day. Did what was necessary in the bathroom in just over a minute, then wriggled his way into his unmade bed. His pillow smelt vaguely of something unpleasant – unwashed hair perhaps, or sadness, or something of that sort. Turning it over didn't help matters.

He set the alarm clock for half past six, and switched off the light.

Linden? he thought. If I book a room in a hotel, at least I won't have to sleep in dirty sheets for a few nights.

Five minutes later Maarten Baudewijn Verlangen was snoring, with his mouth open wide.

3

Belle rang next morning just as he was coming out of the shower. As usual, the very sound of her voice set something alight in his chest. A spark of paternal pride.

Apart from that, the call did not give him much cause to be cheerful. They had more or less agreed to meet at the weekend. To spend a day together. Possibly two. He had been looking forward to it – in the grimly reserved way he ever dared to look forward to things nowadays: but she had now been invited along on a boat trip out to the islands instead. So if he didn't mind . . . ?

He didn't mind. Who was he to begrudge a seventeen-year-old daughter he loved more than anything else in the world the opportunity of going on a boat trip with like-minded friends – instead of having to trudge around with an overweight, prematurely grey-haired and frequently drunk old fart of a father? God forbid.

'Are you sure?' she wondered. 'You're sure you won't be upset? Maybe we can meet up next weekend?'

'Quite sure,' he assured her. And he claimed that strictly speaking, next weekend would be better for him as well. He had rather a lot of work to get through at present.

Maybe she believed him. She wasn't all that old yet.

She sent him a kiss down the line, then hung up. He swallowed to remove a small lump from his throat, and blinked away a trace of dampness from his eyes. Went down to the corner shop to buy the *Allgemejne*. Have your breakfast and read the paper, you big softie! he told himself.

And that is exactly what he did.

He was at Aldemarckt in Linden by a few minutes past nine, and a quarter of an hour later he had found his way to Kammerweg. He parked diagonally opposite Villa Zefyr, wound down the side window and settled down to wait.

Linden was not much more than a small provincial town – round about twenty or thirty thousand people. A few small industries. Quite a well-known brewery, a church from the early thirteenth century, and housing estates that mainly sprang up after the war – little family houses and occasional blocks of flats, within easy commuting distance of Maardam. He recalled having met a girl from Linden when he was a teenager: she was cool and pretty, but he had never dared kiss her. She was called Margarita. He wondered what had become of her.

But there wasn't much more to Linden than that. The sluggish little beck Megel – no doubt also cool and pretty, and if he remembered rightly a tributary of the River Maar – meandered its way through the town and then over the plains to the north-west. To the south of the beck was a ridge, and that was the location of Kammerweg – a good four kilometres from the centre of Linden with a town hall, a police station, a square, and all the trimmings of civilized living. Plus that thirteenth-century church.

And a brewery – he began to feel thirsty.

Verlangen sighed, put on his dark glasses although the sun had not yet succeeded in breaking through the greyish-white clouds, and lit a cigarette. Gazed at the house, which could only just be made out behind the rows of trees and flowering shrubs that had been planted alongside the street precisely to prevent passers-by from peering in, and tried to assess its market value.

Not less than a million, he decided. Probably not even less than one-and-a-half. Mind you, they were only renting it, if he had understood fru Hennan correctly.

The situation was ideal in many respects. A large plot with some kind of woods or overgrown park at one end, and another plot at least as big at the other end, with a house that was also half hidden among greenery. He guessed that must be where the Trottas lived – the pilot family with the awful children – but you can never tell for certain.

On the side of the street where he was parked there were no buildings at all, just a steep slope down to an asphalted cycle path alongside the beck into town.

Rather splendid isolation, in fact, decided Verlangen with an involuntary stab of envy. The Hennan house that he could just about see in among the greenery was pale blue – not the prettiest colour he had even seen, but what the hell? His own forty-five-square-metre flat contained more glaring nuances than Kandinsky could ever have dreamt of . . . And just to the right of the house was a clinically white diving tower – or at least, that's what he thought it must be.

So they had a swimming pool as well. And why not a tennis court and a sizeable cocktail terrace round the back? He couldn't help wondering how easy it might be to torch the whole set-up – preferably with G surrounded by flames on all sides while the private dick played the hero and rescued the young wife, carrying her over his shoulder to safety. But he was forced to cut short all such thoughts when a shiny blue Saab glided slowly out between the two black granite pillars that marked the entrance to the drive of the house. They stood there like two immobile but well-dressed and somewhat ominous lackeys, making no attempt to hide their silent disapproval of any unwelcome visitors.

The only occupant was the male driver, and Verlangen had no doubt that it was none other than Jaan G. Hennan himself – despite the fact that he only had a very vague impression of him.

Who else could it possibly have been? Surely one could take it for granted that Barbara Hennan had given Verlangen the correct address . . .

He gave the Saab a fifty-metre start, then switched on the engine of his faithful old Toyota and began tailing him.

A classic set-up, he thought with an intentional lack of emotion.

Hennan parked in one of the narrow alleys behind the church, then walked the hundred or so metres down towards the square and vanished through the main entrance of a three-storey block of shops and offices of typical beige-coloured fifties design. Verlangen managed to squeeze his Toyota into a cramped space on the other side of the street. Switched off the engine, lit another cigarette and wound down the window again.

He fixed his gaze on the row of featureless rectangular windows in the storey above the ground-floor shops – a shoe shop, an undertaker's, a butcher's.

After a couple of minutes one of the windows over the undertaker's opened: Jaan G. Hennan leaned out and emptied half a cup of coffee onto the pavement below. Then closed the window.

Typical, Verlangen thought. Born a bastard, always a bastard. He didn't even bother to look down and see if he might be pouring the coffee onto a passer-by.

He adjusted the back of his seat so that he could lean back in comfort, took out the sport section of the *Allgemejne* and checked his watch. A quarter to ten.

So there we are, then, he thought. Out working again.

When he had read even the obituaries for the second time and smoked about ten cigarettes, Verlangen began to regret his decision to have an alcohol-free day.

It was twenty minutes past eleven, and he reconsidered his position and adjusted his abstinence to the morning. Surely he could allow himself a couple of beers with his lunch – always assuming he had any lunch – after enduring these blue-grey hours keeping an eye on his suspect. It would be as boring as meditations in a Buddhist monastery. A good friend of Verlangen's had gone off on one of those jaunts a few years ago. Tibet or Nepal, or some such bloody place . . .

Hennan was also more or less invisible. He had appeared once more in the window, but that was all. Stood motion-less for a few seconds, staring up at the clouds as if he were thinking hard about something. Or perhaps just suffered a minor stroke. Then he had turned away and vanished from Verlangen's horizon.

His prey. The object of his surveillance. The reason why Verlangen was sitting around here in his worn-out Japanese oven of a car frittering away his worn-out life for three hun-dred guilders a day. Carpe diem, my arse.

He returned to thinking about Hennan. The impressions he had registered of him – not very màny, to be sure – during the preliminary investigation into his crimes a dozen years ago.

The actual process had been quite painless. Once a few underlings had been pressurized into starting talking, the proof of Jaan G. Hennan's misdeeds had been overwhelming. Over a number of years he had bought and sold cannabis, heroin and amphetamines via couriers, built up an efficient network and had probably tucked away a million or two – especially in view of the fact that he seemed not to have been a drug user himself.

Not an especially remarkable story, in other words, but it was mainly thanks to the assiduous efforts of Verlangen and his colleague Müller that the case had been successfully concluded. That G had got what he deserved – two years and six months – and that as a result it was presumably highly unlikely that they – G and Verlangen – would ever exchange birthday or Christmas cards. Not even if they lived for another five hundred years.

He recalled Hennan's ice-cold, almost personal contempt during the interrogations. His unreasonable refusal to ascribe any kind of moral aspects to his dirty work. 'There's no space inside G for morals,' Müller had once suggested, and there was something in that. His self-confidence – and the desire for revenge that occasionally flared up in his dark, somewhat oscillating gaze – had been such that one simply could not sweep it aside.

And his comments. Like some forgotten B-film from the forties: 'I'll be back one of these days. You'd better look out then, you damned cretins!'

Or: 'Don't think I'll forget you. You think you have won something, but this is only the beginning of a defeat for you. Believe you me, you bloody lackeys, clear off now and leave me in peace!'

Self-assured? Huh, that was not nearly a strong enough term for it. Thinking back now, Verlangen couldn't recall any-body or anything more stubborn and egotistic during all the years he had served in the police force. Fourteen of them. There was something genuinely threatening about Jaan G. Hennan, wasn't that the top and bottom of it? A sort of slowly smouldering hatred that simply could not be shrugged off. A bone-chilling promise of reprisals and retribution. Obviously, threats of various kinds were bread and butter as far as police officers were concerned; but in Hennan's case they had seemed unusually real. Nothing less than a form of evil. If Hennan had been an illness rather than a person, he would have been a cancer, Verlangen thought: no doubt about it.

A malignant tumour in the brain.

He shook his head and sat up straight. He could feel pains coming on at the bottom of his spine, and decided that a short walk was called for. Just a little stroll to the square and back: that was no more than fifty metres or so, and he could do that without even letting his prey out of his sight.

In any case, if Hennan was really interested in shaking him off his trail, it would be the easiest thing in the world. All he would need to do was to nip out of the rear of the building and vanish. No problem.

But why would he want to do that? He didn't even know he was being watched.

And the man keeping him under observation had no idea why he was doing so.

Good God, thought Maarten Verlangen as he closed the car door. Give me two reasons for staying sober in this world we live in.

At half past twelve Jaan G. Hennan went out for lunch. Verlangen left his car once again, and followed him over the square and to a restaurant called Cava del Popolo. Hennan chose a window table, while Verlangen sat down in a booth

further back in the premises. There were not many customers, despite the fact that it was lunchtime. The shadow
had a good view of the person he was shadowing, and optimistically ordered two beers to go with the pasta special of
the day.

Hennan sat there for forty minutes, and all that happened
was that he read a newspaper, ate some kind of fish soup and
drank a small bottle of white wine. Verlangen also managed a
coffee and a cognac, and it was with a pious hope of being
able to sleep for an hour or even an hour-and-a-half that he
walked back to his car.

And that is exactly what happened in fact. He woke up at
about half past two when the sun finally forced its way
through the clouds and found its way in through his dirty
windscreen. It was like an oven inside the car, and he noticed
that his intake of alcohol had begun to hammer nails into his
skull. He checked that Hennan's dark blue Saab was still
parked where it had been before, then walked down to the
kiosk in front of the town hall and bought a beer and a bottle
of mineral water.

When he had finished drinking them it was ten minutes
past three. The sun had continued to dominate the afternoon,
and his clothes were clinging stickily to his body. Hennan
had appeared in the window again for a few seconds with a
telephone receiver apparently glued to his ear, and a traffic
warden had been snooping around in the hope of being able
to allocate a ticket. But that was all.

Verlangen took off his socks and put them in the glove
compartment. Living felt slightly easier, but not a lot. He lit

his twenty-fifth cigarette of the day, and wondered if he could think of something to do.

After number twenty-six, the building had still not exploded and it had not become any cooler. Verlangen walked as far as the telephone kiosk outside the butcher's and phoned his employer. She answered after one-and-a-half rings.

'Good,' she said. 'It's good that you've rung. How's it going?'

'Excellent,' said Verlangen. 'Like a dance. I didn't think there was much point in ringing the first morning. He's in his office, and he's been there all day, in fact.'

'I know,' said Barbara Hennan. 'I've just spoken to him on the telephone. He's coming home in an hour.'

'You don't say?' said Verlangen.

'Yes I do. That's what he said, at least.'

I see, thought Verlangen. So why the hell should I hang around here, waiting for death to knock on my door?

'I think you can pack it in for today,' said fru Hennan. 'We'll be together all evening, so it will be okay if you start keeping an eye on him again tomorrow afternoon.'

'Tomorrow afternoon?'

'Yes. If you are in place after lunch tomorrow, and keep an eye on what he gets up to during the afternoon and the evening . . . especially in the evening . . . Well, it's especially important for me that you don't let him out of your sight then.'

Verlangen thought that over for two seconds.

'I'm with you,' he said. 'Your wish is my command. I'll give you another report the day after tomorrow, will that be okay?'

'That will be fine,' said Barbara Hennan, and hung up.

He stayed for a moment or two in the stuffy telephone kiosk, then noticed that the female traffic warden's funereal grey uniform was approaching, and he hurried off to his car.

Life, where is thy sting? he thought, switched on the engine and drove off.

Although he had more time than was available in the forecourt of Hell, Verlangen chose not to drive back to Maardam. The alternative of clean sheets was too tempting, and at a quarter to five he checked in at the Belveder, a simple but clean hotel in Lofterstraat, behind the town hall.

Between seven and eight he had dinner in the sepia-brown dining room together with a swimming club from Warsaw. Some sort of ragout that reminded him vaguely of his former mother-in-law. Perhaps not so much of her as of the Sunday dinners she used to prepare, and it was a memory he could have done without. He bought two dark beers to take up to his room, managed to overcome an increasing desire to telephone his daughter, then fell asleep in the middle of an American police series some time between eleven and half past.

The sheets were cool and newly ironed, and even if the day

ended up being somewhat less alcohol-free than originally envisaged, at least he was not quite up to the limit of ten beers a day.

Quite some way short of that, in fact.

4

The restaurant was called Columbine, and after two swigs of beer it looked like any other restaurant in any country of the world.

It was evening at last. The old Maasleitner clock hanging over the bottles of whisky at the bar showed twenty-five to eight. On this completely cloud-free Thursday Hennan had stayed on at the office until seven o'clock, for some damned reason or other. Verlangen had been feeling worn out since about four.

But he was used to exhaustion. It had been his constant companion for the last four years, and sometimes it felt as if it was time – nothing else – that got on top of him. A sort of old, smelly item of clothing that he couldn't wait to cast off. To sleep off the hangover, wake up to something different and at long last put on a new era. In which the seconds and minutes actually tasted of something.

But there was never a new era the following morning. Just the same old unwashed garment that clung stickily to his skin, day after day, year after year. There was nothing he could do about it, and the few evenings he dared to go to bed in a sober state it was always impossible to get a wink of sleep.

He drained his glass and looked over towards Hennan. There were only two tables between them, but sitting at one of them was an unusually loud and exuberant group: four chubby young men aged around twenty-eight, each with a moustache, who repeatedly broke out into roars of laughter, leaning back on their chairs and slamming their fists down on the table. Judging by their broad accents Verlangen concluded that they came from somewhere down among the southern provinces. Groenstadt, most probably. Or Balderslacht, somewhere of that sort.

There were quite a lot of other customers, so a certain degree of concentration was needed in order to keep a close eye on the object of his surveillance. Despite everything. But on the other hand, it seemed fairly obvious that Hennan intended to have a meal and stay put for quite some time. He had hung his jacket over the back of his chair, and was working his way through the menu while sipping away at a colourless drink – presumably a gin and tonic – and seemed to be in no hurry at all. Perhaps he was waiting for somebody: the seat opposite him at his table for two was empty. Maybe a woman, Verlangen thought. That would be the most likely possibility, after all. And that was the outcome he had predicted from the start.

Anyway, all he could do was remain where he was, and see what happened. Verlangen decided to have a meal as well. He attracted a waiter's attention, ordered another beer and asked for a menu. The way things looked, he might well be sitting there for quite some time.

★

Two hours later Jaan G. Hennan was still alone at his table. Verlangen had passed close by him twice on the way to the gents, and established that his quarry seemed to have indulged in a substantial meal. At least three courses and two different wines, and just now he was puffing away at a thin, black cigar, gazing out through the window and somewhat absent-mindedly twirling around a brandy glass. As far as Verlangen had seen he hadn't exchanged words with a single person all evening, apart from the waiter. He had been to the toilet once, but what the hell was buzzing around inside his head – or why he was hanging around here instead of spending the time at home with his lovely wife – well, goodness only knew.

At least it didn't look as if he was waiting – or had been waiting – for somebody. He had checked his watch now and then, true enough, but apart from that there had been no indication that a companion had failed to turn up: no calls from the telephone in the lobby, no delays before placing an order, no apologetic explanations to the waiter. Nothing at all.

Nor had he spent time reading a book or a newspaper. Neither had Verlangen, come to that, but then he was there on business, as it were. For a few minutes he toyed with the idea of walking past Hennan and spilling beer over the back of his neck. Or trying to bribe somebody else to do that. There was no shortage of slightly drunk young people sitting around, and no doubt it would have been possible to persuade one of them.

Simply in order to make something happen. Verlangen's

feeling of being worn out had caught up with him again. He had eaten something that was alleged to have been veal – but in that case it must have been from the world's oldest calf.

He had washed it down with four or five beers, and in the end given way to temptation and followed Jaan G. Hennan's example. Coffee and cognac.

He lit another cigarette, despite the fact that his previous one was still glowing away in the ashtray.

Looked at the clock: ten minutes to ten.

Bugger this for a lark, he thought as he turned away yet another customer who wondered if the seat opposite him was taken. Drink up your damned cognac and pay your bill! And get the hell out of here!

It was just as he looked up after thinking these pious thoughts that he saw Hennan was on his way to his table.

Eh, what's all this? he had time to think.

'May I join you?'

'Please do.'

'Hennan. Jaan G. Hennan.'

'Verlangen.'

Hennan pulled out the chair and sat down.

'Verlangen?'

'Yes.'

'Not Maarten Verlangen, surely?'

'Yes, that's me.'

'I thought so.'

'What do you mean? I'm not at all sure . . .'

'Sure about what?'

'That I know who you are.'

Hennan put his cigar down on the ashtray, and leaned forward with both elbows on the table.

'Come off it, Maarten Verlangen. I know all too bloody well who you are, and you know just as well who I am. Why are you sitting here?'

Verlangen took a sip of cognac and thought for a moment.

'That's a very good question.'

'You think so? But you're welcome to answer it, in any case.'

'Why I'm sitting here?'

'Yes.'

'Because I've had dinner, of course.'

'Really? And is that the only reason?'

Verlangen suddenly felt anger boiling up inside him.

'How about you telling me what the hell you're after? I haven't the faintest idea who you are, nor what you're getting at. If you don't have a satisfactory explanation, might I suggest that you clear off before I ask the staff to throw you out!'

Hennan sat there without saying a word, just screwing up his eyes slightly. No trace of a smile. Something told Verlangen that there ought to have been one. He noticed that he had instinctively clenched his fists and pushed his chair back a couple of centimetres.

So that he could stand up quickly and defend himself if necessary.

Don't be stupid, he thought when he realized what his

imagination was pushing him into. He can't start fighting inside here, for God's sake. That would be pure . . .

'Fuzz. You are still the fuzz, I take it?'

Verlangen hesitated for a tenth of a second, then shook his head.

'What about you?'

'Eh?'

'What about you? What do you do? What did you say your name was, by the way?'

Hennan made no reply, simply twisted his lips into a contemptuous grimace. Verlangen looked away. Leaned back and stared up at the ceiling instead. There followed a few moments of silence.

'Why are you no longer a copper? Did you get the sack?'

Verlangen shrugged.

'I packed it in.'

'Voluntarily?'

'Of course. Explain what the hell it is you want, or go back to your own table. I've no desire to sit here any longer and be . . .'

He hesitated as he searched for the right word.

'Be what?'

'Bullied.'

He clenched his fists and prepared to defend himself again.

'You were a real touchy bastard, always keen to claim you were being harassed by me,' said Hennan, and suddenly his face broke out into a beaming smile. 'But in fact I'm the one who should be feeling pissed off with you. Not the other way round.'

Verlangen lit a cigarette.

'Pissed off? Why?'

'Jaan G. Hennan. Do you still claim that you don't remember?'

Verlangen shook his head. A little too fiercely – he could feel the room shaking. Damn and blast, he thought. I'm too drunk.

'I've no bloody idea.'

Hennan rested his chin on his hand and seemed to be thinking things over.

'Shall we go and sit in the bar instead? Then we can sort this out. Let me buy you a whisky.'

Verlangen hesitated briefly, then nodded cautiously and stood up.

'You can have ten minutes,' he said. 'Not a damned second more.'

While they were drinking their first whisky Hennan explained why he had recognized Verlangen and remembered his name.

As they sank the second one, Verlangen recalled the twelve-year-old investigation and said it had completely vanished from his memory – but now that Hennan had raised the matter, well . . .

While they were drinking the third one Hennan took the initiative once again and went on at length about what it was like, spending two-and-a-half years in prison despite being innocent.

Innocent? thought Verlangen, beginning to feel annoyed again. You were more guilty than Crippen, you arsehole!

But he didn't start arguing. Merely said that he could no longer remember any details of the case – he'd had so many to deal with over the years. He noticed that he was beginning to have difficulty in articulating, and immediately laid down a rule that he swore he would stick to, come what may, for the rest of the evening: Don't let Hennan have the slightest idea why you are here! No matter what. Be faithful to your employer!

Hennan went on about all kinds of things, but the fourth whisky evidently had a detrimental effect on Verlangen's hearing. He was simply incapable of understanding a meaningful series of sounds any longer – but nevertheless made a point of muttering and humming and hawing inventively during the pauses. When he next looked at the clock, it was twenty-five minutes past midnight. Hennan also seemed to have had enough.

'Home,' he said. 'Time to go home.'

Verlangen agreed and slid down from the bar stool.

'I'm staying just down the road,' he said.

'I must order a taxi,' said Hennan.

The bartender, a gigantic young man with red curly hair, intervened and informed them that there were always taxis queuing up just round the corner. A mere fifty metres away – that was easier than phoning and ordering.

They went out together into the warm early-summer night. Verlangen had some difficulty in keeping his balance, but Hennan put an arm round his shoulders and kept him more or less upright. When they came to the row of yellow-and-black cars, Hennan said goodnight without further ado, clambered into a back seat, waved, and grinned broadly through the window.

Verlangen raised a hand as he watched the taxi drive off. He suddenly felt a painful stab of repugnance, which he had difficulty in pinning down. On the whole Hennan had behaved reasonably, and the reason why his wife wanted him to be kept under observation was more enveloped in mystery than ever.

But he had fraternized with his quarry. In no uncertain terms. He had babbled on and hummed and hawed and drunk way too much whisky . . . On top of all the beer and cognac – and God only knew what he might have said and not said.

On his way back to the hotel he took wrong turnings several times, and ended up in the cemetery where he made the most of the opportunity of emptying his bladder between what seemed to be a mortuary and a collection of dustbins.

But he eventually managed to find his way back to the Belveder hotel, and by the time he staggered up to his room it was a quarter past one. That was a point in time that had not registered on Verlangen's consciousness, but with the aid of a few independent witnesses and observations, it could be established later with a high degree of certainty.

5

Police probationer Wagner yawned and looked at his watch: twenty-five to two.

Then he looked at his crossword puzzle. It was unsolved.

Almost totally, at least. He had filled in eight squares. Two words. But he wasn't sure if either of them was correct.

In order to pass the time he counted up the number of empty squares.

Ninety-four. He could hardly claim that he had made all that much progress . . . He wondered for a moment if he ought to go and kip down for a while. You didn't need to be awake just because you were on call. It was sufficient to be in the right place, and able to answer the phone if anything happened. The instructions in that respect were just as clear and unambiguous as everything else in the police station.

Linzhuisen's police station, that is. Wagner had been working there for almost a year now, and liked it. He was twenty-five years old, and could well imagine himself being a police officer for the rest of his life. Especially in a little place like this one. Everything was well organized, the pension terms were advantageous, and there was no crime to speak of.

And pleasant colleagues, to boot: Gaardner, his boss, and Willumsen, with whom he often played tennis.

Linzhuisen was not an independent police district, but was a part of Linden, which was run by the chief of police, Chief Inspector Sachs. Linden had slightly more staff: two inspectors and three or four constables and probationers.

But they shared emergency coverage. It was obviously unnecessary to have a probationer or an inspector sitting half asleep throughout the night in both Linden and Linzhuisen – it was only twelve kilometres between the two places, and if a call-out became necessary whoever was on duty would need to summon assistance in any case. Wake up colleagues on stand-by at home, or telephone to Maardam.

As far as Wagner was concerned, this meant he was on emergency duty at the police station four nights per month, and he had no complaints about that.

On the contrary. There was something rather special about these lonely nights that quite appealed to him. Sitting here in the blacked-out police station keeping an eye on law and order while the rest of the world enjoyed its well-deserved sleep. Ready to arrange a call-out as soon as any stricken citizen in need asked for assistance. Indeed, was it not that role that was the most important reason – albeit not the one he talked about most – why he joined the police force four years ago?

Watching over people's lives and possessions, and being the ultimate guarantee of their safety.

Sometimes when he found himself thinking such thoughts, Probationer Wagner told himself that maybe he ought to write them down. Perhaps they would come in useful for teaching and recruitment purposes. Why not?

And that was probably also why – when all is said and done – he didn't like to lie down and fall asleep. Mind you, if nothing happened – and there were hardly ever any alarm calls – he would probably give way and have a lie down in the early hours, he knew that. It was almost impossible to keep awake after half past two or so, even with the assistance of all the crossword puzzles in the world.

He chewed his pencil, took a drink of coffee and tried to concentrate.

Four down, seven letters, the second one might be 'a': 'Literary bloodhound in Paris'.

I suppose one ought to read a book now and then, Wagner thought with a sigh.

Checked the time again: a quarter to two.

Then the telephone rang.

Chief Inspector Sachs dreamt that he was a dolphin.

A young, fit and handsome male dolphin swimming around in cool emerald-green seawater surrounded by a whole school of female dolphins. They all rolled and romped around, swam close to one another, made impressive leaps towards the sun over the glittering surface of the water then dived down to the bottom of the seabed. Rubbed breasts and backs and stomachs against one another in an ever more joyful dance.

This is where I always want to be, he thought. I always

want to be an elegant male dolphin surrounded by randy females.

The sound of the telephone cut through the marrow of his spine and his cerebral cortex like the blade of a saw. He picked up the receiver without even opening his eyes.

'Sachs.'

'Chief Inspector Sachs?'

'Hmm.'

'Wagner here.'

'Who?'

'Probationer Wagner in Linzhuisen. I'm on emergency duty and have just received a—'

'What time is it?'

'Seven minutes to two. I've just had a phone call – at 01.45 to be exact – about a dead woman.'

Sachs opened his eyes. Then closed them again.

'And?'

'It was a man. Who rang, that is. And his wife is dead . . . Hennan, that's his name . . . Jaan G. Hennan. They live in Linden, and so I thought—'

'Hang on a minute. I'll go to the other phone.'

Sachs stood up and tiptoed out to his study. Picked up the receiver of the telephone on his desk.

'Go on.'

'Well, I'll ring the medics and the rest of them, but I thought I ought to inform the chief inspector first.'

'Good. But what exactly has happened? Try to calm down a little bit, if you can.'

Wagner cleared his throat and took a deep breath.

'Her name's Barbara Hennan. They live in Kammerweg –
that's some way away from the centre of town . . .'

'Linden, you said?'

'Yes.'

'I know where that is.'

'Of course. Anyway, this man, Jaan G. Hennan, had evidently come home pretty late – at about half past one – and
found his wife in the pool.'

'The swimming pool?'

'Yes.'

'Drowned?'

'No, on the contrary.'

'On the contrary? What the hell do you mean by that?'

'She was lying . . . She was lying on the bottom, he
said . . .'

'Without having drowned?'

'Yes. There is no water in the pool, it seems.'

Sachs was staring straight ahead, and found himself looking at the framed photograph of his children, which was
hanging on the wall over the desk. They were twins, but
apart from the fact that their skin was the same colour and
they had the same parents, they were as different as two
people can possibly be.

'No water?'

'No, that's what he said. She's lying at the bottom of the
pool, he says she must have fallen in and killed herself.'

Sachs thought for a moment.

'All right. What instructions did you give him?'

'That he should stay at home and wait for us to come.'

'Is there any reason to suspect foul play?'

'Well . . . Not as far as I know, but I thought it was best to—'

'Yes, of course. Did you get any more information out of him? What did he sound like?'

'A bit drunk, I think.'

'Really? How drunk?'

'I don't know. It's hard to say – but pretty drunk, I think.' Sachs sighed.

'So in fact it could be a hoax? Somebody having us on? In theory, at least.'

'In theory, yes. But that's not the conclusion I reached. And in any case, I suppose we have to—'

'Yes, of course. Of course. What was the address, did you say?'

'Kammerweg 4. And his name is Hennan, as I said.'

Sachs managed to find a pencil and noted it down.

'I'll see you there in about ten minutes,' he said. 'If you arrive before I do, don't go in until I get there. Ring the doctor, but we'll wait with the rest until we've been able to check up on the situation. Is that clear?'

'Everything clear and understood,' said Wagner.

'Excellent. Let's go!' said Sachs, and hung up.

He went back to the bedroom. When he switched on the bedside lamp in order to be able to find his clothes, his wife, Irene, turned over and muttered something in her sleep. He eyed her briefly.

It's actually true, he thought. She really does look like a dolphin.

Her face, at least.

He gathered together his clothes, switched off the light and crept out into the kitchen.

Wagner hadn't yet arrived, but Dr Santander, the forensic medical officer, was already there. As Sachs made his way through the rather overgrown garden, he could see Santander standing next to a little collection of deckchairs at the edge of the swimming pool, talking to a sturdy-looking man in his fifties.

He could see them very clearly even though he was still some distance away, because the whole of the pool area was bathed in light. Several spotlights were attached to trees all the way round, and when the chief inspector emerged from the darkness the doctor gave a start and seemed almost scared. Just for a moment Sachs had the feeling that he had barged in on the set of a film being recorded, and it was not easy to shake off this impression despite the fact that Santander broke into a broad smile as soon as he recognized the newcomer. He introduced Sachs to the broad-shouldered man.

'Welcome,' said the latter. 'My name is Hennan. Jaan G. Hennan. It's my wife lying down there.'

He pointed with the hand holding a thin, black cigar between his index and long fingers. He was holding a glass in the other one. Sachs went up to the edge and looked down.

At the bottom of the empty and unexpectedly deep pool, a few metres out from one of the narrow ends, was a woman's body lying on its stomach. She was wearing a red bathing costume, her arms were stretched out at odd angles, and a small pool of blood had spread underneath her head, in stark contrast to the white tiles. Her hair was also reddish, but a somewhat lighter shade. Sachs did not doubt for one second that she was dead, despite the fact that she must have been lying some fifteen to twenty metres away.

'How do you get down there?' he asked.

'There's a ladder over there.'

Now it was Santander doing the pointing.

'I've had a quick look at her,' he explained, adjusting his heavy, horn-rimmed spectacles. 'It seems to be as Hennan says: she must have fallen down and . . . well, died instantly.'

Sachs alternated his gaze between the doctor and Hennan several times. Hennan put down his glass.

'What time was it when you found her?' Sachs asked.

Hennan checked his gold wristwatch.

'Just over an hour ago,' he said. 'I came home and couldn't find her anywhere, so I went out, and . . . well . . .'

He thrust out his hands in an uncertain gesture. Turned round and looked down at the body at the bottom of the pool for a moment. Sachs tried to make eye contact with Santander, but the latter had opened his medical bag and was busy taking out various instruments.

'It's diabolical,' said Hennan, taking a puff of his cigar. 'Absolutely bloody diabolical.'

Sachs nodded and tried to form an opinion of him. He was obviously drunk, but at the same time he kept himself detached and under control in a way that seemed almost absurd in the circumstances – as if they were talking about a sick dog or something of the sort, rather than a dead wife. He was wearing light-coloured cotton trousers and a short-sleeved blue shirt hanging down over his waistband. And bare-footed – Sachs assumed he had taken off his shoes and socks before beginning to look for his wife.

Suntanned and trim. Dark, short-cropped hair with a touch of grey here and there, but not at all receding. A powerful-looking face with a wide mouth and very deep-set eyes.

'How do you feel?'

Hennan seemed to weigh up various alternative answers before actually speaking.

'I don't really know,' he said. 'I suppose I'm not completely sober, unfortunately.'

Sachs nodded.

'But I assume you must have had quite a shock . . . Of some kind.'

'The reaction usually comes later,' said the doctor. 'It often takes quite a while.'

'Obviously I need to have a detailed discussion with you about what has happened,' said Sachs. 'But I suggest we wait until my colleague arrives – he should be here at any moment.'

'Why do you need—?' began Hennan, but Sachs interrupted him.

'It looks like an accident, of course. But we can't exclude the possibility of something else.'

'Something else?' said Hennan, but the penny seemed to drop immediately. 'You mean . . . ?'

'Exactly,' said Sachs. 'One never knows. Ah, here comes my colleague.'

Wagner emerged out of the darkness and greeted everybody present. Sachs noted that his uniform looked as if it had come from the tailor's a mere ten minutes ago.

'I've rung for assistance from Maardam,' said Santander. 'But you might like to go down and take a look before they get here?'

Sachs thought for a moment.

'No,' he said. 'I'll wait. But take Wagner down with you, and I can have a chat with Hennan in the meantime.'

If there is any reason to suspect foul play, he thought, it will be the Maardam CID who take charge of things anyway. And his young eyes are better than my old ones.

The doctor and the probationer went off towards the ladder at the far end of the pool. Sachs gestured towards the deckchairs. Hennan nodded somewhat nonchalantly, and they sat down. Sachs took out his notebook.

'I'm going to ask you a few questions,' he said. 'It's pure routine. We have to proceed in this way, so don't take it personally.'

'I understand,' said Hennan, relighting his cigar that had gone out.

'Your full name?'

'Jaan Genser Hennan.'

'And your wife's name?'

'Barbara Clarissa Hennan.'

'Her maiden name?'

'Delgado.'

'Age?'

'She . . . She was due to celebrate her thirty-fifth birthday in August.'

'A little younger than you, then?'

'Fifteen years. What does that have to do with it?'

Sachs shrugged.

'Nothing, presumably. And you live here?'

'Yes, of course.'

'Children?'

'No.'

'A nice place. How long have you been living here?'

Hennan puffed at his cigar and fingered his glass without picking it up.

'We just rent it. My wife is . . . was . . . American. We lived in Denver for many years, but we moved here last spring.'

'You come from here, I gather?'

'I was born and grew up in Maardam.'

'I see. What is your work?'

'I run an import firm.'

'Where?'

'Here in Linden. It's just a little office at Aldemarckt so far.'

'What do you import?'

'Various things. Stuff that pays well – mainly electronic products from south-east Asia. Components for music systems, pocket calculators and things like that.'

Sachs nodded and decided that would do for background notes.

'Tell me what happened this evening,' he said.

Hennan crossed his legs, and seemed to hesitate.

'There isn't much to tell,' he said. 'As I said, I came home and found her down there . . .'

'Did you go down to check that she was dead before you rang the police?'

'Yes, of course. I even took her pulse, although it was obvious that there was no hope. She was ice-cold.'

'Has the doctor said how long she might have been lying there?'

Hennan nodded.

'Several hours,' he said.

'And what do you think happened?'

Hennan raised his eyebrows and stared at the chief inspector for a few seconds.

'Surely it's obvious. She fell down . . . Or maybe dived.'

'Dived? Are you saying she might have taken her own life? Why do you think—'

'I'm not saying that at all!' interrupted Hennan indignantly. 'Think what you're saying, damn you! My wife is lying dead down there, and I don't want to listen to a lot of crap about her possibly having jumped down intentionally . . . That's out of the question. Completely out of the question, do you hear that?'

'I hear that,' said Sachs. 'But I think it's a bit odd that she would—'

'There's no water in the pool,' said Hennan angrily. 'Perhaps you've noticed that?'

Sachs wrapped his hands round his right knee and paused.

'What are you trying to say?' he asked.

'That she forgot, of course.'

'Forgot what?'

'That I'd had the pool emptied earlier today.'

'Really?'

'"Really?" What the devil do you mean by that?'

'You had the pool emptied, you say. Why?'

Hennan snorted and shook his head melodramatically to underline the chief inspector's ignorance.

'Because you have to do that occasionally. There are a few repairs that need doing – some tradesmen are coming to see to it tomorrow. Today, rather . . .'

He looked at his watch. So did Sachs.

Ten minutes to three.

'So you drained all the water out of the pool. Your wife forgot that it was empty, and dived in. Is that what you think happened?'

'How else could it have happened, for Christ's sake?'

Sachs waited for a few seconds, trying to judge the probability of Hennan's theory.

'Somebody might have pushed her,' he said eventually. 'You, for instance.'

Hennan's face turned a few shades darker.

'What a lot of crap,' he said. 'I've been in Linden since this morning.'

'In your office?'

'Yes. I sorted out the emptying of the pool first – that takes a few hours. I was in my office soon after eleven, if I remember rightly.'

'And your wife?'

'She drove to Aarlach early this morning. She was going to look for some porcelain statuettes – we collect them. She thought she might be able to find a few bargains at Hendermaag's.'

'Hendermaag's?' said Sachs, who was not exactly well up in porcelain statuettes.

'Yes. I'm starting to get a bit pissed off by all this, Chief Inspector. I come home and find my wife dead, and when I call in the police you start interrogating me as if . . .'

'As if what?'

'As if I were a suspect, somehow or other. I've never had much confidence in the forces of law and order, I'll admit that: but this exceeds my—'

'Come on, now,' said Sachs, interrupting him. 'Don't take it like that. I said at the start that it's just routine. I only have a few more questions, and then I'll leave you in peace. What were you yourself doing earlier this evening?'

Hennan underlined his objections by saying nothing and smoking for quite some time before answering. Sachs observed him patiently and bided his time.

'As I've already said, I went out for a meal when I'd finished for the day. We'd agreed on that – my wife didn't know what time she would get back from Aarlach, but there was no way she'd be back early enough to prepare an evening meal.'

'Were you in touch with her during the day?'

'No.'

'Or during the evening?'

Hennan shook his head.

'Not at all?'

'No. I rang home in the late afternoon, but there was no reply.'

'What time was that?'

'Five o'clock or half past, I'd guess.'

'So you don't know what time your wife got back from this outing to Aarlach?'

'No idea,' said Hennan, emptying his glass. 'Not the slightest bloody idea.'

Sachs decided to try a different line.

'It's an unusually big swimming pool,' he said.

Hennan nodded vaguely and muttered something.

'And deep. I don't think it's usual to have diving towers either, is it?'

'That's down to the bloke who built the bloody thing,' said Hennan.

'What do you mean by that?'

'The bloke who owns the house. His wife was a diver. He gave her this damned pool – and the diving tower – as a wedding present. My wife . . .'

'Go on.'

'My wife also enjoyed diving. Do you know how far it is from the top of the tower down to the bottom of the pool?'

Sachs shook his head, and felt a sudden shooting pain down his spine when he looked up at the dazzlingly white concrete construction.

'Fourteen metres. Ten plus four. Fourteen metres, do you understand that? No wonder she bloody well killed herself.'

Sachs closed his notebook and sat upright.

He's right, he thought. No wonder she bloody well killed herself.

They could hear footsteps approaching from the darkness of the garden but the chief inspector had time for one more question before the team from Maardam appeared.

'But why didn't she see?' he asked. 'Why didn't she see there was no water in there?'

Hennan seemed to wonder whether he ought to answer or not.

'It must have been dark,' he said. 'It was me who switched on the spotlights when I started looking for her. I think she was a bit drunk as well.'

'What makes you think that?'

'Because that idiot of a doctor says so. Anyway, enough is enough now, for Christ's sake.'

'All right,' said Sachs. 'Thank you for your cooperation.'

He stood up in order to welcome the pathologist Meusse, whom he'd known since he was about ten years old without ever really being able to understand the man. But he gathered that he was by no means alone in that.

'Good evening,' he said.

'Good morning,' said Meusse. 'Where's the body?'

'My wife is lying at the bottom of the swimming pool,' said Hennan, who also stood up. 'Is this going to be a bloody full-scale invasion? I'm off to bed now.'

Meusse observed him with interest for a few seconds, over the top of his spectacles.

'Do that,' he said, stroking his hand over his bald head. 'Sleep well.'

6

When Chief Inspector Van Veeteren came out into the street with Bismarck, it had just turned half past six in the morning and the sun had not yet managed to climb over the top of the line of dirty brown blocks of flats on the other side of Wimmergraacht.

Even so, it seemed like quite a decent morning. The temperature must have been round about twenty degrees, and bearing in mind that he lived in a city where near gale-force winds blew three mornings out of five and it rained every other day, he couldn't really complain.

Not about the weather, at least.

What he *could* complain about was the time. His wife Renate had woken him up with a prod of the elbow, and claimed that Bismarck was whimpering and wanted to go out. Without a second thought he had got up, dressed, attached a lead to the collar of the large Newfoundland bitch, and set off. He was presumably not properly awake until he came to the Wimmerstraat–Boolsweg crossroads, where a clattering tramcar screeched round the curve and scratched a wound in his eardrums.

He was now as wide awake as a newborn babe.

Bismarck forged ahead, her nose sniffing the asphalt. The goal was obvious: Randers Park. Five minutes there, ten minutes examining the plants and relieving herself in the bushes, then five minutes back home. Van Veeteren had been on this outing before, and wondered if the faithful old dog really was all that keen on this compulsory morning walk.

Perhaps she did it to keep the people she lived with happy. They needed to get out and have some exercise every morning, taking it in turns: it seemed a bit odd, but Bismarck did what was required of her in all weathers, rain or shine.

It was a worrying thought: but she was that type of dog, and how the hell could one know for sure?

At the beginning there had been no question of Van Veeteren being involved in the morning exercise. Bismarck was his daughter Jess's dog, and had been ever since she acquired her eight years ago. After eleven months of insistent pestering.

She had been thirteen at the time. Now she was twenty-one and was studying abroad for a year at the Sorbonne in Paris. She lived in a tiny little room in a student hostel where keeping Newfoundland dogs was not allowed. Nor any other animals, come to that. Not even a French boyfriend was permitted.

So Bismarck had to stay behind in Maardam.

There was also a son in the house. His name was Erich, he was fifteen years old, and liked going out with dogs in the mornings. He was allowed to do that now and again after his big sister moved to Paris, but this morning he was not at home.

God only knows where he is, it suddenly struck Van Veeteren.

He had phoned at eleven o'clock the previous night, spoken to his mother and explained that he was out at Löhr and would be spending the night at a friend's house. He was in the same class – or possibly a parallel one – and his friend's father would drive them straight to school the following morning.

What was the name of the friend? Van Veeteren had wanted to know when his wife hung up and explained the situation.

She couldn't remember. Something beginning with M, but she couldn't recall having heard the name previously.

Van Veeteren also wondered if Erich had some clean underpants and a toothbrush with him, but hadn't bothered to pester his wife any further.

Bismarck turned into the entrance of the park, ignoring with disdain a neatly curled poodle who was on his way back home with his boss after a satisfactory outing.

I must have a chat with Erich one of these days, thought Van Veeteren, taking a packet of West out of his jacket pocket. It's high time I did so.

He lit a cigarette and realized that he had been thinking the same thought for over a year now. At regular intervals.

He had breakfast together with his wife. Neither of them uttered a word, despite the fact that they spent a good half-hour over the kitchen table and their newspapers.

Perhaps I should have a chat with Renate as well one of these days, he thought as he closed the front door behind him. That was also high time.

Or had they already used up all the available words?

It wasn't easy to know. They had been married for fifteen years, separated for two without having managed to go their separate ways, and then been married for another seven.

Twenty-four years, he thought. That's half my life, more or less.

He had been a police officer for twenty-four years as well. Perhaps there was a sort of connection, he thought? Two halves of my life combining to form a whole?

Rubbish. Even if you have half a duck and half an eagle, that doesn't mean that you possess a whole bird.

He realized that the image was idiotic, and during his walk to the police station he tried instead to recall how many times he had made love to his wife during the past year.

Three times, he decided.

If he interpreted the word 'love-making' optimistically. The last occasion – in April – didn't seem to come into the category of 'making love'.

And to be honest, in no other category either.

That's life, he thought – and avoided stepping into a pool of vomit somebody had left on the pavement by a hair's breadth. It could have been worse, to be sure; but for Christ's sake, it could have been considerably better as well.

★

On his way up to his office on the third floor he bumped into Inspector Münster.

'How's the Kaunis case going?' he asked.

'Full stop,' said Münster. 'Neither of those interrogations we talked about is going to be possible until next week.'

'Why not?'

'One of them is in Japan, and the other is going to be operated on this morning.'

'But he'll survive, I hope?'

'The doctors thought so. It's for varicose veins.'

'I see,' said the Chief Inspector. 'Anything else?'

'Yes, I'm afraid so,' said Münster. 'Hiller will no doubt be on to you. Something's happened in Linden, if I understood it rightly.'

'Linden?'

'Yes. If we don't have anything more important on – and we might not have now that—'

'We'll have to see,' said Van Veeteren. 'You'll be in your office if I need you, I take it?'

'Buried under a drift of papers,' said Münster with a sigh, and continued down the corridor.

Van Veeteren entered his office, and noted that it smelled rather like a working men's lodging house. Not that he had ever lived in such an establishment, but he had been inside quite a few in the course of his duties.

He opened the window wide and lit a cigarette. Inhaled deeply. Another morning and I'm still alive, he thought, and it struck him that what he would like to do more than anything else was to go and lie down for a while.

Was there anything in the rules and regulations that said you were not allowed to have a bed in your office?

'Yes, well, it's that business in Linden,' said Hiller, pouring some water into a pot of yellow gerbera. 'I suppose we'll have to drive out there and take a look.'

'What's it all about?' asked Van Veeteren, contemplating the chief of police's plants. There must have been about thirty: in front of the big picture window, on the desk, on a little table in the corner and on the bookshelves. It's beginning to look like an obsession, he thought, and wondered what that was a sign of. Growing roses was a substitute for passion – he had read that somewhere; but Hiller's display of plants in his office on the fourth floor of the police station was much more difficult to pin down. Van Veeteren's botanical knowledge was limited, but even so he thought he could identify aspidistra and hortensia and yucca palm.

And gerbera.

The chief of police put down his watering can.

'A dead woman,' he said. 'At the bottom of a swimming pool.'

'Drowned?'

'No. Certainly not drowned.'

'Really?'

'There was no water in the pool. It's rather difficult to drown in those circumstances. Not to say impossible.'

A slight twitch of the mouth suggested that Hiller was indulging his sense of humour. Van Veeteren sat down on the visitor chair.

'Murder? Manslaughter?'

'Probably not. She probably fell in by sheer mischance. Or dived in by mistake. But it seems to be not straightforward, and Sachs has asked for assistance. He's not quite himself after that little haemorrhage he had – no doubt you remember that? He seems to be aware of that himself. But he only has one more year to go before he retires.'

Van Veeteren sighed. He had met – and worked with – Chief Inspector Sachs on three or four occasions. He had no special views about him – neither positive nor negative – but he knew that Sachs had suffered a minor cerebral haemorrhage a few months ago, and that it might have affected his judgement to some extent. At least, that is what had been alleged: but if it really was the case, or if it had more to do with Sachs's lack of confidence after being a millimetre-thin blood-vessel wall away from death – well, that was difficult to say.

'When did it happen?' asked Van Veeteren.

'Last night,' said the chief of police, running his fingers over the immaculate knot in his tie. 'You could delegate it to somebody, of course; but if you're not too snowed under I think you ought to drive out there yourself. Bearing in mind Sachs's situation. But there's nothing to suggest anything irregular, remember that. It shouldn't need more than a few hours and a bit of common sense.'

'I'll go myself,' said Van Veeteren, standing up. 'A car drive might do me good.'

'Harrumph!' said Hiller.

'Jaan G. Hennan!' exclaimed Van Veeteren as Münster started manoeuvring them out of the underground labyrinth that was the police station garage. 'I can hardly believe my eyes.'

'Why?' wondered Münster. 'Who is Hennan?'

But Van Veeteren didn't reply. He had received a three-page summary of the case written by somebody called Wagner and including a short statement by the pathologist Meusse. He was holding the documents in his hand and trying to absorb the contents. Münster glanced at his boss and realized that it was pertinent to wait, and meanwhile concentrate on driving.

'Hennan,' muttered the Chief Inspector, and started reading.

Wagner's report revealed that the dead woman was called Barbara Hennan, and that the police had been summoned to the scene (Kammerweg 4 in Linden) by a telephone call (received 01.42) from the dead woman's husband. A certain Jaan G. Hennan.

The police had arrived at 02.08, and established that the woman was lying on the bottom of an empty swimming pool, and was in fact dead. Hennan had been interrogated immediately and it had transpired that he had arrived at home about 01.15, and been unable to find his wife until he discovered her lying in the said empty swimming pool. Both local doctor Santander and pathologist Meusse from the Centre for Forensic Medicine in Maardam had examined the dead body, and their conclusions were identical in all respects: Barbara Hennan had died as a result of extensive injuries in her head, spine, nape and trunk, and there was everything to suggest that all the injuries had been a consequence of falling into the empty swimming pool. Or possibly diving into it. Or possibly being pushed into it. The post-mortem was not yet complete, so further details could be expected.

The time of death seemed to be between 21.00 and 23.00. Hennan maintained that at this time he was in the restaurant Columbine in Linden; he had seen his wife alive for the last time at eight o'clock in the morning when she left home in order to drive to Aarlach. It was not known when she had arrived back home after that outing, nor how she had ended up in the empty swimming pool. All information received thus far had come from the said Jaan G. Hennan.

Meusse's brief statement merely confirmed that all fractures and injuries were consistent with the assumption that the dead woman had fallen (or dived, or been pushed) down into the pool; and that the alcohol level in her blood was 1.74 per mil.

'So she was drunk,' muttered the Chief Inspector when he had finished reading. 'A drunk woman falls down into an empty swimming pool. Kindly explain to me why the Maardam CID has to be called out to assist in a situation like this!'

'What about this Hennan character?' wondered Münster. 'Didn't you say you couldn't believe your eyes, or something of the sort?'

Van Veeteren folded up the sheets of paper and put them in his briefcase.

'G,' he said. 'That's what we called him.'

'G?'

'Yes. I was at school with him. In the same class for six years.'

'Really? Jaan G. Hennan. Why . . . er . . . why did he only have one letter, as it were?'

'Because there were two,' said Van Veeteren, adjusting a lever and leaning the back of his seat so far back that he was half-lying in the passenger seat. 'Two boys with the same name – Jaan Hennan. The teachers had to distinguish between them, of course, and it always said Jaan G. Hennan on class lists or in class registers. If I remember rightly we called him Jaan G. for a week or so, and then after that it was just G. He quite liked it himself. I mean, he had the whole school's simplest name.'

'G?' said Münster. 'Yes, I have to say that it has . . . well, a sort of something to it.'

The Chief Inspector nodded vaguely. Fished out a toothpick from his breast pocket and examined it carefully before sticking it between the front teeth of his lower jaw.

'What was he like?'

'What was he like? What do you mean?'

'What sort of a person was he then? G?'

'Why do you ask?'

'Well, you seemed to suggest that there was something odd about him.'

Van Veeteren turned his head and looked out through the

passenger window for a while before answering. Tapped his fingertips against one another.

'Münster,' he said in the end. 'Let's keep this to ourselves for the time being, but I reckon Jaan G. Hennan is the most unpleasant bastard I have ever met in the whole of my life.'

'What?' said Münster.

'You heard me.'

'Of course. It was as if . . . I mean, what does that imply in this context? It can't be completely irrelevant, surely? If you—'

'How are things with you and the family?' said Van Veeteren, interrupting him. 'Still as idyllic as ever?'

The family? wondered Münster and increased his speed. Typical. If you've said A, under no circumstances must you say B.

'As a man sows, so shall he reap,' he said, and to his great surprise the Chief Inspector produced a noise faintly reminiscent of a laugh.

Brief and half-swallowed, but still . . .

'Bravo, Inspector,' he said. 'I'll tell you a bit more about G on some later occasion, I promise you that. But I don't want to rob you of the possibility of your forming an independent impression of him first. Is that okay with you?'

Münster shrugged.

'That's okay with me,' he said. 'And that business of him being the biggest arsehole the world has ever seen, well, I've forgotten all about that already.'

'Of course,' said the Chief Inspector. 'No preconceived

ideas – that is our credo in the police force. In any case, we'll have a word with Chief of Police Sachs first. Whatever you do, don't recall the fact that he recently had a cerebral haemorrhage when we meet him.'

'Of course not,' said Münster. 'An interesting call-out, this, no doubt about that.'

'No doubt at all,' agreed Van Veeteren.

7

On Friday Verlangen was woken up by a firework.

It went off inside his own head, and its scintillations were somewhat monotonous – a non-stop battery of glowing white explosions. Let me die, he thought. Please God, let me die here and now.

His prayers went unanswered. He carefully opened one eye in an attempt to pin down those two coordinates: here and now.

Here turned out to be an unfamiliar room. Presumably in a hotel. He was lying in a bed amidst a mass of crumpled sheets and blankets, and didn't recognize the location. The room looked comparatively neat and tidy, and warm morning sun was pouring in through the windows.

Now was 09.01. There was an alarm clock on the bedside table, peeping away. He recognized it: it was his own travelling clock, bought at the Merckx supermarket a few months ago. Not that he did a lot of travelling, but you never know . . . Cost: 12.50.

He thought for a moment. There was presumably a little button cunningly concealed at the back of the clock that could be used to switch the bloody thing off. He lashed out with his right fist and the clock fell on the floor and was silent. The effort increased the intensity of the explosions inside his head.

Bloody hell, he thought. Here we go again. Where am I? What day is it?

Three hours later he had accomplished a great deal.

He had staggered to the bathroom, thrown up, had a pee and drunk a litre of water.

And somehow swallowed three headache tablets.

Found his way back to bed and fallen asleep again.

This time it wasn't the alarm clock that woke him up. It was a small, dark-skinned chambermaid who stood in the doorway, apologizing profusely.

She was young and pretty, and he decided to make an effort to tell her so.

You mustn't apologize, he wanted to say. You are young and as fresh as a dew-covered lily . . . You are looking at a seventh-rate swine. Learn the lesson.

But all he could produce was a hoarse whisper. His tongue was as supple as chicken wire; and the air coming from his tobacco-laden lungs, which was intended to create an attractive resonance in his dried-out vocal cords, was not much more than a hot puff from a dying desert fire.

Shut the door so that you don't have to look at me, he thought, and tried to do something with his face. To smile, or something of that sort. It hurt.

Now she apologized again. Wasn't he supposed to be

checking out today? she wondered. Before eleven o'clock – that was the set time. Not just in this hotel, but in each one in the chain, as explained in the information leaflet.

It was twelve noon now.

He understood now. Bitch, he thought, and felt the iron band tightening around his head once more. You were just an illusion, you as well.

'Ten minutes,' he managed to croak. 'Give me ten minutes.'

She nodded and left. Verlangen took a deep breath. Uneasy squeaking sounds emerged from his bronchial tubes. He rolled out of bed and staggered into the bathroom.

He had a simple brunch at a cafe by the name of Henry's. Two cups of black coffee, a beer and a small bottle of Vichy water. The fog inside his head slowly dispersed, and when he managed to smoke a cigarette as well, he began to realize at last that he was probably going to survive today.

Whatever good that would do him.

Thanks to the blessed return of nicotine into his veins, he found himself able to recall what had happened the previous day – certain parts of it, at least – and the role he had to play in this hellish dump of a town.

Linden, for Christ's sake, he thought. I've never felt so awful as I do here.

He left Henry's after half an hour, managed to find his Toyota in the hotel car park, flung his bag onto the back seat and walked past Aldemarckt to Landemaarstraat and Hennan's office. It was a little cooler today, thank God: clouds had started to build up from the south-west, and if he hadn't misjudged all the signs it would start raining before this evening.

He stopped at his usual place and contemplated the characterless windows above the row of shops. Checked his watch: a quarter to two. One could hardly claim that he had fulfilled his guard duties all that efficiently or enthusiastically today.

He remembered that he had promised to give Barbara Hennan some kind of report, and spent some time wondering how he was going to present it.

What the hell could he say?

That he had sat for a few hours fraternizing with his quarry? Drunk whisky after whisky after whisky with him in that confounded restaurant, whatever it was called? Eventually collapsed into bed as drunk as a lord at God only knows what time. Always assuming that God had been awake then to notice.

It was hardly the sort of thing one expected of a serious private detective – even Maarten Verlangen could see that.

At least he hadn't given himself away, he was sure of that. Despite everything he'd had the presence of mind not to tell Hennan that his precious wife had hired him as a private dick in order to find out what her husband was up to when she was unable to keep an eye on him herself. It was crucial that he shouldn't give himself away on that score, and he hadn't done so.

So all was well in that respect. But what would he be able to say about the current situation?

That he had spent half the day in bed with a third-degree hangover that unfortunately prevented him from working as usual? That he didn't have the slightest idea where his quarry was at the moment?

Would Barbara Hennan really be interested in continuing to employ him after such obvious negligence? And pay him for his efforts? Hardly.

So what should he do?

The car, he thought! Hennan's blue Saab.

Of course. Verlangen lit a cigarette and began walking optimistically around the block. If Hennan was in his office, the car would be parked somewhere close by. As sure as amen in church and the whores in Zwille.

After quite some time walking around the central parts of Linden, Verlangen was able to state with confidence that Hennan's car was nowhere to be seen. Nowhere was there a well-polished blue Saab – two other Saabs, but neither of them blue and neither of them noticeably well polished.

It looked as if Hennan hadn't come to the office today, in other words. A conclusion that fitted in well with last night's intake of whisky, Verlangen decided, and, after the purchase of a new bottle of soda water at the kiosk in the square, he sat down on a bench to think things over. He didn't have the telephone number of Hennan's company, didn't even know what it was called, so there was no chance of getting in touch with him in that way.

He emptied the bottle of soda water in two swigs, and belched loudly. He remained sitting on the bench for a while until he seemed to feel a drop of rain on the back of his hand, and decided to take a chance and make contact with his employer. He might as well take the bull by the horns, he thought.

Always assuming he wanted to continue coiling in these easily earned payments, and he did.

Once again he rang from the kiosk outside the butcher's shop. He let it ring ten times, then concluded that nobody was at home in Villa Zefyr. Or that nobody intended to answer the telephone, at least. He left the kiosk and put his hands in his pockets. It had turned three now, and it seemed pointless to waste any more energy on Hennan than he had already used up today. Especially as at the moment he had extremely limited resources of energy and patience.

Because of the circumstances.

And because it was now raining properly. Not all that heavily, but persistently and penetratingly. He decided to have something to eat, then go home. His agreement with Barbara Hennan dictated that he should only keep watch over Jaan G. on weekdays: there were only a couple of hours left until Friday evening, and so if he made another attempt to telephone her from Maardam, he could then pack up for the weekend and start work again on Monday morning. All bushy-tailed and raring to go.

No sooner said than done. He had a mediocre pizza at the Ristorante Goldoni, drank a large beer, and felt that his spirits were beginning to perk up again. At a quarter to five he clambered into his faithful Toyota, switched on the engine and set off for Maardam.

An hour later he made another attempt to call Villa Zefyr, but again nobody answered; and since nothing seemed to be working this godforsaken Friday, he went to bed shortly after nine o'clock.

A working week in the life of Private Detective Maarten Verlangen had come to an end.

'An accident,' said Chief Inspector Sachs, stroking his fingers carefully over his thin moustache. 'That is obviously the most likely explanation. But of course, you never know.'

'Very true,' said Van Veeteren. 'Maybe you could give us a summary in broad outline? We shall be talking to Hennan later, of course, but it's always good to know the lie of the land before you actually walk on it. As it were.'

Sachs cleared his throat.

'Yes, of course. Incidents like this when somebody falls and kills him or herself are very tricky.'

'Tricky?'

'Tricky, yes. Let's assume that A and B are standing on a balcony high up in a skyscraper – or on the edge of a precipice, or anywhere at all. A few seconds later B is lying dead fifty metres lower down. How the hell can you prove that A pushed him?'

Van Veeteren nodded.

'Or that he didn't push him.'

'Motive,' said Van Veeteren. 'You find out if there is a motive. If there is, you keep on interrogating the suspect until he gives up. There's no other way – no better one, at least.'

'But in this case,' said Münster, 'she was alone in the house, wasn't she?'

'As far as we know, yes,' said Sachs. 'But that's only because nothing suggests otherwise so far. Fru Hennan seems to have been sitting around drinking, all by herself, and then got it into her head that she should go for a swim . . . Alternatively to take her own life by diving down into the empty swimming pool.'

Van Veeteren took a drink from his mug of coffee, and produced a toothpick.

'Not all that likely,' he said.

'What?' wondered Sachs.

'That she took her own life. How was she dressed?'

'Swimming costume. A red swimming costume. You mean that . . . ?'

'Yes. In the first place it's a damned unpleasant way of dying. And uncertain.'

'I don't know if—'

'There's a distinct risk that you might survive,' said Van Veeteren. 'And in all probability that would mean you'd be crippled for the rest of your life. A wheelchair would be the very least you could expect.'

'I'm with you. It's a point of view, of course.'

'But if we assume she did decide to do that anyway, why the hell would she put on a swimming costume?'

Nobody spoke for several seconds.

'Because she wanted it to look like an accident,' suggested Münster.

'Not impossible,' said Van Veeteren. 'We'll see eventually if there's anything to support such an alternative, but for the moment it would surely make more sense to hear a summary of the situation, as I said before. The Hennans' circumstances, that sort of thing – assuming that you have had time to gather a few details.'

Sachs nodded and put on a pair of thin reading glasses. He thumbed back and forth once or twice in the notebook lying on the table in front of him.

'There isn't a lot,' he explained apologetically. 'The Hennans have only been living here since April. Barely two months. They arrived from the USA in the middle of March and stayed at a hotel in Maardam for a week or two while they were looking for a house to rent – obviously this is information I was given by Hennan himself, but I can't see that there's any reason to question it.'

'Not so far,' agreed Van Veeteren.

'He was born here in Maardam, but he has spent the last ten years in various places in the States. New York. Cleveland. Austin. Denver. He has a company registered here in Linden under the name G Enterprises. There is an office in Lande-maarstraat only a stone's throw from here. So he's some sort of businessman. According to what he says, he has always indulged in that kind of activity. He and his wife chose to move to Europe because trading conditions are better here, or so he says. I don't know, I'm not all that well up in that kind of thing . . .'

'I think we can forgive you for that,' said Van Veeteren. 'But we know what kind of business he indulged in before he crossed over the Atlantic: mind you, it's possible that he's cleaned up his act since then. What do we know about his wife? They met and got married in Denver, is that right?'

'Yes,' Sachs confirmed. 'Barbara Clarissa, née Delgado. Fifteen years younger than her husband. We don't know anything about her, but I expect we shall be able to dig out some information . . . In any case, they rented that house in Kammerweg. The owner is called Tieleberg, and lives somewhere in Spain. It's probably one of the most expensive homes in the whole of Linden, to tell you the truth. Eight or ten rooms plus kitchen, a few thousand square metres of garden, and a completely private situation – and with a swimming pool and diving tower. Kammerweg is where the crème de la crème live. He must be rather well off, this Hennan.'

'Hmm,' muttered Van Veeteren crossly, and broke off the toothpick. 'And what does he have to say about this so-called accident?'

'That it definitely was an accident. He's absolutely certain of that. His wife had no reason to take her own life, and as for somebody pushing her down – who could that have possibly been? She knew next to nobody. And why? Hennan says that they had an excellent relationship. He loved her, she loved him . . . They'd been married for just over two years, and were thinking about having children soon. She was only thirty-four, after all.'

'What about the alcohol?' wondered Münster. 'Why does she sit and drink herself silly if everything in her garden is lovely?'

Sachs took off his glasses and rubbed his thumb and index finger over the bridge of his nose.

'He's a bit vague on that question,' he said. 'I thought so, at least. Presumably she had drunk several gin and tonics plus quite a lot of sherry; but Hennan maintains that she didn't normally drink anything like as much as that. He admits that she did sink a few glasses now and then – even when she was on her own – but not that kind of quantity.'

'1.74 per mil is a pretty high percentage,' said Münster.

'It certainly is,' said Sachs. 'And Hennan let slip that she tended to lose control when she'd had too much to drink – which suggests that it must have happened before. He said she had more body than head when she was drunk. That seemed to mean that she was capable of standing up straight and walking, but not so good at thinking straight.'

'Hmm,' said Münster. 'That would fit in with her being able to climb up to the top of the tower and dive down, without checking to see if there was enough water in the pool.'

'Yes indeed,' said Van Veeteren. 'It fits in exactly. But I don't think we should forget the source of all this information.'

Münster nodded, and Sachs turned over a few more pages in his notebook.

'As far as Hennan himself is concerned,' he continued, 'he was in that restaurant. The Columbine. It's just behind the town hall. From about half past seven until half past mid-night, he maintains. We haven't got round to speaking to the staff there yet, but that is being organized. I'm expecting a report from Inspector Behring later this afternoon. He may well have an alibi. It would take at least half an hour to drive from there to Kammerweg and back – maybe forty minutes. Anyway we'll see what they have to say. Barbara Hennan died at some time between half past nine and half past ten, if I understand it rightly.'

He looked inquiringly at Van Veeteren.

'That's correct,' said Van Veeteren. 'I phoned Meusse, and he guesses around ten o'clock. He's rarely more than half an hour out. What was your overall impression of Hennan? Is he concealing something?'

Sachs closed his notebook and placed his hands in his armpits. Leaned back in his chair and thought for a while.

'God only knows,' he said eventually. 'He was drunk when I spoke to him, but nevertheless . . . well, incredibly calm and collected, somehow. If he was in shock or something of the sort – and let's face it, he ought to have been – he didn't show it at all. But . . . Well, I have to say that I'm not at all sure about my impression of him. I'm grateful for the fact that you are here and will draw your own conclusions as well. As I said, I'm inclined to think that it was an accident, of course – but you never know.'

'And there were no indications in the house suggesting that she'd had a visitor? Somebody else, that is.'

'Nothing that we found, at least. There was just one used glass, and it had her prints on it. But of course we haven't

been through the house with a fine-tooth comb. There wasn't
. . . There didn't seem to be any need.'

Van Veeteren nodded, and took hold of the arms of his
chair.

'All right,' he said. 'Let's see what Inspector Münster and I
come up with. If there is anything of immediate importance
maybe we can call in here on our way home. Otherwise we'll
be in touch by phone.'

'You're always most welcome,' said Chief Inspector Sachs,
thrusting out his arms. 'Good hunting, as they say.'

8

A few seconds before coming face to face with Jaan G. Hennan, an old Borkmann rule came into Van Veeteren's head.

It was not the first time. Chief Inspector Borkmann had been his mentor during the early years up in Frigge, but at that time he had not realized how many of the old bloodhound's understated comments would accompany him throughout his career.

But they did. Irrespective of the type of investigation, there was more or less always a relevant piece of advice from Borkmann to fish up from the well of memory. It was just a case of devoting sufficient time to thinking about it. Sometimes – as on this occasion – he didn't even need to go fishing: he could hear his mentor's calm voice as clear as day inside the back of his head, echoing down through two decades of messy and clamorous police work.

This time – just as he and Inspector Münster were slowly approaching the somewhat portly figure up on the terrace of Villa Zefyr – it concerned the ability to keep quiet.

'Learn how to stay silent!' Borkmann had urged. There

was nothing as uncomfortable for anybody with anything on their conscience as silence.

And Borkmann had elaborated: 'If you can just keep your trap shut, a mere look or the raising of an eyebrow can induce any killer or bank robber to lose his composure and let the cat out of the bag. From sheer nervousness. Make silence your ally, and you will come off best in every single interrogation!'

Just before they were within hearing distance, Van Veeteren poked Münster with his elbow.

'Don't say too much,' he said. 'Let me run this conversation.'

'Okay,' said Münster. 'Message understood.'

Hennan was wearing wide white trousers and some kind of blue sailing jumper. Or possibly a golf jumper, Münster found it difficult to decide which. He looked grim and easily irritated. Close-cropped, dark hair. A suggestion of grey at the temples. A powerful-looking face. When he shook hands, his grip was firm – as if it involved some kind of marking of territory.

'VV,' he said. 'Long time no see.'

'G,' said Van Veeteren. 'Yes, it's been a few years.'

'Münster,' said Münster. 'Detective Inspector.'

They sat down at a table made of high-grade hardwood. Probably teak. Standing in the middle of it was an ice bucket with several bottles of beer pressed down inside it.

'A glass of beer?' Hennan suggested. 'It's on the warm side today.'

'It'll probably rain,' said Van Veeteren. 'But yes please.'

Hennan poured out three glasses. They each took a swig, then sat in silence for ten seconds.

'Well?' said Hennan.

Van Veeteren produced a packet of West, took one out and lit it with a theatrical flourish. Münster folded his arms and waited. It struck him that it was much easier to conduct an effective interrogation if you were a smoker.

'A sad story,' said Van Veeteren, blowing out a cloud of smoke.

'You can say that again,' said Hennan.

Five more seconds passed.

'I wonder how the hell it happened,' said Van Veeteren.

'What do you mean by that?'

Van Veeteren shrugged, and contemplated Hennan for a while. Hennan didn't move a muscle.

'Don't you?'

'Don't I what?'

'Wonder how it happened.'

Hennan drank a sip of beer, and took a slim black cigar out of a wooden case lying on the table. Also teak, Münster decided. Or possibly walnut – the grains were not quite the same.

Hennan lit it, and removed a flake of tobacco that had stuck fast to the tip of his tongue.

'I don't understand why you have come here,' he said. 'My wife has died as a result of a terrible accident. I've spent half the night talking to stupid police officers, and now it seems the same nonsense is going to continue.'

Van Veeteren took a puff of his cigarette, and nodded very slowly and very thoughtfully.

'How long were you in jail?' he asked.

Jaan G. Hennan's facial expression stiffened significantly, Münster noted. As if somebody had pulled his ears backwards and stretched the skin on his face and somehow or other made it thinner. A sort of facelift, but sideways. The image of a wolf flashed through Münster's consciousness.

Van Veeteren yawned and blew his nose. He took a little yellow notebook out of his inside pocket and wrote something down. Hennan observed his actions with increasing annoyance.

'What the hell do you want?' he exclaimed in the end. 'If you have something to say, for Christ's sake come out with it! But if you simply intend to sit here and play at hard-nosed idiotic coppers, I shall leave you to it. I have quite a lot of things to see to.'

'Really?' said Van Veeteren. 'What, for example?'

'Eh?'

'What do you have to see to?'

'That ...' Hennan hesitated for a second ...'That has nothing to do with you.'

He pulled up the sleeves of his sailing-golf jumper and revealed two powerful, tanned lower arms. Van Veeteren leaned a bit further forward over the table.

'Why are you so nervous?' he asked in a friendly tone of voice. 'Is there something you forgot to mention to the police last night?'

Hennan turned his head and spat out another flake of

tobacco onto the grass. Crossed his legs and began drumming his fingers on the arm of his chair. A few more seconds passed.

'Your lickspittle here,' he said, pointing at Münster. 'Is he dumb, or what?'

'I have a sore throat,' said Münster. 'Carry on, you two. I'll say something if there's anything that needs saying.'

Van Veeteren nodded sympathetically in Münster's direction before once again concentrating on Hennan.

'G,' he said. 'I've never liked that letter.'

Hennan did not react.

'Do you really think your wife died in the way you tried to convince the police it happened last night?'

Hennan didn't move a muscle of his face. But he kept on drumming his fingers. Van Veeteren waited. Münster waited.

'Would you kindly explain what the hell you mean by that?'

The Chief Inspector raised a smile.

'What do I mean? I wonder if she was blind, of course. What was her IQ?'

'What the devil . . . ?' Hennan began to protest.

'Don't you also think there was somebody who pushed her?'

'Why should I think that?'

'No sensible person dives into an empty swimming pool.'

'Barbara did it by mistake.'

'That's what you are trying to make us believe, yes.'

Hennan seemed to be arguing with himself for a few

seconds. Then he stood up and pushed his chair backwards so that it toppled over onto the lawn.

'I've had enough of this now,' he said. 'I'm not going to sit here and be castigated any longer. Not another word without a solicitor present.'

Van Veeteren stubbed out his cigarette. Then he took a drink of beer. Then he stared at his former schoolmate with astonishment written all over his face.

'A solicitor? Why on earth should you need a solicitor? Surely you aren't hiding something from us?'

'I have no intention . . .'

Van Veeteren stuck a warning index finger up into the air, and turned to look at Münster.

'Do you think herr Hennan is hiding something, Inspector?'

Münster thought for a moment.

'I can't think what that could possibly be,' he said.

'Get out of here!' said Hennan. 'Leave me in peace. This was the damnedest—'

'I'll just finish off my beer,' said Van Veeteren, raising his glass. 'It wasn't up to much, but it's drinkable. Cheers, and I look forward to our next meeting.'

'Not too bad,' said Van Veeteren when they were back in the car. 'Round one to us, all the judges agree.'

'So do I,' said Münster. 'But I don't really understand what you're getting at.'

'Really?' said Van Veeteren in surprise. 'And what do you mean by that, Inspector?'

Münster started the engine.

'Are you suggesting that it's Hennan who's behind all this? Or what? Have we forgotten that he seems to have an alibi?'

'Bah!' exclaimed Van Veeteren. 'Alibi? We haven't had confirmation of anything yet. He could easily have slipped out of that restaurant for thirty or forty minutes . . . Let's wait until we have the staff's version before we start talking about an alibi.'

'All right,' said Münster. 'I'll wait for that.'

'Or he could have had an accomplice,' said Van Veeteren. 'He could have hired a gorilla who went to the house and pushed her into the pool.'

Münster sighed.

'Are you really being serious?'

Once again he received a surprised look from his superior.

'Münster, I know that Barbara Hennan's death looks like some sort of accident, and there's a damned good reason why it should look like that as well.'

'Really?' said Münster. 'And what's that?'

'That G wants it to look like an accident.'

Münster said nothing.

'Surely you don't think that I'm mistaken?' said Van Veeteren, winding down the passenger window a couple of centimetres. 'It seems to be raining now – what did I tell you?'

'It would never occur to me to question your judgement, Chief Inspector,' said Münster diplomatically. 'We don't have any facts to go on as yet, so it's okay to speculate as much as you like.'

'Speculate?'

'Yes.'

Van Veeteren said nothing.

'But he seems a hard nut to crack, that Hennan,' said Münster. 'I'll give you that.'

'Even hard nuts can be cracked open,' said the Chief Inspector, staring hard at a broken toothpick. 'Just wait.'

'It will be interesting,' said Münster. 'And those old insights into his psychology that we spoke about . . . What was it you said? The most unpleasant bastard . . . ?'

But Van Veeteren merely gestured dismissively with his hand.

'Next week,' he said. 'Let's enjoy a restful weekend first. How are Synn and little Bart?'

He drives me up the wall at times, thought Münster.

Maarten Verlangen had an alcohol-free day on Saturday. He changed the bed sheets, washed three machine-loads of laundry, and took all his rubbish out to the communal bins. In the afternoon he went jogging for one-and-a-quarter kilometres in Megsje Bois, then telephoned a woman he knew.

Her name was Carla Besbarwny, and exactly as he had hoped and expected she said he was welcome to visit her if he felt like it. She would need to walk the dogs first, but any time after eight would be fine. He thanked her and hung up. Breathed a sigh of relief. It's good that Carla exists at least, he thought.

He had known her for rather more than three years: they had met about half a dozen times, and on each occasion had spent more or less all the time in her generous waterbed. He knew that she probably had quite a few other men who came to visit her in similar circumstances, but so what? You couldn't own women like Carla. She lived at the far end of Alexanderlaan in a large four-roomed flat, together with three dogs, a few cats and an unknown number of small birds, guinea-pigs and Japanese dwarf-mice. Goodness only knew how she made a living, and from a purely clinical point of view she was probably mad.

But that didn't much matter either. He wasn't going to visit her that evening for spiritual fellowship. Nor would that be why she received him.

He rang her doorbell at a quarter past eight on Saturday evening, and exactly sixteen hours later left her in an ambivalent state of lax harmony and bad conscience. Exactly the same as usual.

'Why don't you get married, Carla?' he had asked her at one point during the night. 'A woman like you?'

'Are you proposing to me?' she had wondered.

'No,' he had answered. 'I . . . I'm not mature enough to get married yet.'

'There's your answer.'

He returned to the loneliness and clean sheets of Heerbanerstraat. Thought about phoning his daughter, but put it off. He didn't want to contact her too often. He didn't want her to feel that she had a duty to meet him or talk to him. Quality is better than quantity, he used to tell himself. A bitter and somewhat heroic thought, in fact, for surely a certain level of quantity was necessary if any kind of level of quality was to be achieved?

Except in connection with Carla Besbarwny, perhaps?

He shelved all such thoughts and instead tried once again to telephone Villa Zefyr. It wouldn't be a bad idea to get some instructions about how he should go about his work in future, he thought, and in any case, he still hadn't delivered his Friday report.

If it was G who answered he could always hang up.

It was G.

As far as Verlangen could judge, in any case. He sounded gloomy. For a couple of seconds Verlangen toyed with the idea of disguising his voice and saying that it was a wrong number, but he decided that to do so would be too risky.

He swallowed, and hung up.

Strictly speaking I don't actually start work again until tomorrow, he decided. The Sabbath day should be respected – and sufficient unto the day is the evil thereof, as the Good Book says.

He fetched a beer from the refrigerator and switched on the television.

When Van Veeteren put on Pergolesi's *Stabat mater* late on Sunday evening, he had been longing for that moment all weekend.

There had been so many domestic obligations to cope

with. Dinner with Renate's brother and sister-in-law on Saturday evening – and breakfast and lunch with the same dodgy pair on Sunday, since they lived up in Chadow and had spent the night with the Van Veeterens. A serious discussion with Renate about Erich's situation at school (and in life generally) on Sunday afternoon (but without the main character himself, as he was out with some of his mates), and then – for two hours in the evening – a damned dishwasher he had been promising to try to repair for a month now. It was much more broken when he had finished with it than it had been to start with.

What had he said to Münster? Something about a restful weekend?

He hadn't even had time to glance at the chess problem in the *Allgemenje*.

But at half past eleven he flopped down at last in the armchair with Pergolesi ringing in his ears. Dark in the room. Renate in bed, Erich in bed. The disc was fifty-eight minutes long – he had checked that before switching it on. It also contained the Orpheus cantatas.

Good, he thought. At last an hour of high-quality life.

And at last an opportunity to think about his relationship with G.

What could be a better-quality accompaniment to that than the Dolorosa duet, sung by Julia Gouda and Anna Faulkner? He took three deep breaths and floated back thirty-five years in time. That was where it was – his strongest memory of G.

Blacker than black.

★

Autumn term at Manneringskolan on the banks of Poost-lenergraacht, to be more exact. Age: early puberty. Main characters: G, VV and a little Jewish boy by the name of Adam Bronstein.

G: the big, strong and feared young man. Adam Bronstein: the gifted, spectacles-wearing, quick-thinking, anaemic one. VV: the hesitant one who didn't dare to pick a fight with G, didn't dare intervene and put a stop to the bullying of those weaker than himself. It is not only Adam Bronstein who suffers, but he is the main victim.

The terrible deed takes place after a PE class. When the teacher (the immensely unpopular herr Schwaager) has left – and when most of the boys have finished the necessary washing and clothes-changing and left the gym that smells strongly of sweat (located in an old wooden building between the school itself and the canal) – G forces Adam Bronstein to lie down on the large grey mat that is used for practising somersaults and similar useful exercises. The skinny little boy does as he is told and G rolls him up inside the mat. It becomes a large, compact cylinder, just over a metre high and just over a metre in diameter. A leather strap fastened around it prevents it from unrolling. Thanks to his own considerable strength and the assistance of one of the boys still left (his name is Claus Fendermann and he is destined to become an outstanding pianist), G stands the cylinder upright – with Adam Bronstein's head at the bottom. His arms are pressed closely against his sides, his feet in a pair of pitiful blue-grey socks with worn-out elastic tops sticking a few centimetres out of the top. The boy is stuck there in a sort of dark, iron-hard vice: his head is slowly filled with blood, it becomes increasingly difficult for him to breathe – and the boys leave him there in that state. G, Claus Fendermann, VV and several others. They gather together their things and hurry off to their conventional classroom. G is the last to leave, and closes the door behind him.

There is no class in the gymnasium the following period, so Adam Bronstein stays inside the cylinder for almost an hour. It is a cleaner who finds him. He is still alive, but only just. He spends two months in hospital. Never comes back to school.

The news breaks in January that he has hanged himself.

It is not usual for thirteen-year-olds to hang themselves. Not at that time, at least.

He might just as well have died straight off in the bloody mat, says G. The little Jewish swine.

Stabat mater.

The Quis est homo movement began, and Van Veeteren realized that he was sweating profusely in his armchair. Cold sweat. Adam Bronstein was only one of the memories associated with G. There were more. But perhaps that one was sufficient to be going on with?

He tried to concentrate on Friday's confrontation instead.

What had it signified? In fact?

Why had he chosen that absurdly hard-boiled line during the conversation at Villa Zefyr? Silence and polished steel.

Why? There was no doubt that he had overdone Borkmann's rule of silence.

And why had he been so convinced of Hennan's guilt when he spoke to Münster about it afterwards in the car? The inspector had sounded sceptical, and rightly so.

Did he really think that G had got rid of his wife? Killed her? Hand on heart.

Wasn't it rather a sudden urge – and a sudden opportunity out of the blue – to give G what he deserved? To put things to rights and punish him thirty-five years later? Once and for all.

Was it really as simple as that?

In any case, it was difficult to ignore these private motives for revenge – but maybe it was good that he had allowed himself to wallow in them? From the very start. Motives that you didn't recognize were more difficult to cope with than those you dragged up to the surface, he was aware of that. It was something even Borkmann had pointed out on one occasion or another – although in that case it had to do with the motivation of a criminal rather than that of a police officer investigating a case.

But if he could now – in theory at least – ignore the deep-seated disgust he felt for Jaan G. Hennan, push it to one side for a moment, what were the facts of the circumstances surrounding Hennan's wife's death?

Was there any real reason to suspect a crime?

And if there was, was there any objective justification for directing those suspicions at G?

Van Veeteren closed his eyes and tried to relax. The

questions were pointless. They were being asked too early. Of the traditional puzzle-pieces Motive-Method-Opportunity, only the second was anywhere close to being identified. If in fact it was the case that Barbara Hennan had been murdered, there was not much doubt about the method. The way in which it had been carried out. A push in the back – or as much violence as could be considered necessary to make her lose her balance and fall down from the diving tower.

Another matter, of course, was getting her up there in the first place. That would probably not have been due to brute strength. Cunning, more likely . . . Presumably some kind of very subtle cunning.

Or perhaps she had been knocked unconscious by a blow to the head? It would have been difficult to carry her up the steps to the top of the diving tower afterwards, but no doubt not impossible. He made a mental note to ask Meusse if one might be able to distinguish between a wound that had been inflicted slightly earlier than – and in a different way to – those that were the result of her crashing down into the bottom of the empty swimming pool.

That was more or less all that could be said about the method, Van Veeteren thought. He wondered if he ought to go and fetch a beer from the kitchen, but decided against it.

What about Opportunity? Well, it wasn't especially difficult to speculate about that.

Anybody at all who might have been in the vicinity of Villa Zefyr at about ten o'clock on Thursday evening would have had an opportunity – hypothetically at least – to carry out the murder in the way spelled out above. The problem was that the most interesting figure in this context – Jaan G. Hennan – appeared to have an alibi for this time.

Appeared. Obviously, it remained to be seen how solid this alibi really was. Sachs and his team ought surely to have had enough time to sort out this matter by now.

That left Motive. Who had had any reason to kill Barbara Hennan? And more specifically: what motives might G have had?

Van Veeteren decided that if there was one question he ought to examine rather more closely in the next few days, it was this one.

If there is even a fraction of a possibility that he is behind this, the Chief Inspector thought, gritting his teeth . . . If G has anything at all to do with the death of his wife, I shall put him behind bars for it. For Adam Bronstein's sake and all the other poor devils he has tortured in one way or another during his life.

It was quite simply his duty. An absolutely imperative duty.

What am I doing? he thought in horror. I'm sitting here, hoping that an accident can be transformed into a murder. Purely in order to satisfy my own private instincts for vengeance. Talk about objective police work! Talk about motives!

He listened to the end of the Pergolesi CD, both *Stabat mater* and the Orpheus cantatas. It was a quarter to one when he crawled down into the double bed next to his wife. Quietly and carefully so as not to wake her up.

I don't love her any more, he suddenly thought. I haven't done so for ages now. Why do we continue to maintain this conventional spectacle?

For whose sake?

It was an idiotic question to ask himself just before falling asleep, and an hour later he was still awake.

9

When Maarten Verlangen opened up his office in the morning of Tuesday, 9 June, it was the first time he had set foot in there since Wednesday the previous week.

As a result, if nothing else, he had the last five editions of *Neuwe Blatt* to read. In accordance with an unwritten gentleman's agreement, a neighbour – the widow fru Meredith – always posted her copy through his letter box after she had read it and cut out the evening's television programmes. The gesture was a thank-you for what Verlangen had done eighteen months earlier to track down some pervert who had spent some time posting his own excrement through her letter box – a young and at times promising banking lawyer, it transpired, who had undergone a personality change after cycling headfirst into a tramcar on Keymer Plejn. After nailing him, Verlangen had felt a certain degree of sympathy with the poor, confused young man, and had visited him regularly during the six months he had spent in the Majorna mental hospital.

Despite everything, it seemed there were some people worse off than he was . . .

He arranged the newspapers chronologically in a pile on

his desk, lit a cigarette and listened to his telephone answering machine. Nothing from Barbara Hennan. Only three messages, in fact: one from the insurance company, one from somebody called Wallander who would ring him back, and a wrong number.

He dialled the number of Villa Zefyr.

No answer.

He read the Wednesday edition of *Neuwe Blatt* and tried again.

No answer.

Lit another cigarette and worked his way through the Thursday and Friday editions of the newspaper.

Third time lucky, he thought.

The hell it was. The ringing sounded as desolate as his own thoughts. He replaced the receiver, and wondered what to do next. Was there any point in continuing to keep an eye on Hennan?

Was he under any obligation to do so?

Hardly. He had been working on the case for three days (or at least been on hand in Linden for three days), his daily rate had been three hundred guilders and he had been given a thousand by fru Hennan. Bearing in mind his hotel bill and other odds and ends, one could say that the pay more or less covered his input.

Perhaps it would be as well to leave it at that. Forget about the elegant American woman and her shady husband, and devote his attentions to something else.

But on the other hand: another thousand for a few days of less than strenuous effort was not to be sniffed at. Especially as he had no other commitments at the moment. Apart from a so-called 'pay by results' job he had been toying with for several months: a gang of graffiti-producing vandals had been making a nuisance of themselves in Linden, and local shop-owners had clubbed together to offer a reward of 5,000 guilders to anybody who could apprehend them. But although Verlangen had one or two possible names and a few possible faces in mind, there was a long way to go before he could collect the reward.

He sighed. Opened the day's first beer and decided on one final compromise in the Hennan question: first he would glance through the Saturday and Sunday editions of *Neuwe Blatt*, and then make another call to Villa Zefyr.

The article was on page five of the Saturday edition.

Woman found dead was the headline, and he read the short text with roughly the same feelings he used to have at the Gerckwinckel pub when he realized that the sweaty, red and swollen face in the mirror over the toilet was his own.

Was it possible? he wondered.

Who else could it be, for Christ's sake?

A woman aged about 35, it said.

Of American origin.

Found dead at the bottom of an empty swimming pool.

On the outskirts of Linden. Unclear circumstances, but as far as one could tell she had thought the pool was full and dived in from a considerable height.

No witnesses of the accident. No suspicions of foul play.

Verlangen read the article – no more than sixteen lines in a single column – three times while drinking the beer and smoking another cigarette.

American woman?

How many American women could there be in Linden? Not many, he thought.

And he remembered that diving tower. What an incredibly pointless way to die.

Hell's bells, he thought. What the devil is the significance of this?

Thursday night? Dammit all, that was the night he had sat and . . .

For a few seconds Maarten Verlangen could feel his mind changing into that famous tablet of soap in the bathroom that it was impossible to grasp hold of, and that not even a louse could cling to. After another deep draught of beer, however, he managed to restore a modicum of order into his thoughts, and two possible courses of action crystallized out.

Or at least, two first moves in two possible courses of action.

Either he could phone the police – that would of course be the most sensible thing to do.

Or he could drive out to Linden one more time and see what he could find out there.

After five seconds of simulated thinking, he chose the second alternative. He could ring the police at a later stage, and it would be stupid to get involved before he had established that it really was the right woman. That it was in fact Barbara Clarissa Hennan who had been found lying dead in the swimming pool.

No sooner said than done. He left his office and half-ran to his car.

'Really?' said Van Veeteren. 'Is it that bad?'

He listened intently to what was emerging from the telephone receiver with the expression on his face becoming ever more gloomy. Like a trough of low pressure, thought Inspector Münster, who was sitting opposite his superior and running the tip of his tongue over a back tooth from which he had lost part of a filling the previous evening. An English toffee – it wasn't the first time.

'I see,' muttered Van Veeteren. 'Ah well, I suppose it was only to be expected . . . Good God no, we're not going to drop the matter as quickly as that. I'll be in touch again shortly.'

He listened for a short while longer, then said goodbye and hung up. Leaned back on his chair and glared at Münster.

'Sachs,' he said. 'They've spoken to people at that restaurant now.'

'And?' said Münster.

'Unfortunately it seems he was in fact hanging around there all the time, our friend G.'

'Oh dear. But maybe he—'

'The whole evening.'

'Are they certain of that?'

The temperature in the area of low pressure fell by several more degrees.

'Apparently. Damn and blast!'

Münster shrugged.

'So that's that, then. I suppose we can—'

'But who knows? He arrived at about half past seven – he'd rung in advance and booked a table. As if he were determined to set himself up with an alibi, the swine.'

Van Veeteren stared hard at Münster.

'And then what?' wondered Münster, as was presumably the intention.

'Then? Well, he had dinner, drank a fair bit with it, then moved over to the bar, they reckon. He evidently took a taxi at about a quarter to one: they're trying to track down the driver. Damn and blast, as I said.'

Münster nodded.

'So he's clean, it seems? It's not possible that he slipped out for an hour or so, I take it?'

'How should I know? Nobody was keeping an eye on him all the time, but given how long it would take to get to Kammerweg and back . . . Well, I suppose it's not totally out of the question. It would have had to be after he'd paid his bill in that case, and he presumably did that at about half past nine . . . Hmm . . .'

'Was there anybody with him?'

'Not while he was at his table. Apparently he spoke to somebody or other later in the bar . . . Maybe even several, but our colleagues in Linden haven't bothered to look any closer into that. No, we shall have to try to find some other way of solving this, Münster.'

'What, for example?'

The Chief Inspector snapped a toothpick and looked out through the window.

'Theoretically . . . Theoretically he could have nipped out at around half past nine, driven like a madman to Kammerweg, pushed his wife into the empty swimming pool and been back in the bar at Columbine's thirty or forty minutes later. But as I said, if you can think of a better solution, that's fine by me.'

Münster said nothing for a while.

'That business ten years ago . . .'

'Twelve,' said Van Veeteren. 'Nineteen seventy-five.'

'Twelve years ago. Were you involved in it in any way?'

Van Veeteren shook his head.

'Not at all. The drugs squad dealt with all aspects of it, I only heard about it. It's a pity they didn't manage to get him locked away for longer – I suspect he should have got much more than two-and-a-half years . . . If they don't appeal, that's usually an indication that they were lucky.'

Münster squirmed in his chair.

'Forgive me for asking,' he said, 'but how come you are so sure he is guilty this time as well? Despite everything, it does seem—'

'I've never said I'm sure,' interrupted Van Veeteren, annoyed. 'But I'm damned if I'm going to exclude that possibility at this early stage.'

'There is a variant,' said Münster after a short pause.

'A variant?' said Van Veeteren. 'What do you mean by that, Inspector?'

Münster cleared his throat and hesitated for a moment.

'Well, how about this?' he said. 'It's purely hypothetical, of course. Hennan leaves the restaurant, let's say at a quarter to ten. He goes out and meets his wife somewhere in central Linden. He hits her and kills her and puts her body in the boot of his car. It takes about ten minutes. Then he goes back into the restaurant. When he gets home – at about one o'clock – he takes her out of the boot and throws her into the swimming pool. Then he phones the police.'

Van Veeteren worked away at his lower jaw for a while with a new toothpick before answering.

'That's among the most unlikely thing I've heard since Renate got it into her head that . . . anyway, that's irrelevant. What the devil do you mean?'

'I did say that it was a bit forced.'

'Do you know how G travelled home that night?'

'No, I—'

'Taxi. He took a taxi. Are you suggesting that he stuffed her into a body bag and put her in the back seat, and then got the driver to help him carry her into the house?'

'Stop,' said Münster. 'We haven't yet had it confirmed that he really did take a taxi, have we? We only know that he said he did.'

Van Veeteren eyed him critically.

'All right,' he said. 'You have a point. We can check with Meusse if the injuries could have been caused by something different from the fall. We need to do that in any case, of course. But if it did happen in the way you describe, I hereby promise to clip your toenails for a whole year.'

'Excellent,' said Münster. 'I look forward to that. But you're the one who's so keen to get G locked up, not me.'

'Rubbish,' said Van Veeteren. 'We're only discussing matters hypothetically, I thought you were capable of doing that. You have to try out any number of theories – if you don't do that, you'll never get anywhere.'

Münster remained seated for a few seconds, thinking things over. Then he stood up.

'I have quite a lot of other things to see to, if you'll excuse me. Shall I tell you what I really think about Barbara Hennan's death?'

'If you feel you have to.'

'Thank you. An accident. As clear as crystal. The Chief Inspector can put away all his nail scissors.'

Van Veeteren snorted.

'Inspector Münster, bear in mind that you are not employed in the CID to investigate accidents. Your job is to uncover and fight crimes. Not to turn a blind eye to them.'

'Understood,' said Münster. 'Anything else?'

'And to play badminton with your immediate superior. When do you have time? Tomorrow afternoon?'

'Understood,' said Münster again, and slunk out through the door.

He's getting better and better, thought the Chief Inspector when he was on his own. In fact.

But then, he has such a good mentor.

Inspector Münster had been working for the Maardam police for just over ten years, but had only been a detective officer for three. He moved to the CID at around about the same time as Van Veeteren took over from old Chief Inspector Mort, and Van Veeteren had noticed – especially during the last year – that more and more frequently Münster was the one he most wanted to have around. In cases where it was possible to pick and choose among colleagues, he almost always chose Münster.

There was nothing seriously wrong with Reinhart, deBries, Rooth, Nielsen or Heinemann, of course, but it was only with Münster that he could develop the mutually fruitful teacher–pupil relationship – a game that was all too often misunderstood nowadays, he thought, and which he no doubt linked with Hesse's *Das Glasperlenspiel* – a work he assumed would never appear on any reading list for courses on criminology.

And which didn't really fit in exactly with the slightly dissonant tone which occasionally seemed to arise between them as if they were two unequal siblings.

Enough of that, he thought, looking out over the town, which was once again bathed in generous sunshine. Speculations and would-be-wise psychology. And this was not a good time to be thinking about Hesse, in fact. Nor Münster, come to that. It would be better to try to find a way of handling that confounded G.

He realized that this was also easier said than done, put on his jacket and went down to the canteen for a coffee.

★

Verlangen drove slowly past Villa Zefyr and stopped fifty metres further on. Sat at the wheel for five minutes while he smoked a cigarette and wondered what to do. Had the distinct feeling that he ought not to do anything rash. Not to draw any conclusions before he was certain about the basic facts.

Was it Barbara Hennan who died last Thursday evening, or was the newspaper article about some entirely different woman?

During the drive from Maardam he had wondered how best to go about finding out the answer to that question, but no simple, straightforward course of action had sprung to mind.

He could phone one of the editors on the local newspaper, of course, but in all probability they would decline to release the name of the woman involved.

He could march in on Jaan G. Hennan and ask him straight out, but something about this bold initiative scared him. Instinctively. When he thought more closely about it, he also realized that his fear could well be justified. From a purely objective point of view. If Barbara Hennan really was dead, there was obviously something fishy going on. She had commissioned a private detective to shadow her husband, and even if the newspapers said that the police did not suspect foul play – well, come off it! Maarten Verlangen was not born yesterday. Far from it. Hennan was a slimy customer – had been just that twelve years ago, and his behaviour at the Columbine had hardly indicated any improvement in his character.

Just trudging into Villa Zefyr like an innocent Jehovah's

Witness seemed an excessively naive thing to do. Not to say stupid.

What other possibilities were there?

He could telephone the police and spin them a yarn. That might be a reasonable alternative, provided he could find a satisfactory yarn. But there was another way that seemed significantly easier, and which he decided to try first.

The neighbours.

Neighbours always knew everything, that was an old and reliable rule. Verlangen got out of his car and headed for Villa Vigali, which was evidently what the Trottas' house was called. It was the only plot adjacent to that of the Hennans, and as Barbara Hennan had said that they had made social contact with the Trottas, it would be very odd if they knew nothing at all about what had happened on Thursday night.

What *might well* have happened, that is.

He crossed over the street and passed by Villa Zefyr again, this time on foot. At that very moment a black Peugeot approached from the opposite direction and came to a halt just outside the entrance to the neighbouring house. A man in a dark suit got out – and even if Verlangen had not had the background he did have, he would have had no trouble at all in identifying him as a police officer. Without so much as a glance in any direction the man strode in between the brick pillars that marked the entrance to Villa Vigali, and was soon swallowed up by the luxuriant greenery inside the grounds. Verlangen stopped in mid-stride.

Oh dear, he thought. Perhaps this isn't the best time for them to receive another visitor.

But on the other hand: if a CID officer felt obliged to pay a visit to Barbara Hennan's neighbours, that surely indicated that he didn't need to bother to go to the same trouble. The situation was crystal clear.

He returned to his car. Made a U-turn and set off back to the centre of town. A quarter of an hour later he telephoned the police station from a kiosk outside the railway station. A female secretary answered, and he asked to speak to the chief of police.

He had to wait for a minute, but then had Chief Inspector Sachs on the line.

'Good morning, my name is Edward Stroop,' explained Verlangen in a friendly tone. 'I have some information to give you about the Barbara Hennan case.'

Silence for three seconds.

'I see,' said the chief of police eventually. 'Are you in Linden?'

'Yes.'

'May I ask you to come to the police station as quickly as possible?'

'Of course,' said Verlangen, and hung up.

So everything was clear. Crystal clear. His employer, Barbara Clarissa Hennan, had met her maker at the bottom of an empty swimming pool. Verlangen left the station building and remained standing for a couple of minutes on the steps while he lit a cigarette and wondered what to do next.

And what the hell was going on.

10

'All right, all right,' said Münster. 'Of course I know about that. I know the Linden police have already been here and spoken to you, but I'm from the Maardam CID. My chief inspector is a very meticulous gentleman, and he insisted that we also ought to have a chat with you. I trust you have nothing against our trying to do our job as well as we can?'

Amelia Trotta eyed him doubtfully. Her large, smooth face looked worried, despite the fact that there wasn't the slightest trace of a wrinkle in it anywhere. Her shoulder-length hair, dyed blonde, was immaculate and reminded Münster of a forgotten, clean-living film star from his early teens. He assumed that was roughly the impression fru Trotta was trying to give. Or had tried – now she was about forty-five, large and somewhat irritated.

'What's the point?' she asked. 'I have nothing useful to say.'

She made a vague sort of gesture that could mean anything at all. Münster made the most of the opportunity and walked past her into the living room.

'He's very insistent, my boss,' he said apologetically and sat down in a cretonne armchair. 'And he's known for leaving nothing to chance.'

She nodded doubtfully and sat down on the edge of cretonne armchair number two. Smoothed down a few creases
in her dress and sighed.

'Just a few minutes, then,' she said. 'I have quite a few
things to see to.'

Münster took a notebook and pen out of his briefcase.

'Thank you,' he said. 'I shall try to be brief. Anyway, Barbara Hennan. How well did you know her?'

'Not at all,' said Trotta.

'Not at all?'

'Well, hardly. As I explained to the inspectors who were
here yesterday. We've been living here for fifteen years, the
Hennans moved in in April. We've had dinner in each other's
house, but that's all. The sort of thing you do as good
neighbours.'

'Of course,' said Münster. 'And were they?'

'Were they what?'

'Good neighbours.'

She shrugged.

'I suppose so.'

'Suppose?'

'Yes. There was nothing for us to complain about. It's just
that they weren't really our style.'

'I see,' said Münster non-committally, taking a quick look
round the spacious, very tidy room. Sofa with matching arm-
chairs, and television. Two large, pale oil paintings, their colours
matching the upholstery and the curtains. And a set of book-
cases in solid oak containing all kinds of things but no books.

Style? he thought. Hmm.

'What do you think about the accident?'

Fru Trotta tried once again to frown.

'I don't think anything at all, of course,' she said. 'What is there to think?'

'Do you know if fru Hennan might have been depressed?'

'I've no idea. Why do you ask that?'

'There's always a possibility that she might have arranged the accident, as it were.'

'That she took her own life, you mean?'

'We can't exclude that possibility. It's a very odd way to die, don't you think?'

Amelia Trotta spent a few seconds thinking over how to answer that.

'People do die in odd ways nowadays.'

Nowadays? Münster thought. Hmm, I suppose she might be right. He recalled having read not long ago about a prostitute in Oosterdam choking herself to death on a condom.

'Did you like her?' he asked.

She shrugged once again.

'Not all that much then?' he said.

'I've already said that we didn't know them. Neither him nor her.'

'But you had no desire to expand your contact with them, beyond being good neighbours?'

She hesitated for a moment.

'No,' she said. 'I suppose we didn't.'

'Your husband as well?'

'Yes.'

Münster waited.

'There was something . . . something cheap about them.'

'Cheap? What do you mean by that?'

'I'm sure you understand what I mean.'

'No,' said Münster frankly. 'Can you explain in a little more detail?'

She sighed, and moved further back in the armchair.

'I don't know,' she said. 'You just noticed it. She was tattooed, for instance.'

'Tattooed?' said Münster.

'Here,' said Trotta, pointing at a spot high up on her left arm, under the sleeve of her dress. 'A bird or something. You can say what you like about tattoos, but it's not attractive.'

Münster nodded and made a note.

'When did you see her last?'

'On Saturday.'

'On Saturday?' said Münster in surprise. 'She was already dead then.'

'I know that, of course. But I was at the mortuary to identify her. There has to be somebody from outside the family as well.'

'In certain circumstances, yes,' said Münster. 'But let's concentrate on the living. When did you last see her before the accident?'

'The same morning that she died,' said fru Trotta without hesitation. 'Shortly after eight o'clock. She drove off towards town. We just said hello – I was out with Ray.'

'Ray?'

'Our dog. A Pomeranian.'

'I see,' said Münster. 'And you never saw her again after that?'

'Not until I identified her at the mortuary.'

'And herr Hennan. What about him?'

'What about him?'

'Did you see him at all on Thursday?'

'No. As you might have noticed, we can't see into each other's gardens.'

'Yes, I have noted that,' said Münster. 'They had two cars, is that right?'

'Yes, of course,' said fru Trotta, as if fewer vehicles than that was unthinkable in Kammerweg. 'A Saab and a little Japanese thing. She used to drive the little one.'

'Yes,' said Münster. 'Of course. Were you at home on Thursday evening?'

'We were at a little party arranged by some good friends of ours, but we were back home by about ten. The girls need a good night's sleep.'

'I'm sure they do,' agreed Münster. 'Did you notice anything unusual about Villa Zefyr when you came home?'

'No.'

'Nor later on that evening?'

'Nothing at all. We can't see into their garden, as I've said.'

'Did you see if anybody was at home? If there were lights on, anything like that?'

'As I keep saying, we can't see into their garden. We can't see from here if there are any lights on or not.'

She was becoming irritated again. Münster looked down at his notebook and thought for a few seconds.

'Jaan G. Hennan,' he said eventually. 'Could you give me your personal opinion of him?'

'Why?'

'Because I'm asking you to.'

She considered that weighty argument for some time, while examining her fingernails – of which there were ten, varnished beige.

'He's not our type.'

'I've gathered that. Could you be a bit more precise?'

'Not our type at all. Pushy and . . . well, unreliable. He doesn't create a pleasant impression.'

'Impertinent?' wondered Münster.

'Maybe not quite that. But our girls don't like him. They can usually detect that kind of thing. Do you have children of your own?'

'Yes,' said Münster. 'A little boy. Do you know anything about Hennan's background?'

'Only that he's lived in America for ten years. Some kind of businessman.'

'What was the relationship like between herr and fru Hennan? Did you notice anything at all?'

She scraped a speck of something from off her little finger-nail before answering.

'She was more or less the same as him,' she said. 'They seemed to suit each other. Mind you, he was older, of course.'

'But no dissension, as far as you know?'

She shook her head.

'I don't think so. But it wouldn't surprise me. Are you

suggesting that . . . that he might have had something to do with her death?'

She tried to ask that question in the same neutral tone of voice she had been using throughout their conversation, but Münster could hear undertones of fascinated interest.

'We are not excluding the possibility,' he said. 'My boss doesn't like excluding any possibilities at all.'

'I see,' said Trotta, and forgot for a second to close her mouth.

'But nothing dramatic?' Münster asked. 'No quarrels or anything like that you happened to be present at?'

It was obvious that fru Trotta would have liked nothing better than to have witnessed a quarrel between her neighbours. She sat in silence for a few seconds, scouring her memory – but soon her better self took command.

'No,' she said. 'Nothing like that. Mind you . . . mind you, it's a long way from here to their house, as I've said.'

Münster nodded.

'Did they drink?' he asked. 'To excess, I mean.'

Amelia Trotta was unable to provide any dramatic information on that point either. Instead she sighed, and looked at the clock.

'I think . . .' she began, but then lost the thread, overcome once again by that tantalizing possibility. 'Surely you don't think . . . ?' she wondered instead. 'Surely you can't seriously think that . . . ?'

She was unable to put her question into words, but the thought remained suspended over the table in that neat and tidy living room. Like a ketchup stain on a white linen tablecloth, Münster thought as he prepared to take his leave of the idyll.

'We have no definite theories as yet,' he explained, rising to his feet. 'But exploring various possibilities is a part of our work in the CID. I might want to have a chat with your husband in due course – do you think he would have any objections to that?'

'I'll warn him,' said fru Trotta, showing willing to assist. 'But he's away on his travels quite a lot, so you'll need to arrange a time well in advance. He's a pilot.'

'I appreciate the problems,' said Münster. 'What's your profession?'

'I'm a dermatologist,' said Trotta, standing up straight. 'But I'm at home for as long as the girls are at school. They need to have me around.'

I wonder, thought Münster, trying to recall what on earth a dermatologist did. Something to do with skin, he thought. But it might just as well be freshwater fish, or mites.

He decided to look it up when he had the chance. Then he thanked fru Trotta for being so helpful, and left Villa Vengali. As he walked through the garden, he had confirmation of what she had said about visibility between the two houses. He couldn't see so much as a glimpse of the light-blue facade of Villa Zefyr. Only a narrow strip of the white-painted diving tower could be made out through a narrow gap in the thick mass of greenery.

It's reminiscent of this case as a whole, he thought as he clambered into his car. The bottom line is we can't see much at all.

*

Van Veeteren stared at a broken toothpick he was holding in his left hand.

In his right hand he was holding a telephone receiver, and that was what he really wanted to be staring at. But since his physiognomy, in some respects at least, was quite normal, that was an impossibility.

Assuming, that is, that he didn't want to prevent himself from hearing Chief Inspector Sachs's voice: and he didn't. Not in these circumstances.

'What the hell are you saying?' he bellowed. 'A gumshoe?'

'Verlangen,' said Sachs. 'His name is Maarten Verlangen. He used to work for you in the past, he claims.'

'I couldn't care less if he did,' said Van Veeteren. 'But he says he's been commissioned to keep an eye on Jaan G. Hennan, is that right?'

'Yes indeed,' said Sachs. 'Commissioned by his wife – the woman who's now dead. Wednesday, Thursday, Friday last week – although he wasn't exactly overworked on Friday. The devil only knows what this means, but the most remarkable thing is that he was sitting there keeping Hennan under observation all last Thursday evening and into the early hours. At that restaurant. Columbine's. Well, I have to say I don't know how we should interpret that . . .'

'Interpret!' snorted Van Veeteren. 'We're not going to interpret anything. Where is he?'

'Who?'

'The gumshoe, of course. Where is he now?'

'Er. . . .' said Chief Inspector Sachs.

'What?' said Chief Inspector Van Veeteren. 'Speak up!'

'He . . . He's left. But I—'

'You mean you've let him go? What the hell . . . ?'

'I have his name and telephone number, of course. I said we'd be in touch.'

Van Veeteren crumpled up the remains of the toothpick and stabbed himself in the thumb.

'Ow!' he groaned. 'What else did he say? Surely he must have had something to—'

'Not a lot,' interrupted Sachs. 'He had no idea why he was supposed to be shadowing Hennan. Apparently he spent most of the time in his car, gaping up at Hennan's office window. Apart from Thursday evening, that is.'

'And it was Barbara Hennan who employed him?'

'Yes.'

'Why?'

'He didn't know, as I said.'

'I'm not deaf. What did he think?'

'Nothing.'

'Nothing?'

'No, that's what he said . . .'

'Stupid berk. Anyway, let's have his telephone number so that we can sort this mess out.'

'By all means, here we go,' said Chief Inspector Sachs, and read out Maarten Verlangen's numbers, to both his home and his office.

'Thank you,' said Van Veeteren. 'That'll be all for now, I've no more time to waste on you.'

*

He started with the home number.

No reply.

Then the office number.

No reply – apart from a recorded message regretting that Verlangen's Detective Agency was closed at the moment, but that they accepted commissions of all kinds at reasonable prices, and that callers could leave a message after the tone.

Van Veeteren thought carefully about the wording of his message while he was waiting for the tone.

'Maarten Verlangen,' he growled when the peep eventually sounded. 'If you are keen to carry on living, for God's sake make sure that you contact Chief Inspector Van Veeteren at Maardam CID. Immediately!'

He remained sitting there for a while, cursing to himself and contemplating his injured thumb – until the reality behind Chief Inspector Sachs's revelation slowly but surely calmed him down.

The actual content of the message – the fact that the dead woman, the corpse in a bathing costume lying on the bottom of that confounded swimming pool in Linden, had hired a private detective just a few days before she died.

A private dick who was supposed to keep an eye on what her husband was getting up to. That accursed Jaan G. Hennan!

Van Veeteren rummaged around, produced a cigarette, and lit it. What the hell? he thought. What the hell does this mean? Let's face it, she must ... she must have suspected something. Isn't that what it must mean? Come on, ring damn you, you godforsaken gumshoe!

He glared at the silent telephone. Realized that it was barely a minute since he recorded his hard-hitting message, and that one could scarcely expect Verlangen to turn up at his office with such exemplary timing. He inhaled deeply and checked his watch.

Half past two. High time he set off for his badminton match with Münster, in other words. He stubbed out his cigarette, stood up and dug out his racket and his sports bag from the cupboard.

Look out, Inspector, he thought. I'm not to be trifled with today.

On his way down in the lift, it dawned on him that he knew who Maarten Verlangen was. And why he had left the force.

11

When Verlangen left the police station in Linden, he had had three more or less incompatible feelings inside him.

The first was that it was a relief to have this confounded Hennan business off his back. It was precisely a week since the beautiful American woman had turned up at his office: now she was dead, and what had actually happened was a matter for the police to sort out, not Maarten Baudewijn Verlangen.

The second was that he felt somehow empty deep down inside. As if he had given up something: it was not clear what, exactly, but he could hardly deny that he had somehow failed in his task. If a private detective had any sort of moral function in a society, it was to be able to step in and put things to rights when the police force had failed to do so. That was how he usually justified his existence, at least, when he needed to boost his ego and stiffen his backbone.

His theoretical backbone. You have to take life as it comes, and Maarten Verlangen understood the importance of adjusting his motives in order to cope with it. He was no better or worse on that score than any other so-called honest, upright citizen.

But when it came to Barbara Hennan, he had failed to live up to his principles, that could hardly be denied. She had come to him with a somewhat obscure cry for help: he had done absolutely nothing, now she was dead, and he had shuffled off the responsibility into the hands of the police. Whatever it was, it was not an honourable retreat.

Damn and blast, he thought. I'm a seventh-rate shit.

The third feeling was of a more trivial, everyday kind. He was thirsty. He was absolutely desperate for a large beer, and before he drove back to Maardam he dropped in at Henry's bar and ensured that, if nothing else, that particular problem was solved.

Every cloud has a silver lining, he thought. One thing at a time.

Director Kooperdijk at the insurance company F/B Trustor was reminiscent of a little bull.

He was also reminiscent of – and indeed could almost have been mistaken for – Verlangen's former father-in-law, and it was always with a feeling of unease that he tried to cope with the strength emanating from those steel-blue eyes. The man as a whole radiated energy that was so intense, it could not be suppressed. It occasionally forced its way out in the form of aggression or insults. A sort of safety valve, Verlangen used to think. To prevent him from boiling over. Martha's time bomb of a father had been just the same: if there was one thing about which he had no regrets after the divorce it was the end of the confrontations – and the far from subtle

insinuations about his son-in-law's shortcomings and negligence – at the obligatory monthly Sunday dinners in their
large mansion up in Loewingen.

Another case of every cloud . . .

But Kooperdijk's pistol-like gaze over the desk in the lux-
urious office in Keymer Plejn always reminded him of it.

Like now. It was half past two in the afternoon: Verlangen
had arrived fifteen minutes late, and blamed parking problems in the centre of town as it would have been a tactical
error to admit that what had actually delayed him was the
beer at Henry's bar.

'Sit down,' said Kooperdijk. 'We have a problem.'

Verlangen sat down in the low armchair in front of the
desk. The director's chair was at least fifteen centimetres
higher, which was of course no accident.

'A problem?' said Verlangen, popping two throat tablets
into his mouth. 'What kind of a problem?'

'Two problems, in fact,' said Kooperdijk.

'You don't say,' said Verlangen.

'The first has to do with your work.'

'My work?'

'The so-called work you do for us. We have begun to
reassess the situation. It leaves much to be desired.'

'My understanding is that my input has been satisfactory,'
said Verlangen.

'That is debatable.'

'I don't follow you,' said Verlangen. Come to the point,
you little twerp, he thought.

'I can understand that most of what you have done has

been satisfactory from your point of view,' said Kooperdijk, clasping his hands in front of him on the desk. 'But not always from ours.'

'For example?' wondered Verlangen.

'The Westergaade affair,' said Kooperdijk. 'Not exactly satisfactorily concluded. That business with the firm of solicitors. Not satisfactory at all.'

Verlangen thought.

'You can't expect me to produce rats when there is no smell of any rats,' he said.

'Oh no?' said Kooperdijk without moving a muscle. 'That is no doubt a point of view that can be debated. And then there is the matter of your personal conduct.'

'What?' said Verlangen, trying to sit up in the chair so that his eyes were at least level with the desk top. 'My personal . . .'

Kooperdijk leaned forward, resting on his elbows.

'Fru Donck, one of our investigators, saw you at Oldener Maas two weeks ago. Your behaviour did not show you in a favourable light.'

Verlangen said nothing.

'In fact, you were as drunk as a lord, she says. Apparently you molested her companion in the bar.'

Isn't that why women sit in bars? thought Verlangen, sinking back down into his armchair. In order to be molested?

'There must be some kind of misunderstanding,' he said.

'No doubt,' said Kooperdijk. 'The question is, on whose part?'

Verlangen closed his eyes for a second and wondered if he

ought simply to stand up and leave. He suddenly found himself wishing he were on some Greek island. But not Crete, he'd had enough of minotaurs.

'I understand,' he said. 'It won't be repeated.'

'Presumably not,' said Kooperdijk. 'In any case, we are wondering whether we really want to make use of your services in future. Have you any comments to make in that respect?'

'None at all,' said Verlangen.

'Unless, of course, we begin to detect signs of some sort of improvement. That would naturally put things in an entirely different light.'

'I hope so,' said Verlangen.

'But as I said, we have another little problem.'

'Yes, I recall your saying that.'

'Or rather, a big problem.'

'Really?'

'If you could pull something out of the hat in connection with this matter, then of course that would change the situation quite a lot.'

Verlangen cleared his throat. As it was forbidden to smoke in the presence of Kooperdijk, he popped two more throat tablets into his mouth.

'Let's hear it, then,' he said optimistically. 'A big problem?'

Kooperdijk opened a red file and produced a sheet of paper. He made heavy weather of putting on a pair of reading glasses, which made his bull-like physiognomy look slightly less aggressive.

'Harrumph!' he said. 'A life insurance matter. Rather expensive, if we don't play our cards right.'

Verlangen waited.

'One point two million, to be precise.'

'One point . . . ?'

'. . . Two, yes. A lot of money. A hell of a lot too much money. And there's a strong smell of rat, to quote a dodgy source. A bloody enormous rat, by the look of things.'

'Really?' said Verlangen. 'Well, if this is how the land lies, then of course I'm prepared to do whatever I can. What does it look like?'

Kooperdijk removed his reading glasses.

'It doesn't look good,' he said. 'Not good at all. We signed up to a life insurance policy for a certain person a month ago. The first instalment was duly paid, no problem: but now it seems that the insured person has passed on.'

'Died, you mean?' said Verlangen.

'Yes, died,' said Kooperdijk, blowing his nose into a multi-coloured handkerchief he took out of his trouser pocket. 'Expired. Given up the ghost, shuffled off this mortal coil. However the hell you might like to put it.'

'I'm with you,' said Verlangen.

'Trustor has always maintained high standards,' said Kooperdijk, looking up in the direction of the array of diplomas hanging on the wall opposite. 'Signed up to insurance policies that other companies have rejected. High risk factors, and premiums in accordance with that. Our reputation has been at the top of the heap for at least thirty years . . .'

If he starts going on about insurance policies for Holly-wood actresses' dogs, I shall light a cigarette and walk out, Verlangen thought

'Obviously, I don't need to spell all that out for you. But there are limits, and there are customers that don't hesi-tate to take advantage of our liberal policy. This business is no doubt one of those cases. The name of the insured is Barbara Hennan – perhaps you have read about her in the newspapers?'

Verlangen's heart stopped beating.

'Barb . . . ?' he managed to whimper.

'Barbara Hennan, yes. She died last week. If we can't stop it, the insurance payment will go to her husband, somebody by the name of Jaan G. Hennan. One point two million.'

Verlangen swallowed the throat tablets, and his heart started beating again.

'What's the matter with you?' wondered Kooperdijk.

'With me?' said Verlangen. 'Nothing. I just felt a bit dizzy.'

'Felt dizzy when you're sitting down?' said Kooperdijk. 'How old are you?'

Verlangen tried to sit up straight again on his chair.

'I've just had a bout of flu,' he explained. 'Nothing to speak of. Hen . . . Hennan, did you say?'

I'm dreaming, he thought: but he didn't dare to pinch him-self in the arm while Kooperdijk's penetrating bull-like eyes were directed at him.

'Hennan, yes. The whole business stinks of fraud – even a donkey can see that. The police are involved, speaking of donkeys, but they seem to think that it was an accident.'

'Do they?' said Verlangen. 'And what are the terms? Of the insurance, I mean.'

'Natural death. Unfortunately accidents are included under that heading. If anybody helped to push her over the precipice, or if she jumped, then we are not liable. Manslaughter, murder, suicide . . . any of those will do. That's where we should be syphoning it off to.'

Syphoning it off to? Verlangen thought. The man's out of his mind.

'Are you clear about the prerequisites?' wondered Kooperdijk, glaring at him.

Verlangen didn't answer. I've had more prerequisites than you could ever imagine, little man, he thought. But I don't understand them.

I'll be damned if I understand them.

'You had better go and talk to Krotowsky, and he will be able to put you in the picture in more detail,' said Kooperdijk. 'Damn it all, if you can sort out this little matter for us, we can forget all about what might have happened in the past. I'm sure I don't need to point out that it can cost whatever it costs . . .'

Verlangen heaved himself up out of his armchair, and really did feel dizzy for a moment.

'So I should see Krotowsky now, right away – or . . . ?'

'Yes, now, right away,' said Kooperdijk.

Inspector Münster won all four sets in the badminton match with Van Veeteren. As usual. There was just a short period early on when things could have gone either way, but from 5–5 he proceeded via 9–6 and 12–8 to a confidence-inspiring 15–11. The other sets were secured in more business-like fashion: 15–6, 15–8 and 15–4.

'It's that pulled muscle in the small of my back,' said the Chief Inspector on the way to the shower. 'It's hampering me. Next week I'll wipe the floor with you.'

'We'll cross that bridge when we come to it,' said Münster.

'That Hennan business is nagging away at me as well,' said Van Veeteren. 'I can't make head nor tail of it. If I were an up-and-coming young inspector I would no doubt get my teeth into it and show what I was made of.'

'Message received and understood,' said Münster.

He had been informed of the latest development in the case while they were driving to the sports hall. The private dick lark, as the Chief Inspector had chosen to call it. He had also mentioned that he knew who Maarten Verlangen was – one of those police officers, it seemed, who was incapable of distinguishing between right and wrong in the long run – and who had resigned with his tail between his legs and headed off towards an uncertain future. Apparently. Five or six years ago. If the Chief Inspector remembered rightly.

Münster could only agree: it *was* a peculiar situation. He thought more about it after dropping Van Veeteren off at Randers Park, and was stuck in the traffic jams on the way to the suburb where he lived.

If Barbara Hennan really had employed a private detective to keep an eye on her husband, there must surely be some reason for doing so. But what? Münster thought. *What?* Perhaps she had suspected that she was somehow in danger. Surely that had to be the case. Maybe she had suspected that her husband was going to attack her in some way. In any case, this Verlangen must have relevant information to pass on.

And the Chief Inspector was brooding over it. Münster had begun to realize that Van Veeteren's suspicions and intuitive whims were not to be scorned. Three years ago, when he had first been transferred to the CID, Münster had found it hard not to be irritated by the Chief Inspector's odd behaviour and bizarre ideas, but as time passed his doubts had grown into respect.

Respect and a degree of reluctant admiration.

Because of the fact that he was hardly ever wrong. In case after case it seemed that Van Veeteren always managed, unerringly, to pull the right strings. To pick out precisely the person who needed to be interrogated again, or to demand a more detailed account of what herr X or fru Y or fröken Z had been doing on Wednesday evening the previous week.

Among this mish-mash of information and misinformation that accumulated quicker than the blinking of an eye in every new case.

Intuition, as it was called. It had to be acknowledged that Van Veeteren possessed this controversial but gold-plated quality. In spades.

And it had also to be acknowledged, Münster thought as he turned off the motorway and became stuck between a bus and a van transporting fish, that his boss had a point in the current case as well.

If Van Veeteren thought that this remarkable character G

was behind the death of his wife, then no doubt that was true. In one way or another.

But *how*? How had he managed to do it? A good question. Had he slipped out of that restaurant for as long as was necessary? Was that possible, given the time scale? Or had he had a henchman?

The latter possibility seemed more credible. A contract killer? That would be unusual, very unusual – unless they were in the sphere of so-called organized crime, and surely the Hennans were not part of that world? Or?

And how should they go about nailing him?

There were a lot of question marks, Inspector Münster acknowledged as he parked in the street outside his terraced house.

A lot of questions that were probably impossible to answer just yet, he decided. Certainly not before he knew rather more about what the private eye and former copper Verlangen had to say for himself. And what the information about Hennan that the Chief Inspector had ordered from the USA might reveal.

It would be stupid to start speculating too soon – that was a well-established fact. It would be better to devote his attention to his wife and child instead.

That was a much better rule to follow – especially if one had a wife called Synn who was the most attractive woman on the planet. And a son called Bart who about thirty seconds from now would come running up to him, laughing away, and jump into his arms to be lifted up to the heavens, squealing in delight.

Good Lord, Inspector Münster thought. I'm the happiest bloody copper in Maardam – how come I sometimes almost forget that?

Not long after midnight, when they had finished making love, he told Synn the Hennan story and asked what she thought. She lay for a while with her head on his arm, breathing directly into his ear, before answering.

'I would never jump out into the darkness from a diving tower,' she whispered in the end. 'Never ever.'

'Exactly what I thought as well,' said Münster. 'Let's go to sleep now.'

12

On Wednesday morning Chief Inspector Van Veeteren had a quarrel with his wife. It was far from crystal clear what the problem was – presumably they were talking at cross purposes. In any case, it was Renate who had the last word, in that she slammed the palm of her hand down on the table and declared that it was no wonder Erich was as he was, with a father like his.

Van Veeteren would have liked to respond by saying that his mother's good genes and qualities could perhaps compensate for his father's inadequacies, at least to some extent, but she had already left the kitchen by then. As he solved the chess problem in the *Allgemenje*, he wondered yet again why they didn't bring matters to a head and separate once and for all – and what effect such a development might have on their wayward son.

Things couldn't become any worse, he concluded. You always knew what you had but you never knew what you might get. As everybody knows.

The minor controversy over breakfast had one good outcome, he realized as he emerged into the sunshine in Wimmerstraat. It had banished G from his mind for a while, and that was very much needed. It was not normal for investigations to nag away at him like this – and so far as Hennan was concerned it was not even an investigation yet. The case, if one could call it a case, was still on Chief Inspector Sachs's desk in Linden. The Maardam CID were involved in a sort of advisory capacity, but they had not yet taken over the case.

Not yet? he thought as he paused on the pedestrian bridge over the Wimmergracht and lit a cigarette. What do I mean by that? If it is only a matter of time, there's surely no reason to keep extending it?

Especially as I lie awake at night, thinking about it. Damn it all!

He had at last got in touch with Verlangen the previous evening, but did no more than get confirmation of what Chief Inspector Sachs had told him, apart from arranging a meeting with the private detective in his office at the police station.

This morning. Half an hour from now, to be precise, he realized as he passed by Keymerkyrkan and glanced up at the large pale yellow clock face on the tower.

That ought to clarify quite a lot. At least, Verlangen ought to be able to put a sufficient amount of meat onto the bare bones of the case for Van Veeteren to decide whether or not to take over the investigation. Whether it was worth setting up a preliminary investigation featuring that damned G character in the leading role, and get things moving at last.

But it was certainly an odd situation. Extremely odd indeed. With regard to the peculiar way in which Barbara Hennan had died, and the dubious role played by this private eye. He wondered how he would have assessed the situation and what action he would have taken if it had been anybody other than G involved.

At least he would have avoided this annoying appointment, he told himself – but surely the private aspect did not necessarily mean that he would be influenced by vague prejudices? Not necessarily. Knowing people involved in an investigation was an advantage, of course. Provided one was able to handle the fact correctly; to keep it at arm's length, as it were.

He resolved to try to remember to keep personal knowledge at arm's length. Paused outside Kooner's bookshop for a moment, gazing up at the cloudless sky and wriggling out of his jacket. The sun was very warm, and the crowds of tourists in Keymer Plejn were growing bigger. He contemplated the scene in the square. The obligatory South American folk music group were setting up their instruments outside Kellner's, despite the fact that it was only half past nine. Two girls aged about twelve were scampering diagonally over the square with ice creams in their hands, already clusters of blue-haired ladies and pot-bellied gentlemen were sitting at tables outside the cafes, drinking breakfast.

Summer, he thought. It even looks as if we're going to have a summer this year. Well, I'll be damned.

Private detective Verlangen was ten minutes late, but even so had evidently not had time to shave. Probably not yesterday either, Van Veeteren decided as he asked his visitor if he would like coffee.

He would. Van Veeteren suspected he had only had time for a beer for breakfast, and ordered a couple of ham sandwiches as well as coffee via fröken Katz in the front office downstairs.

'Thank you,' said Verlangen. 'I was a bit late getting up this morning. It's sometimes impossible to get a wink of sleep.'

The Chief Inspector noted that his visitor looked distinctly scruffy. A short-sleeved washed-out cotton shirt with a button missing. Worn-out black jeans and down-at-heel sandals. Bags under his eyes and lank, rat-coloured hair that ought to have been cut or perhaps shaved off ages ago.

Evidently Maarten Verlangen had not exactly been living on a bed of roses since he left the police force five years ago. Van Veeteren hadn't expected anything else, but nevertheless felt a pang of sympathy for the decrepit-looking man who was glancing around listlessly as he felt in his pockets for a cigarette.

'Do you mind if I smoke?'

'Please do,' said Van Veeteren. 'There'll be coffee and sandwiches shortly, as I said.'

Verlangen lit a cigarette and inhaled deeply.

'I didn't sleep at all last night, in fact,' he said. 'It's a hell of a peculiar story, this fru Hennan business.'

'Why didn't you contact us earlier?' asked Van Veeteren. 'Nearly a week has passed now.'

'I apologize,' said Verlangen. 'But I didn't realize what had happened until Monday – the day before yesterday, that is. You mustn't think that I . . . That I have a bone to pick with you after what happened five years ago. That was my fault, and I've learned my lesson.'

'I know about what happened,' said the Chief Inspector. 'People sometimes find themselves in situations they can't cope with. You took the consequences, and that's that as far as I'm concerned.'

Verlangen stared slightly unsteadily at him for a few seconds.

'Thank you,' he said. 'Water under the bridge. But I suspect we're on the same side when it comes to a little rat like Hennan, no matter what. He's an unpleasant bastard, and nothing would please me more than putting him behind bars once again.'

Van Veeteren nodded.

'If I understand it rightly, you are the one who nailed him last time?'

'That's true,' said Verlangen. 'Me and a colleague. He got two and a half years, but he should probably have had double that.'

'I agree,' said Van Veeteren. 'But sometimes you have to be thankful for small mercies.'

'That's something I've learned as well,' said Verlangen, allowing himself a wry grin. 'During the last few years, for instance. But shall we run through the facts now? I also have a splendid bit of news, but I think we should leave that until last.'

'A bit of news?' said Van Veeteren. 'About Hennan?'

'A bombshell,' said Verlangen. 'You can no doubt prepare to put quite a lot of resources into this lark – but shall we start at the beginning . . . ?'

Van Veeteren switched on the tape recorder, but switched it off again immediately as there was a knock on the door and fröken Katz came in with coffee and a plate of sandwiches. Verlangen waited until she had left the room, took two bites of a sandwich, washed it down with a swig of coffee, then began.

It took half an hour, with questions from the Chief Inspector, extra details and repeats – especially when Verlangen got as far as Thursday evening and the Columbine restaurant. When Van Veeteren said he was satisfied with what he had heard so far, it was time for the bombshell.

'F/B Trustor – does that mean anything to you?'

'The insurance company?'

'Yes. I work a bit for them as well – or used to do, at least. I was called to see the director yesterday afternoon. For two reasons, in fact. One was to give me the sack because they were not satisfied with my efforts, but the other was to give me an opportunity of rehabilitating myself . . . As it were. Can you guess what that entailed?'

The Chief Inspector shook his head. How the hell could I be expected to guess that? he thought.

'Jaan G. Hennan.'

'Hennan?'

'Yes, indeed. The man himself. The fact is that, a month ago, he signed up for a life insurance policy on the life of his wife. If it turns out that she died of natural causes in that empty swimming pool, he will collect one point two million.'

'What?' said Van Veeteren.

'One million two hundred thousand. What do you say to that?'

Van Veeteren stared at Verlangen.

'A million . . .'

'And two hundred thousand, yes. For Christ's sake, it's lunacy. If there has ever been a man who had a motive for getting rid of his wife, it's Jaan G. Hennan . . . Getting rid of her by natural causes, that is.'

Van Veeteren realized that he was sitting there with his mouth wide open. He closed it, and shook his head slowly.

'That's just . . .' he said. 'And you said nothing about it on the telephone last night. Why the hell . . . ?'

'Come on, it was you who said that it would be best to talk face to face. Besides, I needed a bit of time to think about things as well.'

'Why? Think about what things?'

Verlangen looked embarrassed for a brief moment.

'My own role, of course. With regard to Trustor. If I can nail Hennan without anybody else's help, my daily bread is assured for some time to come . . . If you see what I mean. But I eventually decided that we might be able to give each other a helping hand.'

'For Christ's sake,' snorted the Chief Inspector. 'You sound like a self-conscious American crime movie from the nineteen forties.'

'It goes with the territory in my job,' said Verlangen. 'I'm sorry. Anyway, now you know as much as I do. It was fun to call in at the station again.'

'I can understand that,' said Van Veeteren. 'And it probably won't be the last time, either.'

'No,' said Verlangen. 'Presumably not. The fact is that I'm dead keen to see that swine put behind bars. To be honest . . . Well, to be honest, he scares the shit out of me.'

Out of me as well, thought Van Veeteren – but he didn't say so.

After the conversation with Maarten Verlangen the Chief Inspector took the lift down to the basement and spent an hour in the sauna. That was presumably a variation on yet another Borkmann rule.

'When you feel that your head is about to burst thanks to an excess of thoughts and energy, hop off the train for a while and calm down,' Borkmann had advised him some twenty years ago. 'It's very seldom that haste is linked with reason and perspicacity.'

But as he sat there on the bench, sweating and pondering, nothing became any clearer – apart from the fact that this rule was especially relevant in this particular case.

Haste was the last thing he needed, he decided as the sweat really began to flow. If G – somehow or other – had taken his wife's life, he had done so in order to collect the insurance money – one point two million! Van Veeteren was very tempted to investigate the state of judgements and mental contortions at F/B Trustor.

But no doubt they would refuse to cough up anything at all while a police investigation was taking place, that was clear.

Jaan G. Hennan would gain nothing by doing a runner, or trying to hide himself away. Insurance companies were not renowned for tracking down people and asking permission to pay them lots of money.

Van Veeteren poured more water onto the hot stones so that the steam produced was very close to the limits of tolerance.

The only option open to G, therefore, was to wait. To wait while the mills of justice ground away at their usual extremely slow pace. As far as the police and the prosecution services were concerned, their job was to ensure that a preliminary investigation was launched, and then allow time to pass. Allow G to sweat and wonder what was happening. Two months was the normal time stipulated, but if more time was needed no doubt the prosecutor could be persuaded to grant a month or two extra.

Assuming that incriminating evidence had not been produced, that is: and of course he would make damned sure it was. Surely to God he would be able to dig up sufficient incontrovertible proof to condemn this exceptionally unpleasant person. The murderer Jaan G. Hennan!

And no doubt sufficient resources would be made available.

He poured another scoop of water onto the hot stones, and suddenly the image of an animal appeared in his mind's eye. Some sort of mental – or perhaps psychophysical? – hybrid of a dragon and a sphinx, as far as he could judge: with evil spurting like white-hot lava out of its eyes and mouth, and he himself, the indefatigable and incorruptible

Chief Inspector Van Veeteren like a ... well, like a noble knight embodying goodness and light, spurring on his white steed with the long arm of the law like a lance or vehement sword ...

Everything was swimming before his eyes, and he staggered out of the sauna. Good Lord! he thought. What's the point of boiling your brain as well?

Before meeting Chief of Police Hiller he drew up guidelines together with Münster. It was not all that complicated: Münster made notes and was eventually able to sum up by stating that they should proceed along six different paths. To start with, at least.

First of all they should make a thorough search of Villa Zefyr. With technical teams, vacuum cleaners, the lot: it was true of course that G had had aeons of time in which to clean up, but nothing should be left to chance.

Secondly they needed to establish in as much detail as possible what Barbara Hennan had been doing on that fateful Thursday. Had she really driven to Arlach? If so, what had she done there? When had she returned to Linden? Why had she drunk so much alcohol? And so on. There was an apparently endless list of question marks, and if they could remove some of them, so much the better.

In the third place they needed information about the couple's background in the United States. For now they could no doubt wait for the arrival of the information that had already been asked for: with luck that should arrive later today, or tomorrow. On the basis of what it said, they could then decide if it was necessary to follow that path up in more detail.

Fourthly, Jaan G. Hennan's circle of friends and acquaintances should be investigated. What exactly had he been doing since his return from the USA? What contacts had he made? Were there any friends and acquaintances left from the seventies? And had the Hennans really had no other social contacts apart from the Trottas, with whom they hadn't seemed to get on particularly well?

Fifthly – and here it was Münster who insisted – it would be useful to keep in touch with the private detective Verlangen. Perhaps he might have forgotten some detail in his conversation with the Chief Inspector? Perhaps he could be useful in other ways as well? As he had insisted, they were very much on the same wavelength as far as this case was concerned: Verlangen had a personal interest in nailing Hennan, and it would be a pity not to take advantage of that fact. In one way or another. Even if it was a pretty down-at-heel private eye they were working with.

Van Veeteren thought for a few seconds about Münster's argument on this point, then expressed his approval. At least it could do no harm.

Sixthly – and for now finally – it was of course absolutely essential to deliver the crucial body blow, as effectively as possible: the interrogation of Jaan G. Hennan. They could not afford to put a foot wrong. Even during that first conversation Van Veeteren had suspected that there would be a trial of strength in the offing, and needless to say G was not exactly in the dark about what lay ahead. He must be just as aware of it as he was of the quality of his breath on a Monday morning, the Chief Inspector thought.

No kid gloves. No silly making allowances. Van Veeteren knew that Jaan G. Hennan was guilty, and Hennan knew that he knew.

It could hardly be any clearer.

Or harder.

As there was no urgency, Münster and Van Veeteren agreed to delay the first important confrontation for a few days. It would be better to let the scene-of-crime technicians put him under the microscope first. Better to let him wait and wonder. Van Veeteren decided provisionally on Friday evening: that was two days ahead, and whenever possible it was always an advantage to interrogate a suspect at an un-usual time of day.

In fact Van Veeteren would have preferred to pick G up in a Black Maria in the middle of the night – he sometimes couldn't stop himself from imagining what it would have been like to be a chief inspector in the Soviet Union of the thirties instead – but he desisted from mentioning this possi-bility, in view of Inspector Münster's innocent soul.

'That's that then,' he said instead, collecting the notes from Münster. 'I suppose it's about time for a visit to the King of the Flowers. Would you like to come too?'

Münster smiled and shook his head.

'I take it there won't be a problem in getting the required resources?' he asked.

'I wouldn't have thought so,' said the Chief Inspector. 'This is one hell of a case . . . I'll buy you a beer once we've got him under lock and key.'

Now it's serious then, thought Münster. Deadly serious.

13

Having explained the situation in broad outline to the chief of police – and been promised all the resources available – Van Veeteren retired to his office with a cup of coffee and a packet of cigarettes.

The first thing that struck him after he had taken off his shoes and put his feet up on his desk was that they had forgotten to include the Trustor insurance company on Münster's list of things to do. To avoid unnecessary complications he picked up the telephone and asked to be connected directly to herr Kooperdijk.

He was in a meeting, he was informed eventually, but would ring him back as soon as it was over. In ten minutes or so.

Van Veeteren smoked two cigarettes and emptied his cup of coffee while waiting, but after twenty minutes he had the director on the line at last.

The Chief Inspector summed up his conversation with Verlangen, and in tactfully chosen words wondered if it was permissible to sign up to insurance policies based on even the most stupid of conditions.

Of course it was, Kooperdijk informed him haughtily. It

was all a question of investments and calculated risks. A business arrangement between the company and the client – two independent parties in a free market.

Van Veeteren asked for more relevant details concerning Barbara Hennan's life insurance policy, and soon discovered that it was exactly as Verlangen had said. The whole amount – one point two million – would be paid to the beneficiary – Jaan G. Hennan – the moment F/B Trustor had it in black and white that the cause of death did not come into the categories of manslaughter, murder or suicide.

The Chief Inspector wondered if it was usual to use those particular categories.

Kooperdijk assured him that it often happened. One had the right to include whatever conditions the parties concerned wanted in the policy. It was a matter exclusively between the company and the policy-holder. In principle it was possible to have a policy which would be paid out only if the insured were the victim of murder or manslaughter – but that was not exactly common practice, he claimed: it was only possible *in principle*. He had never come across such a policy, and he had been in the business for over thirty years.

Thirty-one-and-a-half, to be precise.

Van Veeteren said he would get back to Trustor in due course. Thanked the director for his cooperation, and hung up.

I must check what company my own insurance policies are with, he thought. If it's Trustor, I shall cancel them tomorrow.

Then he checked his watch and realized that he wouldn't have time for lunch before his meeting at two o'clock.

He found a sandwich among the debris left behind after Verlangen's visit, went to fetch another cup of coffee and convinced himself it was better than nothing.

All but two of those on the list attended the meeting – Intendent Nielsen was busy with an arson case out at Sellsbach, and Inspector deBries was on leave.

But all the others were present in the conference room. Intendent Heinemann. Inspectors Reinhart and Rooth, and the newly appointed probationer Jung. And Münster, of course. Six qualified CID officers, including Van Veeteren himself. Not bad: but it remained to be seen how many footsoldiers were available: he reckoned they would need rather a lot for several days, but all being well things should ease off after that. Intendent le Houde, who was in charge of the technical team, was already informed and satisfied with the situation. A meticulous search of Hennan's house at Linden would begin the following day.

Van Veeteren cleared his throat and welcomed everybody. Urged all present to pin back their ears and listen with both halves of their brains switched on for the next ten minutes. Then there would be a coffee session, and the allocation of duties.

Any questions?

There were none.

He recounted the case chronologically – not in the order

that it had come to his notice, but from the arrival of the Hennans in Linden until Verlangen's visit to the police station that morning.

When he had finished, Reinhart commented that it was the most outrageous situation he had come across for as long as he could remember. Rooth claimed it was the most obvious set-up he had heard for twice as long as that, and the timid Heinemann was of the view that it was a most intriguing case.

'What do we do if this Hennan character simply flatly denies everything?' wondered Jung.

'He will flatly deny everything,' said the Chief Inspector. 'It doesn't matter how much circumstantial evidence we find, or however many pointers we discover aimed straight at him. He will never confess to anything. Everything seems to be just as obvious as Rooth says – but the problem will be to make it stick in court.'

'I appreciate that,' said Rooth. 'Didn't you say that the comments session was supposed to coincide with coffee?'

Van Veeteren picked up the telephone and spoke to fröken Katz.

The discussion, coffee and allocation of duties took an hour. As it was taking place Van Veeteren noticed to his surprise how he gradually lost interest. Questions about Barbara Hennan's trip to Aarlach, about the couple's social circle and how they might go about checking it – it all slowly drained away from his mind in a very strange way. A cloud of lethargy which slowly but surely enveloped his consciousness, and seemed impossible to resist.

Too much coffee and nicotine, he thought. Tomorrow I shall eat an orange.

Instead it was mainly Münster and Reinhart who made sure that no detail was overlooked. Workloads within the CID were already relatively onerous – Rooth and Jung had been working intensively over the last few days in connection with a robbery out at Löhr, and there were inevitable questions about priorities. Reinhart, for instance, was owed so many days off that he would have time to circumnavigate the globe twice, he maintained.

'By air?' wondered Rooth.

'By bicycle,' said Reinhart.

What distracted Van Veeteren more than anything else, and dominated his phlegmatic thoughts, was the imminent interrogation of Hennan. No doubt about that. When the meeting was over he went back to his office to think again about the priorities for this important meeting.

If there was any aspect of police work that he excelled in above all else, this was it. Interrogation techniques. It was an opinion shared by all his colleagues, he was aware of that, and only false modesty would make him deny that fact.

He knew how to deal with people who had things on their conscience, that was what it boiled down to. It had been suggested that – in eleven cases out of ten, as somebody put it – after just a few leading questions and answers, a few hesitant looks or exaggerated expressions of self-confidence, he could be certain of whether his interviewee was guilty or not guilty. It was a gift, of course. A knack about whose provenance he had no idea – but something that never let him down and could save hundreds of hours' work in an investigation.

Once you have the answer to the question *Who?*, all other aspects of a case shrink and are reduced radically. It becomes a different ball game. Usually man against man. Eye to eye over a rickety hardboard table. *We know you did it. Look me in the eye. You can see that I see, can't you? You can see that I know. We are in complete agreement – I see that you know that I know. Are you going to confess straight away, or are you going to carry on dancing around for a while longer? All right, I have all the time in the world . . . No, you may not smoke. Two more hours, okay? Then I shall lock you up in your cell for the night, and visit you again tomorrow morning . . . No, I'm afraid there is no coffee left.*

A slow pace, with pauses. It has its own brand of beauty. A sort of cruel aesthetic reminiscent of bull-fighting, or the vain fight to the death of an encircled beast. He didn't usually try to analyse why he enjoyed it.

And now it was all about G.

He wondered once again about the business of antipathy and keeping one's distance. How it would affect the interrogations – he didn't doubt for a moment that there would be several. The fact, that is, that he had such a deep-rooted dislike, not to say hatred, of the suspect. That he regarded him, to be honest, as an enemy.

It was hard to say. There was a private level and a professional level – perhaps the fact that they coincided in this case would be a strength? After all, he thought, it must be easier for a boxer or a duellist to defeat his opponent if he hates him than if he doesn't? Surely that must be the case?

It was a warped and confusing comparison, and he decided to proceed no further down that path. It would be better to keep a tighter rein on his approach. To ask rather more penetrating questions.

Was Jaan G. Hennan really guilty of his wife's death? Was there any doubt?

Was it *beyond reasonable doubt*, as the law put it?

He produced a sheet of paper and a pencil and wrote down the usual hobby horses once again.

Motive?

Method?

Opportunity?

It was a copybook case if ever there was one, of course. There were no end of motives. At least one point two million. And method was basically just as straightforward: a push in the back and a fourteen-metre fall onto a white-tiled concrete floor – or possibly a blow to the head first before heaving the victim over the edge.

Opportunity was less straightforward. As all human experience suggests that a person cannot possibly be in two different places at the same time, Jaan G. Hennan could not have carried out the deed himself if he was sitting at the Columbine restaurant in the centre of Linden when the murder took place.

And it would be necessary for a prosecutor to have con-demnatory evidence – overwhelmingly convincing evidence – on all three points. Not just one. Not just two.

Ergo? thought Chief Inspector Van Veeteren as he won-dered whether to fiddle with a cigarette or a toothpick.

Does this mean that I am doubtful about his guilt?

He selected the toothpick, and began poking it into his teeth.

Not at all. He is as guilty as Cain.

Ergo again?

He thought for five seconds.

Ergo there were two alternatives.

One: that G had in fact left Columbine at some point during the evening in question, despite everything. Despite the fact that Verlangen had been keeping an eye on him – presumably a slightly drunken eye.

Two: he had an accomplice.

It was the tenth time in the last twenty-four hours that he had reached the same conclusion.

Excellent, he thought. The analysis has progressed by leaps and bounds.

He noted that it was now half past four, and decided to go home. As it was Wednesday he had at least one game of chess against Mahler down at The Society to look forward to.

As he stood in the lift on the way down to the exit, he wondered if G played chess.

I hope not, he thought, and wondered simultaneously why he hoped not.

*

It turned out to be three games. One win, one loss, one draw. Spanish, Russian, Nimzo-Indian. The draw ought to have been another win, but he frittered away an extra pawn at the end. It was half past eleven when he left The Society's premises in Styckargränd, and he could feel that the summer warmth from that morning was still in the air.

Not the kind of evening to go and lie down in a dodgy marital bed, he thought as he strolled homewards along Alexanderlaan and Wimmergraacht. Certainly not. So what should he do? What was the alternative?

The answer struck him as he passed by his parked car some twenty metres from his front door: he felt in his pocket for the car keys and found that they were in fact there.

Why not? he thought and unlocked the driver's door. What's one hour here or there?

Villa Zefyr seemed as silent and remote as a mortuary when he parked in Kammerweg twenty-five minutes later. He switched off the engine and observed the greenery behind the metre-high brick wall. No sign of any lights inside there. Was G at home? Presumably not – if he had been, surely there would have been a light on somewhere. Indoors or out-doors, and the bushes and branches couldn't be *that* dense: some little strip of light would have shone through. On the other hand, he might be asleep in bed. It was turned mid-night, and it was not impossible that G had the occasional good habit as well. Even if that seemed unlikely. Van Veeteren wound down the side window, but even so he could see no outlines, either of the diving tower or the house itself.

Ideal, he thought. An ideal place in which to get rid of one's wife.

He got out of the car and lit a cigarette. Toyed for a moment with the idea of climbing over the wall and taking a closer look at the heart of darkness, but decided not to. Melodramatic nocturnal break-ins were not his style, and coming up against a wide-awake murderer could hardly serve any useful purpose. He started walking along the street towards Villa Vigali instead, and found that it seemed just as lifeless there as well: a street light cast a dirty yellow beam a few metres into the garden, but that was all. He dropped his cigarette onto the pavement and stamped out the glow. What am I doing here? he thought. What are the powers I am trying to appeal to?

He shook his head and returned to his car. And suddenly felt hungry.

How the hell can I possibly think about food in the middle of all this? he wondered. There must be something wrong with my body fluids.

So as not to ignore the signals from his body altogether, he drove back towards the centre of Linden and found a hamburger bar that was still open. He somehow managed to generate enough willpower to go in and order something called a Double Hawaii Burger Special. He ate half of it while sitting on a bench in the square, and threw the rest to the pigeons. Two women whose intentions were as obvious as they were morally questionable hovered around while he was sitting there, but neither of them made a serious attempt to seduce him. With a sudden pang of shame he recalled the only visit he had ever paid to a whore: he was nineteen years old, and along with a friend had called in at a brothel in Hamburg. In a room filled with the smell of sweet perfume and deep-fried fish he had endured the most painful twenty minutes of his life. His friend had found the experience moreish, however, and their friendship ebbed away as fast as when you remove the plug from a sink full of dishwater.

It was ten minutes to one by the time he crept back into his clapped-out Ford, and during the drive back to Maardam weariness and an urge to be sick fought an unresolved battle inside him.

For Christ's sake, he thought, a Hawaii Burger. Never again.

14

'My name is Rooth,' said Rooth. 'Detective inspector. It was me who rang.'

The woman in the doorway looked somewhat shifty. She was pale and thin, and he would have thought she was a little over fifty, if he hadn't known. Her hair was the same colour as a soft cheese he usually ate in the morning, and hung down like two washed-out, worse for wear curtains on either side of her face. She was wearing jeans and a baggy grey jumper. Rooth realized that he was smiling at her in the hope of preventing her from falling to pieces.

'Well?' she said.

'May I come in?'

She stood there in two minds. Her broad mouth twitched slightly, but no words came out. Rooth coughed in some embarrassment.

'It's just a matter of a brief chat, as I said,' he explained. 'You don't need to worry.'

'I don't know . . .'

'If you think it will be awkward, you can say no. But it would be very helpful to us if I could ask you a few questions.'

She bit her lip.

'Are you a police officer, did you say?'

Rooth took out his wallet and handed her his ID. Allowed her to study it carefully for a while, from all angles.

'Detective inspector?' she said. 'What does that mean?'

He took back his ID card and put his wallet back into his inside pocket.

'If we can go in for a few minutes, I can explain.'

She stared at him for a few more seconds with wide, help-less eyes. Then she stepped back into the hall and allowed him in.

'I don't understand what this is all about. I have no contact with him any more. And I don't feel very well today.'

Rooth nodded and turned to the right into the kitchen.

'In here?'

'I don't know if . . .'

She followed him in, and they sat down opposite each other at a little table with a blue-and-white checked oilcloth. She moved aside a magazine and a half-empty mug of tea with a heart on it.

'Elizabeth Hennan?' said Rooth. 'I take it that's you?'

'Yes,' she said hesitantly, as if that were a secret that shouldn't become generally known.

'You have a brother called Jaan Hennan? Jaan G. Hennan?'

She nodded without speaking.

'You think that this is awkward, I can tell. But I can promise you that we shan't misuse anything you say in any way.'

What the hell is she so afraid of ? he thought.

'I don't socialize with him and I know nothing about his life.'

Rooth assumed an understanding expression and waited for a few seconds.

'You are his only living blood relative, if we have understood the situation correctly?'

'Yes.'

She looked down at the table. Rooth twiddled his thumbs.

'What has he done?'

'Haven't you read the papers?'

'You mean . . . You mean that business with his wife? It was his wife, wasn't it?'

'Barbara Hennan, yes,' said Rooth. 'She died last week, and that's why we need some information about your brother.'

'Why? I don't want anything to do with him.'

'Fröken Hennan,' said Rooth seriously, leaning towards her over the table. 'It will be easier if you don't ask so many questions. We police have certain routines, we have to collect as much information as possible when we are busy with a case. It's not always easy to tell what's relevant and what isn't – if you understand?'

She thought about that for quite a while, first clasping and then unclasping her hands.

'What do you want to know?' she asked in the end.

'Two things really,' said Rooth in a friendly voice. 'Firstly a bit about his general background, as it were. What things were like when you were growing up, and so on. And secondly, what contact you've had with him since he came back from the USA.'

'Can I answer the second question first?'

'Of course.'

'I haven't had any contact with my brother since he came back. None at all. I discovered three weeks ago that he was apparently living in Linden, because a . . . a friend of mine rang and told me about it.'

'A lady friend?'

'Yes.'

'What's her name?'

Elizabeth Hennan hesitated.

'Doris Sellneck. She was married to him at one time, twenty-five years ago. It lasted for five months.'

Rooth noted it down.

'Do you have her address and telephone number?'

'I want you to leave her in peace.'

'All right,' said Rooth generously. 'We shall respect that.'

It shouldn't be difficult to find somebody by that name in a place the size of Linden, he thought.

'And your brother never got in touch with you after he came back here?'

'Of course not.'

Rooth thought for a moment.

'I have four brothers and sisters,' he said. 'They are not all that keen on me, but they do ring several times a year. All of them. There must be something seriously wrong with the relationship between you and your brother.'

Elizabeth Hennan made no reply.

'Did you have any contact at all while he was in the USA?'

She shook her head.

'Why not?'

She unclasped her hands and stared at her palms. A bus came to a halt just outside the kitchen window: it looked as if there was a bus stop there, and a flock of schoolchildren scampered out. Their happy cries and laughter had just about died away when she got round to responding.

'Jaan and I have not spoken to each other for twenty-six years.'

'Twenty-six years?' exclaimed Rooth. 'Why on earth . . . ?'

'Not since my eighteenth birthday.'

'Yes, I understand,' said Rooth. 'But you must explain to me why things turned out like that.'

'I moved away from home on that day.'

'Really?'

'My mother died when I was four. I grew up with my father and my brother – I don't really want to talk about this, and you must leave me in peace when I've finished, I'm not feeling well . . .'

She's using a different voice now, Rooth noticed. He gathered that something was about to burst, and he tried to look like a kind welfare officer or some sort of confessor. It wasn't exactly second nature to him, but that didn't matter as she stared hard at her hands all the time.

'My brother was six years older than I. My father was ill – I didn't realize that until I grew up and he was taken into a home. They took it in turns to have their way with me from when I was ten onwards. Every evening for five years, every single evening, did you hear that? Ernst Hennan and his son screwed little Elizabeth Hennan every bloody evening for five years! Is it any wonder that I don't send my brother a New Year's greetings card? Do you still wonder why I don't invite him and his bloody wives to dinner? Leave me in peace now, I've nothing more to say!'

She fell silent. Her face was ablaze now. Rooth swallowed. Five seconds passed.

'Thank you,' he said. 'Thank you for telling me that . . . And I apologize for having been forced to squeeze it out of you. Can I . . . Is there anything I can do for you?'

Why on earth am I asking that? he thought in confusion. *If I can do anything for her.* It must be far too late for that.

She stroked her hair to one side, looked briefly at him and shook her head. Rooth stood up, but she made no effort to accompany him to the door.

'Goodbye, and thank you for allowing me to come in.'

'Goodbye.'

When he had closed the door behind him, the sun was shining into his face. He did not feel that he had done anything to deserve that.

Maarten Verlangen celebrated his birthday on Thursday. His forty-seventh – he was reminded of this unbelievable but uneven number by his daughter Belle as early as half past seven in the morning, when she telephoned him and woke him up. She sang a snatch of 'Happy Birthday to You', congratulated him from the bottom of her heart, and explained that she had to rush off to school now. She hadn't quite got round to sorting out a present yet – but they would be meeting on Saturday: could he wait until then?

He assured her that he could, and went back to sleep.

The next person to congratulate him didn't ring until half past three in the afternoon. By then Verlangen had been in his office in Armastenstraat for three hours, drunk two beers, smoked about ten cigarettes, and thought so hard about how he might be able to proceed further with the Barbara Hennan case that his head was aching.

A private detective's resources were somewhat restricted, after all – and he had no particular desire to telephone Chief Inspector Van Veeteren at the police station to discuss the case, or to offer his services. That would have felt presumptuous – but if the request came from the other party, that would be an entirely different matter, of course.

But that did not happen. Nobody at all called Verlangen's Detective Agency that warm June afternoon – until Bertram Grouwer rang to wish him a happy birthday.

It was probably true, as Verlangen frequently suspected, that there was only one person in the world who would mourn his loss if he were to disappear from the face of the earth (his daughter Belle), but Bertram Grouwer would no doubt attend the funeral at least. Verlangen had the impression that people who remember birthdays usually turned up at funerals as well – although it was not certain that this general rule was relevant in the case of Grouwer. His birthday was on the same day as Verlangen's, and he was the same age as well.

Apart from that coincidence – and the fact that they had

been in the same class at Weivers grammar school – they didn't have much in common.

Although they were both divorced, and had not signed up to the temperance pledge.

That was why Grouwer rang. He had also been congratulated over the telephone by his children that morning (two boys, aged fourteen and twelve), and was feeling rather lousy. Might it perhaps be an idea, he wondered, to hit the town that evening and share their gloomy thoughts about life and its intolerable brevity while partaking of a beer or two?

Grouwer was a freelance journalist on *Neuwe Blatt*, and liked to string words together. Verlangen thought for a few seconds, then announced that he thought it sounded like a damned good idea.

They started at Kraus. Devoured an expensive but value-for-money (according to Grouwer) fish soup, drank two bottles of Riesling and a cognac with the coffee. What the hell (according to Grouwer), you only celebrated a birthday once a year, and had an obligation to indulge yourself now and again.

They went on to Adenaar's, where they sank a few beers and ended up discussing the essential nature of women. Grouwer had been together with a tall, tasty beauty several times over the last six months, but she was a complicated character, it transpired. As beautiful as sin, wonderful in bed, but a bit on the nervous side, it seemed. And she objected to his going to football matches twice a week, and his desire to smoke a cigar with his morning coffee.

Verlangen felt quite drunk when they left Adenaar's and would have preferred to go home, but Grouwer insisted that they ought to round off the evening with a visit to the jazz club Vox in Ruyders Allé. After a short internal struggle Verlangen agreed, and they headed over there. There was a queue outside the club, and they had to stand for twenty minutes in steady drizzle before they were allowed in. This sobered Verlangen up quite considerably, so when they discovered a couple of seats in a quiet corner, they each ordered a substantial whisky. That was needed in order to squeeze the dampness out of their bodies. Four coloured musicians were playing on the stage, and it was cramped in the smoke-filled room: but it was not long before Verlangen caught sight of Jaan G. Hennan at a table a few metres away. He was sitting with a few other men and women, but they didn't seem to be a group. There was a shortage of seats, and people simply sat down wherever they could find a vacant chair.

'Well, I'll be damned,' said Verlangen, lighting a cigarette.

'Eh?' said Grouwer.

'I'll be damned,' said Verlangen again. 'There's a murderer sitting over there.'

'What the hell are you talking about?' said Grouwer, looking round.

Verlangen realized straight away that what he had said was idiotic, but sometimes there were things that simply had to be said and couldn't be suppressed. 'There's a murderer sitting over there' was very definitely one of them.

'I was only joking,' he said. 'Cheers.'

Grouwer didn't touch his glass.

'Like hell you were,' he said. 'Who do you mean?'

Verlangen took a swig of whisky. I'm an idiot, he thought. He won't give up until I tell him who it is. Not Grouwer.

'I need to go to the loo,' he said. 'Excuse me for a minute.'

Grouwer nodded.

'While you're away I'll work out who you meant,' he said. 'If I guess right, you owe me a beer. If I'm wrong, I owe you one.'

Verlangen stood up and felt that his drunkenness had returned in spades. Glanced at Hennan, who was sitting there smoking and seemed completely absorbed by 'Take the A-Train' which was currently being performed on the stage.

'Go to hell, damn you!' he said and headed off towards the gents.

When he came back Grouwer was sitting there looking like the cat that got the cream.

'It's that bloke in the striped shirt,' he said, with a conspiratorial wink.

'Who?' said Verlangen, looking around once again.

Grouwer signalled with his head.

'Diagonally behind me. Just beside the stage. Next to that bird in red.'

Verlangen peered in the direction described, and saw the person Grouwer meant. A thin little man in his fifties with neatly combed black hair and an ugly little moustache.

'Like hell it is,' he said. 'You owe me a beer.'

'Oh dear,' said Grouwer, grabbing the arm of a waitress

who happened to be passing. He ordered two lagers and a tub of peanuts.

'Well, the least you can do is to tell me who you really meant,' he said. 'If I also go to the loo I want to know whether or not I'm standing there having a piss next to a murderer or not. I reckon you owe that to me.'

Verlangen sighed. Thought for a while about the pluses and minuses while Grouwer stared expectantly at him. Emptied his glass of whisky.

Huh, he thought. What difference does it make?

It was a few minutes past half past one when Maarten Verlangen finally collapsed into his bed at home in Heerbanerstraat after his birthday celebrations. He had exceeded his ten-beer limit by quite a lot, he could feel that without any question. But he hadn't been asleep for more than half an hour before he woke up and felt as wide awake as a new-born babe.

What the hell? he thought as he started rummaging after his address book in the desk drawer. How on earth could I not have thought about that?

He found the number after searching for a few minutes, but when he dialled it and waited for about twenty rings, it dawned on him that he was wasting his time.

Some people get up and answer when the phone rings at two in the morning; others don't.

15

It was Friday before the report requested from the USA was spat out of the fax machine in Maardam police station.

To make up for the delay it was unexpectedly comprehensive: six densely typed pages written by a certain Chief Lieutenant Horniman of Denver Police District. Van Veeteren was given the documents shortly after ten o'clock, and he immediately shut himself into his office to scrutinize and meditate on them.

He didn't really know what he had expected – but in any case not, and in no circumstances, this remarkable information, he thought after he had only read half a page. Good Lord, no!

It began with details about Barbara Clarissa Hennan, née Delgado. She came from a little town in the backwoods of Iowa, Clarenceburg, with a population of barely a thousand souls. She was the youngest of eight siblings, the family was deeply religious and members of an obscure sect that Van Veeteren had never heard of: *The Sons and Daughters of the Second Holy Grail.* However, Barbara had abandoned both her faith and her family and run off with a long-distance truck driver a few weeks after her sixteenth birthday. After that, it seems, she had spent ten years travelling around from city to city and state to state; then she had joined some other dubious sect around the beginning of the seventies, and disappeared more or less without trace for several years. Probably in California, Horniman thought. Around 1980 she turned up in Denver, Colorado, where she worked for some years at a beauty parlour before meeting Jaan G. Hennan.

They had married in 1984 and lived together in Denver until the spring of 1987, when they emigrated to Europe. Apart from a few speeding tickets and a prosecution for the possession of cannabis, which was eventually dropped, there were no known blemishes on Barbara Hennan's character.

The same applied to her husband, in fact: but Van Veeteren could read between the lines and sensed that Chief Lieutenant Horniman had serious doubts about G's honesty.

Hennan had come to New York in the autumn of 1979 with a three-month residence permit. He managed to acquire a work permit that very same winter, had several short-term jobs and worked on a number of different business projects in New York and New Jersey, as well as Cleveland and Chicago. In 1982 he had married a woman by the name of Philomena McNaught and moved to Denver. At some point during the summer of 1983 his wife disappeared while on a car journey in Bethesda Park in the Rocky Mountains: Hennan was suspected of having had something to do with her disappearance, but there was no proof and he was never charged. In June 1984 Philomena McNaught was declared officially dead, and Hennan collected 400,000 dollars from an insurance policy on her life. Both the Denver police (and, judging by the formulation of the report, Van Veeteren guessed that Chief Lieutenant Horniman had been personally involved in the case – deeply involved, it seemed) and the insurance company's detectives had made a formidable effort to investigate the circumstances surrounding fru Hennan's fate, but had failed to produce sufficiently incriminating evidence to take Hennan to court. The marriage between Jaan G. Hennan and Barbara Delgado took place a month after the insurance payment was made, and about a year later Hennan liquidated his firm G Enterprises, which had been devoted mainly to the importation of conserved fruit from south-east Asia. The couple continued to live in Denver until they emigrated to Europe in the March of that same year.

Van Veeteren read through the report twice.

Then he stood in front of the open window and lit a cigarette.

Incredible, he thought. Absolutely incredible.

And now the bastard is planning a repeat performance.

After lunch Reinhart and Münster had also acquainted themselves with Horniman's report, and they assembled in the Chief Inspector's office to discuss it.

'One thing is crystal clear,' said Reinhart as he filled his pipe. 'I haven't come across anything more suspicious than this in the whole of my career. If Hennan isn't guilty I shall kiss the ground the Chief Inspector stands and walks upon. And the inspector as well, come to that.'

Münster recalled the promise Van Veeteren had made

about clipping his toenails, but refrained from joining in the competition to do more and more outrageous things.

'It's so obvious that you have to be astonished,' he said instead. 'How the hell does he dare?'

The Chief Inspector flopped down on his desk chair.

'That's the problem,' he sighed. 'He seems to be prepared to dare anything at all, and he knows damned well that we have the problem of proving anything.'

Reinhart nodded.

'In fact you can kill off a large number of women,' he said, 'provided you do it in the right way. What's the name of that English king? Henry the what . . . ?'

'Eighth,' said Van Veeteren.

'The Eighth, yes. But he wasn't after insurance money, if I remember rightly. He just wanted male heirs. He hadn't studied genetics.'

'And he didn't need to worry too much about laws and regulations and CID officers either,' said Münster. 'Things were a bit different in those days.'

'Are you suggesting that our friend G is worried about the law?' wondered Van Veeteren sarcastically. 'That's a new one on me.'

'Not worried about,' said Münster. 'But aware of.'

Reinhart lit his pipe.

'In any case, we don't need to draw up a list of possible suspects,' he said. 'Every cloud has its silver lining. Anyway, what do we do next? Arrest the bastard? That's the least one could ask for.'

The Chief Inspector dug down into his breast pocket for a toothpick and looked grim.

'I'm not so sure about that,' he said. 'G knows of course that he'll be arrested sooner or later. He's prepared for the whole rigmarole – he's been through it all before, dammit, in the land of milk and honey. As a sort of rehearsal. We'll have to get in touch with this Horniman character – maybe there's something else that we can get our teeth into . . .'

'Some hope,' said Reinhart. 'But of course, I can phone him if you like.'

'Please do,' said Van Veeteren. 'The paradox is of course that this report doesn't change our views all that much. We're just that bit more certain what kind of a person G is, and ninety-nine jurymen out of a hundred would be convinced of his guilt. But that doesn't help us. What matters in a court of law is proof, not belief, as you gentlemen may be aware: so that's what we have to produce. Proof.'

'Beyond reasonable doubt,' muttered Reinhart, blowing out a cloud of smoke. 'This case feels almost classical in a way – or do I mean clinical?'

'I couldn't care less what you mean,' said the Chief Inspector. 'But what we need to do in any case is to prove how he goes about throwing his wife down into that swimming pool. And as far as I can see there is one possibility that is more likely than any of the others. Don't you think?'

'An accomplice,' said Münster.

'Exactly. We must find the bastard who did this on his behalf – or else we must destroy his restaurant alibi. This Verlangen seems very dodgy, to say the least . . .'

'Maybe we could get him to shut up?' suggested Reinhart.

'That would probably not be impossible,' said Van Veeteren with a nod. 'But maybe a bit unethical. He's important for the alibi after all ... But you have to agree that it's remarkable that the victim created an alibi for the murderer in this way ...'

'And that to crown it all, it's very much in Verlangen's interest for us to nail Hennan,' said Münster. 'Yes, I have to agree that it's remarkable.'

'The gods are playing games with us,' said Van Veeteren, tossing a used toothpick out of the window. 'But I think it will be difficult for us to maintain that Hennan left Columbine's for a whole hour – with or without Verlangen. Remember that we have to prove that he did so, not simply show that he had the opportunity. And besides, our private dick wasn't the only one who noticed his presence.'

No one spoke for a while.

'There are not many unknowns in this equation,' said Reinhart eventually, looking thoughtful. 'We have more or less all the cards in our hand, and yet—'

'Like hell we have,' interrupted the Chief Inspector in irritation. 'We have only one card in our hand; a very large and very scornful joker by the name of Jaan G. Hennan, who enjoys taking the mickey out of us.'

'All right,' agreed Reinhart. 'That's the way it looks. When are you thinking of interrogating him?'

The Chief Inspector pulled a face.

'Soon.'

'I hope so,' said Reinhart. 'Don't underestimate your interrogation skills. He might break down and confess.'

'Do you really think so?' said Van Veeteren.

'No. But shouldn't we perhaps keep an eye on him anyway? If we're not going to bring him in immediately.'

Van Veeteren stood up to signal that perhaps they had been discussing the situation for long enough now.

'Already done,' he said. 'I've had him followed since yesterday morning.'

'Really?' said Münster. 'Who's the shadow?'

'Constable Kowalski.'

'Kowalski!' exclaimed Reinhart. 'Why the hell Kowalski? He's about as subtle as . . . as a randy Labrador after a bitch on heat.'

'Exactly. That's why,' said Van Veeteren.

Reinhart thought for a moment.

'I get it,' he said.

Meusse the pathologist stroked his hand over the top of his head and adjusted his spectacles.

'Have you finished?' asked Van Veeteren.

'As close to finished as you could hope.'

'And?'

'Hmm. There was one thing above all else that you wanted to know, if I understood you rightly?'

'That's correct,' said Van Veeteren. 'Let's hear it.'

'It's not possible to be sure,' explained Meusse. 'But then again, it's not possible to exclude anything either. The injuries are bound to be pretty extensive after a dive like that.'

'So it's possible that she might have been knocked unconscious first?'

'I don't regard that as out of the question, as I said. But that's all I can say. In any case, she landed head-first.'

'Would it be complicated to push her over and get that result?'

'Not at all. Especially not if she was unconscious to start with.'

'I understand,' said Van Veeteren. 'Anything else?'

'What do you want to know? Degree of intoxication? Stomach contents?'

'I know that already.'

'Perhaps there's one thing,' said Meusse, flicking through the file lying on the table in front of him. 'She had given birth.'

'Given birth?' said Van Veeteren.

'Yes,' said Meusse. 'Only one child, presumably. I thought that might be worth mentioning.'

'Really?' said Van Veeteren. 'It could be. Was that all?'

Meusse shrugged.

'Of course not. You have the full report in this file. Here you are, no need to say thank you.'

I ought to have offered him a beer, realized the Chief Inspector after he had left the office.

A child? he thought when he had returned to his room. Did it say anything about any children in Horniman's report?

He read it for the third time, and established that there was no such mention.

Shouldn't there have been something about that? he wondered, but he had no time to reach a conclusion on that point. He realized that it was gone four o'clock, and high time he was in the conference room for the run-through.

The run-through after two days of intensive work on the Hennan case.

The G File.

He didn't really like that description, but was well aware that this was how he would always refer to it. Both while it was under investigation, and in the future.

The G File.

16

'If we are going to stick to the normal procedure,' began Van Veeteren, 'we should start with the technical evidence. But we don't have any yet. I've just spoken to le Houde, and there will be a report on Monday or Tuesday. They have been going through Villa Zefyr with a fine-tooth comb for a day and a half, but as they don't know what they are looking for I find it hard to believe that we shall achieve a breakthrough on that front.'

'A bloody fingerprint on the diving tower would be quite useful, don't you think?' suggested Rooth. 'Left by somebody who's in our files.'

'Le Houde would have mentioned it if there'd been anything like that,' said Van Veeteren. 'Who'd like to start? Heinemann?'

Intendent Heinemann changed his glasses and consulted his notes, which thanks to the habit of a lifetime were written in flimsy violet-blue exercise books. Reinhart had a theory that he had been presented with a gross of them as a prize for good work and excellent progress at some point in his schooldays, and there was nothing to suggest that the theory was wide of the mark.

'Yes, hmm, well . . .' began Heinemann. 'Shall we start with that visit to Aarlach, perhaps?'

'Why not,' said the Chief Inspector.

'Hmm. Well, it's crystal clear that fru Hennan left her home in Linden by car at about eight o'clock on Thursday morning. The woman next door can swear to that. She filled up with petrol at Exxon on the slip-road to the motorway – they remember her: she bought a mug of coffee and a sandwich with cheese and—'

'Carry on,' said the Chief Inspector.

'Of course. It's also been established that she was at the ceramics shop Hendermaag's in Keyserstraat in Aarlach between about twelve noon and a quarter to one. She examined quite a lot of china, and eventually ordered two sets of crockery – they didn't have them in stock – from a series by the name of Osobowsky, royal mint-green – six soup bowls and six ordinary plates. She paid a deposit of a hundred guilders, with the remainder to be paid on delivery – yes, well, she will never be able to . . .'

'And then?' wondered Reinhart.

'Then she left the shop.'

'And?' asked Reinhart.

'I don't know where she went after that.'

'How long does it take to drive up to Aarlach?' asked Münster. 'Three hours?'

'At most,' said Reinhart. 'She could have been back home by four. What does this tell us?'

'We haven't managed to establish when she actually

arrived back home, have we?' asked Münster. 'She might have done other things as well.'

'Of course,' said the Chief Inspector. 'Bought a few bottles of sherry, for instance. Anything else, Heinemann?'

'She didn't call in at Exxon on the way home as well, did she?' wondered Rooth.

'I'm afraid not,' said Heinemann.

'Anything else?' repeated the Chief Inspector.

'Yes,' mumbled Heinemann, thumbing through his note-book. 'I've looked into that company of his, as we said. Hennan's company, that is . . . G Enterprises – he's used the same name as he used in the USA, apparently there's nothing to prevent that. However, it doesn't seem to have been doing very much . . . It was registered at the beginning of May and he rented some small premises in Landemaarstraat in Linden, but that's all.'

'What?' said Rooth.

'What are you saying?' wondered Reinhart. 'A company that doesn't actually do anything?'

'That's not forbidden,' said Heinemann. 'Obviously it's usual for a company to carry out some kind of business, but this one doesn't seem to have done so.'

'Don't you have to indicate what kind of business you are going to do?' asked Münster. 'For the tax authorities, at least?'

'Yes, Hennan specified "trading" on his registration form. But that doesn't tell you very much. I'll look further into this, of course.'

'Of course you will,' said the Chief Inspector with a deep sigh. 'Is that all so far?'

Heinemann took off his glasses and began polishing them with his tie.

'Yes,' he said. 'So far.'

'Brilliant,' said Reinhart.

'Yes indeed,' muttered the Chief Inspector. 'Anyway, let's continue. Rooth and Jung, perhaps?'

Rooth reported in a somewhat subdued tone on the visit to Elizabeth Hennan, and concluded, to sum up, that if the world had ever seen a prize prat more repulsive than any other, who deserved to waste away under lock and key, his name was Jaan G. Hennan.

'If you start by raping your little sister for five long years, you have no doubt set the tone for the rest of your career,' said Reinhart with disgust in his voice. 'By Christ, if we can't nail this monster I'll be very tempted to go and finish him off with my bare hands.'

'Steady on,' said Van Veeteren. 'I have even better grounds for catching him than those, but we had better stick to the rulebook in this case as in every other.'

Reinhart looked up at the Chief Inspector in surprise.

'You've lost me now,' he said. 'What reasons could you possibly have that are better than mine?'

'We can talk about that some other time,' said Van Veeteren. 'In any case, it would be good if we could catch him with the means at our disposal and nothing else. Are we agreed on that?'

'All right,' said Reinhart. 'It was metaphorically speaking.'

'Carry on, Rooth. The sister is his only relative, I assume?'

'Correct,' said Rooth. 'His father died in a mental hospital fifteen years ago. And his mother died even earlier, as we know. Anyway, then we worked through the list of names of those who knew him when he was arrested the first time, in 1975. We've tracked down a few of them, but none had the slightest idea that Hennan had come back . . . Or so they claim. Well, we've interviewed only a couple of them so far, but neither Jung nor I had any reason to doubt what they told us, it seems—'

'Hold on,' said Reinhart, interrupting him. 'It's in this category that he could well have found an accomplice. An old friend from his drug-taking days. We must be very thorough here – I hope that's clear to you?'

'Of course it's clear,' said Rooth crossly. 'Our two boys are called Siegler and deWylde. Siegler's in jail in Kaarhuijs for bank robbery, and he wasn't out on parole last Thursday. DeWylde was up in Karpatz – we've checked that as well.'

'Good,' said Reinhart.

'How many names do you have on the list?' wondered Münster.

'Six or seven so far,' said Jung. 'Plus those two. But no doubt we'll have more to add as time goes by.'

'Let's hope so,' said the Chief Inspector. 'But I assume you've also noted that the Hennans don't seem to have had much of a social life.'

'We have indeed,' said Rooth. 'We haven't yet found a single berk who admits to having said as much as "Good morning" to Monsieur Hennan. Not during the last fifteen years, in any case.'

'We mustn't forget the neighbours,' said Heinemann quietly. 'The Trottas. Didn't they have dinner at each other's place? They must surely have had something to talk about . . . Maybe that could give us a lead?'

'Quite right,' said the Chief Inspector. 'We'll be in touch with them again.'

'I've already broken the ice there,' said Münster. 'But I only spoke to the wife. What about his office? There must be people around there, surely?'

Jung cleared his throat.

'He rented it after replying to an advertisement. The property is owned by the man who runs the undertaking business on the floor below. His name is Mordenbeck, and he's not exactly a cheerful type. Apparently he and Hennan have exchanged about twenty words since the latter moved in.'

'What about the house?' asked Reinhart. 'In Kammerweg . . . How did they get that?'

'Through an estate agent,' said Münster, who had looked into the matter. 'The Tielebergs, the family that owns the place, live in Almeria in Spain, and didn't even need to come up here to sign the papers. The Hennans have only signed a contract for six months, by the way . . . The whole situation gives the impression of being stage scenery, as it were.'

'Stage scenery, yes,' said the Chief Inspector glumly. 'Roughly made backdrops so that he could strike and earn one point two million. I need hardly mention that both their cars were rented – both the Saab and the Mazda.'

'Holy shit,' said Reinhart. 'I can't believe this is true.'

'But it is true,' insisted the Chief Inspector, looking distinctly ill-humoured. 'Absolutely bloody true. And Barbara Hennan has been murdered. And we are the CID officers investigating the case. Would you like to hear some more facts?'

'Yes, please,' Rooth was so bold as to request. 'That would certainly liven things up.'

Van Veeteren glared at him and stubbed out his cigarette, which was beginning to burn the tips of his fingers.

'All right,' he said. 'Münster, let's hear about Columbine's.'

Münster stretched.

'By all means,' he said. 'It will be a pleasure. It's not yet one hundred per cent certain, but I'm afraid it looks as if the staff there can give Hennan an alibi for the critical moments. Barbara Hennan died at some time between half past nine and half past ten, and one of the waiters at the restaurant is certain that Hennan paid his bill at a quarter to ten – plus or minus five minutes. The barman is just as certain that he served him a whisky shortly before half past ten. That was when he stopped working. So there's a gap of forty-five minutes at most – but there are others who can probably fill it. Our friend Verlangen, for instance.'

There followed several seconds of silence. Then the Chief Inspector stood up and walked over to the window.

'I take it you gentlemen realize what this means?' he said in a tired-sounding voice.

'That he didn't do it,' said Reinhart. 'Jaan G. Hennan can't have murdered his wife.'

'Exactly,' said Van Veeteren. 'At least we have reached one definite conclusion. Any comments?'

'Does that mean it's time for coffee?' wondered Rooth.

The second half of the run-through was also an uphill struggle.

Van Veeteren summarized the report from Horniman, and those who had not yet become familiar with it (Rooth, Jung and Heinemann) reacted in more or less the same way as those who had perused it already (Van Veeteren, Reinhart and Münster), earlier in the day. The Chief Inspector also recounted what had emerged from his conversation with the pathologist, Meusse, and a theory was produced with regard to the child that had not been mentioned in the report.

'She had it while she was mixed up with that damned sect, of course,' maintained Rooth. 'Stillborn, presumably – they all live on roots and grasshoppers and don't get sufficient nourishment.'

Rooth's hypothesis was not greeted by applause, but nor were there any serious objections.

Münster reported that renewed contact with the insurance company F/B Trustor had revealed that fru Hennan had not been present when the policy was signed, and that current practice did not require her presence. To round things off the Chief Inspector read out a two-page report from Constable Kowalski – containing forty-two spelling mistakes, but they were not noticeable when the text was read aloud – regarding the suspect Jaan G. Hennan's actions and doings from Thursday morning up to and including lunch on Friday of this week. No criminal (or otherwise notable) behaviour had been observed, despite careful and intensive observation – with the possible exception of a visit by the said Hennan to the jazz club Vox on Thursday evening, during which he had offered his shadow a so-called double whisky at the bar. In order to avoid any unnecessary suspicions, the shadow had accepted the drink, and had also spoken to his quarry about general and neutral matters for about ninety seconds.

After the report from Kowalski, Van Veeteren declared the meeting closed.

'It's not going all that well,' said Münster when he and the Chief Inspector were ensconced with a Friday beer each at Adenaar's half an hour later.

'No,' said Van Veeteren. 'You can say that again.'

In both his voice and the expression on his face were a trace of resignation that Münster was not used to. A sort of introspection, in fact, which was quite unlike the usual intense concentration that Münster had grown familiar with over the years. He wondered what lay behind this. There was a purely personal aspect between G and Van Veeteren that had been hovering in the background, but just how it was more than the fact that they had been at school together thirty or forty years ago, he didn't know. After hesitating for a while, Münster asked outright how he was feeling, and the Chief Inspector admitted that he wasn't exactly on top form.

'Mort used to talk about this,' he added when they had tasted their beers. 'Did you ever meet Mort?'

'Just a few times, very briefly,' said Münster. 'I never spoke to him.'

'He grew very tired during his last few years. It happened quickly, as if he had suddenly walked into a wall. He talked about it . . . but in a vague sort of way – I don't know if he really wanted to discuss it, but in any case, it was the job that finished him off.'

'What exactly was it about?' asked Münster.

Van Veeteren lit a cigarette and looked out through the window for a while before answering.

'A case like this one, presumably. Or several of them, perhaps. Investigations in which he knew exactly what had happened, but he couldn't prove anything. And so he had to let the perpetrator go free.'

'That's something that happens to all of us,' said Münster. 'It's just a matter of finding a way to cope with it.'

'Of course,' said the Chief Inspector. 'But sometimes you can't find a way. I think it was something purely personal in Mort's case as well. I had the impression that a close relative was involved, but he never went into any details. As I said.'

Münster thought for a while.

'There's an expression in the USA – Blue Cops: are you familiar with that?'

Van Veeteren nodded but said nothing.

'Police officers who burn themselves out,' said Münster. 'There's an over-representation of such cases in the suicide statistics that is scary to say the least . . . I read about it a few weeks ago.'

Van Veeteren took a swig of beer.

'Yes, I know about the phenomenon. Perhaps what you need is an armour-plated soul – but unfortunately you wouldn't get very far even with one of those. You sort of lose the ability to see, unless you have a certain kind of darkness inside you . . . I think Churchill wrote about this, in fact. He wrote that, in a way, he *understood* Hitler. You need to have an emphatic insight into even the most damnable of psyches, don't forget that, Münster.'

Münster said nothing, but thought for a while.

'So G has one of those dark souls, does he?'

Van Veeteren raised an eyebrow and seemed surprised by the question.

'Without a doubt. Always assuming that he has a soul.'

'And so we must . . . ?'

Münster broke off and started laughing, but the Chief Inspector still looked serious.

'Is it the case . . . ?' asked Münster hesitantly. 'Is it the case that there is a personal aspect in this business as well? Just as there was for Mort. Have you had dealings with Jaan G. Hennan before?'

Van Veeteren didn't seem keen to follow the thread, and Münster assumed he had gone too far. He took another drink of beer and leaned back on his chair. Glanced discreetly at his wristwatch and established that he ought to be setting off for home shortly.

Or that he ought to have set off already. He had promised

Synn that he would be home before six, they were expecting guests – her sister and her husband, but even so . . . And wasn't he supposed to buy something on his way home as well . . . ?

'Yes, of course,' said the Chief Inspector interrupting his train of thought. 'Of course I've had dealings with him before. Donkeys years ago, of course, but it was a woman . . . Or rather, a girl.'

'A girl?' said Münster.

'A girl, yes. Nineteen, twenty years old . . .'

'Really?' said Münster, and his curiosity was so strong that he couldn't camouflage it.

'As I said,' said the Chief Inspector. 'But we'll take that another time.'

I very much doubt that, thought Münster, and suppressed his curiosity. No point in persisting, obviously. He emptied his glass of beer, and prepared to leave Adenaar's.

'When are you intending to interrogate Hennan?' he asked.

Van Veeteren stubbed out his cigarette and also drained his glass.

'Tonight,' he said. 'I intend to bring him in late this evening.'

'Tonight?'

'Yes. If you are interested, you're welcome to watch the performance through the two-way mirror. About eleven o'clock. Reinhart will be there, but there's no harm in having an extra pair of eyes and ears present, I suppose.'

Münster thought for a moment, then made up his mind.

'I'll be there,' he said. 'Eleven o'clock?'

'Maybe not before half past eleven,' said Van Veeteren, getting to his feet. 'I thought the night might be a suitable setting for this sort of lark. But only if you have time.'

'I shall make time,' promised Inspector Münster, and followed the Chief Inspector to the exit.

17

In addition to Reinhart and Münster, Inspector Rooth was also on parade in the cramped area in front of the two-way mirror when the interrogation of Jaan G. Hennan was due to begin. Rooth's so-called date had rung and announced that she was ill, he explained, and this promised to be at least as entertaining as a bad television crime series.

Hennan had been collected from his home by Constables Kowalski and Klempje shortly before half past ten. He had accompanied them quite eagerly and with a smile on his face, and then had the doubtful pleasure of spending forty-five minutes on a chair in the stark interrogation room before Van Veeteren entered through one of the two doors and sat down opposite him.

'About time,' said Hennan, but with no trace of irritation in his voice.

Van Veeteren didn't respond. He messed around for a while with the tape recorder and lit a cigarette, then read out Hennan's rights and asked if he wanted to have a lawyer present.

Hennan leaned back, smiled broadly and announced that he needed a lawyer about as much as one needs a wart in one's arsehole. The Chief Inspector nodded and switched on the tape recorder. Stated the time, place and nature of the interrogation, and asked Hennan to give his full name, birthplace and date of birth. Hennan obliged, smiling all the time.

'Right,' said the Chief Inspector, hanging his jacket on the back of his chair. 'You are here because you are suspected of murdering your wife, Barbara Clarissa Hennan. You are not yet under arrest, but that's only a matter of time.'

'Murdering? Arrest?'

'Yes,' said Van Veeteren. 'Would you like to confess right away, or do we have to make a meal of it?'

'Rubbish,' said Hennan.

'I didn't understand your reply,' said Van Veeteren.

'Rubbish,' said Hennan again.

'Now I understood it,' said Van Veeteren. 'Should I interpret it as meaning that you are surprised at the fact that we suspect you?'

Hennan rested his chin on the knuckles of his right hand and thought for three seconds.

'Both yes and no,' he said. 'I am well aware of the overall incompetence of the police and have long since ceased to be surprised by it; but in this case you appear to have excelled yourselves.'

'Expound,' said the Chief Inspector.

'Certainly not,' said Hennan. 'If it needs expounding, you can do so yourself. Personally I would prefer to be driven home and go to bed.'

'That's not what we had in mind,' said the Chief Inspector. 'How long were you married to Philomena McNaught?'

Hennan's response came without any obvious surprise.

'Just over a year.'

'She died while on a car journey in Bethesda Park, is that right?'

'I don't know anything about that. She disappeared, and was eventually pronounced officially dead.'

'If I were to tell you that her body had been found, would that surprise you?'

Hennan hesitated for a moment. Then he smiled again.

'No,' he said. 'They were bound to find her sooner or later. How did it happen?'

'What do you mean?'

'I wonder where they found her, of course. And in what circumstances. As she was most probably killed by a large beast of prey, it's a bit surprising to hear that a whole body has been found, I'll give you that. My God, do you really think that I haven't been around long enough not to know when a member of the filth is sitting there lying to me?'

Van Veeteren sat in silence for a while, gazing at a point on the wall just above Hennan's head. He didn't move a muscle.

'Are you so stupid,' he said in the end, 'so *incredibly* stupid, that you think you can get away with the same ruse twice? We know that you have killed two women, and that you will be in jail for the next twenty-five years of your life. I suggest that you get yourself a lawyer without delay, since you don't seem to understand the situation you find yourself in.'

'Crap,' said Hennan. 'I don't need a lawyer. But on the other hand, I do need to go to the loo.'

'Five minutes,' said Van Veeteren, and switched off the tape recorder.

'I must disappoint you on one point,' said the Chief Inspector when Hennan had returned.

'Really? How sad.'

'Even if you hadn't been caught, you wouldn't have been able to collect any insurance pay-out.'

'You don't say?' said Hennan with a smile. 'Well, I suppose I shall have to listen to your insinuations since we are sitting here. Go on, I'm all ears.'

'Thank you. We shall prove that it wasn't an accident – the murder of your second wife, that is – and hence the appropriate clause in your insurance policy kicks in.'

Hennan shrugged.

'You have every right to try to prove whatever you like, of course. Don't let me get in your way. But it would astonish me if you were to succeed.'

'She was unconscious before she was pushed down into the empty swimming pool,' said Van Veeteren, lighting another cigarette. 'But you have evidently decided to carry on pretending to be stupid – I must say I had expected rather better opposition.'

'Opposition?' said Hennan in histrionic surprise. 'What the devil are you rambling on about now, Chief Inspector?'

'You're boring me,' said Van Veeteren with a yawn. 'You raped your little sister regularly for five years, is that right?'

'What?' said Hennan.

'I asked if you raped your sister, Elizabeth Hennan, regularly for five years. Or was it for longer than that? Why did you stop? Do you think fifteen-year-olds are too old?'

It took several seconds before Hennan was able to gain control over his facial expression. Then the smile reappeared, albeit a thinner version of it.

'Perhaps I ought to have a lawyer after all,' he said. 'You seem to have taken leave of your senses.'

'Perhaps you prefer to answer that question at the trial instead,' suggested the Chief Inspector. 'Do you still meet at all? Like brothers and sisters usually do, I mean?'

Hennan made no reply.

'Can you give me the names of some of your friends and acquaintances?' asked Van Veeteren.

'Why should I?'

'Perhaps you could do with somebody to speak up on your behalf, for instance. Can you give me the names of a few people who can confirm your good character?'

'No,' said Hennan. 'It's up to the police to find witnesses.'

'Maarten Verlangen, perhaps?' suggested the Chief Inspector.

'Verlangen? Who the hell is he? – Oh, do you mean that ex-copper? What have I got to do with him?'

'You met him the evening your wife died.'

Hennan thought for a moment.

'Yes, that's right. We had a few drinks. A sad type – he's gone down in the world.'

'How come you are acquainted with him?'

Hennan burst out laughing.

'You know that full well. We had a score to settle a few years ago. He had me locked up – I was innocent, but I spent some time in jail thanks to him. But that's all forgotten now. I don't hold grudges.'

'I take it you know what he does for a living nowadays?'

'I've no idea,' said Hennan. 'I'd like a cigarette now.'

'By all means,' said Van Veeteren. 'Verlangen works as a private detective.'

Hennan looked surprised.

'A private eye? He didn't say anything about that. Still, I suppose it's not easy for sacked coppers to find a decent job.'

Van Veeteren allowed a few seconds to pass in silence.

'But no doubt you knew that your wife was also acquainted with him?'

'My wife? Acquainted with whom?'

'With Verlangen.'

Hennan almost succeeded in concealing his surprise by lighting a cigarette.

'Rubbish,' he said. 'Why should Barbara be acquainted with somebody like Verlangen?'

'If she were still alive, she could have explained it to you. But of course Verlangen will fill us in at the trial.'

Just for a moment, for a fraction of a second, Van Veeteren had the impression that Hennan was about to give the game away. Perhaps it was an illusion, but for an instant the Chief Inspector felt that he could see right through Hennan – and if he had ever had the slightest doubt that he was guilty, that unguarded moment would have been sufficient. Jaan G. Hennan had Barbara Clarissa Delgado's life on his conscience, alongside that of Philomena McNaught. He thought quickly about how one could put into words that all-embracing revelation, that all-embracing guilt reflected in those eyes – for a jury, for instance: but all he could envisage was the deep abyss that separates insight and action. It wasn't the first time.

He was brought back down to earth by Hennan clearing his throat.

'Is it full steam ahead for the police to make up any lies they like during an interrogation nowadays?' he asked.

Van Veeteren snorted.

'G,' he said. 'Sitting with and talking to a murderer are one thing; but I find that having to converse with a hopelessly stupid murderer is extremely boring. We'll take a break for half an hour.'

Hennan shook his head and made as if to stand up.

'No, no,' said the Chief Inspector. 'You will stay here. There's a floor if you want to lie down for a while.'

'I'm reluctantly impressed,' said Inspector Reinhart during the break. 'But I think it might be as well if we didn't go out of our way to broadcast our methods.'

'How did you rate his reaction to Verlangen?' wondered the Chief Inspector. 'There was some uncertainty there – I didn't notice it until afterwards.'

'Uncertainty?' said Münster. 'What kind of uncertainty?'

The Chief Inspector shook his head and stuck a toothpick into his mouth.

'I had the impression that he was pretending to be surprised – but only half pretending . . . And I'm wondering which half was genuine.'

'That Verlangen . . .' sighed Rooth. 'We have no idea what he said and didn't say at the restaurant. He was presumably pretty drunk – Hennan might have extracted God only knows what out of him.'

'Absolutely right,' said Van Veeteren. 'We still don't have an answer to that question. But why on earth did she go to a private detective? That's a more important question. Is it enough that she felt vaguely threatened in some way? I don't think so. It ought to be possible to pin it down more precisely.'

'But if Verlangen himself doesn't know the answer, how can we find it?' said Rooth. 'The one who knows is dead.'

'I'm aware of that,' said Van Veeteren.

'What's the plan for the next round?' wondered Reinhart.

'A one-hundred-and-eighty-degree turn,' said the Chief Inspector. 'Come and fetch me in a quarter of an hour's time: I'm going to go and put my feet up on my desk for a while. Keep an eye on what he's doing in there.'

Münster looked at the clock. It was twenty-five to one.

'I want you to concentrate now,' said Van Veeteren. 'That's why you've got that cup of coffee.'

'I'm overwhelmed,' said Hennan.

During the whole of the break he had sat leaning back on his chair with his arms folded over his chest and his eyes closed. His smile had vanished now, but otherwise he looked calm and collected.

'First let's get confirmation of a few facts for the record. Twelve years ago you were sentenced for drugs crimes and spent two-and-a-half years in prison. Is that correct?'

'I've already—'

'Answer yes or no.'

'Yes,' said Hennan with a shrug.

'And almost ten years ago you emigrated to the USA?'

'Yes.'

'As soon as you were released?'

'More or less.'

'In 1983 you married a certain Philomena McNaught?'

'Yes.'

'She disappeared a year later, and you collected four hundred thousand dollars on a life insurance policy. Correct?'

'Correct,' said Hennan.

'Did your then wife know that you had insured her life for such a large sum?'

'Of course.'

'In 1984 you married Barbara Delgado?'

'Yes.'

'This year you moved back to Europe and you immediately signed up for a large insurance policy on her life. One point two million. Is that true?'

'Yes.'

'Did she know that you had taken out that policy?'

'Naturally.'

'But she wasn't present when you signed it?'

'She was busy doing something else at the time.'

'What?'

'I don't remember.'

'I'll note that down. A month after you paid the first premium, your wife was found dead in the swimming pool of the house you rent in Kammerweg in Linden?'

'Yes. What do you mean—'

'No questions, if you don't mind. As I have already said we shall be able to prove that your wife did not die a natural death. The insurance will not be paid. You must now choose one of two possible lines to take.'

'Really?' said Hennan. 'What the hell do you mean?'

'You will have to make exactly the same choice at your trial, so you might as well start practising now.'

Hennan didn't respond, but his left eyebrow twitched.

'Either you elect to cooperate in order to help us catch the killer,' explained the Chief Inspector, 'which is what ninety-nine out of a hundred men would do. Or you elect to be obstructive. That can only be interpreted in one way: that you yourself are responsible for your wife's death. One in a hundred, as I said. Is that clear?'

'Huh,' said Hennan drily.

'Which line are you going to take?'

'Obviously I would never dream of taking a line which would obstruct a police investigation,' said Hennan with treacle in his voice. 'I don't understand how you could possibly imagine my doing such a thing, Chief Inspector.'

'Excellent,' said Van Veeteren. 'Give me the names of your closest friends.'

'We don't have any friends.'

'Who has been to visit you at Villa Zefyr since you moved in?'

'The Trottas,' said Hennan. 'Nobody else.'

'Nobody else?'

'Not as far as I recall.'

'You're lying,' said Van Veeteren.

'Well, maybe the odd delivery person,' admitted Hennan. 'The removal men, of course – I could probably extract some names from the firm . . . Our cleaner . . .'

'Which of your former so-called friends have you been in contact with since you came back?'

'None at all.'

'Think carefully now.'

Hennan smiled but said nothing.

'Listen here, young man,' said the Chief Inspector. 'I don't think the jury will understand which line you chose – but there is one thing they will comprehend, you can be quite sure of that.'

'What?'

'That it was you who helped your wife over the edge of the pool that evening.'

'I think there is a snag,' said Hennan.

'Really? What might that be?'

'As I understand it, I have an alibi.'

'What?' exclaimed Van Veeteren. 'You think you have an alibi? Who has tricked you into believing that?'

Hennan hesitated for a second.

'I have an alibi because I happened to be at the Columbine rest—'

'Stop!' interrupted the Chief Inspector. 'That no longer has any significance. You seem to have forgotten that we know how the murder actually took place.'

'What?' said Hennan. 'What kind of idiotic . . . No, I've had enough of this crap now.'

'Are you going to explain or shall I?' asked the Chief Inspector.

'Explain what?'

'How it happened?'

Hennan glared at him for a few seconds, then once again folded his arms over his chest and closed his eyes.

'Switch off the lights when you leave, if you don't mind,' he said. 'I have nothing more to add.'

Van Veeteren remained seated for a minute. Then he switched off the tape recorder, took out the cassette and stood up. Paused for a few moments and contemplated Hennan, then left the room without switching off the light.

'Forty-eight hours,' he said to the others when he had closed the door behind him. 'We have forty-eight hours. Make sure he's put under lock and key. I'll sleep in my office and cross swords with him again tomorrow morning.'

'He'll soon give up,' said Reinhart. 'That last ploy was a pretty effective booby trap.'

The Chief Inspector stared at him, his eyes slightly screwed up.

'I'm glad to hear that you are an optimist,' he said. 'Good night, gentlemen.'

18

He was woken up by the telephone. At first he wasn't at all clear about where he was, but then he felt a pain at the base of his spine and realized that he must have been asleep on the sofa in his office.

He looked at the clock: a quarter to eight. With considerable difficulty he staggered over to his desk and answered. It was Reinhart.

'Do you read the *Neuwe Blatt*?' he asked.

'No,' said Van Veeteren. 'Do you?'

'Very rarely,' said Reinhart. 'But I have done today. I happened to run past a placard.'

'Run?' said Van Veeteren.

'I was out jogging – I usually do that on Saturday mornings. Anyway, I think you should.'

'Go out running?' said Van Veeteren.

'Well, yes,' said Reinhart. 'But what I meant is that you should read today's *Neuwe Blatt*. There's an article about Hennan.'

'What? Why is there an article about . . . ?'

'A whole page. Somebody called Grouwer has written it. Devilishly well informed – we have a leak.'

'A leak?' said the Chief Inspector, trying to straighten his back. 'What the hell are you on about? Have you started working for the security services?'

'Buy the rag and read it for yourself,' urged Reinhart. 'Are you going to stay at the station?'

'I think so.'

'I'll be there in an hour. I'll just have a shower first. Then we can discuss it.'

He hung up. The Chief Inspector stood there with the receiver in his hand, staring into space for a while. Then he dialled the duty officer and asked for a copy of *Neuwe Blatt* to be sent up to his office.

Then he did the same as Reinhart: went for a shower.

Reinhart had certainly not provided him with false information, that was immediately obvious. At the top of the front page was a headline in bold print: *Cold-blooded murder in Linden?*

At least they've used a question mark, thought the Chief Inspector. Every cloud . . . Both Barbara Hennan and Jaan G. Hennan were named in the introductory paragraph. As directed, Van Veeteren turned to page five which was devoted entirely to the case: *The accident reported on from Kammerweg in Linden last week could well turn out to be an extremely cunningly planned murder*, it said underneath a large picture of Villa Zefyr with the magical diving tower just visible behind the greenery. A photographer had simply snapped the mansion from the other side of the road, Van Veeteren established. He steeled himself in order to be able to cope with the pathetic language used, and continued reading.

It was as Reinhart had said. Devilishly well informed.

The macabre scene in the empty swimming pool was described in accurate detail, and then followed by a discussion about the insurance policy. Jaan G. Hennan, it said, without any second thoughts, had signed up to a sky-high life insurance policy for his young American wife, only a few weeks before she was found dead in her home. Herr Kooperdijk, the director of F/B Trustor, had expressed severe doubts regarding the honesty of Hennan, and hoped that the police would bring him to court as soon as possible. The author of the article implied that there was no doubt the situation involved fraud and even more serious criminal activity.

Towards the end of the article it was stated that Hennan had a criminal past, and that he had spent almost a decade in the USA, but it was not at all clear what he was doing during that time. In conclusion Grouwer stressed how important it was that the Maardam CID, which was now responsible for the case, should not mince matters but had an obligation to make public vital information.

Had the police something to hide? came the rhetorical question. Why had there been no arrest? When would the first press conference finally take place? There was a murderer on the loose.

It did not state explicitly that this Jaan G. Hennan was the supected murderer, but any seven-year-old able to read could work that out between the lines.

Van Veeteren drank two cups of coffee while reading the

article. Also tried to eat a cheese sandwich with paprika rings and a rather sad lettuce leaf, but was unable to force it down.

Ah well, he thought. Now the hacks are snapping at our heels as well. Let the circus begin.

As an immediate confirmation of this assumption, the telephone rang at that precise moment. A mildly irritated editor by the name of Aronsen from the *Telegraaf* wondered what the devil and what the hell? . . . Van Veeteren explained that he was just about to conduct an important interrogation and referred the editor to a press release that would be issued before noon.

'Have you got him?' asked Aronsen.

'Of course,' said the Chief Inspector in a neutral tone of voice. 'He's down in the basement.'

He concluded the call then rang the switchboard and gave instructions that nothing from the mass media should be passed on for the next few hours, then went to brush his teeth.

By the time he got back, Reinhart had appeared.

'A great story, don't you think?' he said, pulling a face.

'Terrific,' said the Chief Inspector. 'I've promised a press release before noon. Do you feel fit enough to cobble one together?'

'Nothing would please me more,' said Reinhart. 'Give me seven minutes and a cup of black coffee. Where the hell has he got the information from?'

The Chief Inspector shook his head.

'No idea. How many of us know about it?'

Reinhart counted them up.

'Six, I think. Plus the odd half-informed constable and probationer, of course. But I find it hard to believe that one of us—'

'Damn and blast!' interrupted Van Veeteren. 'Verlangen, of course! That private dick's the one who's let the cat out of the bag. When you've finished with the press release, can you phone him and check?'

'I'll do it the moment it's finished,' said Reinhart. 'You're probably right. It wouldn't surprise me if he's the culprit. I think . . . I think this changes the situation quite a bit, in any case.'

'What do you mean?'

'If there's a murderer on the loose and people know his name, that will increase the pressure on us to do something.'

'You don't say,' said Van Veeteren with a sigh. 'Yes, you're probably right. I suppose we'd better ring the prosecutor pronto . . . before they ring us . . . That usually makes a good impression.'

'Do you think they read the *Neuwe Blatt*?' asked Reinhart.

'Maybe they are out jogging,' said the Chief Inspector.

Reinhart smiled wryly.

'Okay. Ring them. When are you thinking of having another go at Mr Murderer himself?'

Van Veeteren did three or four half-hearted back stretches.

'In pain?'

'That sofa.'

'Serves you right. Well, when?'

'I don't really know,' said Van Veeteren. 'I had thought of continuing this morning, but I think I'll postpone it for an hour or two. Would you like to be present?'

'Do you mean at the table or outside the window?'

'At the table,' said Van Veeteren. 'It could be interesting to expose him to a bit of crossfire.'

'Absolutely,' said Reinhart. 'You can count on me.'

Then he left the room, and Van Veeteren dialled the number of the public prosecutor.

When Reinhart had composed and dispatched the press release – a not exactly detailed document comprising fifty-five words which revealed no more than a third of what had already appeared in the newspaper, plus the fact that a press conference would be held on the Monday – he telephoned the *Neuwe Blatt* and was given the home number of Bertram Grouwer.

It sounded as if Grouwer hadn't yet opened his eyes properly, but he had enough presence of mind to protect his source. As they say. Reinhart asked if it might possibly have been Maarten Verlangen, whereupon Grouwer hung up.

Bloody muckraker, thought Reinhart, whose relationship with the fourth estate was somewhat strained. You're not much of an actor.

Verlangen sounded not much more wide awake than Grouwer – until he grasped what the call was about.

No, he hadn't yet read a newspaper today. But yes, he did recall sitting talking to his good friend Grouwer on Thursday evening. They had been out celebrating their joint birthday, as it were, and had no doubt sunk a glass or two.

'How soon can you get here?' Reinhart wondered. 'Ten minutes? We need to talk to you.'

He didn't know if that really was necessary, but he certainly had no intention of allowing a loose-tongued berk to lounge around in the sun for hours on end on such a pleasant early summer day as this. Certainly not, dammit.

Verlangen sounded apologetic and promised to start moving immediately, and to be at the police station within an hour.

Get going, then, thought Reinhart. Hung up and lit his pipe. If I can get hold of Heinemann, he can spend the whole day interrogating you!

The prosecutor's name was Silwerstein. Van Veeteren had dealt with him several times before, and knew that he did not like to be telephoned on matters to do with work on his Saturday off. He preferred to play golf. He reiterated this preference the moment he came in through the door. Van Veeteren explained that for his part, he never indulged in that activity; but that as far as possible he too tried to avoid working weekends.

But what could one do? He promised to keep things as brief as possible. Then he poured Silwerstein a cup of coffee and explained the situation in ten minutes. He concluded by asking the prosecutor if he happened to be a loyal reader of the newspaper *Neuwe Blatt*.

He most certainly was not, Silwerstein assured him, and wondered why on earth the Chief Inspector wanted to know that.

Van Veeteren handed over a copy of the paper, and as the prosecutor read the article his eyebrows were raised and his jaw dropped.

'I see,' he said when he had finished. 'The man in the street's sense of justice demands, and so on . . . Why have you released this information to the press?'

'Somebody boobed,' said the Chief Inspector. 'The information didn't come from us.'

The prosecutor took off his spectacles.

'So where did it come from, then?'

Van Veeteren snapped a toothpick and gazed out of the window. Silwerstein sighed and gave up.

'I see. And what about proof? Can you make it stick?'

'It's hard to say,' said Van Veeteren. 'Not as things stand at the moment, but we have only interrogated him properly once so far.'

'He denies it?'

'Yes. And he'll continue to deny it.'

'Are you sure?'

'I'd bet a golf course on it.'

Silwerstein said nothing.

'I don't think we can count on any kind of arrangement or compromise. It's not that sort of case.'

'It seems pretty obvious that he did it. Doesn't it?'

'There's hardly any doubt,' said Van Veeteren. 'I would have preferred to carry on working away from the glare of publicity for a while longer, but after this newspaper article, well . . .'

'I understand,' said Silwerstein. 'And you have him in custody now?'

'Since yesterday evening.'

'What do you want, then? A warrant of arrest on the spot?'

'What do you think?' asked the Chief Inspector, folding up the newspaper.

Silwerstein thought for a moment and looked at his watch.

'I don't like to rush things,' he said. 'But I take it you'd like to keep him in custody?'

'His name has been in the press,' said the Chief Inspector. 'There'd be an outcry if he were allowed back on the streets.'

'Hmm, yes,' said the prosecutor, scratching the bridge of his nose. 'I must do my homework. If you get another forty-eight hours, we can reassess the situation on Tuesday evening . . . By then you ought to have put some flesh on the bare bones of the case, I take it?'

'We'll do what we can,' promised the Chief Inspector.

On second thoughts Intendent Reinhart decided it would be best for him to take charge of the discussions with Maarten Verlangen. Quite apart from the inquisition aspect, there were a few things he would like to discuss with him in more detail. And Heinemann would doubtless have things to do on a free Saturday.

Verlangen slunk into Reinhart's office like a repentant sinner. He looked worn out and dishevelled, and seemed to be suffering from a lingering hangover.

'I'm sorry,' he said. 'I didn't mean to . . .'

'Sorry?' said Reinhart. 'You have undermined our efforts in a way that it's impossible to assess. If Jaan G. Hennan goes free, he'll come and thank you on his bare knees.'

'What?' said Verlangen.

'If Hennan goes free, he will—'

'Yes, I heard you,' said Verlangen. 'But it's not possible – all I did was summarize the situation as it was, and—'

'Sit down,' said Reinhart. 'You stink of booze.'

Verlangen sat down.

'It got a bit late last night. I—'

'Last night as well? And no doubt you took the opportunity of telling the tale to another hack?'

Verlangen shook his head and stared down at the floor.

Poor bastard, Reinhart thought. He's a complete wreck.

'Get a grip,' he said. 'I want to talk to you about a few other things quite apart from that newspaper blunder. Are you hung over? Do you need a cup of coffee?'

'I've already had some,' said Verlangen. 'I'm really sorry, as I said. What do you want to talk about? It would be good if it didn't take too long – I'm supposed to meet my daughter shortly.'

'Let's see how it goes,' said Reinhart.

'Thank you,' said Verlangen.

'Barbara Hennan. I want to talk to you about her.'

'I see. Why?'

'Because we need to be clear about why she came to see you in the first place. She must have had a reason, and the only reason I can think of is that she suspected something was going on . . . That she suspected her husband was trying to get at her in some way or other. What do you say to that?'

Verlangen frowned.

'I don't know,' he said. 'I've naturally been thinking along those lines as well, but she never spoke about what lay behind her request . . . Why I should keep an eye on him, that is.'

'We know that,' said Reinhart. 'But if we accept the theory that she was frightened of something, and you think about that, knowing what actually happened – well, can it be true? Did she give any indication that it could be?'

Verlangen dug a crumpled packet of cigarettes from out of his pocket.

'That she might be afraid? No, I can't say she did. She adopted an extremely business-like approach all the time. Controlled, you could say she was. I thought . . . well, I suppose I thought she was incomprehensible.'

'Incomprehensible?'

'Yes.'

'But what did you decide? You must have come to some conclusion about what was going on, surely?'

Verlangen lit a cigarette.

'No, not really,' he said. 'Although I suppose I probably thought it was the same old story. That he was being unfaithful, that is.'

'That you should check on whether Hennan was seeing some other woman?'

'Yes. Although . . .'

'Well?'

'Although there was nothing about her behaviour which indicated that. It was just a guess on my part, because that's nearly always what it's about.'

'I understand,' said Reinhart. 'And Hennan didn't meet any other women while you were shadowing him?'

'No, he didn't.'

'How long were you keeping a watch on him?'

Verlangen shrugged.

'Only two days. Wednesday and Thursday. It was extremely monotonous – apart from Thursday evening, of course.'

'What did he do?'

'Do? He went to his office in Landemaarstraat . . . Sat there, had lunch, sat there again and drove home.'

'Was that all?'

'Yes.'

'Did he meet anybody?'

'Not that I noticed. Somebody might have visited his office, but I don't think so.'

'What about his lunches?'

'There was only one. Wednesday. He ate all on his own.'

'Marvellous,' said Reinhart, annoyed. 'And it was the same again at that restaurant on Thursday evening, was it?'

'The same again.' said Verlangen. 'As far as I know, I was the only person he spoke to.'

'As far as you know?'

'Yes, I was the only person he spoke to,' confirmed Verlangen.

Reinhart sighed.

'For Christ's sake . . .' he said. 'Have you any ideas? Anything that's occurred to you since we last spoke?'

Verlangen took a drag of his cigarette and thought for a few seconds.

'He did it,' he said. 'I'm sure it was Hennan who set her up, but I don't know how. I suppose the only possibility is that he had an accomplice. I can't see any other alternative.'

Reinhart swung round forty-five degrees on his desk chair and stared up at the ceiling. Pondered for a while, then swung back again.

'No,' he said. 'Neither can we. If you can tell us where we can find his accomplice, we'll forgive you for that newspaper cock-up.'

Verlangen squirmed and looked at the clock.

'Was there anything else?' he asked tentatively.

'Not for the moment,' said Reinhart. 'Did you say you were going to meet your daughter?'

'Yes.'

'How old is she?'

'Seventeen.'

'May I give you a piece of advice?' said Reinhart.

'Eh? Yes, of course.'

'Go home and freshen yourself up a bit before you meet her. No seventeen-year-old wants to be seen together with somebody who looks as if he's slept on a park bench.'

Verlangen promised to take that advice to heart and slunk out of the door. Reinhart shook his head and opened the window.

Ten seconds later the Chief Inspector rang.

'Have you finished?' he asked. 'I thought we could have another go at Hennan now.'

'Yes, I've finished,' said Reinhart. 'I'll be there in a minute.'

19

It was five o'clock on Saturday afternoon when he got home, and the only one there to greet him was Bismarck.

At least she was pleased to see him. On the kitchen table was a note from Renate to say that she had gone to Chadów to congratulate her mother on her birthday. She might stay on until Sunday – if he was interested in knowing, he could always ring.

As for Eric, he had gone to the coast with some mates. She had made him promise to be home before midnight, but whether or not he would keep that promise, she had no idea. It would have helped if his father had been around to assist her.

Van Veeteren tore the note into four and threw it into the waste-paper basket. He felt a sudden irritation flaring up inside him, and an urge simply to get into the car and drive away from it all. From work, home, wife, son – all the oppressive, stifling aspects of his life which could only be compared to a chronic, nagging pain. Deep down under his skin and into the depths of his soul. It was a primitive and childish feeling: he knew that, but it only made matters worse.

It was as if this was the basic condition of life, he thought.

The primeval swamp out of which you constantly had to crawl, and fight against with all means at your disposal. Every morning, every day until the end of time. The moment you lowered your guard you lay there again, kicking and squirming. Back to square one.

He drank a beer, had a shower and put on some clean clothes. That helped slightly. He went for a walk through Randers Park with Bismarck. The weather was tolerably pleasant: cloudy but no wind, and the temperature was certainly above twenty degrees. He decided to eat out.

And in no circumstances to ring his wife.

But it was silly to keep on trying to fool himself, he also thought. Naive to pretend that she was the villain in the plot.

That was not Renate. He was the real villain.

He got back home at about nine o'clock, and once again there was only the dog there to welcome him. They went for another walk through the park, now in persistent light rain; but when they returned home, he requested Bismarck to go and lie down, so that he had an opportunity to think a few human thoughts in peace and quiet. Bismarck nodded, yawned and lay down on her favourite armchair in Jess's old room.

Van Veeteren read the *Allgemejne* and listened to Sibelius for half an hour, but switched off after *Valse triste*. Checked that there wasn't a late film on the box that might be of interest, then went to fetch his briefcase and a beer.

He took out the tape, put it in the tape deck and made himself comfortable in his chair. Switched off the light. Poured out a glass and pressed the start button.

Might as well, he thought. If you are a self-tormentor, you do what you have to do – I'll have to do it sooner or later anyway . . .

After the usual introductory statements about the time, place, subject matter and those involved, they got down to business. It was no more than six hours since they had completed the actual interrogation at the police station, but he noticed immediately that the changed environment – the stage-managed setting versus the dark living room, the well-worn armchair, the late hour and being on his own – somehow changed the circumstances. Transformed what had been presumed and somehow shifted the perspective in ways he couldn't put his finger on.

Or perhaps it was just confirmation of the simple fact that you can sometimes hear better if you can't see.

He closed his eyes and listened to his own voice.

VV: Welcome to a new conversation, herr Hennan.

G: Thank you.

VV: Let me make it clear from the start that neither I nor Intendent Reinhart are here because we have nothing better to do. If you have nothing to say, or don't want to answer questions, we can shut up shop without more ado.

G: I'm naturally at your service, gentlemen. The sooner we can establish that my wife died as a result of an accident, the better.

R: Why do you refute in such a casual manner that there might be other forces at work? I listened to the recording of your earlier conversation last night, and I find it difficult to see the logic of your reasoning.

G: I've no doubt that's true. I'm sorry, what did you say your name was?

R: Reinhart.

G: All right, Constable Reinhart. You are looking for what you want to look for, and you see what you want to see. That logic is so obvious that even you ought to be able to understand it.

R: Rubbish.

G: My wife died as a result of an accident.

VV: I hear what you are saying. But as I've already said, we have sufficient evidence to indicate that there is quite a different explanation. If you refuse even to consider the possibility that somebody killed her, we can only conclude that you yourself played a part in what happened. I thought you'd had time enough to think about that and realize the facts of the situation.

G: I'm afraid I must disappoint you on that score. And I'm afraid you underestimate me.

R: Has it not occurred to you that you are behaving in rather an odd manner?

G: Has it not occurred to you – both of you – that you are

treating me in rather a strange way? Not to say
improperly.

R: Explain.

G: By all means. I have just had my wife taken away from
me in traumatic circumstances. One can hardly say that
you have been very considerate thus far.

R: Really? If you'll forgive me for saying so, you seem to
have controlled your sorrow and sense of loss rather
well.

G: That is something you know nothing about, Constable.
Why should I lay bare my soul before my executioners?

R: Executioners? Good God . . .

VV: So you mourn the loss of your wife?

G: Of course.

VV: More than you mourned the loss of your first wife?

G: I have no yardstick for making such comparisons.

R: So there's no difference between one or two dead
wives?

G: I have no comment to make on that kind of
insinuation.

R: I'm not surprised.

VV: Your firm was a bluff, wasn't it?

G: A bluff? Why should it be a bluff?

VV: What type of activities are you concerned with?

G: Business, of course.

E: What kind of business?

G: Import and sales.

VV: Of what?

G: I have been investigating various possible markets so far

... I don't think these are the kind of realities that you have a clue about. In any case, that's irrelevant. When are you thinking of letting me go?

R: Letting you go? Why the hell should we let you go?

G: Do you think I don't know my rights? I've asked you not to underestimate me – that would only cause you problems.

VV: How long is your rental contract at Villa Zefyr?

G: Six months, automatically renewable. If it isn't cancelled, it runs automatically for another half-year.

VV: Have you cancelled it now?

G: Why should I have done that?

R: Because your wife is dead, for example.

G: I haven't thought about that yet.

VV: In view of the fact that you are likely to be in jail for a few decades, perhaps you ought to do so.

G: Rubbish.

R: And you are thinking of carrying on with your so-called firm, are you?

G: That's not something I need to discuss with you. But I'm thinking of contacting a lawyer if you insist on being unreasonable ... Or at least not observing the limits of your authority.

VV: What time did your wife get back from Aarlach on the evening of the murder?

G: The evening of the murder?

VV: Don't split hairs when it comes to words. What time did she get home?

G: I don't know.

R: Didn't you ring home to check if she was back?

G: I've already said that I did.

VV: At what time?

G: Several times. She didn't answer.

VV: When was the last time you rang?

G: About half past six.

VV: Why do you think she contacted a private detective?

G: I've no idea. I don't believe any of this.

VV: You've had a whole day to think about it. Surely you must have thought of some reason?

G: As I said, I don't believe it.

R: And she hadn't made any similar arrangements previously?

G: Of course not.

VV: What did you talk about that evening, you and Verlangen?

G: Nothing important.

R: What do you mean by that? Football? Brands of whisky? Women?

G: For example.

VV: But you recognized him?

G: There are some coppers' phizogs you never forget.

R: Were you engaged in drug trafficking in the USA as well?

G: I've never been engaged in drug trafficking.

VV: Did your wife have any enemies?

G: Enemies? Why should she have any enemies? She hardly knew anybody in this country.

R: So you didn't have a social life?

G: We didn't want to have one yet.

VV: Why?

G: That was our business. Are you as bored by all this as I am?

R: You can bet we are. Prize idiots don't have all that much in the way of entertainment value.

VV: Claus Dorp – can you tell us a bit about him?

G: Claus Dorp? Why should I tell you anything about Claus Dorp?

VV: Because he's an old friend of yours, isn't he?

G: I wouldn't say that.

VV: I don't suppose he would either. But you were both found guilty in that drugs business twelve years ago. Isn't that the case?

G: So what?

VV: Have you been in contact with him since you came back?

G: No.

R: What about Christian Müller? Ernst Melnik? Andreas van der Heugen?

G: Bravo! Clever coppers! No, I haven't seen any of them for twelve years.

VV: When you got home and found your wife at the bottom of the empty pool, can you tell us exactly what you did then?

G: I've already answered that question several times. If you really want to hear it all again, maybe you could dig out your tapes and listen to them.

R: You'll have to say it all again at the trial in any case.

G: All the more reason why I shouldn't do it now. But there won't be a trial – you know that as well as I do.

R: Shall we have a bet on that?

G: What?

R: One point two million, perhaps? That's a nice round sum.

G: You like to joke, don't you, Constable.

R: Of course. But I don't want to have a bet with you. I don't get involved with any old riff-raff.

G: I'm glad to hear it. Can I tell you something? Man to man, as it were.

VV: Please do.

G: You are pretty ropey actors – I don't know which of you is worse. You know full well that the case you are trying to build up against me would be laughable in a courtroom. You know that and I know that. A flimsy house of cards. It would only need a third-rate defence lawyer to sneeze, and the whole thing would collapse. Why don't you admit that it's the case? So that we don't have to carry on with these ridiculous pirouettes?

R: What's it like to rape your little sister? Do you feel good afterwards?

There was a long silence. Only the sound of Jaan G. Hennan lighting a cigarette, and Reinhart tapping a pen absent-mindedly on the table. Van Veeteren switched off.

I don't want to hear any more, he thought. Reinhart can listen to it and see if he picks up anything.

Picks up what? he asked himself immediately. What is there to listen for, in fact?

An unintentional slip of the tongue?

Something G happened to let slip without meaning to? A ray of light that could at least indicate where it might be fruitful to dig a bit deeper?

He didn't think so. To be honest he didn't think so, he realized that, and to be honest he agreed with G on one point. These interrogations – or conversations – were pointless.

Because the circumstances were clear.

They *knew* that G was behind the death of his wife.

And G *knew* that they knew.

It wouldn't even harm him significantly if he happened to slip up and admit that he had done it, Van Veeteren thought. The only thing that would harm him would be if he let slip *how*.

Or *who*, perhaps. That G came out with the name of the accomplice that – when all was said and done – he must have had.

Hoping for something of that sort seemed almost idiotic.

He switched the light on and took the tape out of the machine. Spent a couple of minutes searching through his collection of records, and eventually decided on Bartók's second piano concerto. He knew that sooner or later he would have to think through that Christa business as well, and it was time now: he could think of no better accompaniment that Bartók.

★

It wasn't only Adam Bronstein, it was Christa Koogel as well. That's the way it was.

Christa Koogel, who had opened up inside him a room of whose existence he had never known. The room of love. A place and a situation in which it was possible to love a woman, and be loved in return. Far away from . . . what had he called it? . . . the primeval swamp of existence.

He was twenty-one, she was nineteen. For four months – a summer and a little longer – he had lived there . . . A magic circle of enhanced vital sensuousness. He could find no alternative way of expressing it, high-flown though the words might seem. An existence, it had seemed to him, in which every object, every action, every look and every touch and mundane chore had been filled with a profoundly meaningful and magically real significance.

Over and over again. Just knowing that she was there in the vicinity, in the same town and the same life, that it was sometimes possible to stretch out his hand and touch her arm or hair or back, and receive a look from her in acknowledgement, gave him – had given him – an incomprehensible feeling of ease and invulnerability. And *substance*.

Twenty-one and nineteen.

Kissing her and feeling her willingness and her naked skin, gently stroking with the back of his hand along her outstretched arm, then continuing over her breasts and her gently rounded stomach . . . he could still – after almost thirty years, it was incredible! – still recall the bodily sensation of that movement and touching. His left hand, her right arm.

The red room of love. Ease and substance. Just over a

summer. And then came her hesitation, and he discovered something else. The black hole of absence. Square one.

They never broke off their relationship formally. They didn't need to.

They simply agreed to meet less often. She needed to think over her emotions. A week later he saw her in a cafe. He saw her, she didn't see him. Her eyes were preoccupied by something else. She was sitting at a table together with a young man, a different young man. They were drinking wine, and their heads were very close together. They were talking and laughing. He was holding his hand over hers. They were both smoking – she had never smoked when she had been together with Van Veeteren in the red room of love. They had hardly ever drunk wine either. The new man was G.

They never broke off their relationship formally. They didn't need to.

And she taught him a third thing.

The feminine defect. That horrific and incomprehensible trait. The fact that a beautiful and gifted and much loved young woman can fall for an utter shit who is not fit to kiss the ground she walks and stands on.

And the door to the room of love was closed. Several years later he met her by pure chance, and rashly plucked up the courage to ask her why she had bothered to open it. The door to love. Or was the bottom line that she could open it to anybody who happened to come along? Was it as simple as that?

They spoke for quite a long time. She cried and said that

she regretted what she had done. That G had treated her very badly. He had made her pregnant, then abandoned her. After the abortion she didn't believe in the room of love either. She said – and he believed her – that she wished that they had stayed together and that she had never met G.

But by then it was too late. Renate was in her seventh month, and circumstances were no longer what they had been.

So there it was. That was roughly how it could be put into words. It wasn't even all that remarkable. Quite a run-of-the-mill melodrama, no doubt. An experience that pretty well everybody had been through – and perhaps that was the aspect which was saddest of all.

He checked the time: a quarter past twelve. Erich hadn't rung, nor had Renate. Bartók had finished, but he couldn't be bothered to prise himself out of his armchair and put on something else. He emptied his glass of beer instead, and hoped to rinse Christa Koogel out of his memory.

Or to shift her into the place where she belonged: alternative paths through life that had never been embarked upon. Closed rooms.

But that left G.

That left Jaan G. Hennan.

As a sort of macabre incarnation of all possible devilry and the errors that had scarred one's earlier life. Downright evil: a person with no redeeming factors.

I hate him, he suddenly thought. If there is any bastard on this earth that I hate, it's G. I could throw him into a fire without a second thought, as one would do with a cockroach. I really could.

He sat there in the darkness for another half hour. Then he made up his mind and went to bed.

20

Chief of Police Hiller felt nervous.

That was clear from a series of minor indications that Münster had no difficulty in interpreting. He licked his lips with the tip of his tongue after every tenth word. He clicked his Ballograph pen non-stop. He was sweating despite the fact that the temperature inside his office was nothing out of the ordinary, and he kept shuffling around on his chair as if he had a thistle between his buttocks.

He's a buffoon, Münster thought.

It wasn't the first time he had thought that. Or something along the same lines. Hiller had spread out in front of him on his large desk an array of daily newspapers. After the article on 'The Pool Murder' in Saturday's *Neuwe Blatt*, a whole host of features had appeared. The *Allgemenje, den Poost* and the *Telegraaf* had carried large spreads on Sunday, and today – on Monday morning – Grouwer had once again taken the stage and demanded that the police at last, and for once, should satisfy the demands – the minimal demands! – that the general public and the taxpayers – not to mention the insured! – had a right to expect of them. There was a limit to what the people's sense of justice could take. People like Jaan G. Hennan should simply not be allowed to go free!

'A good point!' said Hiller, mopping his brow with a paper towel. 'He has a point, that damned journalist! We must sort this out. The situation is blatantly obvious: he has eliminated his wife in order to collect the insurance money!'

'He was sitting in a restaurant when she died,' pointed out Van Veeteren quietly.

'He has an alibi,' added Reinhart.

'That doesn't matter,' said the chief of police, sweeping his arm over the newspapers. 'Just look at all this! We shall be portrayed as flat-footed incompetents if we don't solve this. For Christ's sake, the man has done exactly the same thing once before!'

'Very true,' said Van Veeteren. 'He succeeded on that occasion as well. We won't be the only ones having to bear the shame.'

'Shame!' snorted Hiller. 'There will be no question of any shame as far as we are concerned! Hennan will be arrested and found guilty of this, so we need to produce evidence that will stand up in court. I've spoken to the prosecutor this morning.'

'I spoke to him on Saturday,' said Van Veeteren. 'He is in complete agreement with our approach.'

'No matter what, we need to bring him to court,' said Hiller, tapping with his Ballograph on one of the few empty spaces on his desk. 'No matter what. I managed to persuade the prosecutor of how necessary this was . . . even if the level of proof is not what it might be.'

'He was convinced of that on Saturday,' said Van Veeteren. 'I don't think we need to sit here all morning going on about this – the situation is quite clear, after all. It must—'

'Hennan must have had an accomplice!' the chief of police interrupted. 'I have read up on the case and come to the conclusion that this is the only possibility.'

'Really?' said Reinhart.

'Some sort of hit man, yes. The prosecutor agreed. Your job is to find this contract killer, or to put pressure on Hennan so that he comes clean. We shall devote as much as possible in the way of resources to this, no stone must be left unturned. All Hennan's contacts must be hunted down and interrogated! He has a record, after all.'

'We know,' said Reinhart. 'We are not idiots. But given the way things stand at the moment . . . Well, is the prosecutor prepared to go ahead with the little we have?'

The chief of police nodded seriously and wet his lips.

'Yes. We need to have him arrested this afternoon. At an appropriate time before the press conference. The Chief Inspector and I will take that, the same policy as usual. Frankness and restraint. We don't want to have the media against us in this case. We're all on the same side – I assume I don't need to go on about that?'

'Hardly,' said Van Veeteren with a sigh, checking his wrist watch. 'Was there anything else? Press conference at three o'clock, is that right?'

'Fifteen hundred hours,' said Hiller. 'Well, if you don't have any questions, that was that, then.'

★

'So there,' said Reinhart, lighting his pipe. 'That was that, then, to quote a well-known sage.'

He was sitting on one of the two visitor chairs in Van Veeteren's office. Münster was on the other one, and the Chief Inspector himself was standing with his back to his colleagues, gazing out over the town through the open window. The sky was unsettled: an area of low pressure had drifted in from the south-west in the early hours of the morning, and put the damper on summer – but perhaps it was a better reflection of the mood in the office, in fact.

'Well,' said the Chief Inspector, 'unfortunately we have to admit that he summed up the situation quite well for once. We've come as far as we're going to get for the time being, and if we don't get any further it will be up to the prosecutor to show that the evidence we have is sufficient – but God only knows how he'll do that.'

'What has le Houde discovered?' asked Münster.

The Chief Inspector shrugged without turning round.

'Not a lot,' he said. 'Or nothing at all, to be exact. Nothing from the diving tower apart from some fingerprints of herr and fru Hennan. Especially from her, which doesn't exactly strengthen our case. Ditto inside the house . . . The occasional fingerprint from persons unknown – but that's normal. They had a cleaner, for instance. Heinemann has spoken to her: she came just once every other week, and there was never anybody at home . . . Three times in all – they hired her at the beginning of May.'

'No sign of anybody else being there that evening?'

'Nothing at all.'

'Pity,' said Reinhart, blowing out a cloud of smoke. 'But I suppose that was only to be expected.'

'It can sometimes be wise to dampen down our expectations,' said the Chief Inspector.

'Has anybody spoken to Denver yet?' wondered Münster.

Reinhart sighed.

'Yes. I got hold of Lieutenant Horniman last night. He had just returned from his mother's funeral, and wasn't exactly in high spirits. As far as Hennan and Philomena McNaught are concerned, he had a theory I'm inclined to believe without more ado. He thinks Hennan killed her during that holiday out in the wilds – strangled her or shot her or cut her head off with an axe, you name it – then buried her one metre deep – or a yard, to quote the source – and reported that she had disappeared. That damned National Park is about as big as Ireland and it would involve a hell of an effort to find her.'

Van Veeteren stopped contemplating the weather and sat down at his desk.

'That's something we've always known,' he said.

'What is?' asked Münster.

'If murderers in general had the sense to dispose of the bodies of their victims properly, we wouldn't catch very many of them. We must be thankful that people haven't been bright enough to adopt that simple rule. Had he anything helpful to tell us – Horniman, that is?'

'Zilch,' said Reinhart. 'But he's just as sure as we are that Jaan G. Hennan is a blackguard of the first order.'

'Blackguard?' muttered the Chief Inspector and glared at

Reinhart. 'Do you no longer distinguish between a black-guard and a murderer?'

'It's very easy to be both,' said Reinhart. 'How's it gone for Rooth and Jung in their search for an accomplice? That's surely where we are going to make a breakthrough.'

'No luck there either so far,' said Van Veeteren, gazing out of the window at the overcast sky again. 'Unfortunately. They have a list of about twenty names, and when they've gone through them all I'll also have a chat with the ones who seem potentially interesting. I've asked Rooth to produce five names in any case – even if there isn't a single prat who is really interesting.'

'Find the one who knows something,' said Münster. 'It's not the first time we've been looking for a key of that kind.'

'No,' said Van Veeteren. 'The problem in this particular case is that the one with the knowledge happens also to be the murderer. Which could possibly mean that he might prefer to keep silent.'

'That's hardly the first time either,' said Münster.

Reinhart nodded and looked impotent.

'It's so damned simple that it could drive you mad,' he growled. 'That bastard hires a gorilla who does the job for him, receives a substantial sum of money, and we don't arrest him. Neither of them. Could there be some charge other than murder, by the way? If he wasn't the one who literally did the deed?'

'Of course,' said Van Veeteren. 'Incitement, for instance; but there are several options to choose from. They could result in eighty years at least. But you are forgetting a few small details.'

'I'm aware of that,' said Reinhart.

'In the first place,' said the Chief Inspector, 'we have to be able to demonstrate that Barbara Hennan didn't die as a result of an accident, as G maintains. In the second place we have to prove that Hennan really did hire a contract killer. And to be honest, we haven't really got very far on either of those obligations – don't you agree?'

'I know, I know,' said Reinhart. 'I wasn't born yesterday. Damn and blast! . . . But in a way I'm beginning to think that it was a good thing that our private eye let the cat out of the bag after he'd taken a drop too much.'

'Why?' wondered Münster.

'Because it would have felt even worse to have been forced to let Hennan go free at this early stage. All the fuss means that there will at least be a trial.'

'Yes,' said Van Veeteren. 'I'm inclined to agree with you. But of course there's a risk that the judge will intervene and dismiss the case if he thinks the evidence is insufficient. Even if the prosecutor seems to be willing to give the circus a green light. We don't know who the judge will be yet, but there are a few who care as much about public opinion as a killer bear worries about a flea.'

'Poetic,' said Reinhart. 'Are you thinking about Hart?'

'I suppose I am,' said Van Veeteren. 'Anyway, at least we have a few weeks in which to dig deeper. And of course we have stumbled upon bits of information before. All initiatives are welcome . . . And anybody who feels up to sitting eye to eye with G is welcome to do so – just let me know in advance.'

'I don't think I would like that,' said Reinhart.

'What you would like is not very relevant in this case,' said the Chief Inspector.

The press conference came and went.

The decision to arrest Hennan was of course a goody that the reporters were only too pleased to gulp down, and Van Veeteren was reminded yet again of the rather-nail-him-than-bail-him mentality that always seemed to prevail in the media at this early stage of a case. The first priority was to find the murder, the spectacular crime, and they had done that. Then there was a race to point out the murderer: that was the detail the next day's billboards and headlines would feature. In Act Three, they liked to do a complete about turn (if that was possible, and the Chief Inspector had no doubt that there were circumstances in this case that would make it possible) – and try to stand up for the accused. Was he really guilty? Had the police in fact arrested the wrong man? Should an innocent man be found guilty? Could one have faith in the rule of law?

And then, if the accused was in fact found guilty: was it possible to write stories about him? His childhood and teenage years and a mass of extenuating circumstances?

That is how things would proceed, and over the years Van Veeteren had learned how to accept the inevitable. If he had been a journalist rather than a detective chief inspector, he would presumably have played the game according to those rules, just as now – as far as possible – he tried to act in accordance with the terminology that formed the framework of a CID officer's work. There was a temptation to skirt round them from time to time, from case to case, but so far – after almost a quarter of a century in the trade – he had never overstepped the mark. Not flagrantly, at least.

After the tussle with the press, which lasted less than half an hour, he withdrew to his office and spent some time chewing over these circumstances. Wondering about if, one day, he might reach a point when he felt the urge to take the law into his own hands. When the circumstances were such that doing so might be justified. Morally and existentially.

Even in the private sphere of his own ruminations, he tried to keep his thoughts on a theoretical level. Tried to avoid dragging G onto the stage – so that the question remained at the level of what one *ought* to do, rather than what one *would like* to do. To echo Reinhart's words.

That was easier said than done, and when he realized that he was wishing he could roll Jaan G. Hennan up in that old gymnastics mat that had squeezed the life out of Adam Bronstein's fragile soul, he gave up.

Reminded himself of the previous day's decision to have a serious talk with his wife, and left the police station.

That also came and went.

When they had more or less concluded that the split between them was a sort of inevitable fact, they were suddenly able to talk to each other again – but he wondered deep down if this somewhat melancholy mutual respect was in fact the clearest indication that the fate of their marriage was sealed, once and for all. When they were no longer able to allow their emotions to spill over into an out-and-out quarrel, he found it hard to believe that there was any foundation left on which to build. Whatever it was that he had envisaged and desired half a lifetime ago, it was certainly not this lukewarm and cheerless stand-off.

Perhaps in fact Renate felt the same: but they didn't discuss this aspect of their putative coexistence. Instead they came to a sort of half-hearted agreement: this was – if he understood it rightly – that they should continue for another six months, and see how things developed.

And that they should accept a shared responsibility for Erich, who – and it was at this point he saw that Renate was on the point of bursting into tears linked with her bad conscience – was very much in need of all the parental support he could be offered. They were touchingly in agreement on this, and if only their vulnerable son had been at home that rainy Monday evening, they would no doubt have had a serious conversation between the three of them.

But he wasn't. And when at about half past eleven Van Veeteren heard him sneaking in through the front door and into his room, Renate was already asleep. He let sleeping dogs lie.

I know so damned little about his life, he thought.

What does he think about? What are his dreams and plans and fantasies?

Why don't I know more about my own son?

And with the bitter taste of neglect in his mouth he fell asleep.

21

Early summer became high summer.

If it had to do with private or professional reasons he was never quite sure, but for the next three weeks he took part in no further interrogations of G.

Reinhart and Münster played the Nasty Cop-Nice Cop game on a few occasions, with Reinhart playing the role of the unpleasant officer and Münster the rather more humane one. It was an old ruse and easy to see through, but it sometimes paid off even so. To some extent, at least. When a person is treated with friendliness and understanding after aggression and animosity, he finds it hard not to give way and unburden his mind. Irrespective of whether or not he realizes that it was all an act.

But not in this case. After a few long and fruitless sessions, Reinhart and Münster agreed that Jaan G. Hennan regarded their visits mostly as a sort of welcome – and almost entertaining – relief in the tedium of waiting for the trial to begin that had become his everyday routine, and they agreed to put a stop to it. If it was not possible to extract any information by interrogating him, then perhaps the loneliness and isolation might make him wobble slightly.

The Chief Inspector took upon himself the task of speaking to people recommended by Rooth and Jung for a follow-up interview. He had asked them for the names of at least a handful of people who might just possibly have information about what Hennan had been getting up to after his return from the USA, and they had obeyed the order. They had given him a list of five names. Not six or seven: he realized that if he had asked for at least three, he would have received precisely that number.

The whole operation had cost several working days, and afterwards Van Veeteren was able to confirm that the time had been wasted just as Inspector Rooth had claimed it would be. None of the five – nor any of the other twenty-two interviewees – had had any contact with Hennan whatsoever in recent times. At least, none of them admitted to being in touch with him; and on the day before the trial was due to begin in the Linden courthouse, when the Chief Inspector attempted to sum up the result of a month's work aimed at throwing light on the circumstances surrounding Barbara Hennan's death, he came up with the round but deeply unsatisfactory number of zero.

Absolutely nothing. They knew no more now than they had known at the beginning of June. Nothing had been refined from a suspicion to a certainty, nothing had turned up from an unexpected quarter – as sometimes happened as a sort of reward for valiant drudgery.

Things had not gone their way, to put it in a nutshell, and it was probably this grim truth that was nagging away in the back of his mind when he decided to confront the leading character one last time. One early Monday morning, when he sat down opposite him yet again in the bleak interrogation room, it felt as if he were in the closing stages of a hopeless game of chess, with so few pieces left and the situation so deadlocked that the only possible moves remaining were repetitive and leading nowhere apart from an inevitable draw.

And it was presumably because of this that he decided to change the routine a little.

'Your lawyer?'

Hennan shook his head.

'Not necessary. I don't want to expose her to this nonsense.'

'All right. Then I suggest we have a conversation off the record.'

'Off the record?' said Hennan. 'Why?'

'Because it could be interesting,' said Van Veeteren. 'No tape recorder and no witnesses.'

'I don't understand the point.'

'That's neither here nor there. Let's go to another room.'

'By all means. But just for a change. As far as I know you even have bugs in the loos.'

'You have my word,' said Van Veeteren.

'Your word?' Hennan burst out laughing, and stood up. 'Okay! Off the record, if you think it will make any difference.'

The Chief Inspector chose one of the so-called discussion rooms on the first floor. He asked if Hennan fancied a beer, and rang down to the canteen and asked them to come up with two.

'Shouldn't we have a lie-detector test?' asked Hennan after taking his first swig. 'That might be interesting, don't you think?'

'I don't see the point,' said Van Veeteren. 'I know you are lying even so.'

'Yes, I've gathered that you think that. But next week at this time, when I'm a free man, don't pretend that you didn't understand the fact of the matter.'

'Your conception of time is a little out of joint,' said the Chief Inspector. 'In my judgement you'll have to wait for fifteen years. Not a week.'

Hennan smiled.

'We'll see about that,' he said. 'My lawyer says that she has seldom if ever seen a prosecutor as naked as this one.'

'Does she, indeed?' said Van Veeteren. 'Anyway, I suggest we abandon these clichés and get down to some serious talking instead.'

'Serious?' said Hennan. 'Off the record?'

The Chief Inspector nodded and lit a cigarette.

'Exactly. I think you need to get things off your chest, and you have my word that whatever you say will not be used against you.'

Hennan looked at him for a brief moment with something that seemed like interest.

'Why should I need to do that?' he asked.

'Basic psychology,' said Van Veeteren, pausing briefly while he rolled up his shirtsleeves.

'Psychology?' said Hennan. 'It stinks of desperation, if you'll excuse—'

'Rubbish. Let me explain. You are regarding this as a sort of trial of strength . . . between you and us. You are obsessed by the thought of winning. But if you really were innocent, being exonerated would hardly be a feather in your cap, would it?'

Hennan said nothing. Took a drink of beer.

'One point two million goes quite a long way, of course: but your triumph would be getting away with it despite the fact that you are guilty. And so it would be a plus-point – a big plus-point – if one of us . . . me for example . . . knew exactly what the facts are. Are you with me? It has to do with aesthetics.'

Hennan leaned back and smiled briefly again.

'Of course,' he said. 'Of course I'm with you. But if what you say is correct, you seem to be convinced already that I am behind the death of my wife. Isn't that enough? If I'm satisfied with the money, can't you be satisfied with the fact that you know?'

'Not really,' said Van Veeteren. 'I am a scrupulous person, and there are certain question marks. I don't quite have the whole picture clear before me.'

'Really?' said Hennan. 'So the Chief Inspector wants some details. How I actually did it. How I could sit in that restaurant and even so kill my wife. Have you considered hypnotism?'

The Chief Inspector nodded.

'Of course. But you are no more hypnotic than a donkey.'

'Thank you,' said Hennan. 'No, I admit that it didn't happen that way.'

'Good. So that's one thing we agree about at least. How did it happen, then?'

'You want me to reveal that?'

'Yes.'

Hennan turned his head and contemplated the wall for a while, and for a second – or a tiny fraction of a second – the Chief Inspector had the impression that he was about to reveal all.

To explain how he had in fact taken the life of his wife, Barbara Clarissa Hennan, née Delgado – in a way that was so clever and ingenious that no detective chief inspector in the whole wide world could possibly imagine it.

Then that split second disappeared into its shell like a mussel; and looking back, it was not possible to say if it had been imagination or not. Hennan slowly straightened his back and took a deep breath. Directed his gaze once more at Van Veeteren, and eyed him with an expression of mild contempt.

'It seems to be nice weather out there.'

'Could be worse.'

'Thank you for the beer. Perhaps I can return the compliment next week. I know a good place in Linden.'

Huh, I hate that bastard, thought the Chief Inspector. I really do.

That night he dreamed he was making love to Christa Koogel.

They were married, had four children and lived in a big

house by the sea. Behrensee, as far as he could make out, south of the pier. Just how this came to him in a dream was unclear, to say the least; but it was a fact even so. It was not a sudden, frenzied bout of intercourse, but calm and tender love-making with a woman who had been his life's companion for many years; and when he woke up it was clear to him that he had been on a journey in search of one of those alternative paths through life. A possibility that had not become reality, a direction his life could have taken if only something else had not intervened instead.

If he had not made different choices. Or if he had made them.

He looked at the clock. It was only half past five. He noticed that he was covered in sweat: if this was a result of his illusory love-making, or if it was the cold sweat caused by the angst of what might be in store in the day to come, he didn't know. The dream lingered on inside him like a stab of sorrow, and he knew that he would be unable to go back to sleep.

He got up carefully – so as not to wake up his actual life's companion – and had a shower instead. Stood there for ages, hoping the water would wash away some of the slag inside his body as well: but it was doubtful if he succeeded in that. When he sat down at the breakfast table with the *Allgemejne*, it was twenty minutes to seven. The trial in Linden was not due to begin until ten o'clock, and he realized that he had a long day ahead of him.

The first of many.

22

In addition to places for those actually involved in the trial, the courtroom in Linden had room for about fifty observers, including authorized representatives of the media; and when the doors were closed before proceedings began, the number of those interested in attending but unable to do so because of the lack of space was about three times as great as the number who could be fitted in.

In view of the interest aroused by the case of the dead American woman, there had been some discussion about transferring the trial to Maardam, but Judge Hart had dismissed any such suggestion. This is not a football match, after all, he had declared, and the rule of law was not dependent on such irrelevant factors as public interest and media coverage. In no way.

The Chief Inspector had described Hart as an apathetic toad with an intellect and education equivalent to about half a dozen Nobel Prize-winners, and when Münster contemplated his slim figure up on the podium, he suspected that this was probably a fitting assessment. He looked as if he had been most reluctant to get out of bed that morning, and if he hadn't slept in his ceremonial robes, they clearly hadn't been ironed for the last six months. He began by clearing his throat very loudly and changing his glasses three times. Then he slammed his hammer down on the statute book, producing a cloud of dust, and instructed the prosecutor to open proceedings.

Prosecutor Silwerstein stood up and presented his case. It took just under forty-five minutes, and the gist was that he intended to show how the accused, Jaan G. Hennan, with malice aforethought and ice-cold execution, murdered – or arranged the murder of – his wife, Barbara Clarissa Hennan, née Delgado, on Thursday, 5 June, by pushing her – or arranging for her to be pushed – into the empty swimming pool in the grounds of the pair's rented home, Villa Zefyr, at Kammerweg 4 in Linden. He intended to make it clear, beyond all reasonable doubt, that Hennan was guilty of this unscrupulous deed, despite the fact – and this was being stated openly and unhesitatingly at this early stage of pro-ceedings – that it was not the intention of the prosecution to base its case on so-called technical proof, since such proof – strictly speaking – could not be found in a case of this kind. It was as simple as that.

Instead the prosecution intended to base its case on cir-cumstantial evidence – but it was exceptionally telling circumstantial evidence whose implications were crystal clear, and whose combined weight and significance could hardly leave anybody in doubt – especially not any of the five esteemed members of the jury – about who had instigated, staged and carried out the said murder. Likewise – here too in more than merely convincing fashion – the flagrant motive for the crime would be revealed, and placed in razor-sharp relation to what had happened to a previous wife of the accused quite recently in the United States of America. For the second time in the course of four years, the wife of the accused had died in mystical circumstances (at this point a few semantic nit-pickers in the public gallery reacted with half-suppressed giggles), and for the second time Jaan G. Hennan was now hoping to collect a considerable – very considerable! – amount from the company that had insured her life. One point two million!

The prosecutor had no doubt that all those present in this courtroom, once all the facts had been revealed and presented, would be totally convinced that Jaan G. Hennan was not only guilty of one wife's murder, but of two. It was the duty of all concerned to make sure that he was given a long and justified sentence.

For most of this introductory harangue, Münster kept a close watch on the five members of the jury – three women and two men (a proportion which perhaps, but presumably only peripherally, according to the Chief Inspector, might work to Hennan's disadvantage, since women, thanks to tradition and their concern for their own sex, were less inclined to find wife-murderers not guilty than men were) – and tried to assess from their facial expressions and subtle reactions how they were thinking on the starting line, as it were.

It was of course impossible to obtain a clear indication on that basis. When Silwerstein had just finished his verbose introduction, one of the two men on the jury – a grey-haired gentleman aged about sixty-five who reminded Münster vaguely of the actor Jean Gabin – took out a colourful handkerchief and blew his nose with a muffled but audible trumpeting noise, and it seemed to Münster that if he had to interpret it, it was not an especially good omen for the outcome.

As for the main character himself, Jaan G. Hennan, he sat for almost all the prosecuting counsel's speech with his head bowed and his hands demurely clasped on the table in front of him. He was wearing a discreet, medium-grey suit with a black band on its lapel. White shirt and black tie. It was not hard to understand that he was trying to look as if he were in mourning.

Nor was it difficult to see that he had succeeded rather well in this respect.

After the prosecutor, it was the defence counsel's turn.

She was a woman, which perhaps restored Hennan's position. If a woman was prepared to defend an alleged wife-killer – well, there was something in all normal women (the Chief Inspector had maintained with a worried sigh), a faint biological voice whispering that the accused couldn't be a wife-killer in fact.

Fru Van Molde said nothing about whether or not the prosecutor was naked under his gown, but she did not mince her words. For rather more than half an hour she devoted herself to describing the so-called case for the prosecution as a badly constructed house of cards without so much as a single trump. She described her client, Jaan G. Hennan, as an upright and honest man who had suffered a terrible loss –

yet again! – and instead of sitting here in the dock defending his honour, he should be set free immediately and in the interests of common decency allowed to get on with making the funeral arrangements. In the most tragic circumstances imaginable he had been robbed of his wife, and it was nothing short of a scandal that – without so much as an ounce of proof! – he had been taken to court, and in the grim light of all the facts there was only one verdict that could to some degree restore one's faith in the judiciary. The case should be dismissed without further ado, and the accused set free immediately.

Münster couldn't read any unambiguous reactions on the part of the jury to this demand either, and Judge Hart did not dismiss the case. Instead, he changed his glasses once again, yawned, and stated that it was time for lunch. Proceedings would resume at two o'clock.

During the afternoon session both Chief Inspectors Sachs and Van Veeteren spent half an hour in the witness stand. Sachs reported in detail about what he and Probationer Wagner had done during the night when Barbara Hennan had been found dead, and Van Veeteren gave a very different account, covering other details of the case. He explained the dubious input of the private detective, Verlangen; Hennan's background; the mysterious death of Philomena McNaught, and the business of the insurance policy. Münster could see that the Chief Inspector was not exactly enjoying himself, neither with regard to the infantile leading questions from the prosecutor, nor to the defence counsel's somewhat arrogant tone of voice as she attempted to portray the police input into the case as amateurish.

'But for God's sake, why didn't you drop the investigation when you didn't manage to find the slightest bit of technical proof?' she asked at one point.

'Because we CID officers consider it to be our duty to catch and lock up murderers,' said Van Veeteren. 'Unlike you, fru Van Molde, who are keen to set them free.'

Then it was Meusse's turn. If it were possible, he seemed to enjoy sitting in the dock even less than the Chief Inspector – but then again, Münster couldn't recall ever having seen the introverted pathologist enjoying himself. Not in any circumstances. In any case, he described the unclear situation with crystal clarity. There was nothing to support the suggestion that Barbara Hennan had been pushed from the diving tower, and nothing to suggest that she had been rendered unconscious first: but on the other hand there was nothing to contradict either possibility. The injuries to her head, neck, nape and spine were extensive, Meusse asserted: but a little push in the back seldom resulted in any marks at all. Not in general, and not in this case either.

Neither the prosecutor nor the defence counsel had many questions to put to the pathologist, since they had both – so to say – been given carte blanche for their respective points of view, and Meusse was able to leave the witness stand after less than fifteen minutes. Despite the fact that it was only half past three, Judge Hart declared proceedings closed for the day. He wished everybody a pleasant evening, urged the members of the jury not to discuss the case with one another nor with anybody else, and expected to see all those involved in court by ten o'clock the following morning.

'Perhaps one could have expected a little more of the prosecutor,' said Münster in the car on the way back to Maardam.

'Silwerstein is an ass,' said Reinhart from the back seat.

'That may well be,' said the Chief Inspector. 'But we can't do anything about that. And in any case, what happened today isn't what will decide the outcome.'

'Let's hope not,' said Reinhart. 'Are you saying that the outcome depends on Hennan? I thought he managed to look pretty broken-hearted today, the berk. As if he were attending a funeral . . . Or sitting in a dentist's waiting room, or something of that sort.'

Van Veeteren sighed.

'What the hell did you expect? If he was stupid as well, on top of everything else, he would have been in jail for a long time by now.'

Reinhart thought for a moment.

'What had I expected?' he said eventually. 'Okay, I'll tell you. I'd expected that by now we would have found that damned accomplice . . . The one who actually killed Barbara Hennan. We've been looking for him for a month now, and I don't think I've ever been involved in anything that produced so few results. Or what do you have to say?'

Neither Van Veeteren nor Münster had any comment to make.

'We have Kooperdijk and Verlangen as well,' said Münster after a while.

'That's true,' muttered the Chief Inspector. 'Witnesses for the prosecution. Let's hope that they don't turn out to be henchmen for the defence . . .'

'Hasn't fru Van Molde called a single witness?' wondered Münster.

'No,' said Van Veeteren. 'She hasn't. Let's hope that Silwerstein is able to score a point on that fact, at least. That it was not possible to find a single character witness to speak in favour of Hennan. That says quite a lot, after all.'

'It's not compulsory to produce character witnesses,' said Reinhart. 'When the accused doesn't have a character, it could be stupid to do so.'

'That's what I'm saying,' said Van Veeteren. 'For God's sake, let's go to Adenaar's. You have time for a beer, I hope?'

Münster checked his watch.

'Well, just a small one,' he said. 'At least the trial didn't drag out all day. Every cloud, and all that.'

'One must be grateful for small mercies,' said Reinhart. 'When the big ones are a cock-up. So, full steam ahead for half an hour at Adenaar's. We need to talk a bit of crap instead of going on and on about this damned case.'

23

The building was on Westerkade, almost as far out as the Loorn Canal, and when Verlangen saw it he didn't understand why the local authorities hadn't insisted on demolishing it ages ago.

Nor did he understand how anybody could consider living in it. The dirty and decrepit brick building had four floors, but the street frontage was no more than twelve to fifteen metres long; on one side of it was a scrapyard, and on the other some sort of warehouse made of rusty corrugated iron. Nevertheless, when he entered through the disintegrating wooden front door he couldn't help but feel a little twinge of satisfaction: despite everything there were evidently folk who lived in worse conditions than he did himself.

Inside the vaulted entrance hall it was as dark as inside a sack of coal, and he was forced to light a match in order to find the door leading into the stairwell. There were no name plates on any of the doors he passed, but The Wheelchair had said the top floor, so he assumed he should continue up the stairs. He found it hard to believe that anybody lived in the flats he passed, but of course you never can tell. A sort of dirty, dusky half-light filtered in through a broken window, and the whole place was suffused with a smell of pissoir and decay. Lumps of plaster had fallen off the ceiling and walls here and there, and something that must have been a large rat slunk into a hole in the wall between the first and second floors.

At the top of the stairs were three doors, but two of them were covered by heavy planks nailed onto the frames. After hesitating for several long seconds, he pulled himself together and knocked hard on the third one.

Nothing happened, so he knocked again, even harder.

More time passed, then he heard a sort of shuffling noise from inside. As if somebody was dragging a piano or a coffin over the floor. That same somebody started coughing and hawking up phlegm, and then there was a rattling noise from a security chain and the door opened ten centimetres.

'Kekkonen?' said Verlangen.

Kekkonen wasn't really called Kekkonen, but he was the spitting image of an old president of one of the Nordic countries, and nobody called him anything else.

'Verlangen?'

'Yes.'

He unhooked the chain and opened the door. A grey-spotted cat slunk out, and Verlangen slunk in. Kekkonen closed the door. Verlangen looked around. The flat comprised one room, a window, a humming refrigerator and a mattress on the floor. There might have been a toilet as well – it smelled like it.

'Welcome, for God's sake,' said Kekkonen. 'What the hell do you want?'

'Do you live here?' asked Verlangen.

'At the moment,' said Kekkonen. 'Have you got a fag?'

Verlangen gave him one and watched him lighting it with shaking hands. Kekkonen had aged enormously since Verlangen had last seen him. He looked like a hunched little old man, despite the fact that he couldn't have been more than about forty-five, and his completely bald head, which in the old days at least had a certain lustre about it, was now more reminiscent of a skull. He wondered what drugs Kekkonen was on, and how many years he had left. Or months.

'What do you want?' he asked again, flopping down onto the mattress among all the blankets, crumpled daily papers and something that must once have been a sleeping bag. Verlangen had no desire to join him, and remained standing.

'I thought The Wheelchair had explained. Hennan. Jaan G. Hennan.'

'I don't know him,' said Kekkonen.

'Don't talk crap. You've told Duijkert and The Wheelchair that you've met him, and I've been looking for you for over a week.'

'I don't know anybody called Hennan,' said Kekkonen.

Verlangen dug out a fifty-guilder note from his pocket, and dangled it in front of Kekkonen's nose.

'You helped us to nail him last time, and we let you go free as a thank-you gesture. Have you forgotten that?'

He could see that Kekkonen's memory did not extend all that far back in time, but fifty guilders were fifty guilders no matter what.

Kekkonen sat up, leaning against the wall, and took a few puffs of his cigarette.

'A hundred,' he said.

'Fifty,' said Verlangen. 'This is only a tiny matter. I gather you met Hennan somewhere or other: what was it about?'

Kekkonen grabbed the note and tucked it underneath the mattress.

'Not met,' he said. 'Saw.'

'Okay, saw. Out with it – surely I don't have to cross-examine you?'

'I'm not sure.'

'Not sure?'

'Yes. That it was him.'

'That it was Hennan?'

'Yes, it was . . . a bit unclear. I could have been somebody else.'

'That's not what you said to The Wheelchair.'

'I couldn't care less about The Wheelchair.'

'I'm sure that's true. Come on now, out with it.'

'You're not a cop any longer, is that right?'

'You know that I'm not a cop any more.'

'Congratulations,' said Kekkonen with a grin. 'It's always good to know that people are making progress in life. How about another fag?'

'For Christ's sake, you haven't even finished that one yet,' said Verlangen, nodding in irritation at Kekkonen's right hand.

'Good Lord,' said Kekkonen in surprise, and took a puff. Dropped the butt into an empty bottle and was given another cigarette.

Please, God, Verlangen thought. I can't take much more of this.

'Come on, now,' he urged. 'You say you saw Jaan G. Hennan: tell me about it, and then I'll leave you in peace.'

Kekkonen coughed for quite a long time, then he sat absolutely motionless for several seconds, with his mouth half-open and staring into space. Verlangen realized that he was trying to pull himself together for a big mental effort.

'Yes, I saw him,' he said. 'If it really was him.'

'Go on,' said Verlangen.

'In the park, that bloody park . . . what's its name . . . Wollersparken, something like that?'

'Wollerimsparken?'

'Wollerimsparken, yes. I slept there for a few nights not long ago . . . I sometimes sleep outside when the weather's good.'

'I'm sure you do,' said Verlangen. 'So you saw Hennan together with somebody else, is that right?'

'Yes,' said Kekkonen. 'He came with that bloke who was in Maardam then for a few days . . .'

'Who?' said Verlangen.

Kekkonen shrugged.

'When?'

'God only knows. A month ago, or thereabouts. A big bloke with a ponytail . . . a killer if ever I saw one . . . a dangerous bastard, no doubt – I think he was an Englishman . . . or an Irishman, something like that . . .'

'Name?' said Verlangen.

'No idea,' said Kekkonen. 'I think they called him Liston, something like that . . .'

'Liston?'

'Yes. That's a boxer. Or was . . .'

'I know,' said Verlangen. 'So he was coloured, was he?'

'Not at all,' said Kekkonen. 'But he certainly seemed to be a strong bugger.'

'I see. Anyway, what did Hennan and this Liston fellow do in the park?'

Kekkonen furrowed his brow and concentrated again.

'They sat on a bench,' he said. 'They sat there talking . . . for quite a long time . . . I was sort of lying in the bushes behind them. I remember that they carried on talking for ages – I needed to go for a piss, but I didn't dare, sort of . . . It was in the morning. A lovely morning, lots of birds twittering away and all that – that's what's so brilliant about—'

'Did you hear what they were talking about?'

Kekkonen shook his head.

'Not a word,' he said. 'I just lay there, waiting. I very nearly pissed myself, but I just managed to avoid it. When they left he got a great bloody big envelope . . .'

'Who got the envelope?'

'Liston, of course. That big bloke . . . He got an envelope from the man who might have been Hennan, and then they left.'

'And what happened next?'

'I went for a piss.'

Verlangen thought for a moment.

'Was that all?' he said.

Kekkonen snorted.

'For Christ's sake, of course it was,' he said. 'I told you it was nothing . . . Anyway, you know all there is to know about it. Are you sure you're not a cop any longer?'

'I'm not a cop,' Verlangen assured him. 'This Liston, did you see him again afterwards?'

Kekkonen thought that over.

'No,' he said. 'I don't think so. I'd seen him once before, that's all . . . At Kooper's, I think.'

'But not with Hennan?'

'No, not with Hennan. God, but you do go on and on . . .'

'All right,' said Verlangen. 'I won't disturb you any longer. I expect you've got a lot to be getting on with.'

'You can bet your bloody life I have,' said Kekkonen. 'But I think it was worth a bit more than fifty.'

'Kiss my arse,' said Verlangen and left the room.

Huh, he thought when he emerged into the drizzle in Westerkade. What the hell am I supposed to make of this?

He checked his watch: it was half past seven. In less than twenty-four hours he would be giving evidence in the courtroom in Linden.

Liston?

Unless Kekkonen had made it all up thanks to his mashed-up brain, there had been somebody in Maardam in the beginning of June called Liston. Or somebody who was known as Liston, at least.

Who had been given an envelope by Jaan G. Hennan one

morning in Wollerimsparken. *A man who might have been Hennan.*

That was all.

As he was wandering back alongside the canal, he tried to imagine Kekkonen in the witness box. It was not a pleasant sight – or wouldn't be if it was possible to get him there. Probably not, he thought. Kekkonen had an ability to disappear if it was in his interest to do so: that was in fact probably the only ability he had kept intact over the years.

But if by hook or by crook they managed to get him in there, what would Kekkonen say? If Verlangen knew him right he would shut up like a clam, or possibly claim that he couldn't remember anything at all. That's what he used to do twelve years ago, and it was probably what he would do today.

Or perhaps he would say that he had been given a fifty-guilder note by Verlangen to spill the beans, and so he had made something up.

Damn and blast! thought Maarten Verlangen as he made his way home through the increasingly heavy rain. This is pointless.

Utterly pointless.

By the time he finally reached Kleinmarckt he was soaked through. He hesitated for a moment, then slunk into the Café Kloisterdoom and ordered a beer and a gin.

No, it would do more harm than good if I involved that bald-headed halfwit, he decided. KBO – it's best to keep buggering on.

24

Silwerstein started in the simplest possible way.

'Did you kill your wife, Barbara Hennan, in the evening of Thursday, 5 June?'

'No.'

'Had you made an arrangement with some other person to kill her?'

'No.'

Hennan's voice was loud and clear. Van Veeteren noticed that he been sitting there and holding his breath as he waited for the two 'nos', and that everybody else in the courtroom had done the same. It was really the same suppressed excitement you experience at a wedding before the 'I do' from the bride and the bridegroom, and he reflected briefly over how simple and straightforward our fundamental craving for drama is.

A yes or a no, the tipping of the scales.

'Did you kill your then wife, Philomena McNaught, at some point during your journey through Bethesda Park in the USA in June 1983?'

The defending counsel rose to her feet.

'Objection! My client is not accused of anything that happened four years ago.'

Judge Hart changed his glasses and eyed her for a while with something that most resembled scientific interest – a biologist who had stumbled upon a remarkable living organism and was keen to be precise in establishing its species.

'My learned friend no doubt realizes that it could be useful for us to have a little background information,' he proclaimed, pointing at her with the earpiece of his spectacles as if it were a gun. 'Please sit down! Herr Hennan, please be so good as to answer the question.'

Hennan nodded.

'No,' he said. I didn't kill Philomena. It was our honeymoon trip, I loved her.'

A cheap point, Van Veeteren thought grimly. But a point even so.

'What is your occupation?' asked Silwerstein.

'I'm a businessman.'

'A businessman?'

'Yes.'

'And what kind of business do you conduct?'

Hennan leaned forward and placed his hands on the bar. Van Veeteren noticed that he was wearing a wedding ring on this occasion, something he hadn't done during any of the interrogations at the police station.

'As you may know we had just arrived from the USA, my wife and I, when this accident happened . . . I ran an import company in Denver, and it was my intention to do the same here in Linden.'

'An import company?' asked Silwerstein. 'And what do you import?'

'As I was trying to say, I haven't had time to establish myself yet. In Denver I dealt mainly with tinned goods from south-east Asia – fruit and vegetables. But also some technical products. One needs to conduct some research into markets and patents before one can get going.'

During the introductory questions and answers Silwerstein had remained standing on the same spot, three metres in front of the accused: now he took two paces to the side and looked at the jury instead.

'So one could say that your so-called company hasn't yet actually done anything at all?'

'No, you could of course—'

'One could say that it is merely a facade for what was your real intention when you came to reside in this country, couldn't one?'

'I'm afraid I don't understand what you mean.'

'You don't? I think you understand perfectly clearly. Is it not the case, Herr Hennan, that you only had one thing in mind when you moved here from Denver in the USA? That is, doing the same as you had done with Philomena McNaught all over again? Getting rid of your wife and collecting another sky-high insurance pay-out? One point—'

'Objection!' shouted the defending counsel. 'The prosecutor is casting unfounded aspersions around, left right and centre. I really must—'

'Thank you,' interrupted the judge. 'That's enough. Might I ask the prosecutor to calm down somewhat.'

Silwerstein nodded submissively.

'Is it true that you took out an insurance policy on the life of your wife with the company F/B Trustor?'

'Yes.'

'Can you inform the court of the amount the policy involved?'

Hennan cleared his throat.

'One point two million.'

'One point two million guilders?'

'Yes.'

'Do you not think that is an unusually large amount?'

'No.'

Silwerstein turned away from the defendant once again.

'If we were to conduct a survey of these people,' he said, holding out his arm in a theatrical gesture, 'how many do you think there would be with life insurance policies of a similar size? I myself have a policy for a hundred and fifty thousand. I spoke to my insurers yesterday and that is considered to be a relatively large amount. Let me repeat my question, herr Hennan. Do you not think that one point two million guilders is an unusually large amount for a life insurance policy?'

'I don't know,' said Hennan. 'I wouldn't have thought it would be considered all that high in the USA . . . And I've been living there for ten years.'

The prosecutor tried to look pleased. He walked back and forth several times before stopping in front of Hennan again.

'Exactly,' he said. 'You did the same as you had done in

America. Can you tell us how much you collected after the death of your former wife, Philomena McNaught?'

'Objection!' said Van Molde again. 'This has nothing at all to do with—'

'Overruled,' said Hart without so much as glancing at the defence counsel. 'Would you kindly answer the question, herr Hennan.'

'Four hundred thousand,' said Hennan.

'Guilders?' asked Silwerstein.

'Dollars,' said Hennan.

'Four hundred thousand dollars?' repeated Silwerstein in staccato tones. He tapped the tip of an index finger against his chin and pretended to do a calculation. 'That corresponds to about twice that amount in guilders, doesn't it? Eight hundred thousand. Can that be right?'

'More or less,' said Hennan. 'I don't know what the exchange rate is at the moment.'

'You don't? Never mind, if we sum up the situation using approximate figures, we can conclude that within the last four years you have got rid of two wives in unclear circumstances, and that you are expecting to rake in a total of two million guilders in insurance pay-outs. Don't even you find this appears to be a little . . . remarkable?'

Hennan contemplated his wedding ring, but made no reply. The prosecutor paused briefly. Then asked:

'Do you know if your wife felt threatened by you?'

Hennan raised his gaze and looked at the jury. One by one, it seemed.

'She did not feel threatened. To say she did is rubbish.'

'I must object again,' said the defence counsel. 'If the prosecutor doesn't stop making these baseless accusations, what we are doing will no longer be classifiable as legal proceedings.'

'Harrumph,' growled Judge Hart. Changed his glasses and glared at the defence counsel. 'Calm down, fru Van Molde! If you want to object, then by all means object. But let's have no more of this coquetry!'

Van Molde sat down. Hart turned to Silwerstein.

'Explain what you mean,' he said. 'Threatened?'

Silwerstein bowed humbly.

'So you didn't know about it?' he asked.

'About what?' said Hennan.

'That your wife was worried that something was about to happen.'

'She was not worried and she didn't feel threatened, as I have said.'

'So how would you explain the fact that she hired a private detective to keep an eye on you?'

'I have no idea,' said Hennan.

'But you know that she did so?'

'I do now, because the police claim that she did. I didn't know at the time . . . and I very much doubt it.'

'You doubt that your wife hired a private detective to keep a watch on you?'

'Yes. There is . . . There was no reason for her to do so.'

'Really?' said Silwerstein. 'I must say that I disagree completely on that point. If she had gone to a better detective – or why not to the police? – well, she might be alive today.'

'Objection!' shouted the defence counsel, now with an obvious note of despair in her voice.

'Sustained,' said Hart. 'Members of the jury are requested to erase the prosecutor's last comment from their minds.'

Silwerstein went for a short walk again, then stopped by the side of the accused, leaning his elbow on the bar.

'Can you tell us what you did in the morning of the fifth of June?' he asked.

'I had several things to see to at home,' said Hennan. 'I didn't go to the office until after lunch.'

'I'm mainly interested in what you did with your swimming pool.'

'It needed cleaning.'

'Explain what you did.'

'I emptied it. As you know.'

'You emptied out all the water?'

'Yes.'

'Why?'

'You have to do that. It had to be cleaned, and there were some cracks that needed repairing.'

'Did your wife know about this?'

'Of course.'

'Was she at home when you were busy emptying it?'

'No, she had left for Aarlach quite early in the morning.'

'I see. So you had the pool emptied during the morning, and then you drove to your so-called office; and in the evening, when your wife came back from Aarlach, she dived into the pool and killed herself. Is that how you see the situation, herr Hennan? She dived down – head first – from a tower ten metres high into a swimming pool she knew was empty!'

'I have no other explanation,' said Hennan. 'She was lying on the bottom when I came home. What do you expect me to think?'

'I don't care what you think,' said the prosecutor, 'but I do know what you want *us* to think. But we don't, herr Hennan. Can't you see how implausible the whole situation is?'

'I have no other explanation,' said Hennan again.

'But I do,' said Silwerstein. 'An explanation that I am convinced everybody in this room will be prepared to give credence to. Your wife did not die as a result of an accident. She died because first somebody rendered her unconscious, and then he threw her down from the very top of the diving tower. Some accomplice or other that you had hired to carry out the deed. A contract killer. Isn't that in fact a much more plausible explanation than your doubtful—'

'Objection!' interrupted the defence counsel angrily. 'Can the prosecutor produce any evidence to support these horrific claims? A contract killer? Proof, please!'

A degree of unrest became audible in the public gallery, and Hart thumped his hammer down on the desk in front of him.

'Order!' he shouted. 'Objection overruled – but the prosecutor must justify his accusation.'

'Common sense justifies it,' maintained Silwerstein confidently after an artificial pause. 'Common sense! And if necessary: one point two million guilders. And if that's not enough: Philomena McNaught and four hundred thousand dollars! I have no more questions to put to the accused at the moment.'

He bowed discreetly once again, and went back to sit at his desk.

Defence counsel Van Molde stood up.

'Where were you in the evening of June the fifth, herr Hennan?'

'At the restaurant Columbine here in Linden.'

'From when and until when, roughly?'

'I arrived there soon after eight o'clock, and stayed until about half past twelve.'

'Did you leave the restaurant at all during the evening?'

No.'

'Thank you.' She turned to the Judge. 'I have written statements from the staff at the Columbine confirming that Jaan G. Hennan was at the restaurant for the whole of that evening. I haven't bothered to call them up as witnesses because this afternoon we shall hear another witness say the same thing. According to the pathologist Dr Meusse, whom we heard yesterday, Barbara Hennan died at some time between nine thirty and ten thirty p.m. that same Thursday. During that time, and for all the rest of the evening, the accused was at the Columbine restaurant. He cannot – I repeat the word not – have killed his wife. Did you hire some other person to kill your wife, herr Hennan?'

'Of course not.'

'Of course not, no. Did you love your wife, herr Hennan?'

'Yes. We loved each other very much.'

'Thank you. Is it your view that in this country we have a right to take out an insurance policy on the life of somebody we love?'

'I hope so.'

'I hope so too. Thank you, I have no more questions for the accused.'

Before Hennan left the dock he remained seated for a while, as if there was something he would have liked to add. His gaze wandered over the three rows of listeners, and when he came to Van Veeteren in the second row he paused for a moment and gave a sort of thoughtful nod, that was no doubt impossible for most of those present to see. Then he stood up and returned to his seat at the side of the defence counsel.

The bastard! Van Veeteren thought, and fought hard to suppress an impulse to stand up as well. Stand up and leave the courtroom. Why do I find it almost impossible to control this? he wondered. What makes me prepared to go on the attack if he simply looks at me for a second? Damn it all, I really shouldn't have come here today.

He clenched his fists and closed his eyes. Judge Hart changed his glasses again, and summoned Director Kooperdijk into the dock.

The prosecutor's and defence counsel's cross-examination of the dynamic director of the insurance company did not produce any surprises. Kooperdijk's answers were convincing and predictable in every tiny detail, and while he was being questioned, the Chief Inspector wondered – doubtless along with several others of those present – whether he ought to transfer his insurance policies to F/B Trustor after all. If the company was prepared to sign up to such generous deals as the one they had made with Hennan – and if needs be pay out the amount involved (oh yes, Kooperdijk assured the court, they had plenty of capital, enough to pay ten times that amount) – well, perhaps others could benefit from taking out policies with them . . .

Kooperdijk left the dock after just over twenty minutes. It was a quarter to twelve by that time, and Judge Hart decided to adjourn proceedings for lunch until half past one. He urged everybody to be punctual after the break, and thumped his hammer down on the statute book.

Van Veeteren had lunch at the Columbine. After all, there was a limited number of eating places in Linden – and at least they didn't have Hawaii Burger Special on the menu.

Instead he had fillet of veal, and drank two glasses of expensive but value-for-money Rioja while wondering if he might actually be sitting at the same table as Hennan had occupied that Thursday evening – and if he really wanted to be present at the afternoon session in the courthouse.

No, he didn't, he soon concluded, certainly not; but some sort of vague sense of duty compelled him to be present in the public gallery even so, when the time came.

Until the bitter end, he thought gloomily. Let's hope to

God that this hopeless Verlangen character can make a useful contribution despite everything!

However, the next witness to be called by the prosecutor was not Maarten Verlangen, but Doris Sellneck.

25

'Can you tell us, fröken Sellneck, about your relationship with the accused, Jaan G. Hennan?'

Doris Sellneck performed a series of rather strange head movements before answering. As far as Van Veeteren could judge, she seemed to be about fifty years old – a tall, slim woman with an air of introversion about her. As if she were not really present. He remembered who she was the moment he heard her name.

He also remembered why he hadn't bothered to interrogate her.

'I really don't understand why you have called me here,' she began. 'Jaan G. Hennan is a closed chapter in my life. It's over twenty years ago.'

'Precisely,' interrupted the defence counsel. 'I submit that fröken Sellneck should be allowed to leave the dock immediately.'

'Yes, please,' said Doris Sellneck.

'Overruled,' said Hart.

'My dear fröken Sellneck,' said Silwerstein. 'We have talked about this. It's true that it's a long time since you were married to the accused, but we are trying to fill in a little of the background, so to speak. His character, and things like that. If you—'

'He has no character,' exclaimed Doris Sellneck with sudden enthusiasm. 'He is a person without a spine.'

'Objection!' intervened the defence counsel.

'Might I request the witness to be careful with her choice of words,' said Hart.

'Eh?' said Sellneck.

Van Veeteren closed his eyes. The prosecutor cleared his throat.

'So you were married to Hennan very briefly. In 1964, is that right?'

'Yes, 1964,' said Sellneck. 'We got married in May, and separated in October.'

'Can you tell us a little more about your marriage,' asked Silwerstein. 'And about Hennan.'

'He didn't treat me well,' said Doris Sellneck, tossing her head. 'I was the one who filed for divorce. He had somebody else on the side.'

'Another woman?'

'Yes. Her name was Friedel.'

'Really? How did he treat you badly?'

'He deceived me and swindled me.'

'I really must object!' insisted Van Molde yet again. 'It's absolutely preposterous to dig up a witness who hasn't met my client for nearly a quarter of a century. You haven't been associating with your former husband since your divorce, is that right, fröken Sellneck?'

'I wouldn't dream of it,' said Sellneck.

Hart banged his hammer on the table and glared crossly at the defence counsel.

'It will be your turn to put questions to the witness when the prosecutor has finished,' he said. 'Perhaps we can agree on that little detail, at least?'

'By all means,' said fru Van Molde, and sat down.

Silwerstein wiped his forehead with a handkerchief.

'So your husband swindled you, did he?'

Sellneck nodded.

'A large sum of money, yes. I was obliged to buy him out of the flat which we had paid for with my money. Thirteen thousand guilders.'

'I understand. How long had you known him before you married him?'

'Six months. He proposed, and I said yes. I was naive – all he wanted was my money. He had no intention of it ever being more than a bogus marriage.'

'What do you mean?'

'He had that other woman all the time . . . Friedel. He never wanted to go to bed with me. I wasn't good enough. For God's sake, he's an absolute swine!'

There was some muttering and mumbling in the public gallery once again, but Hart only needed to raise his hammer to restore order.

'You have said that he beat you, is that true?' said Silwerstein.

'Objection!' shouted the defence counsel, rising to her feet. 'This witness is as incompetent as it's possible to be. A frustrated woman intent on revenge after a quarter of a century. It's outrageous! Even murder becomes statute-barred after twenty-five years: fröken Sellneck belongs to a different age!'

'Thank you for your views,' said Hart. 'Please sit down, fru Van Molde – but I have no doubt that members of the jury can make psychological judgements on their own account. Would you please kindly answer the prosecutor's question, fröken Sellneck.'

'What question?' wondered Doris Sellneck.

'If Jaan G. Hennan beat you,' said the prosecutor.

'Yes, he did,' said Sellneck eagerly. 'He gave me a punch on one occasion. In my face. It was just after I had filed for divorce. You shouldn't treat your wife like that.'

The defence counsel waved her hand.

'Could my client make a brief comment at this point? For clarification.'

Van Veeteren noted that Judge Hart was beginning to look almost amused. He nodded his approval to Van Molde, and Hennan stood up.

'It's true that I hit my then wife on one occasion,' he said. 'She was clinging onto my arm and wouldn't let go – I had to give her a slap with my other hand in order to get free.'

He sat down again. Doris Sellneck waved her clenched fist at him from the witness box, and many of those in the public gallery shouted out in anger. But not Chief Inspector Van Veeteren.

Reinhart is right, he thought. Silwerstein is an ass. Thank God he didn't drag Hennan's sister into the box as well.

Judge Hart allowed the noise to ebb away before signalling

to the prosecutor that he should continue. But Silwerstein decided that it was best not to take any more risks, and turned to the jury instead.

'I think we have received quite a good insight into the character of the accused,' he said. 'Even more than twenty years ago, he exploited women for financial gain – and he has continued to do so ever since. Doris Sellneck managed to emerge with her life intact: but Philomena McNaught and Barbara Delgado didn't. Thank you, fröken Sellneck, I have no more questions for you.'

But defence counsel Van Molde did. Albeit only a few.

'What's your occupation, fröken Sellneck?'

'I'm on sick leave.'

'Sick leave?'

'Well, I'm on a disability pension.'

'Where do you live?'

'I live at Liljehemmet.'

'I see. That's a home for people with various psychological handicaps, isn't it?'

'It's a nursing home, yes. I'm a disability pensioner.'

'How long have you been living at Liljehemmet?'

Doris Sellneck tossed her head for the last time.

'For eighteen years,' she said. 'It'll be eighteen years this August.'

'Do you like it there?'

'Yes, I do,' said fröken Sellneck. 'It's a lovely little place right next to Seegergracht. We have a film show every Thursday and Sunday.'

After that piece of information, she was allowed to leave the witness box.

Verlangen was clean-shaven, and was wearing a white shirt.

In response to the prosecutor's preliminary questions he informed the court that he worked as a private detective on his own account, that he was forty-seven years old, and that he had previously been employed as a police officer.

Silwerstein asked if he had had any contact with the accused before this case, and Verlangen recounted in considerable detail his contribution twelve years ago when Hennan was found guilty of drugs crimes. Van Veeteren noticed that during his account, on several occasions fru Van Molde seemed to be on the point of objecting, but she remained seated – perhaps because Hennan placed a hand on her arm.

'And then, a month ago, he suddenly turned up in your life once again, did he?' asked the prosecutor.

Verlangen proceeded to give a detailed account of how Barbara Hennan had contacted him, and of the surveillance work he had undertaken in Linden.

'Do you regard yourself as an experienced detective?' asked Silwerstein when Verlangen had finished.

'I've been working for five years as a private detective,' said Verlangen, 'and before that I spent many years in the police force working along similar lines . . . So yes, I think I can say that I am quite an experienced detective.'

'Have you had similar surveillance commissions previously?'

'Yes, several times.'

'What is the usual reason?'

'When it's a question of wives wanting their husbands to be kept under observation, it's usually a matter of the husband being unfaithful. They want to know if their husband has been seeing some other woman.'

'That's the most usual motive, is it?'

'Without a doubt.'

'And how was it in the case of Barbara Hennan?''

'She didn't give a motive.'

'Is that usual?'

'It happens. But they usually say what the reason is.'

'Did you have the impression that fru Hennan suspected something along those lines when she asked you to keep an eye on the accused?'

'Objection!' exclaimed the defence counsel. 'The witness is being invited to speculate.'

'Overruled,' said Hart. 'But members of the jury should bear in mind that the witness has been invited to make his own judgements.'

'I didn't have any specific impression,' said Verlangen after a short pause for thought. 'But I suppose I assumed that there was some ulterior motive.'

'And what might that have been?'

'I don't know. She wanted to be informed about what he had been up to. And I was supposed to report every day.'

'And did you do that?'

'Yes.'

'But your work came to a rather abrupt end after quite a short time, isn't that so?'

'Yes. My client was found dead after two days.'

'Two days after Barbara Hennan had hired you to keep an eye on her husband, she was found dead at the bottom of the empty swimming pool in their garden – is that correct?'

'Yes.'

Silwerstein nodded thoughtfully, and turned to face the jury.

'I'm not going to ask the witness to draw any conclusions, since my dear colleague is so obsessively keen to object. But I feel obliged to ask an open question – about what it would be reasonable to conclude from what we have heard from herr Verlangen, the private detective. Ladies and gentlemen, I submit that there is only one plausible conclusion: Barbara Hennan realized that her husband, the accused, was planning something. She was scared, and worried about her safety, and so she employed a private detective in order to obtain help. Unfortunately he was unable to assist her in the way she had hoped, and two days later it was too late. Is there anybody in this courtroom who has the slightest doubt about who was guilty of her death? I certainly don't. Jaan G. Hennan!'

'Objection!' said the defence counsel in a weary-sounding voice

'Sustained,' said Hart. 'Herr prosecutor, the closing arguments will take place tomorrow, not today. Do you have any more questions to put to herr Verlangen?'

'No,' said Silwerstein, sitting down on his chair. 'No more questions.'

Fru Van Molde approached Verlangen like a cat approaching an injured bird.

'Why did you leave the police force, herr Verlangen?' she began by saying.

'I wanted to do a different sort of work,' said Verlangen.

'A *different* sort of work?'

'Yes.'

'So you left your job as a police officer and became a private detective. Do you call that a different sort of work?'

'You're more independent,' said Verlangen, squirming on his chair.

Remarkable, thought Van Veeteren. She can't really know anything about this – was it just inspired intuition that enabled her to find that sensitive point?

'Objection,' said Silwerstein. 'What is my learned friend trying to imply?'

'Nothing,' said Van Molde before Hart had time to say anything. 'I'll proceed. During the time – the short time – you carried out your so-called surveillance of my client, did he do anything of an illegal nature?'

'No.'

'Did he do anything you thought seemed suspicious?'

'No, he did—'

'It will be sufficient if you simply say yes or no, we'll save

time that way. Did he meet anybody you felt you ought to report to your employer?'

'No.'

'Did he do anything at all – in any way at all – that sug- gested he had criminal intentions?

'No.'

'Was there ever a time while you were keeping a watch on my client when you thought he might be in danger?'

'No, I could—'

'Yes or no?'

'No.'

'Did you notice that at any time Hennan made contact with or spoke to anybody apart from the restaurant staff or similar persons?'

'No.'

'And you were keeping watch on him at the Columbine restaurant at the time when his wife died?'

'Yes.'

'Thank you.'

She turned to look at the jury and the public gallery with an expression of mild astonishment on her face.

'On the basis of what private detective Verlangen has had to say, how on earth could the prosecutor possibly conclude that Jaan G. Hennan had anything to do with the death of his wife? It is incomprehensible, ladies and gentlemen, totally incomprehensible. In actual fact the witness has given my client an alibi, a crystal clear alibi for the time when the lady died. I have to say that I simply don't understand what the prosecution is trying to prove.'

Judge Hart leaned forward over the podium and the defence counsel changed track.

'Is it true that you are acquainted with herr Kooperdijk, a director of the Trustor insurance company?'

Verlangen hesitated for a second, then gave up.

'Yes.'

'In what way?'

'I do various jobs for them.'

'Really? So you also work for F/B Trustor, the company with which my client has his insurance policies?'

'Occasionally, yes.'

'As a sort of insurance detective?'

'You could say that.'

'Thank you. Is it your job, among other things, to try to reveal so-called insurance fraud?'

'Among other things.'

The defence counsel made a rhetorical pause that Van Veeteren reckoned lasted for at least five seconds, to ensure that this information sank into the minds of the jury members.

'So you could say,' she went on, 'that you have a professional interest in my client being implicated in the death of his wife? Because if he is, then the insurance money will not be paid out . . .'

'Of course I haven't—'

'Yes or no, herr Verlangen.'

'No, I have nothing to do with that.'

The defence counsel made another pause, gazing at Verlangen with her eyebrows raised.

'Herr Verlangen,' she said eventually, 'I have spoken to herr Kooperdijk and he has described the situation to me. Is it not the case that the company has not been entirely satisfied with your work as an insurance detective, and that it would be of considerable advantage to you if the company didn't need to pay the sum insured to herr Hennan? Is it not the case that in addition to your professional interests, you also have a personal interest in my client being found guilty?'

'I really cannot—'

'Would you like me to summon herr Kooperdijk to the witness stand in order to verify what I have just said?'

Verlangen made no reply. He simply rubbed the knuckles of his right hand over his chin and cheeks, and looked somewhat confused – as if he were surprised to find his face closely shaved for once. He looked nervously at the defence counsel, the jury and the public gallery. Five more seconds passed.

'I note that the witness chooses not to answer my question,' said Van Molde. 'In that case I think there is no point in continuing. I have nothing to add.'

She sat down. Judge Hart instructed Verlangen to leave the witness stand, then put all his pairs of spectacles into separate pockets, peered at his wristwatch, and declared proceedings closed for the day.

As Van Veeteren drove out of Linden, it started raining. A heavy, thundery rain that had evidently been lying in wait and gathering strength throughout the oppressive afternoon. He drove onto the hard shoulder and stopped, spent some time searching through his collection of cassettes and finally settled on Fauré's *Requiem*. He put it on. Thought for a moment, and decided to take a longer route home – a twenty-minute drive was not enough, he needed at least an hour. He restarted the engine, took the slip-road off to the right and headed south towards Linzhuisen and Weill instead of straight ahead.

We can't go on like this, he thought. No way. G will be set free, and there's nothing I can do about it. Irrespective of how the closing arguments go tomorrow, the jury will find him not guilty. I've known that all the time, and now we are there.

In a way he was surprised to find that he was not surprised. Nor upset. After all, it was the first time he had ever let a murderer go free.

But that had to happen one day, he had been aware of that. Chief Inspector Mort had told him what it felt like when you lost your first case; Borkmann as well. It had been twenty years before Van Veeteren found himself in that situation – that must surely have been some kind of record, but just now he couldn't care less about that aspect of the problem. He had had time to make preparations, plenty of time; but the whole investigation had been unmanageable from the very start, and nothing had gone their way as time passed.

No new evidence had come to light, no interrogations had opened up cracks or changed the circumstances at all: the accursed G had been able to sit back and relax, and wait for the inevitable outcome – a not-guilty verdict, and one point two million guilders.

There was nothing that could be done about it, and it made no difference at all if the jury and the judge and everybody else involved were just as convinced of G's guilt as the Chief Inspector was.

No difference whatsoever. The mills of justice ground slowly in accordance with the letter of the law and accepted practice.

This case was clinical, to use Reinhart's word. All the ingredients had been there from the start: the insurance policy, the alibi, the private detective, Hennan's past – no new facts had been discovered, despite assiduous and single-minded work by the police, which had also been conducted in accordance with the letter of the law and accepted practice. No, it would have made no difference if a hundred thousand people had been convinced that G had hired a killer to murder his wife, the Chief Inspector thought with a sigh. He would have got away with it even so.

Because they had not succeeded in finding the actual killer.

And because they had not succeeded in proving that Barbara Hennan had not died as a result of an accident. Not even that.

It had been a waste of time, in other words. At least, it was easy to come to that conclusion. He wondered if the case would ever have come to court even, had it not been for that confounded Verlangen letting the cat out of the bag and opening the door for the media.

Maybe, maybe not. But as Reinhart had said: at least it felt better not having had to set G free without making a fight of it. Despite everything, it was better that the mills of justice had ground away.

The rain began to ease off when he came level with Linzhuisen and turned off towards Korrim and Weill: a narrow and rarely used road over the flat landscape – he couldn't remember when he had last been on it. He began thinking about how the trial in Linden's courthouse had proceeded, and wondering if he had really expected anything different from the depressing – and also somewhat bizarre – judicial performance he had taken part in and been present at for two whole days.

Presumably not, he decided when he had finished ransacking his unexpressed hopes. It had proceeded as it had to proceed. If, tomorrow or the day after, the jury were to reach the unlikely conclusion that G was guilty, he would not feel any genuine sense of satisfaction, he knew that. A guilty verdict would never survive an appeal: it would only drag things out unnecessarily.

No, it was not the mechanisms and abstruseness of the judicial process that nagged away inside him: it was something different. Nor was it his own failure after twenty years of putative success, or his personal relationship with G – there was a third reason.

A third, he thought. The third factor of the equation? He ought to have become a mathematician instead . . . And he suddenly had the feeling that his woolly thoughts, and the words he was trying to hook and fish them up with, were beginning to become rather abstract – or abstruse. What the hell was he searching for?

What was it that he was trying to glimpse, but had not yet succeeded?

He switched off Fauré and turned into the car park outside the cemetery in the village of Korrim. Got out of the car and lit a cigarette. It had stopped raining altogether now, and the sun was beginning to find its way through the clouds once again.

The accomplice? he thought? The murderer?

The two known factors of the equation: Jaan G. Hennan and Barbara Hennan. And then the third, the unknown one.

Was there a third factor, in fact?

He gazed out over the country churchyard with all its trees and bushes. An elderly man in a blue overall was working away under the dripping braches of the elm and lime trees, raking between the graves. Everything looked so calm and peaceful – and just for a moment he felt envious of the unknown workman. He took three or four puffs of his cigarette as he watched the man raking away, and gave his thoughts free rein.

I don't understand, he thought. I don't even understand the questions I ask myself any longer.

Then he clambered back into his car, and began the drive back to Maardam.

26

He didn't bother to drive back to Linden on the Thursday to be present at the concluding speeches, and when Münster came into his office in the late afternoon to report on the outcome, he was already discussing another case with Heinemann.

'That bastard got away with it,' said Münster.

'Hennan?' said Heinemann.

'Yes, Hennan.'

'It was only to be expected,' said Van Veeteren.

'Yes, I suppose so,' said Münster.

Heinemann blew his nose ostentatiously.

'Do you know how long the jury were out?' asked Van Veeteren.

Münster sat down on the window ledge.

'Less than half an hour, if I understand it rightly. No, it went as you predicted it would. But I can't help but think that it's a scandal that he was found not guilty. And Silwerstein declined to comment about a possible appeal.'

The Chief Inspector closed the file he had been leafing through.

'It would have been an even bigger scandal if he'd been

found guilty,' he said. 'In fact. And of course an appeal would require some new circumstances to come to light.'

'Yes,' said Münster dejectedly, 'you're right. The investigation never . . . never really got anywhere. We needed to find the actual perpetrator – without him it was never going to be possible to nail Hennan. The actual murder was sort of hovering in the air, so to say.'

Van Veeteren made no comment.

'I wonder how one goes about hiring a murderer,' said Münster. 'I really do think we ought to have discovered some intermediary or other. Surely you can't just advertise for a professional killer?'

'I hope not,' said the Chief Inspector. 'But there's nothing to say that we didn't in fact talk to an intermediary. Why on earth should they give themselves away just because we come and ask a few questions?'

'Yes, why indeed?' said Münster.

Van Veeteren folded his arms and leaned back on his chair. Gazed out of the window for a while before speaking again.

'We'll have to shelve this case, Münster. We might as well accept that as a fact. Maybe something will crop up in a year – or five or ten years – which will give us a clue to follow up. But not just now, we've wasted far too many working hours on G already. Go back to your office and get going on something useful instead.'

'All right,' said Münster. 'I've got rather a lot of things to deal with, in fact.'

He stood up, nodded to Heinemann and left the room.

There was silence for a while after Münster had left. The

Chief Inspector could see that Heinemann was brooding over something, and in the end he came out with it.

'That G,' he said, carefully polishing his spectacles with his tie, 'I never really felt that he was the type.'

'What type?'

'The type who would hire somebody else to do a job for him. I don't know why, but I've had that feeling all the time . . .'

The Chief Inspector looked at him, waiting for a continuation, but there wasn't one. Ah well, he thought, opening the file again. Heinemann has always been one to come out with throwaway remarks.

'Shall we get on?' he said.

'What?' said Heinemann. 'Oh, yes, of course.'

Verlangen was not sober when Krotowsky rang on Tuesday evening, but it wouldn't have changed anything if he had been. Although perhaps the dialogue might have been a little different.

'Herr Kooperdijk asked me to ring you,' said Krotowsky.

'Well, I'll be damned,' said Verlangen.

'Perhaps you know what it's about?'

'I haven't the slightest idea.'

'How are you? You sound a little . . .'

'A little what? How do I sound?'

'Never mind,' said Krotowsky. 'The director asked me to phone you in any case, and inform you that we are cancelling your contract – we shan't need your services any more.'

'Services?' said Verlangen. 'What bloody services? He must have said servitude. You heard wrongly, you fucking lap-dog!'

'Steady on now, for God's sake,' said Krotowsky. 'There's no need to get so het up. You knew exactly what the situation was, and—'

'Do you know what you can do, you fucking arse-licker?' said Verlangen, with the wind in his sails now. 'You can take your big fat director and stuff him up your own damned arse-hole – dammit all, do you think I've nothing better to do than sit here listening to your moronic drivel?'

'That's more than enough, for Christ's sake,' said Kro-towsky. 'The next time I clap eyes on you, you might just as well—'

'Piss off!' said Verlangen, slamming down the receiver.

That sorted that lot out, he thought, with a satisfied belch. He reached for the can of beer on the table, and wondered where the hell the TV remote had gone to.

The journalist claimed that his name was Hoegstraa, and that he worked for *den Poost*.

'Why are you ringing me at home?' asked Van Veeteren.

'I tried to get you at the police station, but they said you had already gone home.'

'What do you want?'

'It's about the Jaan G. Hennan case. He was found not guilty today, and they say you have never failed to get your man before ...' He paused, but Van Veeteren made no attempt to fill it. 'Anyway, we are interested in hearing what you have to say about that, Chief Inspector.'

'I have nothing to say.

'But if it really is the case that—'

'Are you hard of hearing? I've just said that I've nothing to say.'

There was silence for three seconds.

'I see,' said the journalist. 'Well, thanks anyway.'

'You're welcome,' said Van Veeteren.

The conversation with Erich took half an hour.

Or, at least, thirty minutes passed from the moment he entered his son's room until he left it. Erich was sitting on his bed, Van Veeteren was sitting on the edge of the desk. What was actually said could have been written down on a serviette or in a sonnet, if it had occurred to anybody to record it – but even so, there was a sort of understanding between them.

He liked to think so, in any case; and as a sort of confirmation of this new and unexpected significance, Erich took the initiative towards the very end of the conversation.

'There's really only one problem,' he said.

'Let's hear it,' said his father.

'I don't feel at home in this world,' said his son. 'What are you supposed to do if you don't really want to go on living?'

At first what Erich had said didn't sink in; but then the words combined to form . . . to form a clenched fist of ice that slowly sank down inside him and eventually came to a stop just underneath his heart.

If you don't really want to go on living.

His own son.

An eternity of small, tiny elements of time passed by as the ice sometimes hardened, sometimes thawed slightly, and while both of them, father and son, seemed to be encapsulated in a sort of private, fundamental loneliness. Square one. Or perhaps square zero.

He could think of nothing to say in response. No words.

Or rather, he thought of a dozen possible things to say, but a sort of half-hearted would-be-wisdom was inherent in all of them, and he refrained from giving them voice. Instead they just sat there, out of respect to Erich's words, and to silence. Five minutes passed, perhaps ten. Then he gave his son an awkward hug, and stood up.

Paused in the doorway.

'Remember that I love you,' he said. 'If I believed that there was a God, I would pray for you.'

'I know,' said Erich. 'Thank you.'

He knew that he wouldn't sleep, so about midnight he went for a long walk with Bismarck. Wandered around in Randers Park for so long that he passed every damned park bench and every damned waste-paper basket at least three times.

Why would anybody not want to carry on living when they were only sixteen years of age? he thought.

He tried to remember if he himself had seen life as something one couldn't cope with when he was Erich's age, but he couldn't remember what the facts were in those days.

We like to believe that children and young people think life is easier than adults do, he thought. It's a sort of precondition of parenthood – but of course in fact it's an illusion and a misunderstanding. Yet another one.

With regard to misunderstandings – totally uninvited – he started thinking again about those wind-blown and would-be-wise theories regarding the equation's third factor that he had succumbed to deliberating about recently – such as Heinemann's intuitive comment on G.

That he wasn't the type who would employ accomplices.

That there might not be a third factor.

I must shelve this, the Chief Inspector thought. For the time being, at least. Otherwise I'll go mad.

He lit a cigarette, turned up his collar to keep the rain out, and started walking home.

Mami had gone away.

A long way away, they said. Both Auntie Peggy and one-eyed Adam, who had come to fetch her and her things.

To another country, perhaps. They didn't really know, but she couldn't continue living at Peggy's. A long time had passed. Days and nights and more days. Much more than a week, as Mami had said, she knew that. Maybe two weeks, maybe more. It had been summer all the time. She had slept at Auntie Peggy's many, many nights, but now Adam had come to fetch her.

She was going to a home, they said.

A home.

No, not to a home where Mami was. A different sort of home – she didn't know what different kinds of home there were. Adam had a large, green, soft bag into which they packed all her things and her clothes. Auntie Peggy had washed everything at least, there was nothing that smelled of pee any more. Adam was wearing a checked vest, one of those with holes in so that you could see that he was very hairy on his stomach and chest. Some on his back as well, it was disgusting.

Mami would no doubt come one day, they said. Come and fetch her from that home, but not just now. Just now she was away some-

where, she had a lot to do and she didn't have time to come and look after her.

It would be great at the home. There'd be other children to play with, she'd have her own bed and a cupboard to keep her things in. Even a little lake to swim in, that was right next to the home – there was a jetty from which you could jump into the water, and it was still summer.

They would drive for a few hours in Adam's car. They'd be there by the evening, and she'd be able to have dinner and meet her new friends.

Auntie Peggy lifted her up and gave her a big hug, with her big titties and nasty smell. Adam adjusted the black patch over his right eye, and told them to hurry up for God's sake, or they'd never get away.

And pack those bloody dolls away in the bag as well.

She unfastened the zip and packed away Trudi, but she kept Bamba under her arm. Bamba was not a doll you could hide away just anywhere, but neither Adam nor Peggy understood that. Adam picked up the bag and they went out through the door.

She didn't know whether to feel happy or sad. It felt odd, and it would be many days before Mami came back, she realized that. But she would never sleep at that damned Peggy's place again.

Never ever.

2002

APRIL-MAY

27

He dreamt that he was sitting asleep in an antiquarian book-shop.

In the winged armchair in the inside room cum kitchen-ette, of course, with an open book on his knee, a mug of coffee in the holder on the chair arm, and with the rain drum-ming away on the metallic sill of the window overlooking the alley.

April, presumably: the cruellest month. It was late after-noon, and if there was a shortage of customers he was seldom able to keep awake for a whole hour between five and six – there was nothing he could do about it, and of course there was no reason why he shouldn't allow himself a little snooze for a quarter of an hour or even half an hour: no reason at all, at his stage of life . . .

The doorbell rang, and he woke up.

He was sitting in the inside room of the antiquarian book-shop with Nooteboom's book on Spain open on his knee. An empty coffee mug was standing in the holder on the chair arm, and rain was drumming away on the window led—

What the hell? he thought. Am I dreaming or am I awake?

Have I just woken up or just fallen asleep?

He shook his head and shivered. What did it mean when reality and dream were identical? Was it the ultimate indication of inadequacy, or was it something else? Something radically different?

He heard somebody closing the door behind them in the main room of the shop. The rustling sound of a raincoat being taken off. A slight clearing of the throat. He decided that he was in fact awake.

'Hello? Is there anybody there?'

He heaved himself up out of his armchair and admitted that he existed.

The woman was blonde, and seemed to be in her thirties. He only needed a quick glance to ascertain that she was not intending to buy a book, but was on some quite different business. It was not clear what. And not clear how he realized that. He waited while she wiped the water from her spectacles with the aid of a blue-grey jumper sleeve.

'Van Veeteren? I'm looking for somebody called Van Veeteren.'

'On what business?'

'Is it you who . . . ?'

She smiled uncertainly.

'It's not impossible. Why don't you tell me what you want, then we can see. Would you like to sit down?'

Later – three or four or five months later – he would like to think that even then he had some sort of a premonition. That as she stood there, trying to find somewhere to put her wet

raincoat, he had an inkling of what was to come. Of what –
for the last time? – he would become involved in.

Yes, it really would have to be the last time.

But this was later, looking at everything in the rear-view
mirror – we understand life backwards, but we have to live it
forwards, he had read in Kierkegaard – and now, as he took
her red jacket and hung it over the chair behind the substantial Hoegermaas desk with the catalogues and the newly
arrived but as yet unsorted piles of books, with the receipt
book and cash box, the ashtray and the old, faded bust of
Rilke . . . well, to be honest, there was no significant gap in
the veil that protected the future. A narrow beam of curiosity, perhaps. A sort of hope, but nothing more.

But you only see certain things afterwards. No doubt that
is just as well. He showed her into the cramped kitchenette,
she took a seat on one of the wicker chairs, and he sat down
opposite her.

'It was Intendent Münster who sent me here.'

'Intendent Münster?'

'Yes.'

'And . . . ?'

'At the CID section of the police station. I spoke to him
yesterday on the phone, and he suggested that I should get in
touch with you – assuming you are in fact Chief Inspector
Van Veeteren?'

He waved a deprecating index finger.

'Both and, fröken.'

'Both and?'

'Yes and no, but mainly no. Once upon a time I really was

a chief inspector; nowadays I am merely herr Van Veeteren, a saviour in times of distress but normally just a seller of second-hand books. That Intendent Münster can't get the facts of the situation into his head . . . But I think it's high time you came out with what it is that you want, fröken – or is it fru?'

'Fru, in fact.'

'Of course. Why should a woman as beautiful as you are be running around on the loose?'

She smiled, and he realized that his words were closer to reality than he had originally intended. She was not a striking beauty, but she was good-looking and there was a warmth and a glint of steel in her eyes.

'My name is Belle Vargas.'

He had the impression that he ought to note that down, but he had neither pen nor paper within reach.

'I'm coming to see you because I'm worried about my father. He has . . . well, I don't really know for certain, but I think one has to say that he has disappeared.'

'Disappeared?'

'Yes. That's why I went to the police yesterday . . . To report him missing. And when I got back home, that intendent rang . . .'

'Münster?'

'Intendent Münster, yes. He suggested that I should look you up and tell you about it, because he thought you would be interested.'

Van Veeteren cleared his throat.

'I'm afraid I don't really understand what all this is—'

'Forgive me. I was called Verlangen before I got married. My father's name is Maarten Verlangen.'

It was a couple of seconds, perhaps three, before the penny dropped. But when it did, it was all the more nerve-shattering. Like – like a knife scraping against the bottom of a saucepan, or a fingernail breaking on contact with a slate. He looked at the clock. There was half an hour still to go before closing time. Belle Vargas was fiddling nervously with something in her shoulder bag: he realized that she was waiting to hear if he was going to listen to what she had to say or not.

'I think . . .' he said. 'I think we need a cup of coffee. What do you say to that?'

I suppose I really am awake? he thought.

'It's fifteen years ago, I hope you are clear about that.'

'I know. Intendent Münster stressed that as well, but I don't need to be reminded. My father has been going downhill for some years now, and it's as well that you are aware of that from the start. I'm not suggesting that it began with that business, but nevertheless it was somehow crucial . . . It floored him.'

She paused, and stirred her cup of coffee.

'Belle?' said Van Veeteren. 'Your name is Belle, is it? I remember him talking about his daughter. How old were you then?'

You should never ask a woman about her age, he thought: but if you wondered how old she was quite a few years ago, that was another matter of course.

'Sixteen or seventeen,' she said. 'That was when he had his private detective agency, my dad; but after that G business it never got going again. He kept his office, of course, until just a few years ago, but he hardly ever had any work . . .'

'I understand,' said Van Veeteren, taking out his cigarette machine. 'I think it would be a good idea if you could tell me what's happened. Now, as it were.'

'Forgive me,' said Belle Vargas, blushing. 'But, in fact, I don't know what's happened . . . Apart from the fact that he's disappeared. I'm usually in touch with him once a week . . . or every other week at least . . . but now it's been a month.'

'Where does he live?'

'In Heerbanerstraat. He's lived in that scruffy little flat ever since they divorced . . . and that was over twenty years ago. No, I'm afraid my father hasn't had much of a life.'

'Perhaps he has realized that, and started all over again somewhere else?'

She laughed.

'My father? No, I can hear that you don't know him. And he would never go away without letting me know. He is . . .' She struggled to find the right words. 'He's pretty lonely. I think I'm the only person of importance in his life. Me and my children – I have a boy and a girl.'

'I understand,' said Van Veeteren again. 'Yes, I had the impression that he was a sort of lone wolf . . . even at that time. Fifteen years ago. But now you think he's gone missing, do you?'

She nodded and swallowed.

'Yes. As far as I know, he hasn't been home since the third

or the fourth. I was at his place in Heerbanerstraat the day before yesterday, and there was an enormous pile of post and junk mail – mainly junk mail, of course. It . . . Something must have happened to him.'

Her voice trembled, and Van Veeteren gathered that she was much more worried than she had appeared to be.

'What was he working at nowadays?'

I ought to have said 'is he working at', he thought, but it was too late.

'He's been out of work for some years now . . . Apart from the occasional little job now and again. I suppose I ought to admit that he's been drinking more than is good for him. I suspect that applied even when you met him. But . . . Well, things haven't got any better.'

Van Veeteren nodded.

'That's the way it can go,' he said. 'I'm sorry for your sake, and I understand that it must be difficult. But I don't really understand why you've come to see me. Or why Intendent Münster thought you ought to come to me. I assume a Wanted notice has been issued?'

'Yes. And they've checked up at all the hospitals and such places . . . I'm quite reconciled to the thought that he might have died in some sort of accident when he'd had a drop too much – but it seems that there are no unidentified bodies that could be him . . . And then, there are a few other circumstances.'

'Circumstances?' wondered Van Veeteren. 'What circumstances?'

She rummaged in the shoulder bag she had put on the

floor in front of her, and dug out an envelope. Opened it, and produced a sheet of paper.

'This was lying on the kitchen table.'

Van Veeteren took it and examined it. A normal A4 sheet, lined, from a spiral-bound writing pad, by the look of it. There were two things written on it:

14.42

and

G. *Bloody hell*

That was all. Rough handwriting. A blue ballpoint pen that had left a few tiny blots. The G was written bigger and more powerfully than any of the other letters – aggressively, no doubt about it. The numbers higher up were underlined. Down at the bottom of the paper, on the right, was a pale yellow stain in the form of a three-quarter circle: his diagnosis was a beer glass.

He returned the sheet of paper, and looked at her.

'Well?'

She hesitated.

'I suppose . . . I suppose it's not all that much, but you must be aware that he was obsessed by that Hennan business. At times, at least. As if that – and only that – was the reason for his personal failure. You can't imagine how many hours I've spent listening to him going on about it . . . He lost his job with that insurance company as a result of it, I don't know if you are aware of that . . . And, well, if it's true what they say and some people need something specific to complain about, then there's no doubt that Jaan G. Hennan is the bugbear in my father's life . . . I take it you know what I'm talking about?'

'I think so,' said Van Veeteren. 'Life doesn't always turn out to be what we'd like it to be. But you said there were several things. Not just this sheet of paper.'

She nodded.

'Yes. These scribbles don't say all that much – but there was a phone call as well.'

'A phone call?'

'Yes. My father rang and spoke to my son, Torben. We've tried to work out precisely when that was, but you know what children are like . . . Torben is ten years old. It was presumably at the beginning of last week, ten or eleven days ago, but he can't remember exactly. He only remembered about it the other day when we were sitting and talking about Grandad, and whether to issue an S.O.S. message . . .'

'What kind of call was it?'

'My father rang, and Torben answered. He was alone in the house, and that's why we think it must have been a weekday when he'd come home from school, but my husband and I hadn't yet got home from work . . . Monday or Tuesday, most likely. Anyway, I've checked everything it's possible to check, and I can vouch for what my son says.'

'So what did your father want?'

She paused briefly before answering. She held his gaze for an extra half-second, and he realized that she was trying to make sure that he was genuinely interested. That he believed what she was telling him.

'He asked Torben to give us a message,' she said. 'Unfortunately, Torben forgot about it for a few days. But my father said: "It's about Jaan G. Hennan. Now I understand how he did it. This evening I'm going to prove it." He repeated it twice, and asked Torben to tell us exactly what he had said.'

Van Veeteren frowned.

'Hmm,' he said. 'And your son forgot about it?'

'Unfortunately. Other things got in the way. But he remembered about it in detail once he did get round to it – you know what ten-year-olds can be like.'

Van Veeteren nodded vaguely.

'"Now I understand how he did it. This evening I'm going to prove it." That's what he said, is it?'

'And that it had to do with Hennan, yes.'

'It sounds a bit . . . well, what could one call it? Melodramatic?'

'I know. He can be like that.'

'Ten to twelve days ago?'

'No more than two weeks, in any case.'

'But you think that he hasn't been at home for . . . How long was it you said?'

'Four weeks, as far as I can judge.'

'And you don't know where he rang from?'

'No.'

'Does he have a mobile phone?'

'No.'

'Did he say anything about contacting the police, or anything like that?'

'No, evidently not. And I'm quite certain that Torben would have remembered if he had done.'

Van Veeteren prised a cigarette out of the machine and said nothing for a while.

'What did he sound like when he rang? Did your son get any impression of that? I mean, in view of—'

'I understand what you're getting at. I obviously asked Torben about that as well, and he maintains that Grandad was sober. He's spoken to him a few times when he wasn't, so he knows what it's all about. He says that Grandad sounded quite . . . well, keen . . . eager . . . as if he were in a hurry. It was a very short call, it seems.'

'And he didn't say anything about ringing again later?'

'No, he didn't . . . Anyway, I don't know what you think about this, but at least I've filled you in. It was that intendent who urged me to contact you . . .'

'Excellent,' said Van Veeteren. 'Thank you. It's absolutely right that you should come to me. Intendent Münster made a completely correct judgement.'

He picked up the sheet of paper and studied it for a while in silence.

'These figures,' he said. '14.42 . . . It looks like a departure time. A train or a bus.'

She nodded.

'Presumably. That's what Intendent Münster thought as well . . . So maybe he's gone off somewhere. But for heaven's sake, this was such a long time ago!'

'And he didn't say anything about where he was calling from? He couldn't have been at home, could he?'

'He could have been absolutely anywhere. Torben is sure that he didn't say a word about where he was.'

'You don't happen to have one of those . . . what are they called? Caller somethings?'

'Caller-ID. No, unfortunately not.'

Van Veeteren leaned back and thought. Belle Vargas finished her coffee and seemed to be wondering if there was anything else she could add, or whether she should thank him for his hospitality and leave. He watched her out of the corner of his eye while thoughts meandered through his brain.

'Damn it all!' he muttered eventually. 'After fifteen years. But then again . . . then again, it's not certain that it means anything at all. He's a bit obsessed by this Hennan business, you said?'

'On and off, at least. I imagine that he might well have become so . . . so incredibly enthusiastic if he really had caught on to something . . . I'm not sure if you understand how—'

'I certainly do,' interrupted Van Veeteren. Cleared his throat and sat up straight on his chair. 'Don't underestimate me, intuition is my speciality. I was responsible for the Barbara Hennan investigation in 1987, and I met your father several times. I shall get in touch with Intendent Münster, and we shall see what we can do about this. Am I right in thinking that your father has never gone missing like this before?'

'Never,' said Belle Vargas emphatically. 'I'm sure something must have happened to him, and I'm extremely grateful that you are taking the trouble to help me. My father is a . . . a quite insignificant person, if you see what I mean.'

'Insignificant?' said Van Veeteren. 'Ah well, not everybody has the distinction of wallowing in the spotlights. But don't expect too much. Let us hope that there is a straightforward explanation, and that we find your father in good condition.'

She nodded. Stood up, shook hands and left the bookshop. Through the display window he watched her turn up the hood of her jacket to fend off the pouring rain, and hurry off in the direction of Kellnerplejn.

When she had disappeared behind a furniture van outside Gestetner's, he finally pinched his arm. It hurt.

A straightforward explanation? he thought five seconds later. Maarten Verlangen in good condition?

He realized that he didn't really believe in either possibility, and when he locked the street door he had a sudden attack of dizziness. He sat down on one of the reading chairs.

G? he thought. Yet again?

The last round?

These were only words that drifted into his head instead of thoughts, he knew that, and he felt a need to hold them at bay. They were too heavy for the slight suspicion that had suddenly emerged inside him. The vague feeling that the only case he had failed to solve in over thirty years of police work might have a verse as yet unsung, despite everything – a suspicion that would never keep afloat if he started examining it in detail, hoping, and planting words.

Caution! he thought. Don't start creating illusions, you bookseller!

He stood up and pulled down the curtain across the door. Went back to the inner room and his armchair. Dug out the bottle of port and a glass from behind the row of Schiller and Klopstock, and filled it to the brim. Made himself comfortable in the armchair and lit the cigarette he had made during his conversation with Belle Vargas but never got round to lighting – and as if to order, the moment he closed his eyes and made himself defenceless, that old image from the gym appeared in his mind's eye.

The frozen image from the gym itself with Adam Bronstein rolled up inside that stinking mat – and then another image from a few minutes later. A devilish moment.

When . . . when they are already on their way from the scene. When G has closed the gym door and is walking off, and when it has occurred to him how he will be able to save the life of Adam. He pauses in the schoolyard, pretending that his shoelace has come undone and needs tying. He crouches down among the red and yellow autumn leaves next to one of the bicycle stands and pretends to be tying a knot – and things proceed exactly as he had hoped: G doesn't stop and wait for him, merely glances in his direction and continues walking towards the school gate with the others.

But then, suddenly, his courage fails him. Instead of staying where he is, allowing G and the others to pass through the dark gate, and then going back into the gym – instead of doing what he knows he ought to do, he stands up and hurries after them.

He's not the one who rolled Adam Bronstein up in the mat.

It's not his responsibility.

It's not . . .

He opened his eyes and the image disappeared.

Is that why I hate him? he wondered. Is it because he implicated me in his guilt? Made me guilty for the first time fifty years ago?

He looked at the clock. It was a quarter past six . . . and he suddenly remembered that they were expecting guests: two of Ulrike's children, his own grandchild Andrea and her mother. Ulrike had thought of serving up a paella, and no doubt needed his assistance in the kitchen.

He could feel a longing for her, a longing to be in the kitchen with her, each with a glass of Chianti and with the smell of bread baking in the oven. A very strong longing.

Good Lord, he thought. I'm sixty-five years of age, but as lovelorn as a teenager.

He stood up and left the bookshop.

Late that night he telephoned Münster. He hadn't spoken to him – nor to any other of his former colleagues – for several months, and it felt almost as if he were intruding. It was remarkable, but that's the way it was.

It transpired that Münster had no information about Verlangen over and above what he had already heard from Belle

Vargas. They had issued a Wanted notice the previous day, but as yet – after rather more than twenty-four hours – they had not received a single response. He agreed to meet Van Veeteren in a few days' time to discuss the situation: if anything significant turned up in the meantime, Münster promised to inform the *Chief Inspector* immediately.

The intendent never actually used the words, but nevertheless Van Veeteren could hear them – as plain as day – on the tip of his tongue.

The *Chief Inspector*.

I would have retired last autumn if I'd stayed on in the force, he thought. Perhaps it was the intention that I would fit in another round with G after all. Perhaps that is what the director had intended all along?

Was that possible? The director?

He shook his head and tried to rinse away the thought with a mouthful of Chianti.

But it wouldn't go away.

28

It was six months since he had last met Münster – and ten months since they had last played badminton – but it turned out to be an unexpectedly memorable meeting even so.

The intendent had been in bed with flu as recently as that same morning (38.3 degrees the previous night) and was a walking corpse. Van Veeteren had no difficulty in winning the first set 15–10, and at 10–3 in the second Münster was forced to throw in the towel, having been sent staggering from corner to corner like a fatally wounded quarry by his ruthless opponent.

'Personally, I'm on rather good form,' maintained Van Veeteren as he gave his defeated opponent a helping hand back to the changing room. 'But perhaps I don't need to mention that.'

Münster was breathing hard, but did not respond. Van Veeteren spent a few seconds trying to think of something sympathetic to say, but failed and thought it was better to say nothing. They showered, got changed and sat down in the cafeteria to drink a beer in one case and ice-water in the other, and to talk about Maarten Verlangen.

'What the hell's going on?' wondered Van Veeteren. 'Might there be something in it, do you think?'

Three days had passed since Belle Vargas turned up at the antiquarian book shop, and Verlangen was just as missing now as he had been then. Münster drank half a litre of ice-water, and looked doubtful.

'As I understand it, it's not possible to think anything,' he said. 'We made a few inquiries about Hennan, just as you suggested, Chief . . . Or rather, we *tried* to make some inquiries.'

'Meaning?'

'We didn't discover anything at all, despite the fact that Krause hammered away at the keyboard until his fingers nearly dropped off. He's not the type to have a website, that Hennan character.'

'That doesn't surprise me,' said Van Veeteren.

'He seems to have left the country a few months after the trial – in 1987, that is. After having collected the insurance money, of course, and . . . well, since then there has been no trace of him. Buenos Aires or Calcutta or Oslo? He could be anywhere in the world, all we can do is guess.'

'I'd rather not,' muttered Van Veeteren. 'Presumably he's acquired several new wives as well . . . It's been fifteen years, after all. And I assume you've also drawn a blank with Ver-langen?'

Münster poured some more water into his glass, and breathed heavily.

'Indeed. But he's certainly not in Calcutta. Krause checked that train time, or whatever it was . . .'

'It was a train time,' said Van Veeteren. 'Possibly a bus, but

I don't think that's likely. Aeroplanes leave at times ending in five or ten. From Sechshafen, at least . . . Or rather, that's when they are supposed to leave, which isn't exactly the same thing . . . But never mind that, we'll say it was a train time.'

'That's all right by me,' said Münster. 'But in any case, there is no train due to leave Maardam at 14.42. Nor one due in at that time, in fact. Not according to the timetable, at least.'

He rummaged around in his inside pocket and produced an envelope.

'But as we are equipped with computers nowadays, well . . .'

He handed the envelope over to Van Veeteren.

'What's this?'

'A compilation,' said Münster. 'As you reckoned it was a train time, we looked up train times. On one sheet of paper you have all the stations in the country at which a train was due to leave at eighteen minutes to three. On the other sheet, stations where trains were due in at that time.'

Van Veeteren folded out the sheets of paper and eyed the columns with the names of the stations somewhat sceptically.

'For Christ's sake . . .' he said. 'What am I supposed to do with this?'

Münster flung out his hands.

'Don't ask me. It only took a minute to get it, according to Krause. Anyway, that's as far as we've got so far.'

'Drink up that bloody water, and let's get out of here,' said Van Veeteren.

★

A few days later, a Tuesday morning right at the beginning of May – and after having struggled with dreams involving G in one way or another for three nights in a row – he had had enough. He telephoned Belle Vargas and asked to meet her again. There was no other possible solution.

It transpired that she was working as a physiotherapist at a private clinic just a few blocks away from Kupinskis gränd, and her lunch hour was at twelve. Van Veeteren suggested one of the pavement cafes in Kejmer Plejn since it was such fine weather, and she thought that was a splendid idea.

She sounded rather hopeful, he thought as he hung up. He hoped she didn't think he would be able to give her some news about her father.

Indeed, he hoped instead that she might have something to tell him.

But that was not the case. Maarten Verlangen was still just as much missing without trace as he had been for over a month now – or about roughly half that time if one accepted the telephone call to his grandson Torben as the last sign of life.

So no real reason for optimism, thought Van Veeteren: but at least it was lovely weather. A warm breeze and twenty degrees or more in the shade. They found a table just underneath the statue of Alexander; and when they had settled down and ordered their food, he could see that she had given up.

It was as simple as that. Belle Vargas had decided that her father was no longer alive. And that decision had given her a sort of strength – it was paradoxical, of course; but he recognized the phenomenon from his time as a detective chief inspector.

For sorrow is easier to bear than uncertainty.

In the long run, at least. There is no attitude you can adopt to cope with uncertainty. No method for handling it, he thought. But death is surrounded by rituals.

'I know he's dead,' she said, as if to confirm his unstated suspicions.

'Perhaps it's best to assume that, yes.'

She looked at him with an expression of mild surprise. He realized that she had expected him to suggest that he wasn't.

'I want . . . I mean, it seems to be important that we find him.'

'Of course.'

'We spoke about this the other day, my husband and I . . . He had read somewhere that the burial ceremony is the oldest symbol of . . . well, of some kind of civilization. That we take care of our dead, and all that.'

'No doubt about it,' said Van Veeteren. 'Besides, it's the only time in life that content and form coincide absolutely. It most certainly is important.'

He could see that she didn't really understand what he had said, but didn't bother to spell it out.

'I have a little request,' he said instead.

'A request?'

'Yes. If you still want me to do what I can in connection with this case. Don't expect anything, though. I'm an old man and out of practice – five years in a dusty old antiquarian bookshop doesn't exactly spruce up your abilities, you must have no illusions about that.'

She smiled.

'I have the impression that you have a few mental faculties that are still working. What do you want me to help you with?'

'I'd like to take a look at his flat.'

She nodded.

'The police have already been there.'

'I know. I'm not assuming of course that I shall find anything they've missed, but it wouldn't do any harm for me to take a look.'

She hesitated for a moment.

'It's . . . It's not a pretty sight.'

'I don't suspect for a moment that it is. But you have a key, I take it?'

'I certainly do. And of course . . . Of course you are welcome to go and take a look if you can be bothered. I think I might even have the key with me now.'

She rummaged around in her handbag, produced a bunch of keys inside a leather holder, and unhooked one of them.

'I hope you don't want me to be present when you go to the flat?'

'Not if you will trust me to be there on my own.'

'Of course I do. When . . . when had you thought of going there?'

He thought for a moment.

'This evening. If I could take a look this evening, then . . .'

'Then I shall call in at your bookshop tomorrow afternoon

and collect the key,' she said. 'I'm most grateful for you taking time to look into this business. I shall pay you, of course, somehow or other. If you can—'

'Nonsense!' he said, interrupting her. 'I don't want any reward at all. I've been involved with this old Hennan case for over fifteen years now. If there's the slightest chance of casting new light on it, I'm only too grateful.'

She looked at him with sudden interest.

'I see. You mean it's been haunting you as well? Not just my father?'

Haunting? he thought. That was putting it a bit strongly, perhaps.

'I haven't been able to forget all about it, that's for sure,' he admitted.

The moment he entered the flat in Heerbanerstraat and closed the door behind him, he was ready to agree with Belle Vargas's judgement.

Maarten Verlangen's home was not a pretty sight.

The hall was two square metres and furnished with a few daily newspapers spread out over the floor, a three-legged mahogany bureau and a cracked mirror. The kitchen was immediately off to the right, and the furniture there was classically simple: a kitchen table with a laminated top but without a cloth, two Windsor-style chairs and about two hundred empty bottles. The latter were all over the place – in crates on the floor, on the table, on the draining board, on top of the lopsided and buzzing refrigerator – he made up his mind not to open it in any circumstances.

The bedroom was to the left. The Venetian blinds were down, but a dirty, dusky light filtered in even so since some of the laths were broken: he could make out an unmade bed and a bedside table, a stone-dead potted plant on a pedestal and a heap of unfolded clothes that presumably concealed some kind of chair.

The living room contained some decent furniture. A lop-sided glass-fronted bookcase, a table, a corduroy sofa and an armchair. A television set and a hi-fi system, both of them so covered in dust that they looked almost mouldy. A modern desk made of white-painted wood with an office chair on castors. On two of the walls were some rather shabby Van Gogh reproductions. The third was covered by a gigantic and somewhat blurred green beer poster, and the fourth comprised a dirty and milky window and a dirty and milky glass door leading out onto a tiny balcony overlooking a multi-storey car park. Newspapers and magazines and advertising leaflets were lying everywhere – only on the desk was there some sign of order among the chaos. If you were trying hard to be kind, that is. Also on it were a telephone, a small, grey metal set of shelves with narrow horizontal pigeon-holes for invoices and other important documents that clutter life's thorny path – and a spiral-bound writing pad (the one from which that page with the train time and the line about G had been torn out, Van Veeteren assumed). A few lottery tickets covered in scribbles suggested that even Maarten Verlangen had hopes for the future. Or *had had*, at least.

But the flat was certainly not a pretty sight.

Nor did the atmosphere appeal to one's sense of smell, alas. There was a quite distinctive odour, Van Veeteren noted. A sweet-sour smell of old food left-overs, old unwashed clothes, filthy old floors, and old man.

And that was all. Apart from a mouldy-smelling bathroom that he only peeped inside and established that the light wasn't working.

He stood in the living room, trying to make up his mind. Dammit all, he thought. I ought to, but I haven't got the strength. What the hell am I doing here?

Had he really thought he would be able to root around in this repulsive midden?

If two CID officers had spent six hours rummaging around and not found anything that could be regarded as a clue, how many hours would a half-petrified bookseller need in order to find anything?

He shook his head. Lit a cigarette and made one more tour of the flat.

Then he gave up and drove home.

Once upon a time I used to be a detective chief inspector, he thought. But that was then . . .

That evening he went to the cinema with Ulrike. They saw two of Kieślowski's *Dekalog* films, and wondered all the time how the hell it had been possible to create something so artistically brilliant with such minimal resources. Absolutely miraculous! he insisted as he and Ulrike walked slowly back home alongside Langgraacht, and she agreed. If only we could see life through a Kieślowski camera, she maintained, then one of these days we might even begin to understand what it's all about.

Later on, some time after midnight, when that miracle of a woman had fallen asleep, he noticed that images of the lugubrious housing estate in Warsaw were still nagging away in his brain, and in some mysterious way were beginning to merge with the images he had registered that afternoon in Verlangen's flat.

He remained lying in bed for a while, trying to fall asleep with that remarkable mixture in his mind's eye; but it soon became obvious that it was impossible. He sneaked out and set up a Preisner CD in the living room instead. He switched on the lamp by the sofa and took out the list he had received from Münster the previous week.

All the places from which a train had left for somewhere or other at 14.42.

And all the places where a train was due to arrive from somewhere or other at that same time.

He remained sitting there for a while with a list in each hand: then he put the list of departures to one side. If one assumed, he thought, or if one dared to assume that Verlangen had set off from Maardam, from where no trains were due to leave at that time, the note must surely refer to an arrival time.

But why would anybody want to bother to note down an arrival time – unless perhaps somebody was going to meet him? Was that perhaps the answer?

Twenty-six. There were twenty-six places in the whole country where a train was due to arrive at 14.42. At seventeen of them every day of the week. Four only on weekdays, three on Sundays and holidays, and two only on Saturdays.

According to Inspector Krause's computer, at least.

He lay down on the sofa. Had Maarten Verlangen travelled to one of these places? Had he been sitting at his filthy kitchen table or perhaps at his desk and noted down those four figures after telephoning the information office at Maardam Central Station?

It was not impossible. By no means impossible. He yawned. Noticed that he was feeling cold and covered himself with the blanket.

When all was said and done, was it here – in one of these twenty-six places – that Verlangen came face to face with the hereafter, this depraved detective?

Face to face with the hereafter? thought Van Veeteren. Depraved? What are these words that come bubbling up from the swampy backwaters of my brain? Where is my imagination leading me? It's time to switch off now. Very definitely time.

He switched off the light and fell asleep.

And in that transparent moment between waking and sleeping it dawned on him how it would be possible to proceed.

It was obvious. Like adding one plus one.

29

'What?' said Inspector Krause. 'I'm not quite with you.'

'All right,' said Van Veeteren. 'I'll say it again. I take it you remember that you pressed a button on your enormous computer last week and produced a list of names of places connected with a specific time in a railway timetable . . . 14.42? It must have been last Wednesday or Thursday, I'd—'

'Of course,' said Krause indignantly. 'That wasn't what I was wondering about. I just thought the *Chief Inspector*—'

'Hang on!' interrupted Van Veeteren. 'I have not been associated with those words for five years now – that ought to have been long enough for you to grasp the fact.'

'I apologize,' said Krause. 'Don't take it personally. But what was that business about the telephone?'

'Do you know that Verlangen rang and spoke to his grandson about three weeks ago?'

'I'd heard about it, yes . . .'

'What I want to know is where he rang from.'

'Really? And how . . . ?'

'It shouldn't be all that difficult, nowadays.'

'But if he rang from his mobile, you can't just—'

'Mobile?'

'Yes.'

'Not everybody has a mobile phone, despite what some people seem to think. Maarten Verlangen didn't have one, for instance.'

'Really? Well, I didn't think—'

'That means he must have rung from a land line. Perhaps from a card- or coin-operated phone, and so it shouldn't be all that difficult for a bright detective inspector to track down where he rang from.'

'I see,' said Krause. 'I'm with you.'

'Good. A telephone call to the Vargas family in Palitzer-straat. Their number is 213 32 35. At some point between the twelfth and eighteenth of April, let's say, to be generous. And then it would be interesting to compare—'

'To compare that with the list of train times,' said Krause. 'I'm with you now – and I'm sorry that we didn't catch on to this earlier. I'll deal with it straight away. Where can I contact the *Chief* . . . Where can I get in touch with you when I'm ready?'

'Krantze's antiquarian bookshop,' said Van Veeteren. 'I'll be sitting here, waiting. I assume you have my number?'

Krause confirmed that he did, and asked if there was anything else.

There wasn't – not for the moment, at least, Van Veeteren assured him, and hung up. Leaned back in his armchair and picked up Nooteboom again.

One plus one, as already said.

★

Couldn't they have worked this out themselves? he wondered while he was waiting. Why had they failed to put two and two together?

A telephone call from an unknown place, and a train journey to an unknown place.

Those were the only two leads they had, but even so they hadn't managed to link them together. How useless can you get?

But on the other hand, perhaps it wasn't all that odd. No doubt Verlangen's disappearance was not very high up among the priorities at the Maardam police station. Perhaps it wasn't even on their agenda at all? Most probably it was just one item among hundreds of others reported to the police – maybe it was more realistic to congratulate Münster on noticing the link with the G File?

The *possible* link. He suddenly began to feel highly sceptical about the whole business, and regretted having sounded so arrogant when talking to Krause. How big were the odds on the two lines of investigation actually crossing? Was it even going to be possible to establish where Verlangen had telephoned from on that day in April? What if there were a dozen calls during the time he had specified, all coming from places on the list? Saaren or Malbork, for instance. What if Belle Vargas's husband's ancient and ailing parents lived somewhere up there, and they were in the habit of ringing every day to discuss this and that, and report on their bowel movements?

I'm a conceited ass, he told himself grimly, going into the

kitchenette to boil some water for coffee. They ought to be grateful that I resigned in good time.

'Two,' said Krause. 'There are two possible alternatives regarding that phone call.'

'Good,' said Van Veeteren. 'I'm grateful that you took the time to look into it.'

'Eh?' said Krause.

'I said I was grate— Never mind. Let's hear it.'

'Yes, well,' said Krause, clearing his throat. 'I've been through all the incoming calls between the twelfth and the eighteenth of April with fru Vargas . . . in accordance with the information I received from the telephone company. And there are two which she thinks are the most likely candidates. The only possibilities, in fact. We might be able to exclude one of them when we've spoken to her husband, but we haven't been able to do that yet . . .'

'I see,' said Van Veeteren. 'What are the two places, then?'

'Karpatz and Kaalbringen,' said Krause. 'On the fourteenth and the sixteenth respectively. I . . . er . . . I'm aware that Kaal-bringen is on the 14.42 list.'

'But Karpatz isn't.'

'No,' said Krause. 'So . . .'

'So one could say that there is really only one alternative?'

'Well, yes,' said Krause. 'If it fits in, yes.'

I knew it, thought Van Veeteren. Dammit all! Thanks to some worn out synapse in my shrivelled mind, I knew it. It's incredible, it's simply not possible to get round or go past certain patterns . . .

'Hello?'

'Yes?'

'Are you still there, *Chief Inspector*? Oops, sorry, I—'

'No problem. So, Kaalbringen it is . . . We'd better not invest too much hope in this lead, but if it's now thought that it's worth the trouble of searching for Maarten Verlangen, well, it's an indication of the way the wind is blowing. Don't you think?'

'Definitely,' said Krause. I must say that I—'

'You and your colleagues will have to take account of your priorities, of course – I understand that completely. Many thanks for your efforts, maybe we shall have reason to discuss the matter further.'

Krause muttered something inaudible, Van Veeteren thanked him once more, and hung up.

He's too young, he thought. He wasn't involved in the Hennan case, and he wasn't there in Kaalbringen.

But Intendent Münster was involved!

In both cases.

He flopped down on his chair.

Both cases? Linden and Kaalbringen? Van Veeteren shook his head. What an arbitrary connection . . .

Needless to say Jaan G. Hennan and the axe murderer in the little northern coastal town had nothing to do with each other: it was only in his own private version of history that the two phenomena were linked.

Kaalbringen and the G File.

But it was remarkable nevertheless. Patterns and conformity to law? he thought. Damn it all! He rolled a cigarette and lit it, wondering whether he should contact Münster straight away, or whether he should give himself a little more time to think things over and consider practicalities. He soon opted for the latter alternative – whatever conclusions and plans of action he decided on, there was no urgency involved. One thing was clear: Verlangen had been missing for at least three weeks, and even if his adventures and fate since leaving Maardam were hidden in mist and murky circumstances, it was likely that his daughter's clear-eyed pessimism was well founded.

There was very little chance of him still being alive.

Van Veeteren sighed. Asked himself on what grounds he could justify that conclusion, but he couldn't find any. He left the kitchenette and went to fetch the bottle of port instead.

Chief of Police Hiller was busy planting two dwarf acacias when Münster entered his office on the fourth floor.

Münster would have been quite unable to judge that the plants were acacias (although he might have guessed that they were a dwarf variant in view of the fact that they were tiny), but Hiller explained the details even before he had time to sit down.

It was almost like a formal introduction, Münster thought. Acacia, dwarf – Münster, Detective Intendent! Pleased to meet you. The chief of police had spread newspapers out over his desk, and was working in his shirt sleeves with his tie thrown back over his shoulder. He was filling terracotta-coloured pots with soil from a large plastic sack, and pressing it down carefully with his thumbs so that the plants were upright and steady.

'This Verlangen business,' he said without interrupting his work or even looking up.

'Yes?' said Münster.

'I heard about it by accident. We mustn't let ourselves be carried away by our imaginations.'

'What exactly do you mean, sir?' asked Münster.

'What I say,' said Hiller. 'Verlangen is an old cheat who has gone missing, that's all. He used to work for us at one time, and he was involved in an old investigation – but that's all history now. History, Münster!'

'History,' said Münster.

'It's ninety-nine per cent certain that he fell into some canal or other in a drunken state – he's had problems with his drinking habits. He'll turn up again one of these days. This is not a matter we can waste our resources on . . . we've got our hands full as it is. What with that confounded business out at Bossingen and those accursed Holt brothers, and—'

'I know what we're busy with,' said Münster, interrupting the flow. 'No, I don't think Reinhart intends to assign officers to chasing up Verlangen. But I'll tell him what your views are as soon as I see him, I promise you that.'

'Excellent,' said Hiller. 'Of course. Where is he, by the way?'

'Who? Reinhart?'

'Yes. Wasn't he the person we were talking about?'

'Yes, of course. I assume he's interrogating racists down at number twenty-two. The ones who burnt that school down.'

'Racists? Ugh, yes. I understand. Anyway, that's all I wanted to say. You can get back to your work.'

'Thank you,' said Münster.

How old is he now? he thought as he closed the door behind him and heard Hiller saying something encouraging to his acacias. Isn't it about time he was pensioned off?

Mahler had set up the pieces and was scribbling away in a black notebook when Van Veeteren came down to their usual table at The Society on Saturday evening.

'New poems?' he asked.

'New is an exaggeration,' said Mahler. 'Poems is an exaggeration. It's modern abstractions concerning the black hole, rather. Unrhymed.'

'That sounds like good fun,' said Van Veeteren.

'I know. I think that's exactly what I shall call it, in fact. What do you reckon?'

'Modern Abstractions Concerning the Black Hole?'

'Yes.'

'It sounds more like a summary of contents than a book title.

Mahler stroked his beard thoughtfully.

'Maybe. Ah well, I suppose I'd better fill it out with some kind of content first. In any case, it'll be my twelfth. I think that will be enough.'

'Your twelfth? Congratulations! A full dozen! . . . How long have you been at it?'

'It's forty years since my debut. According to my calculations that works out at just over two words a day.'

'Two words a day?' said Van Veeteren. 'That can't be all that much of a burden, surely?'

'Rubbish,' said Mahler. 'It's the hardest grind in the world. You're forgetting that each word is chosen from a range of twenty-five thousand: and every time you choose a new word, you have to start again at the very beginning.'

Van Veeteren gestured to the waiter that two more beers were required, and gave that some thought.

'I beg your pardon,' he said. 'You're right, of course. I was a bit too presumptuous. Shall we play?'

'It's your turn for white,' said Mahler, lighting a cigar.

'That was due to a lack of concentration. You ought to have noticed that bishop on G6. Is something worrying you?'

Van Veeteren started setting up the pieces for the next game.

'In a way,' he said. 'It's an old story that seems to have come to life again.'

Mahler emptied his beer glass and dried out his beard.

'Nothing can compete with an old, old story. Is it something I know about?'

Van Veeteren picked up one of the black knights and weighed it in his hand for a while before replying.

'I'd have thought so,' he said. 'The G File.'

'The G File!' exclaimed Mahler. 'The only blot in your copybook. Of course! What's happened?'

There was a disgusting level of amusement and curiosity in the old poet's tone of voice, Van Veeteren thought: but perhaps that was nothing to get upset about. Nor to worry about. If there was anybody – apart from Ulrike, of course – in whom he could confide his irresolution, it was Mahler. That was something he had learned over the years. As far as secrecy was concerned, talking to Mahler was like talking into a well. An unusually talented well, in which words and confidential comments sank down to the bottom and lay there in hermetically sealed silence for all eternity.

And from where a word or two – extremely carefully chosen words – came bouncing back.

He lit another cigarette, and started telling the tale.

'Soup with unknown ingredients,' was Mahler's summary twenty minutes later. 'And the police have no intention of intervening, I gather?'

'No more than routine. They have plenty of other things on their plate, it seems – not least that damned Nazi business, for instance. I have to say that I understand their position. The Verlangen link is about as substantial as a strand of hair.'

Mahler said nothing for a while.

'I don't agree,' he said eventually. 'As far as I can judge, there must be something in this. Don't ask me what and how – but surely it would be even more strange if Verlangen's disappearance *didn't* have anything to do with G? Don't you think? After that note on the kitchen table and that telephone call.'

'I know,' muttered Van Veeteren. 'I'm not senile yet. Not quite, at least.'

'Same here,' said Mahler, looking grim. 'As clear in the head as a mountain stream and as morally aware as a thirteen-year-old. It would presumably be easier to live if one were not like that. What are you thinking of doing?'

Van Veeteren inhaled deeply and thought it over.

'I don't know.'

'Don't know?'

Mahler eyed him critically through the smoke. Van Veeteren said nothing.

'You're lying. You know only too bloody well what you're going to do.'

Van Veeteren turned the chessboard round so that the white pieces were on Mahler's side.

'All right, I'm lying. I intend driving up to Kaalbringen, of course. One of these days. It's your move, herr Poet.'

'That's what I thought you'd do,' said Mahler, adjusting his glasses. 'But hold your tongue now, you're disturbing my concentration.'

30

Ulrike was sceptical.

'I can understand that you are concerned,' she said. 'Of course I can. But I can't understand what you think you can gain by driving up there.'

They had eaten a simple boeuf bourguignon, drunk a bottle of 1997 Barolo with it, and he had told her about the two cases.

Both G and the axe murderer in Kaalbringen. She knew quite a bit about them, but had no idea about his collisions with G when he was a child and a teenager.

Until now. It was good to get them off his chest, he thought, and it dawned on him that this was the first time he had ever spoken to anybody about Adam Bronstein.

This is ridiculous, he thought. Why should anybody hide away sources of agony like that for a whole lifetime? Why should anybody avoid talking about them? For Christ's sake, it was over fifty years ago!

And he wondered about that 'anybody'. Was it a euphemism for 'I' or for 'men'? One of those didn't exclude the other, of course – but perhaps there was some sort of general tendency? Being a woman and a thinking being, Ulrike found it difficult to understand the point of this type of agonizing stricture, and wondered if he had any more skeletons in the cupboard of his soul.

'A whole cemetery,' he assured her. 'But driving up to Kaalbringen is a way of confronting them. One of them, at least.'

But she didn't buy that without any objections.

'I think your soul is shallower than that,' she said with a sudden smile.

'Really?'

'You want to meet that Bausen character again, that's what it boils down to.'

'But I would never—'

'Spend a few evenings playing chess and drinking wine. Come on, own up – you hypocrite! You surely don't really think you're going to find Verlangen up there?'

'I have no intention of answering that question,' said Van Veeteren.

As he sat in his car, driving through the sun-drenched, flat countryside, he thought about her views and objections – and decided that he couldn't have expressed them any better himself.

Did he really imagine that he would be able to achieve anything?

Was he convinced it would be possible to find out what had happened to this drunken ex-private detective? This former cheat of a police officer? Did he really seriously believe that Verlangen actually was/had been in Kaalbringen?

Wasn't this journey rather a sort of . . . symbolic exercise? A wishy-washy gesture?

Kaalbringen. This sleepy little coastal town where he had spent six late summer weeks ten – no, nine – years ago together with Münster, while they were investigating one of the most remarkable cases he had come across during all his years as a detective chief inspector.

Was there any real possibility, then? That Verlangen had come here of all places?

Wasn't it in fact just as Ulrike had suspected – that he longed to see Bausen again? To sit over a chessboard with an old, well-kept wine in his overgrown garden, theorizing over this and that, and re-experiencing a mood and a sort of affinity that he couldn't quite put his finger on, or express in words?

But which had existed even so. To the highest degree. Surely one didn't need to put absolutely everything into words, for God's sake?

He gazed out over the rolling fields, and noticed that he was drumming his fingers on the steering wheel. Was that unease or expectation? Hard to say. And difficult to lay bare motives and private reasons, as always. But it was a remarkable coincidence, that couldn't be denied. The fact that the G File should open up again in this way after fifteen years, and lead him back to Kaalbringen of all places. A coincidence that was so unlikely, one couldn't avoid looking into it in more detail. *Trying* to look into it, at least.

A sign? A key point in the pattern?

It occurred to him that perhaps it was in fact a penitential journey. To make up for the fact that he hadn't saved the life of that Jewish boy fifty years ago. The fact that he had allowed Jaan G. Hennan to go free on that and subsequent occasions.

And the fact that he had not kept in touch with Chief Inspector Bausen as he ought to have done . . . And for Erich's sake?

And now suddenly a door had opened up slightly and given him an opportunity to put things right. Could it be justifiable to see things in that light?

Bullshit, he thought. What could Erich possibly have to do with all this?

It was the same old story. The statistician's presumptuous attempt to understand a set of circumstances about which he didn't have a clue. Five seconds at the scene, and he thinks he can detect the whiff of eternity!

He searched through the CDs and decided on Schnittke. Piercing strings and persistent rhythms that ought to sharpen up his thoughts.

G. This was all about the G File, nothing else, he decided. No vague personal motives, no circumlocutions, just the one familiar question that had been dogging him for fifteen years.

Who killed Barbara Clarissa Hennan?

Or rather, how had Jaan G. Hennan managed her death?

He recalled that somebody had used the term 'classic' during the course of the investigation in 1987. Münster or

Reinhart, most likely. Or was it Verlangen himself? In any case, it was not difficult to agree with that judgement – the business of the dead American woman in the empty swimming pool in Linden was so clinically simple that it almost lacked substance. No complicating circumstances. No confusing leads heading off in different directions. No distorted motives or unclear testimonies.

Just a dead woman and one point two million guilders. And G.

And that Verlangen.

Yes, he had to admit that in fact Verlangen had disturbed the classical set-up. The down-at-heel private detective's role had been perplexing even at the time, and of course it was no less perplexing now.

And what if he was now playing some sort of role again? Was that plausible?

Could it in fact be that Verlangen had discovered a clue implicating G? How? How could that possibly have happened? The most likely circumstance would have to be that he had simply stumbled upon something – especially in view of the state he was in.

And those words on the phone to his grandson.

Now I know how he did it!

Was it true? Was it possible? How the hell had this wretched ex-detective managed to discover the answer to a question that Van Veeteren himself had been struggling with for fifteen years?

Preposterous, he thought, increasing his speed. Absolutely preposterous.

Nevertheless, it was just as difficult to see any other possible solution.

He stopped for lunch at a roadside cafe not far from Ulming. He telephoned Bausen and told him he would be arriving in about two hours. Bausen sounded more energetic than ever. Van Veeteren had trouble in believing that he was turned seventy, but that was the fact of the matter. Perhaps the years he had spent in prison had done him good in some paradoxical way: he had seemed to imply that in the previous day's telephone conversation, and maybe it was not so surprising.

With regard to the concept of penance, that is.

A bank of cloud had slowly worked its way in from the north-west during the morning, and only five minutes after he had set off again after lunch, the rain came pelting down. The countryside, the broad rolling plains, lost both their contours and their colours: he replaced Schnittke with Preisner, and found the right mood music in Kieślowski again.

> *Though I speak with the tongues of men and of angels,*
> *and have not charity, I am become as sounding brass*
> *or a tinkling cymbal.*

That was true. During the last five years he had learned that they were hellishly true, those famous words from the First Letter to the Corinthians.

It had taken almost a whole lifetime, but he had learned that in the end.

Better late than never. He ate two mint pastilles to get rid of the unpleasant taste of old lunch, and started thinking about Erich, his dead son.

And he noticed that it hardly hurt any more.

By the time he parked outside Bausen's house in Kaalbringen it had stopped raining, and he was able to register that it looked exactly as he had remembered it.

More or less overgrown. More or less impenetrable. Now, as then, it was impossible to make out the house from the street: bushes, trees, creepers and tall grass had interwoven to form a living wall, and it was obvious that Bausen had not rented out his house during his seven-year absence. It had simply been allowed to become even more overgrown – and why not?

He entered through the gate, identified the rudimentary opening that was supposed to be a path, ducked down and began walking through the jungle.

Bausen was sitting in a basket chair on the roofed patio, reading a book. Everything here seemed familiar as well: the rattan table with the two chairs, empty crates and all kinds of junk next to the walls. Now as then. A broken bicycle, an oar together with half an oar, and something that Van Veeteren suspected might well be a rolled-up yoga mat. The chessboard and the red-painted box with the pieces was on the top shelf of a wonky bookcase full of tins of paint and various tools.

Bausen saw him approaching, and his face lit up.

'Good God,' he said. 'Younger and more handsome than ever.'

'You took the words out of my mouth,' said Van Veeteren. 'Are you growing old backwards, or how do you do it?'

There was good reason for the flattery, no doubt about that. Bausen did not look like a man of seventy-something. More like the picture of good health itself – short and wiry, in possession of quite a lot of greyish-white hair, and a pair of eyes in his handsomely hewn face that seemed to have been stolen from a fourteen-year-old.

He stood up and shook hands.

'Yoga,' he said. 'That's half the secret. I started while I was in jail, and saw no reason to stop. Forty-five minutes a day – I'm more nimble now than I was when I got confirmed.'

Van Veeteren nodded.

'What's the other half?'

Bausen laughed.

'What the hell do you think? A woman, of course . . . Not a formal relationship, but we meet now and again. It's the main point of being alive, in fact. For God's sake, at my age it's high time to start getting a grip of things. Good to see you. Long time no see.'

'Nine years,' said Van Veeteren. 'Anyway, here I am again.'

'On the trail of another murderer. Whatever, I can assure you that it's not the same one as last time. Would you like a beer and a sandwich? I thought maybe we could have a more substantial meal a bit later on.'

'A beer and a sandwich is precisely what I'd hoped for,' said Van Veeteren. 'I take it we can sit out here?'

'Of course we can,' said Bausen. 'Yes, I remember you were partial to that. Sit down and enjoy the surroundings, and I'll go and fetch the necessary.'

Van Veeteren sat down on the other basket chair, and sighed with pleasure.

What a marvellous jungle, he thought. And what a lovely man.

Bausen studied the two photographs carefully.

'So these are the two gentlemen you are looking for, are they? I can't say off the top of my head that I recognize either of them – but my knowledge of what's going on in town isn't what it once was. For obvious reasons.'

'For obvious reasons,' agreed Van Veeteren. 'No, I can well imagine that. And I'm afraid these photos are not all that up to date, as they say. Hennan is now fifteen years older than that, and Verlangen's daughter didn't have a better one of him than this. It was taken around Christmas four years ago.'

'He looks a bit worse for wear,' said Bausen.

'I don't suppose he's become any better,' said Van Veeteren. 'If he's still alive.'

'Do you think he might not be?'

Van Veeteren shrugged.

'It's just that I can't see any sensible reason for him hiding away. The last sign of life was that telephone call from here three weeks ago.'

Bausen frowned.

'I see. And so the hypothesis is that he's fallen foul of Jaan G. Hennan in some way or other, is that right?'

'Hypothesis and hypothesis,' said Van Veeteren.

'Hmm. What has Hennan been up to for the last fifteen years? Do you know anything about that?'

'I don't, and nor does anybody else. He seems to have left the country at some point during the autumn of 1987, and there's no trace of him after that. Until this little pointer from Verlangen, that is . . . Which would suggest that he's come back.'

Bausen examined the photographs again for a while. Van Veeteren took a swig of the dark beer and leaned back in the creaking chair.

'It's just a passing thought on my part, of course,' he said. 'If it had been anywhere else but Kaalbringen, I'd probably have let it pass.'

'You don't say?' said Bausen with a trace of mild irony in his voice. 'But still, you are here now – and why not? If we can combine your passing thought with a few decent wines and a few decent games of chess, it might be worth the trouble, perhaps? No matter what?'

'That's exactly what I thought,' said Van Veeteren. 'How's the wine cellar? Is it still there?'

'It certainly is. And most of the bottles have benefited from seven years of unintended maturing, I can assure you of that.'

'Excellent. Do you still have good relations with the police force here in town nowadays? It would make things easier if we could get a bit of assistance from them.'

'I don't have much to do with them,' admitted Bausen. 'It was Kropke and Moerk when you were last here – I suppose you remember them?'

'I certainly do,' said Van Veeteren. 'Are they still around?'

'Inspector Moerk is still here. Kropke went off to Groenstadt a few years ago. We have a new chief of police called deKlerk – he's said to be good, but I hardly know him . . .'

'For natural reasons?' wondered Van Veeteren.

'For natural reasons,' said Bausen with a chuckle. 'He took over six months after me in any case – there was some sort of delay. Anyway, I don't think they would put any obstacles in our way if we made an effort to contact them. After all, it's more or less police business anyway, and I don't expect them to be snowed under at this time of year. The tourist season hasn't got under way yet. If Verlangen has been in Kaalbringen, he must have taken a room somewhere, and it shouldn't be too difficult to find out about that detail at least.'

'I hope not. What about Inspector Moerk . . . ?'

'What about her?'

'She was a pretty competent woman, I seem to recall. I assume she hasn't got worse as the years have passed – if you'll forgive me for putting it like that.'

'No problem,' said Bausen, looking thoughtful. 'No, she's no doubt still pretty reliable. And we've sorted out the little difficulties we used to have . . . But this G character – if I understand you rightly you have a rather special relationship with him, is that right?'

Van Veeteren thought for a few seconds before responding.

'A special relationship?' he said eventually. 'Yes, you could say that again. To tell you the truth . . . well, to tell you the truth that bastard has been haunting me ever since I was running around in short trousers. If there's anybody I'd like to see on the scaffold, he's the one. Then I could grow old in peace and dignity.'

Bausen smiled briefly.

'You haven't been working as a police officer for the last few years, is that right?'

'Yes, that's right. I became a bookseller in my old age, as I said. I've responded to requests to help out in a few investigations, but it's really only the G File that could get me working full on again.'

'Really?' Bausen leaned back and observed him with interest. 'So it's not really true, what you said about letting it pass if it hadn't been for the Kaalbringen connection?'

Van Veeteren thought it over again.

'Probably not,' he said. 'I suppose I'd have found it difficult not to follow the scent no matter where it came from or led to. It's one of those stories which prevents you from sleeping at night unless you've searched under every single stone.'

'That happens,' said Bausen. 'There are some things you just can't let drop.'

'I know that you are fully aware of that,' said Van Veeteren.

They drank a toast, then sat in silence for some time.

'Anyway,' said Bausen after a while. 'Let's pay the police station a visit tomorrow morning. But for now, I suggest a game before our evening meal. As you are a guest, you can start with white.'

'Thank you for that,' said Van Veeteren. 'Do I remember rightly that your weakness was the Nimzo-Indian defence? I have that impression.'

'I know nothing about that,' said Bausen. 'But don't build up any hopes. I have no weaknesses at all nowadays.'

31

After a little more thought – and in the clear light of morning from a more or less cloudless sky – Bausen decided that he had no great desire to visit the Kaalbringen police station in Kleinmarckt. He had not set foot inside it for nine years, and after admitting his doubts to Van Veeteren he restricted his input on this occasion to a telephone call, informing his former colleagues of the *Chief Inspector*'s wish to pay them a visit and discuss certain circumstances.

It transpired that Chief of Police deKlerk was otherwise engaged in some other place that Saturday, but Inspector Moerk would be in her office until three o'clock, she maintained, and immediately expressed her great delight at the prospect of meeting Van Veeteren again after all these years.

At least, that is how Bausen described the situation when he had concluded the call, and explained that the coast was clear.

'It's ten o'clock now,' he also said. 'Shall we say that we can meet at the Blue Ship for a bite of lunch at about one? Do you remember where it is?'

'I remember every alley and every lamp-post in this godforsaken dump,' Van Veeteren assured him in a friendly tone. 'Okay, let's say one o'clock.'

Beate Moerk looked as if she had aged about nine months over the past nine years, but nevertheless she had passed a certain borderline, he thought. She made no secret of what lay behind this process of elegant refinement.

'I've settled down,' she informed him after serving coffee and a plate of Danish pastries from Sylvie's Luxury Bakery, which was still next door to the police station. 'I'm married and have two children now. You only live once so I thought I might as well.'

'Very sensible,' said Van Veeteren. 'Pass on greetings to your husband, and congratulate him. I have no doubt he feels that the gods have been smiling down on him.'

'Phuh,' said Moerk, blushing modestly. 'I gather you have something special to discuss, *Chief Inspector?*'

'I'm a bookseller now,' said Van Veeteren. 'I spend my time in an antiquarian bookshop nowadays. Can't we just use first names?'

'Have you left the police force?' she wondered in surprise. 'Bausen said nothing about that.'

'Five-and-a-half years ago. But I must admit that I have a request that falls under the nasty old heading of a police investigation . . . A case that has been haunting me over the years, you could say.'

She suddenly looked genuinely worried.

'Yes, Bausen indicated something of the sort. If we can do

anything to help, then of course we'll bend over backwards to do so. And all that . . .'

Van Veeteren nodded and stroked his hand over his cheeks and chin – and realized that he hadn't shaved.

'I'd be most grateful if you could,' he said. 'Anyway, if I explain the situation in broad outline, perhaps you'll be able to do a few things for me. It shouldn't be too difficult to establish whether I'm on the right track or not. In the first place it concerns a certain person by the name of Maarten Verlangen . . .'

It was the third time in the last few days that he had run through the case concerning G in detail – for Ulrike, Bausen and now Beate Moerk – and it was beginning to dawn on him that he felt more isolated from all that had happened on each occasion that he had to sit down and recount it.

Maybe that wasn't so odd. The book of memoirs he intended writing was going to focus on Jaan G. Hennan, so presumably there was – in addition to all the other traumatic detritus – something mysterious and hidden away in this old story. Something which resisted all forms of description and narration. Or at least resisted his own tentative efforts to do so.

Perhaps it is a sort of therapy that one day will cure me? he thought, somewhat surprised. The effort, that is. But hell's bells, why can't I just amputate the whole confounded business and be rid of it, once and for all?

In any case, Beate Moerk seemed obviously interested. She

asked questions, made notes and asked him to explain things in more detail – so the whole procedure lasted three cups of coffee, the same number of Danish pastries and getting on for an hour.

But it went much more quickly when it came to deciding what the Kaalbringen police could do to help. After all, there was not a lot they could be asked to do. Apart from trying to find Verlangen.

Or at least to find something that indicated that he had been there. Some three weeks ago. Round about 15 April. Moerk promised to start digging immediately: all being well it should only take a few hours to check every hotel and boarding house in the area, and irrespective of the outcome she should be able to ring Bausen some time that evening.

As far as Jaan G. Hennan was concerned, there was nothing much more they could do than something similar – but preferably somewhat more discreet. Mind you, if he really was in Kaalbringen and was using his real name, it should not be especially difficult to find him. But on the other hand, if for some reason or another he preferred to use a different identity, that would change the situation of course.

And they would have to take into account the fact that G – wherever he happened to be – was a free man with the same human rights as everybody else.

Van Veeteren informed Inspector Moerk that – unless something startling happened – he would be setting off for Maardam at some point during Sunday evening, and wondered if he might invite her to a late lunch or early dinner before he left Kaalbringen. Tomorrow, in other words. Presumably together with Bausen.

He thought she hesitated for a moment before accepting the invitation in principle – but she would have to discuss the situation with her husband first.

That was perfectly understandable, of course. She promised to give a definite answer when she telephoned Bausen that evening.

He had just over an hour to fill before meeting Bausen for lunch, and took a walk down to the harbour and marina. He crossed over Fisktorget, and found he remembered the names of all the buildings and streets in or running into the square: Dooms gränd, Esplanaden, See Warf – the hotel he had stayed at for over a month – Hoistraat and Minders steeg.

It felt odd to be wandering around here again – the axe-murderer case was almost a decade ago now: but the years had drained away at an amazing speed, as they usually did when memories had not been kept alive by return visits. The boats bobbing up and down in the marina could well have been exactly the same as the ones all that time ago, he thought, and the same applied to the ice cream kiosk and the girls lounging around in front of it. And when he branched off onto the well-worn pedestrian and cycle path through the trees of Stadsskogen, he found himself expecting to come across the place where one of the victims had fallen foul of the murderer's razor-sharp axe.

But he didn't. He emerged into the Rikken housing estate

without having found the exact scene of the crime, and realized that even when you see again and recognize familiar places, there has to be an allotted portion of illusion and imagination. Of course.

As he tried to find the nearest way up to the Blue Ship restaurant, he thought instead about whether he would recognize G if he happened to bump into him.

It was far from certain, he had to admit. At least if it was just a brief meeting with other people milling about.

And if – against all the odds, he reckoned – G really was here in Kaalbringen and wanted to remain incognito, he had every chance of succeeding in his desire.

In the space of fifteen years you could change every single cell in your body twice over, if Van Veeteren remembered rightly what he had been taught in his biology classes at the beginning of time. You were at the mercy of inherent forces, as it were.

He arrived at the Blue Ship in somewhat low spirits at a couple of minutes past one. Bausen had already found a window table with a good view.

Let's face it, Van Veeteren thought: Ulrike was no doubt right. This is not going to lead anywhere.

But it's good fun to meet an old axe murderer again. No doubt about that.

Beate Moerk set about what she needed to do the moment Van Veeteren left Kaalbringen police station. According to the telephone directory there were twenty-eight different hotels and bed-and-breakfast establishments where one could spend a night or indeed several in the little coastal town of Kaalbringen, but she knew that only about half of them were open all the year round. Exactly which ones were open in the usually rainy and not exactly hospitable month of April was not clear, but she decided to leave nothing to chance and started telephoning them all, one after another in alphabetical order.

After five calls she changed tactics, and decided to use faxes instead of the telephone. Half an hour later she had sent out information to all the establishments unlikely still to be in hibernation – but she did not include a photograph of Verlangen: he looked even worse in a photocopy than he did in reality – like a botched Rorschach test or something of that sort – and in view of the fact that Van Veeteren could see no reason why he would have used a false name, she hoped it didn't matter.

Did they have the name Maarten Verlangen in their register? At some time in April this year – or at any other time, come to that. Please reply to Inspector Moerk at the police station. Preferably before five p.m. Negative or positive. It was a routine matter, but urgent.

By the time she left her office at a few minutes past three she had received eleven responses to the nineteen faxes she had sent out.

All of them negative.

*

Van Veeteren had one victory and one draw in the bag from the games played the previous evening, but by the end of the Saturday afternoon session Bausen had caught up at 2–2. They decided to postpone a deciding game until later in the evening, and combined (but with Bausen very much in charge) to prepare a stew containing rosada fish, hake, mussels, olives, garlic, peeled tomatoes and parsley, which they ate together with saffron rice and thin slices of crispy bacon.

Van Veeteren was inclined to agree with Bausen that it was top hole, as good as it damned well gets. Especially when, as in this case, it was washed down by a bottle of white Mersault, one of the very last of the 1973 vintage in Bausen's cellar.

Black coffee, a calvados and a Monte Canario cigar to round things off – and, Bausen claimed, heavenly bliss would be attained via a few simple but testing yoga exercises recommended by Iyenghir, devised specially for people with stiff loins and excessively short rear thigh muscles. Men over the age of fifteen, in other words.

But not immediately after the food, God forbid. On this occasion it was merely theoretical.

The theory had barely been considered when Inspector Moerk rang to report on progress. Bausen handed the telephone over to Van Veeteren, who was half-lying on the sofa as he heard that seventeen of the nineteen hotels and B&B establishments had responded, and could confirm that they had not had as a customer anybody by the name of Maarten Verlangen – nor anybody corresponding to the description of him – during the past year. Neither in April nor in any other month.

So two establishments had not responded – probably because they had not yet opened for the season, but Moerk promised to look into that the following day. When she was also looking forward to having dinner with the two former chief inspectors at round about six p.m.

'Where?' she wondered.

Van Veeteren consulted his host briefly, and they agreed on Fisherman's Friend. The best ought to be good enough – and it promised to be that sort of occasion.

Inspector Moerk assured them that she was very pleased about the choice of venue, and wished the two gentlemen a very pleasant evening. What were they doing, in fact? Wine and cigarettes and chess, presumably?

What? Yoga exercises?

She wished them sweet dreams and hoped they would soon be feeling better, then hung up. Van Veeteren noticed that he was smiling.

The fifth game was soon abandoned as a draw, and as the time was merely half past eleven – and there was still half a bottle of 1991 Conde de Valdemar on the table – they agreed to make one final attempt at a decider.

And so it was turned two o'clock when Bausen blew out the last candle with a tired sigh. Another draw. Final result: 3–3.

'That's life,' said Van Veeteren when he had settled down in the guest bed and Bausen stood in the doorway to wish him goodnight. 'We're unbeatable, that's the bottom line.'

'I agree entirely,' said Bausen. 'And if that bastard G really is here in Kaalbringen, we'll nail him as well.'

'Let's hope and pray that's the case,' said Van Veeteren. 'If Inspector Moerk has found Verlangen by tomorrow, I'll bet there's another chapter still to be written in this damned story, despite everything.'

But that was not the case.

'I'm sorry,' she said when they had sat down at a table in the conservatory at Fisherman's Friend, 'but it seems this Verlangen character hasn't been here in Kaalbringen after all. Or at least, he hasn't spent a night in any of our hotels or B&B establishments.'

'How carefully have you checked?' asked Bausen.

'As carefully as you could ask for,' said Moerk. 'But it's not a hundred per cent certain, of course. There's a youth hostel, and quite a few private guest rooms as well – but only in the summer months. If he really has spent a few days here, it's possible that he stayed with a friend, don't you think?'

'It's possible,' Van Veeteren agreed, 'but unlikely. For one thing he doesn't have any friends, according to his daughter . . . Not outside Maardam, at least. And for another, a good friend would surely have reported the fact if he'd gone missing. But it's obvious that we're clutching at straws here in any case. He might simply have been passing through, for instance.'

'The phone call to his grandson came from the railway station, is that right?' asked Moerk.

'Unfortunately, yes,' said Van Veeteren. 'A call box. That could mean that he was on his way to somewhere else, of course – or back to Maardam: but I don't think there's much point in speculating about that.'

'But all this doesn't exclude the possibility that he did spend a few days here,' said Bausen optimistically. 'And that's the main point, isn't it?'

Van Veeteren nodded. *The main point?* he wondered as he gazed out over the sea, which was grey and ambivalent in the gathering dusk a hundred metres or so below them. What does he mean by *the main point?*

The waiter came with menus, and there was a pause in the conversation. Van Veeteren leafed through the stiff pages, and was reminded that this wasn't just any old restaurant. It was perched up on a limestone cliff a kilometre or so east of Kaalbringen where the coast became much more hilly – and especially out here in the conservatory one seemed to be floating on air. Seagulls were soaring around in the gentle breeze, and he recalled – or thought he recalled in any case – that he had been sitting at this very same table with Bausen nine years ago. They had eaten turbot, if he remembered rightly, and drunk a bottle of Sauternes . . .

That was before the antiquarian bookshop. Before Ulrike. Before Erich's death.

It wasn't even a decade ago, he thought. But nevertheless my life has changed fundamentally. I'd never have believed it at that time.

Bausen cleared his throat, and Van Veeteren came back down to earth.

'Anyway,' he said. 'Verlangen has presumably been here, at least for an hour or two – but I don't think we're going to get any further than that at the moment. I'm inclined to regard this meal as pleasure rather than business.'

'Objection!' said Bausen. 'Why restrict yourself to either– or when you can have both–and? I assume there's a Wanted notice out on this Verlangen character, and that you and your colleagues at the police station are keeping your eyes skinned.'

There seemed to be a degree of irony in this assumption, and Beate Moerk smiled in order to show that she had realized that.

'We're all eyes, yes,' she said. 'If we discover the slightest trace of Verlangen – or of Jaan G. Hennan come to that – I promise that you will hear about it without delay. Maardam CID, I assume?'

'Well,' said Van Veeteren, digging out a business card. 'I think it would be better if you contacted Krantze's Antiquarian Bookshop in the first place. Discretion is the better part of valour, as they say.'

'I'm with you,' said Moerk, accepting the card. 'But to tell you the truth, I'm feeling a bit peckish. I thought our agreement included a bite to eat?'

'Absolutely right,' said Bausen. 'There's a time for everything, and now it's time to eat.'

During the drive back home he listened to Pergolesi and thought about his memoirs.

Or rather, why he had interrupted them.

The bottom line was that it was not – as he often maintained and used as an excuse – the murder investigation involving G that had thrown a spanner into the works. Of course not. It just so happened that the two things occurred at the same time, and he needed an excuse.

In fact, the need to document his life as a police officer seemed to have deserted him. The need to put things into perspective and put into words his thirty years in the police force . . . The feeling that something had to be justified.

It was like photographs from a disappointing holiday, he had thought: a sort of retroactive authenticity – the actual time had been wasted, and the documentation replaced the experience.

For better or worse, of course. 'It's always possible to make glittering poetry out of the most appalling failures – and thank goodness for that!' was something Mahler had once confided in him, and no doubt there was some sort of parallel to that thought in his memoirs project . . . But the urge had left him, the vague desire to record his deeds in print – and of course Ulrike played a vital role in this. As in so much else.

The words from Corinthians came to him once again, and he wondered what his life would have been like if Ulrike had not sailed into it. *If* and *if not* . . . There was no point in speculating on that as well, of course, and he soon grew tired of trying to find alternative ways through the swamp that was life. His own path had turned out the way it did, and if he thought about it at all nowadays, it was with gratitude. Despite everything.

The year of grace?

He abandoned fiction and tried to think about so-called realities instead – about Maarten Verlangen and about Jaan G. Hennan.

What did he know?

Nothing at all, to be honest.

But what did he think, then?

Or, *What did he have good reason to think?* Preferably with the aid of a reasonably sharp razor blade, presumably.

He thought for a while and replaced Pergolesi with Bruckner.

Something had happened.

Indubitably, as they say.

Verlangen had been on to something. But had come too close to the fire and burnt himself.

Not just burnt himself. Been burnt up.

Been killed.

By G?

That was what he had been telling himself ever since Verlangen's daughter had come to the bookshop and told her tale. But did he really have good reason to believe that?

Did he have any reason at all?

Were the remains of Maarten Verlangen really buried somewhere in the Kaalbringen area (or dumped in the sea) – while the renowned former Chief Inspector Van Veeteren was sitting back in his warm car, fleeing the scene? Was that the reality? For an all-seeing and all-knowing and mildly ironic God?

Good reason? Bullshit.

I shall never sort this out, he suddenly thought. I shall never know how the murder of Barbara Clarissa Hennan was carried out. Nor what happened to Maarten Verlangen fifteen years later.

Nor will anybody else.

It's so damned irritating, but that's the way it is.

Former Chief Inspector Van Veeteren was deceiving himself on this point to some extent; but a whole summer would pass before he realized this – and by then he had long since forgotten that he had given up all hope.

AUGUST–SEPTEMBER

32

The body was found on Saturday, 24 August, by a mushroom picker called Jadwiga Tiller.

It was a beautiful summer's day. Fru Tiller was seventy-five years old and had been out all day in the mixed coniferous and deciduous woodland between the villages of Hildeshejm and Wilgersee several kilometres to the east of Kaalbringen with her husband Adrian. They had parked next to the log piles at the side of one of the many dirt roads running through the forest and down to the sea, and after a few hours had filled almost two carrier bags with top-class cep mushrooms. She used to tell her friends Vera Felder and Grete Lauderwegs how she had a good nose for mushrooms – 'I can smell them a mile off!' she used to say: 'Even when I'm blind I'll still be able to sniff 'em out!' – and thanks to that ability she found herself exploring a little copse of young beech trees, searching around among dead leaves and old husks without finding anything edible, and then stumbled upon a human being.

Or rather, a dead body. In an advanced stage of decomposition – there didn't seem to be much more left than a few rags of clothing and a skeleton, and for a confused moment

Jadwiga Tiller wondered if *that* was the smell that had seduced her. She suddenly felt very dizzy, and had to sit down on a felled tree trunk in order to recover her composure.

That took a few seconds. Then she cupped her hands around her mouth and shouted: 'Kolihoo! Kolihoo!'

That was the call she and her husband had been using in the woods while mushrooming for thirty years or more, and sure enough she heard Adrian's 'Kolihoo!' response from not very far away.

'Kolihoo! Kolihoo!' she shouted again. 'Come here! Now! I've found a dead body!'

There was a crashing and crackling in among the bushes, then Adrian Tiller appeared. He continued walking in the direction pointed out by his wife's shaking index finger and saw what she had seen. Despite the fact that he was an ex-soldier and had seen most of what there was to see, he also felt rather dizzy and needed to sit down. He flopped down beside his wife, took off his checked cap and wiped his brow with his shirt sleeve.

'We must ring the police,' he said. 'It's fifteen thirty-five.'

'I understand that we must ring the police,' she said, 'but why on earth are you telling me what time it is?'

'Because the police always want to know what time it is when they are investigating a crime,' said Adrian Tiller.

Inspector Beate Moerk did not place as much importance on the time of the discovery as herr Tiller had done when she sat in her office at the police station in Kaalbringen that evening, trying to sum up what had emerged about the dead man after the first few hectic hours. The body was rather too old for that to matter.

But in any case, it was a man. Evidently somewhere between sixty and seventy. A hundred and eighty centimetres tall, and at the time of his death wearing jeans, worn-out deck shoes, a simple cotton shirt and a blue denim jacket. All the items of clothing were in quite a bad way, of course. According to a very early estimate by the pathologist, the man had been dead for between four and six months, and the cause of death was almost certainly a shot in the head. The bullet had entered through his left temple, and exited through the right one. The gun had been quite a large calibre, possibly a Berenger or a Pinchmann, and the shot had been from close quarters, only half a metre away. No bullet or empty cartridge case had been found.

Nor were there any identification papers or personal belongings, apart from a packet of chewing gum, Dentro Fruit, with two uneaten tablets remaining, in his right-hand pocket. It was impossible to take fingerprints in view of the advanced state of decay, but the Centre for Forensic Medicine in Maardam would be able to establish his dental profile – the body was on its way there for all the usual tests and analyses.

Nothing of interest had been found at or in the vicinity of the place where the corpse had been discovered, nor was there any trace of a fight or struggle. There was a reasonably accessible and usable track only about thirty metres away from the depression in the ground where the copse was located, so it could be that the body had been transported into the woods by car, either dead or still alive.

There was nothing to suggest with certainty that suicide was an impossibility, but no weapon had been found, and the body had been so well covered by leaves and twigs that it seemed likely that somebody had tried to conceal it from the eyes of the world.

Murder, in other words. Inspector Moerk knew that they were landed with a murder investigation. She had said as much in blunt but restrained terms to Chief of Police de-Klerk, who was unfortunately attending a family gathering in Aarlach that Saturday, but now – at a few minutes past nine in the evening – ought to be in his car on the way back home from there (travelling in the opposite direction to the hearse with the dead body in it, but bound to pass it at some unknown point, Moerk realized with a suppressed smile), and would turn up at the police station before half past ten.

That is what he had promised, at least: it wasn't any old day that they were faced with a murder investigation in Kaalbringen, and if you were chief of police, you had appropriate obligations.

Moerk drank the last drop of tea and put her notes away in a yellow folder. Leaned back on her desk chair and gazed out through the open window into the mild autumnal darkness.

Murder? she thought. And then it dawned on her who the dead man must be.

★

She ought to have realized sooner, of course: but it had been
a stressful afternoon and evening. She had been telephoned
from the police station by Constable Bang shortly after four,
and it had been full steam ahead ever since. For the moment,
at least, the case was the responsibility of the Kaalbringen
police – although the scene-of-crime and pathology officers
had been sent from Oostwerdingen.

It had been all go without much pause for thought: interviews with the elderly mushroom-pickers who had found the
body; detailed discussions with the pathologist Meegerwijk
and with Intendent Struenlee, who was in charge of the
scene-of-crime team; off-putting comments to a few journal-
ists who had somehow (Bang?) got wind of the circumstances
. . . Telephone calls here, faxes there: and it was only now – at
nine o'clock in the evening – that she had the chance to sit
down and think things over for a while.

But that was enough. She suddenly knew who it was that
had been shot in the head out there at Hildeshejm . . . Well,
knew was perhaps a bit of an exaggeration: but if anybody
had asked her to place a bet on the outcome, she would
have had no hesitation in wagering a considerable sum.

It had to be that private detective – what the hell was his
name?

It took her quite a while to dig up the name from the lists
of all the others in the archives of Kaalbringen police station,
but she found it in the end.

Verlangen.

Maarten Baudewijn Verlangen, to be precise – and of
course it was necessary to be precise in a case like this.

So that was the way it was. The missing former private detective whom that renowned ex-detective chief inspector had been here looking for at the beginning of May. But whom they had failed to find. Because there was no trace of him. Full stop.

Moerk nodded decisively to herself. Then she picked up the receiver and telephoned her husband Franek – and for a brief moment when she heard his voice was overcome by a deep-seated longing to be with him.

She told him as much, but he assured her that there was no need to hurry: the two children were asleep, he was busy painting, and was more than happy to wait for her with a bottle of red wine and a big hug until after midnight, if necessary. How was it going with the dead body? he wondered.

She told him she thought she knew who it was – but that she would have to stay at the police station and make a few telephone calls. And also report to deKlerk when he eventually condescended to turn up. But she assured him that as soon as all this was cleared up, she would hasten home and switch off all the lights.

He laughed, and bade her welcome.

She sat there thinking for a while before picking up the telephone again: it was not easy to decide what to do, but she eventually ignored all the objections and rang Bausen's home number. Since she assumed that the antiquarian bookshop in Maardam would not be open at half past nine on a Saturday evening . . .

And since Van Veeteren had not given her his home number.

★

Van Veeteren was telephoned in turn by Bausen half an hour later – and having absorbed the brief, preliminary information he was even more convinced than Inspector Moerk that the dead body really was that of Maarten Verlangen.

There were no especially rational arguments to support that hypothesis as yet, of course: but he had dreamt about Jaan G. Hennan (in a remarkable role as a ruthless, horned judge in some kind of war crimes trial) just a couple of nights ago, and he had solved that day's chess problem in the *Allgemejne* in less than half a minute, which was some kind of record.

There was something in the air, in other words; and after Bausen's phone call he realized what it was.

Water had flowed under the bridge, to use an image referring to another element, and it was time to write another chapter in the G File.

But this really must be the last one, he thought when he had hung up and returned to his sofa, Ulrike and the Finnish film on Channel 4. I really must put a full stop at the end of all this pretty soon.

There was a time for everything, of course, but there were limits.

'Who was that?' asked Ulrike, lifting up Stravinsky and placing him underneath the blanket.

'Bausen,' said Van Veeteren. 'They think they've found Verlangen.'

Ulrike picked up the remote control and switched off the sound.

'The private detective?'

'Yes.'

'Dead?'

'Yes. Since April, or thereabouts. Just as I'd thought.'

'How?'

'How what?'

'How did he die?'

'Shot through the head.'

'What the hell . . . ?'

'You heard right.'

'Good Lord! Up in Kaalbringen, then?'

'Just outside – although they haven't officially identified him yet.'

'But they think it's him?'

'Evidently. It will be confirmed tomorrow.'

Ulrike nodded. Lifted up the cat again and tickled him absent-mindedly under his chin while watching the silent pictures on the television screen. Half a minute passed.

'What are you going to—'

'We'll see,' said Van Veeteren. 'It's a matter for the police.'

'Of course.'

He sat there thinking for a while, wondering what to say next.

'Well, anybody's allowed to go chasing shadows,' he said in due course. 'But assumed murders are not something that should be placed on the desk of an antiquarian bookseller.'

'Of course not,' said Ulrike Fremdli. 'Where have I heard that before?'

33

Chief of Police deKlerk tugged thoughtfully at his right ear-lobe, and glared at Inspector Beate Moerk.

'So, that's the way the land lies, is it?' he said. 'I have to say I'm sceptical.'

Moerk shrugged. She was used to her boss being sceptical. To exaggerate only slightly one could say that it was his most dominant characteristic.

Doubt. She had been working with him for just over six years now, and knew that he never bought a pig in a poke. Never took anything for granted. If somebody came into the police station and told deKlerk that there was a red car parked illegally in the square, he could well ask the complainant if it was certain that it wasn't blue. Or if in fact it wasn't a tractor.

This had irritated her at first, but in time he had somehow gained her respect as a police officer and perhaps also as a person; she had learned to tolerate his scepticism. There had even been occasions when they had discussed the merits of 'healthy scepticism as a method', as he liked to put it: and at times she had been forced to accept that he was right.

But only at times. And he never took it to absurd lengths, thank goodness. Despite everything, Chief of Police deKlerk

389

had a wife and three children – there was no doubt at all about that.

'It's a working hypothesis,' she said, beginning to collect her papers. 'That's all.'

'We don't even know yet if it is Verlangen.'

'That's true.'

'It's fifteen years since that murder at Linden – always assuming it was a murder.'

'I know.'

'That old *Chief Inspector* is a bit obsessed by this business, isn't he?'

'Obsessed?' said Moerk. 'No, I wouldn't say that. But he has a nose that would make any foxhound you like turn green with envy.'

'A nose?' said deKlerk. 'Hmm.'

Inspector Moerk checked her watch: it was twenty past eleven.

'Anyway,' said deKlerk, tugging at the other earlobe in order to balance things out. 'If we really do find Jaan G. Hennan here in Kaalbringen, that would shift the goalposts, of course. But we'd better wait until the dead man has been identified.'

'I'm pretty convinced that it is Verlangen in fact,' said Moerk, stuffing the half-sorted documents nonchalantly into her briefcase. 'My female intuition tells me that.'

'Does it tell you anything else?'

'Oh, yes. It tells me for instance that it will be absolutely essential for us to find witnesses. Witnesses who actually saw him here in April. We'll need pictures in the newspapers, to urge people to get in touch with us, and maybe also—'

'Stop!' said deKlerk. 'Not so fast. We'll think about that if and when we know it really is him. That ought to become clear tomorrow, am I right?'

'If it is Verlangen, that will be confirmed tomorrow, yes. If it's somebody else we shall have to wait a bit longer.'

'You're right,' said deKlerk. 'But it's time to lock up now – it's nearly midnight, for God's sake.'

'But this is a murder investigation,' said Moerk.

He raised an eyebrow, and she could see that she had given herself away – that he realized she was almost enjoying herself.

I'm perverse, she thought. But it's nine years since the last time, so it's surely not all that odd?

On the way home she began to recall what had actually happened nine years ago, and she noticed that the hairs on her lower arms were standing on end.

Detective Intendent Münster had devoted most of Sunday to his children.

In the morning he had driven his daughter Marieke to a farmhouse just outside Loewingen where there were four horses and two of her friends, and soon afterwards he had left his son Bart outside the Richter Stadium, from where a bus would take him to a football match in Linzhuisen.

And now, in the afternoon, he had lain down in the double bed and started wrestling with Edwina, aged fifteen months.

Synn, his wife, was enjoying a day off and he didn't know

where she was. Probably on a beach somewhere with one or two of her friends: it was a fine day with a clear sky and not much wind, and when he had seen her last, in between the trips with his other children, he had caught a glimpse of bath towels and a lunch basket – but part of their agreement was that he wouldn't ask where she was going.

Edwina fell asleep at about three, and Münster a quarter of an hour later.

Edwina was not woken up by the telephone ringing, but her father was.

Van Veeteren.

The *Chief Inspector*.

On a Sunday afternoon? Münster suddenly felt wider awake than he had done for half a year.

'Yes, of course,' he said. 'I do have a moment.'

'Excellent,' said Van Veeteren. 'I'm sorry if I'm disturbing your family idyll at the weekend . . .'

'Cut the crap,' said Münster. 'What's it about?'

I've grown bolder as the years have passed, he thought. Much bolder.

'Verlangen,' said Van Veeteren. 'Maarten Verlangen. I take it you remember who he is?'

'Yes, I remember him,' said Münster, moving out into the hall so as not to disturb Edwina's sleep.

'He's dead,' said Van Veeteren. 'They've found him at last. Up in Kaalbringen – that business last spring was fire as well as smoke.'

Münster tried to recall details of the circumstances surrounding Verlangen's disappearance.

'I see,' he said. 'And he's . . . well . . .'

'Murdered, yes. Shot through the head at close range. The body was found in some woods yesterday, and it was identified officially today. I've spoken to both his daughter and the police in Kaalbringen – Beate Moerk, if you remember her?'

'Good God,' said Münster, and he could feel his face flushing as he heard her name. 'So there's a link, in other words.'

'I would think so,' said Van Veeteren. 'In any case they're going to need some help up there, and bearing in mind that old case of ours . . . well, I think it would be as well if we were to take it over.'

We? thought Münster, conducting a rapid analysis of the implications of that little pronoun.

'I mean the Maardam CID of course,' said Van Veeteren.

Do you really? Münster thought.

'Of course. I can take it up with Hiller if you like,' he said. 'But then, you never know how—'

'I've already spoken to him,' said Van Veeteren. 'There won't be any problems.'

'You've already spoken to—'

'Yes.'

'I see.'

'But it would be as well if the right people were in charge of it, don't you think?'

'What? The right people? What do you mean by that, *Chief*—'

'Somebody with a bit of background knowledge. About both G and Kaalbringen. If you follow me?'

Münster understood all right, but hesitated a few seconds before responding.

'I see what you mean,' he said eventually. 'I suppose you're right. I'd better have a word with Hiller and see what he has to say. I'm up to my neck in quite a lot of other things, but all being well, I suppose . . .'

The *Chief Inspector* cleared his throat and Münster paused.

'Hmm, yes, well – you won't need to. As I already had him on the line, well, you know . . . You'll be driving up to Kaalbringen tomorrow morning, and you'll have Rooth with you. Anyway, I'm pleased that it's you who'll be in charge.'

And he hung up. Münster remained standing for quite some time, staring at the telephone. What's going on? he thought. Didn't he start by hoping he wasn't disturbing my peace and quiet? Remarkable.

Or rather, typical.

He checked that Edwina was still asleep, then went into the kitchen to brew some black coffee.

Beate Moerk felt cold.

And with good reason. She was sitting stark naked on a high, uncomfortable stool; and it could well have been a few degrees warmer in the room.

'That's enough now,' she said. 'I have pains in every single muscle, plus two more that don't exist.'

'Calm down, my lovely,' said Franek. 'Just one more minute – and remember that you are destined to become a part of posterity. Sit still now!'

'Bollocks to posterity! We agreed on half an hour – it must be at least three quarters by now.'

He peered at her over the top of his easel. Closed one eye and screwed up the other one.

'An advantage of nude models is that they can't have wrist-watches on,' he said. 'But all right, we'll shut up shop now. Come and have a look at the miracle. I'll be damned if the outline of your hips wouldn't tempt a Greek god to descend from Mount Olympus!'

'Rubbish!' said Moerk, wriggling into her nightgown. 'Blind paint dauber, he talk through back of nightcap.'

She walked round his easel, crept under his arm and took a look at the half-finished painting. It was beginning to look rather good, and she liked what he had said about her hips.

'But make no mistake about it, it's damned uncomfortable on that stool. I hadn't really appreciated the role of suffering in art until I agreed to be a model for you.'

'Exactly,' he said. 'It can be strenuous, but that's the point. Sinews and muscles have to be working, and be seen to be doing so – there are far too many nymphs who just lie back and relax.'

'Some people would say that there are far too many naked women's bodies in art.'

'That's a misunderstanding,' he said. 'It's a bit like saying that authors should stop using metaphors . . . But maybe they should, in fact?'

He looked seriously thoughtful, as he often did when a stray thought struck home. He sucked at the handle of a paintbrush and puckered his brow. That's why I love him, she thought – because he can take everything, absolutely every-thing, extremely seriously.

Because he is so genuinely interested in everything apart from himself.

She tied the belt of her dressing gown. I overestimate him, she thought. But so what? It'll be good to have a bit to spare when I start to grow tired of him.

But with a bit of luck that moment was still a long way away. Beate Moerk had met Franek Lapter at a party two months after the notorious Axeman Affair nine years ago, and she had become pregnant the second time they made love. 'Glad to hear it,' Franek had said when she told him. 'We could both have done much worse.'

They had got married, bought an old house in Limminger-weg on the way to Groonfelt, had their first child and conceived their second within eighteen months. For about the same length of time she had been on leave from her job as an inspector in the Kaalbringen police district. There were those who thought that a good mother ought to stay at home longer with her offspring, but Franek had his studio upstairs and was very reluctant not to be in constant touch with Leon and Myra. Or at least, not for very many hours at a time. So what the hell?

And now there was a murder to be dealt with again.

I love my husband and my children, she thought. But I love them even more if I'm allowed to follow up my perverse interests as well.

'You're a bit obsessed by that dead body, aren't you?' he said as he started washing his paint brushes in the sink. 'I gather it was that private detective from Maardam – is that right?'

Beate pulled on a pair of thick woollen stockings, sat up straight and nodded.

'Verlangen.' she said. 'Yes, he's the dead man.'

'And so you and the Klerk bloke are going to have to solve it, are you?'

'Do you think we're not up to it?'

He paused for a moment.

'You are. And one genius is enough to solve an equation. The others only need to be on hand to make coffee and not get in the way.'

'An equation?' wondered Moerk with a laugh. 'I never managed more than a C in maths when I was at school. But it's not a matter of equations. It's more about cleaning out the stables. And besides, we're going to get some outside help.'

'Outside help? Is it that serious?'

It dawned on her that while Franek was able to sympathize with the problems of an injured fly, he sometimes found it difficult to assess the significance of more important entities. Perhaps it was a sort of necessity in his make-up. For the sake of balance. For his art.

The outsider's perspective, as it was called.

Nonsense, she thought. I overestimate his world of ideas as well. But that's par for the course when you're in love with somebody, isn't it?

'What do you mean? Surely a murder is serious?'

He had finished washing his brushes now. He dried his hands on his checked flannel shirt and walked towards her with his arms stretched out wide. When he embraced her, she could hear her ribs creaking.

'Of course,' he said. 'Can I have another look at your buttocks? I think there was a line that I might not have mastered completely.'

'Grrr,' she said, and bit his shoulder. 'I'm glad you're no longer employing freelance models.'

They took their time over the love-making, and it was just as satisfying as usual: but when he rolled over reluctantly into his half of the bed and fell asleep, she lay awake for at least another hour.

It wasn't especially surprising, of course. The unknown and well-known names hovered like a mantra inside her head: Barbara Hennan – Jaan G. Hennan – Maarten Verlangen – Chief Inspector Van Veeteren . . .

And Münster! She hadn't met Intendent Münster for nine years. They hadn't even telephoned one another; it was as if they had some kind of unspoken agreement not to. But nevertheless she remembered – as clearly as if it had been yesterday – how close they had come to having an affair. To going to bed together.

In the middle of an axe-killer case! Perhaps it somehow had something to do with the perversity of it all?

And tomorrow he was going to turn up again in Kaalbringen.

It's a good job I've got married and settled down, she thought. Thank God for that.

34

The news about the dead body in the mushroom woods received not only a prominent headline on the front page plus half the available space on the placards, but also a three-quarter-page article in Monday's *de Journaal*, the most important daily newspaper in Kaalbringen and the district.

They also reproduced the old photograph of Verlangen, the one that had been sent round local hotels at the beginning of May, and a message from the Kaalbringen police urging all conscientious citizens to be in touch if they thought they had seen the man in the picture at any time in the spring or early summer.

Or – needless to say – if they had any other kind of information which might be useful in connection with the investigation. The article went on to stress that the quiet little coastal town had been free from serious crime in recent years, but now it seemed as if the real world had arrived here. Nowhere was safe in these global times, not even Kaalbringen, maintained the author of the article Hermann Schalke – who had reported on the notorious axe-murderer case almost ten years ago, and had no difficulty in remembering it. No difficulty at all. Our beautiful world is full of evil and our lives are afflicted by its henchmen and proselytes, he wrote philo-sophically at the end of his gloomy disquisition.

And as early as the morning of this warm August Monday the first three informants duly turned up at the police station, where Chief of Police deKlerk was so kind as to share the duties with Inspector Moerk and Probationer Stiller – the latter was only twenty-four years old, had only just graduated from the police college, and had only been in post and in the seaside town since the middle of February.

However, as things turned out all three informants could be dismissed as of no interest quite quickly. Two of them thought they had seen Verlangen as recently as July, by which time he had been dead for at least a month – and the third was a young but already seriously wayward man by the name of Dan Wonkers. He was obviously quite drunk despite the early hour, and equally obviously unwilling to pass on his red-hot tip unless there was some sort of financial reward hovering in the wings.

There was not, and he left the police station shouting indignantly about bourgeois swine and police fascists – famil-iar phrases he had most probably had imprinted in his brain while drinking his mother's milk and listening to his father, whose name was Holger Wonkers, a red-wine radical from the sixties who had survived against all the odds. He was famous – or rather infamous – in Kaalbringen and beyond.

Shortly after lunch, however – it was a quarter past one and more or less simultaneous with the arrival of Intendent

Münster and Inspector Rooth from Maardam – a witness of a totally different character turned up at the police station.

Her name was Katrine Zilpen, and as Inspector Moerk was acquainted with at least one of their newly arrived colleagues – and Probationer Stiller had not yet arrived back after lunch – it was the chief of police himself who received her in his office.

'Please sit down,' he started by saying. 'I gather you have come in connection with our appeal for information, is that right? I understand your name is fru Zilpen.'

'Correct,' said Katrine Zilpen, sitting down opposite him. 'I don't know if we've met?'

'I very much doubt it,' said deKlerk.

She was quite a powerfully built woman in her forties, and he thought he recognized her – in the way he had begun to recognize more or less every inhabitant of the town. After eight years you might not be able to register and memorize twenty-two thousand faces, he used to think: but quite a lot even so.

And Katrine Zilpen's face was anything but anonymous. By no means. She had a large mop of copper-red hair arranged in a sort of pineapple shape with the aid of a thin yellow scarf. Clean-cut features and green eyes in a shade that reminded him of the salt-water aquarium in Oudenberg where he had worked as a guide for a few summer months in his younger days.

If she were a little less vulgar she would be rather pretty, he thought.

She made a sort of rolling movement with her lips (he

assumed she had applied new lipstick just before entering through the glass doors of the police station, and that doing so before making visits was one of her routines), and she asked if she might smoke. He produced a packet of cigarettes from a drawer and slid it over to her side of the desk. Then he moved his chair a little closer to the open window and asked her to explain why she had come.

'That dead body,' she began after lighting a cigarette. 'I think I've seen him. While he was still alive, that is.'

'Excellent,' said deKlerk. 'Where and when?'

'At Geraldine's. Some time in April, I can't remember exactly when, but it was a weekend in any case.'

'Geraldine's?' said deKlerk, frowning. 'Do you mean that camping site?'

'Camping and camping. Geraldine's Caravan Club, it's called. It only has stationary caravans – I don't know if you'd call that a camping site.'

'Out at Wilgersee?'

'Not quite as far away as that. It's a kilometre or so after Fishermen's Friend. It's a field with ten or a dozen caravans – my husband and I sometimes go there for the weekend. To get away from it all. We've been doing so for quite a few years.'

'April?' wondered deKlerk.

'There's heating in the caravans. In most of them, at least. She lives there all the year round.'

'Who does?'

'Geraldine Szczok. The woman who owns the place.'

DeKlerk asked her to spell the name, and wrote it down.

'So that's where you met the man we want information about, is it?'

'I think so.'

'Think so?'

'I can't be a hundred per cent certain, of course. I'm not an idiot.'

'I understand.'

'Do you? Good. Anyway, I saw that photo in the newspaper this morning, and thought straight away that it was that man. But if you don't think it's reliable enough, it doesn't matter to me.'

'Now, now – we're not that finicky, fru Zilpen. Would you like a cup of coffee, by the way?'

'No thank you. I have to be back at work in a quarter of an hour. But I'm pretty sure it was him, anyway. We exchanged a few words with him as well, both my husband and I. He was living in one of the other caravans – most of them were empty because it was so early in the year.'

'So you spoke to him, did you? Excellent. What about?'

'Nothing special. Just a few politeness phrases really . . . About the weather, about what it was like living in a caravan, that sort of thing. We only stayed for two nights, my husband and I. He'd been there for a few days by the time we arrived.'

'And he was still there when you left, was he?'

'Yes. We packed up and went home on the Sunday afternoon. He was sitting outside his caravan. We said goodbye and wished him all the best, the way one does.'

'Did he say his name?'

'Maybe his first name, but I don't remember.'

'Do you recall what he was wearing?'

Zilpen drew deeply on her cigarette and thought for a while.

'No. But nothing unusual in any case. Jeans and jumper and trainers, most likely . . . But I don't remember, to tell you the truth.'

'Did he say why he was staying at the camping site?'

'I think he mentioned to Horst that he had some sort of job in Kaalbringen.'

'Horst?'

'My husband.'

'I see. Some sort of job?'

'I think that's what Horst said . . . But if you are interested you'd better talk to him instead. Or to Geraldine . . . She must surely know a bit more about him.'

'Of course. We shall be in touch with her . . . And no doubt with your husband as well. What about the timing? Can you possibly pin down which weekend in April it was? If you check on a calendar or in a diary, for instance?'

Fru Zilpen shrugged and stubbed out her cigarette.

'I suppose so. Yes, I can try to do that – if you think it's necessary.'

Chief of Police deKlerk cleared his throat.

'It most certainly is necessary, fru Zilpen. And we are very grateful to you for coming to us with this information. Have you left your address and telephone number in the office, so that we can get in touch with you?'

'Of course,' she said, looking ostentatiously at her watch.

'Just one more moment: will you and your husband be at home this evening?'

She thought for a moment.

'I'll be at home. My husband's on night shift and he'll be leaving around six o'clock.'

'Good. Would it be convenient for us to call round before then and ask him a few questions?'

She nodded and stood up.

'I suppose so. You can always ring first, of course.'

'Naturally.'

DeKlerk also stood up and reached out over the desk. As far as he could judge she hesitated for half a second before shaking his hand.

Ah well, he thought. I didn't exactly fall in love with her either.

Van Veeteren and Inspector Ewa Moreno met Belle Vargas at Darms Café in Alexanderplejn on Monday afternoon. It was Belle herself who had suggested that they meet somewhere in town, and when they had sat down at a fairly isolated table, she explained why.

'I need to get away from home. I've taken some days off work . . . I think people might think it was indecent if they found out that I'd carried on working as usual just after my father had been found murdered. But the fact is that I have nothing to do. Those who know what has happened daren't ring and disturb me, my husband's at work, the children are at school and nursery school . . . What the hell is there for me to do? Sit and mourn? Discuss the burial with the undertaker? – Although I suppose I'm not allowed to do that yet anyway . . .'

'It would be as well if you waited for a few days,' said Moreno. 'As you know there are always delays in a situation like this one . . . But I can quite see that it must be hard for you.'

'The eye of the storm,' said Van Veeteren, observing her with a worried furrow between his eyebrows. 'You're sitting in the eye of the storm, and that's never a very pleasant place to be. How do you feel?'

Vargas sighed deeply and shook her head.

'I don't really know,' she said. 'I assumed from the start that he was dead. And knowing the facts is better than not knowing – but I wish he had met a different end. What has happened is . . . well, it's simply awful.'

She scraped her coffee cup against the saucer and blinked away a few tears.

'Murdered?' she said. 'Good God, my poor solitary dad murdered? Did you suspect that?'

Van Veeteren exchanged looks with Moreno.

'No,' he said. 'But to be honest, we're not all that surprised either. You know as well as we do that he had his reasons for travelling up to Kaalbringen. That old business we talked about in the spring. I think . . .'

He paused, suddenly unsure about what to say next. Vargas blew her nose into a paper handkerchief and managed to take a drink of coffee.

'Please forgive me. I thought I was in control of my emotions, but I'm evidently not. Of course, I was aware that he might be in some sort of danger . . . But even so, it is hard to accept what has happened. Has he been lying dead up there in the forest since April?'

'Presumably,' said Van Veeteren. 'But one hopes that people don't suffer once they are dead. We are the ones who suffer, the mourners.'

She looked at him in surprise.

'You may be right,' she said. 'Anyway, I'm suffering, that's for sure.'

'I hope you accept that we need to ask you a few questions,' said Moreno, changing the subject. 'Your father has been murdered, and we want to catch whoever did it.'

'I know,' said Vargas, taking another tissue out of her handbag. 'I assume you want to catch that Hennan character – I take it he must be the one behind all this?'

'That's not impossible,' said Van Veeteren. 'But we don't know yet.'

'Fire away,' said Vargas. 'What do you want to know?'

Van Veeteren took out his yellow notebook.

'We must start by concentrating on the period before your father disappeared from Maardam.'

'Before he disappeared?'

'Yes, the end of March to the fifth or sixth of April, or thereabouts. No matter how you look at it, something must have happened during that time that made your father follow up some kind of lead in connection with Jaan G. Hennan . . . And he must have discovered something relevant to what happened in 1987. We don't have much to go on at the moment

– only that telephone call to your son and the notes on the sheet of paper on the kitchen table. Perhaps he has left some other tracks?'

'Tracks?' said Vargas, looking thoughtful. 'I don't really know . . .'

'He might have made a note somewhere or spoken to a friend, perhaps,' said Moreno.

Vargas gazed blankly at her for a while before responding.

'I don't think he had any friends,' she said. 'He was a terribly lonely person, my father. Why didn't the police worry a bit more about all this in April?'

'Because . . .' began Moreno – but then she realized what she was about to say and bit her tongue.

'Because the importance of my father has increased out of all proportion thanks to the fact that he's been murdered,' said Vargas. 'I understand exactly how things stand, you don't need to elaborate.'

There ensued a few seconds of silence.

'How exactly can I help you?' asked Vargas eventually with an obvious tone of indignation in her voice.

Van Veeteren cleared his throat demonstratively.

'Well,' he said. 'There may be something in what you say, and you may well feel that we are putting you under undue pressure. But I'm afraid we don't have any choice. Is his flat still undisturbed?'

She nodded and bit her lip.

'I'm sorry, I'm a bit . . . You know. Yes, we've been paying the rent every month, despite the fact that I haven't set foot in the place. If you want to examine it, I happen to have the key with me – the same as last time . . .'

'Good,' said Van Veeteren. 'Why delay matters unnecessarily? We can talk to the neighbours while we're at it. Perhaps there might be somebody who had a bit of contact with him, despite what you say.'

Vargas handed over the same key that he had used four months ago.

'Forgive me for saying things I shouldn't,' she said. 'I don't mean to be obstructive – obviously I want you to find my father's murderer.'

'We agree absolutely on that score,' said Van Veeteren. 'We'll do our best, and I suggest you should start work again tomorrow. Forget all that nonsense about people finding things indecent, that's my advice.'

Belle Vargas smiled at him.

'I'll think about that,' she promised.

'And we'll be in touch again with more questions,' said Moreno.

'I know,' said Vargas.

'That was a damned unpleasant reflection on her part,' said Van Veeteren after they had left the cafe. 'What she said about his importance before and after his death.'

'Yes,' said Moreno. 'Unpleasant is putting it mildly.'

'Quite correct, though, for if – a hypothetical assumption, of course – if we did solve this damned G case thanks to the murder of Maarten Verlangen, well, I have to admit that I would have spontaneous feelings of satisfaction . . . But only if I avoided thinking the kind of thoughts she had.'

Moreno thought for a while before answering.

'I understand what you're saying,' she said in the end. 'But what's done is done. Verlangen has been murdered, and the worst possible outcome would be that it didn't lead us any-where . . . We can't ignore the facts and simply indulge in pious thoughts.'

'I agree,' said Van Veeteren. 'You're as bright as a button, young lady. Incidentally, did you think I acted in the cafe as if I were a member of the police force? I even accepted the key.'

'That thought did occur to me,' admitted Moreno.

'That was a hell of a pretty inspector,' said Rooth. 'Do you know if she's married?'

'I've no idea,' said Münster.

'No idea? Wasn't she around when you were last up here?'

'That was nine years ago,' said Münster in annoyance. 'As far as I recall she wasn't married then.'

'Good,' said Rooth. 'So it's about time she settled down now.'

Münster eyed him incredulously.

'You are outrageous, Rooth. Absolutely outrageous. Don't you think we should concentrate on what we've come here to do rather than go on about your putative love life?'

'By all means,' said Rooth. 'Just this once. What have we come here to do, in fact?'

Münster could see that it was in a way a justified question.

'The same old story, I assume,' he said, holding the lift door open for his colleague. 'We've come to solve a murder case . . . to march uninvited over as many thresholds as we can find, nosey around as much as we can in people's private lives, find a killer and make him confess using every method we have at our disposal. Why do you ask?'

Rooth strode out through the hotel entrance and found the afternoon sun in his eyes.

'It's good weather at least,' he said. 'But there's a bit more to it this time than all that marching and noseying around – come on, admit it. Would you recognize Hennan if you were to bump into him, for instance?'

Münster hesitated.

'I think so,' he said. 'Especially if I had the opportunity to spend a bit of time with him. But it's hard to say.'

'I suppose that's why you've been picked out to come here,' said Rooth. 'Because you were quite active fifteen years ago.'

'Presumably,' said Münster. 'Where the hell did we leave the car?'

'Over there,' said Rooth, pointing. 'But I wonder why they picked me . . . I was very much in the background, hardly visible at all.'

'You are my slave, hasn't that dawned on you yet?' said Münster. 'I devise the strategies and you do all the rough work.'

Rooth put half a bar of chocolate into his mouth and chewed it slowly as they crossed over the square.

'I don't believe that,' he said when he had swallowed

enough for him to be able to speak. 'I reckon they decided this case needed a gifted theoretician with a bit of perspicacity. Tell me when you get stuck – you don't need to be ashamed.'

'Good God,' said Münster as he unlocked the car. 'Have you got the address with you at least?'

'Sure,' said Rooth, taking a slip of paper out of his breast pocket. 'Horst Zilpen, Donners Allé 15. If you drive, I'll read the map.'

35

On the way out to Geraldine's Caravan Club Beate Moerk told Probationer Stiller what she knew about the owner. It was as well to warn him what to expect, she thought. He was new to Kaalbringen, after all, and if one could prevent him from putting his foot in it, that would be an advantage, of course.

Geraldine Szczok, or Van der Hahn as she was called before her marriage, belonged to the so-called beat generation. Read too many novels by Kerouac at an early age and ran away from her well-to-do parents (dealers in shoes and leather goods) to California at the end of the fifties. She was away for a year or so, and came back to Kaalbringen with a little son, who she maintained was fathered by no less than Eddie Cochran during a night of passionate love-making in Salinas. But she had no luck in her efforts to inherit part of the fortune of the dead rock singer, and when she eventually turned up at her parents' mansion in Walmaarstraat, carrying Eddie junior, one rainy day in February, she announced that she wanted no more to do with all that beat crap, and had every intention of settling down for good in Kaalbringen and writing a novel.

Their other child, Geraldine's two-year-younger brother Maximilian – yes, they really were called Geraldine and Maximilian, Moerk assured him: no doubt indicative of their parents' aspirations – had died of congenital leukaemia while she was away, and so her parents (or her mother at least) welcomed their runaway daughter and their grandson with open arms. Geraldine settled down in a wing of the mansion and began writing her novel; and when the older generation died (one after the other with a gap of only eight months) some twenty years later, she was still busy with that project.

When Geraldine reached the age of fifty she discovered that she had no money left, sold the family home, married an adventurous plumber by the name of Andrej Szczok and started the caravan site on the top of the hill a few kilometres east of Kaalbringen. After a few years Andrej disappeared in romantic circumstances with a gypsy woman, and to help her recover from that blow Geraldine invested in an unusually well-appointed caravan and settled down to live permanently on the camping site. If Beate Moerk understood it rightly, this must have been round about the beginning of the nineties.

'She sounds like a remarkable woman,' said Probationer Stiller. 'How did the novel go?'

'She hasn't finished it yet,' said Moerk. 'We'd better treat her with kid gloves. They say she can be a bit temperamental.'

'I can well imagine that,' said Stiller, looking somewhat bemused.

★

Geraldine Szczok lived up to her reputation.

She was a large, well-built woman wearing goodness knows how many layers of brightly-coloured garments, well-fitting sandals, a lilac beret, and with a twenty-centimetre-long gold-coloured cigarette-holder. If Moerk's information was correct, she must be about sixty-five by now – and it was difficult to imagine her in a care home or some similar institution ten or twenty years from now. Very difficult.

The camping site itself seemed to be neat and tidy. About ten caravans of various makes and appearance were scattered over a gently sloping field bordering on a strip of mixed deciduous woodland that stretched down the hill as far as the beach and the sea. Most of the caravans seemed to be occupied. People wearing tracksuits were playing volleyball and badminton, or washing up to the accompaniment of music from transistor radios, or simply lounging around and enjoying the midday sun with their newspapers, beer, or mugs of coffee. A few dogs were chasing one another, and some children aged about five or six were busy trying to dismantle a bicycle. At the edge of the woods a dark-skinned man was practising tai chi movements. It all looks very peaceful, Moerk thought. This is what you might call the embodiment of the quality of life.

The site owner's own caravan was blue and canary-yellow in colour, twice the size of the next-largest, with a television aerial and satellite dish, and a plaque with the word *Reception* in neon green.

Sitting in a deckchair in front of it was the one and only

Geraldine Szczok – with a glass of beer on the table beside her, and a ten-kilo cat on her knee.

'Welcome!' she said without standing up or making any other movement requiring energy. 'I gather you are the people from the gendarmerie. Sit yourselves down!'

She took the cigarette holder out of her mouth and pointed it at two much simpler chairs. Moerk and Stiller sat down.

'That's right,' said Moerk. 'A nice place you've got up here.'

'Nice?' said Szczok. 'You have come to the Freedom Republic, make no mistake about that.'

'Interesting,' said Stiller, looking around warily.

'We need a fair amount of information, as I explained earlier,' said Moerk. 'It's to do with a murder – perhaps you've read about it in today's paper?'

'I don't read newspapers,' said Szczok, screwing another cigarette into the holder. 'But fire away.'

Moerk took out the photograph of Verlangen.

'We're told this person stayed at this camping site some time in April. Do you recognize him?'

Szczok looked at the picture for two seconds.

'Of course I bloody recognize him,' she said. 'But it's a crappy photo.'

'I'm afraid it's the only one we have,' said Moerk. 'Can you tell us anything about him?'

'Tell and tell,' said Szczok. 'What do you want to know? He stayed here for just over a week, then disappeared. A shady type.'

'He's been murdered,' said Moerk. 'That's why we're here.'

'So I've gathered,' said Szczok.

'It would be very useful if you could tell us anything about what he was doing while he was here,' said Stiller. 'Did you chat to him at all?'

Szczok looked him up and down with a deep furrow between her made-up eyebrows. As if she were surprised that he could talk.

'He didn't have much to say for himself,' she said. 'And I leave people in peace if they want to be in peace.'

'But I expect you have his name at least,' said Moerk. 'Date of arrival and suchlike.'

'Of course. It's in the book.'

'The book?'

'In there.'

She pointed over her shoulder with her thumb.

'If you'd like to have a look at it, maybe the constable could nip in and fetch it? It's on the shelf over the fridge. Black.'

Stiller nodded and disappeared into the caravan. Szczok lit her cigarette and adjusted her beret. Stiller returned after ten seconds with a thick, black notebook, A4 size.

'*Vamos a ver*,' said Szczok, shooing away the cat and taking hold of the book. She leafed through the pages for a while. Stiller sat down again, Moerk produced her own notebook and waited.

'Here we are! Henry Sommers, yes, that's him. Arrived on the ninth of April, and left about ten days later. He paid in advance for a week, but if he's dead now that's nothing to get upset about . . .'

'Sommers?' said Stiller. 'So he didn't use his real name, then.'

'In the Freedom Republic you can use any name you like,' declared Szczok, taking a swig of beer. 'Would my gendarme friends like a beer?'

Moerk and Stiller shook their heads.

'No, thank you,' said Moerk. 'Which of the caravans did he live in?'

'The one that burned down.'

'Burned down?' said Stiller.

'Burned down, yes.'

'What do you mean?'

'I mean that the bloody caravan burned down, of course.'

Stiller looked at Moerk. Moerk looked at Stiller. Then she cleared her throat.

'Are you saying that the caravan in which Maarten Verlangen . . . or Henry Sommers if you prefer . . . lived – that it burned down?'

'Exactly. You've hit the nail on the head, Constable. Congratulations.'

'When did it happen?' asked Stiller.

Szczok shrugged.

'A few days after he'd disappeared. Round about the twentieth of April, I would think.'

'Why?'

'Why did it burn down?'

'Yes.'

'How the devil should I know? Presumably there was some

cock-up with the electricity. Or the Calor gas. Or maybe somebody set fire to it.'

'I assume you reported it?'

She shook her head.

'No, I didn't.'

'Why?'

'I didn't want to. I don't like busybody fire authorities coming here and nosey-parkering about.'

'What about the insurance people?' wondered Stiller.

'It wasn't insured. It was the worst caravan on the whole site – he wanted it because it was cheapest. I'm glad to be rid of it.'

'How did you discover the fire?' Moerk asked.

'I woke up, of course,' said Szczok, annoyed. 'It was the middle of the night, and it was burning so fiercely that there was a roaring noise. The whole caravan was in flames, I got up and ran out with the extinguisher . . . It didn't help much, and I didn't have a single guest. But then it started raining, and it was all over by dawn.'

'Was . . . was there anything at all left of it?' asked Stiller.

'Nothing at all. A black mark on the ground and a pile of ashes that fitted into two wheelbarrows. Humboldt helped me to clear up.'

'Who's Humboldt?'

'A neighbour. The farmer from over there – he occasionally comes round to help.'

She pointed with her thumb again.

'Damn and blast!' said Moerk.

'I beg your pardon?'

'I said damn and blast, if you don't mind. We're only human, we police officers.'

'Pretty subhuman, I've always thought,' said Szczok. Leaned her head back and poured the rest of the beer down her throat. Then she wiped her mouth with the back of her hand and smiled.

Or looked pleased, at least. Goodness knows why.

'We had hoped we might find something he'd left behind,' said Moerk after a short pause. 'But you say everything has gone. Presumably all his belongings were still in the caravan when it burnt down?'

'As far as I know. I didn't set foot inside it. I suppose I thought he might come back – he'd only been missing for a few days. And we didn't rummage around in all the ash and soot, neither Humboldt nor I.'

Moerk sighed and turned over a page in her notebook.

'Did you speak to him much while he was here?'

'No, hardly a word.'

'Did he say why he wanted to stay here?'

'Yes: because it was cheap. He'd seen my advert down at the railway station.'

'I understand. But what was he going to do here in Kaal-bringen? Did he say anything about that?'

'No. And I don't poke my nose into other people's busi-ness.'

'So we've gathered. But he must surely have said some-thing? . . . Or implied something?'

'Yes, he said he needed a roof over his head for a week. When the week was up he said he needed the caravan for a

few more days. We agreed that he could pay the balance of
what he owed me when he left.'

'And you didn't get any indication of what he was doing
here?'

'No.'

'Did he have any visitors?'

'Not as far as I'm aware.'

'Did he say where he'd come from?'

'No.'

'And he gave his name as Henry Sommers, did he?'

'Yes. It's written down here in the book.'

She tapped at the black cover with her knuckles.

'How did he spend his days? Was he here at the site, or did
he go off somewhere else?'

She thought for a moment.

'I think it varied. But he was away quite a bit, I believe.'

'Am I right in thinking you didn't have many guests round
about that time?'

'Hardly a soul. A few of the caravans were occupied at
the weekends, but that's all. That's the way it usually is in
April . . . But now it's full, as you can see.'

She gestured proudly at all the caravans.

'Yes, so I see,' said Moerk. 'But the other guests – the ones
who stayed here while Henry Sommers was living in his
caravan: I assume they are all noted down in your book?'

'Of course. Not many of them, as I said – and it can be a
bit sensitive as well.'

'Sensitive?'

'Yes. And I'm not all that bothered when it comes to names. As long as they write something down.'

'Why can it be sensitive?'

'Some of them might be married, others might not be.'

'I understand,' said Moerk. 'But I'm afraid we must ask you for the names even so. Obviously we shall be as discreet as possible. Could we take a look at the remains as well?'

'The remains?'

'The place where the caravan used to stand.'

Szczok leaned back in her chair and chuckled.

'Of course you can, for Christ's sake. It's that grey patch over there in the corner.'

She pointed in the direction of a couple playing badminton. Then she leaned over to her left and fished out another bottle of beer from the bucket standing by the caravan wall. It was obvious that she was beginning to get a certain amount of pleasure from the visit, despite everything. From the discussion with the forces of law and order outside the Freedom Republic. Moerk sighed and stood up.

'I'll go and take a look.'

It won't do any harm for Stiller to look after himself for five minutes, she thought.

When they left Geraldine's Caravan Club a quarter of an hour later, Inspector Moerk felt somewhat resigned.

'Well, that didn't produce much that will be of any use to us,' she said.

'No,' said Stiller. 'Not much at all. What did it look like where the caravan had been standing?'

'A greyish-brown patch on the grass,' said Moerk. 'That's all. It's typical that she didn't even bother to report it. It could well have been arson, but I don't suppose we'll ever know now. Did you get anything out of her when you were alone with her?'

'The names of two people who were here at the same time as Verlangen,' said Stiller, tapping his chest where he had a pocket containing his notebook. 'I assume they were both married to different partners, but they'd stayed with her before. Nothing much apart from that . . . We spoke mostly about her book.'

'What?'

'Her novel – the one she started writing forty years ago.'

'Oh, that . . . What did she have to say about that, then?'

Stiller cleared his throat in some embarrassment.

'She claimed it would soon be finished. She asked if I'd like to read it before she sends it to a publisher . . . Apparently it's over two thousand one hundred pages.'

'Good Lord! Two thousand . . .'

'. . . one hundred, yes. I said I'd read it – maybe I spoke too soon, but I didn't want to offend her.'

'Congratulations,' said Moerk. 'So you know what you're going to be doing every night for the next year.'

Stiller nodded.

'It's no big deal. I read quite a lot anyway – and maybe she'll forget about it in any case.'

Moerk looked furtively at him from the side as she backed

the car out of its parking place, and thought that perhaps he had more strings to his bow than she had suspected thus far. This probationer.

'What are you doing?' said Ulrike Fremdli.

'I beg your pardon?' said Van Veeteren, taking off his head-phones. 'What did you say?'

'I wondered what you're doing. It's a quarter past three.'

'I couldn't sleep,' said Van Veeteren. 'I'm lying here, listening to Penderecki.'

'Really?' said Ulrike.

Van Veeteren sat up and made room for her on the sofa. She sat down.

'What does that mean?'

'What does what mean?'

'"Really?" – The way you said it.'

'How did I say it?'

'A bit like Archimedes in the bath tub. It sounded as if you had just understood something.'

'There's quite a lot I understand – you must have noticed that by now.'

She yawned and tried to rub the sleep out of her eyes.

'Yes, of course,' said Van Veeteren. 'But this presumably had something to do with my sleeplessness.'

'Naturally.'

'Naturally?'

'You're not so stupid as to be unaware yourself about why

you can't sleep, surely? And not so stupid that you think I don't understand . . . Not that latter point, at least.'

Van Veeteren thought for a moment.

'You have a point there.'

'Of course I have. What are you going to do about it?'

'I don't really know. Have you any good suggestions?'

'There is only one solution. Why imagine anything else?'

'You think so?'

'You know full well there is. Don't be silly.'

'I'm never silly. But all right, a few days – if you insist.'

'I don't insist.'

'No? Then I suppose I'll have to make the decision off my own bat, then.'

Ulrike burst out laughing and put him in a stranglehold.

'But we'd better sleep on it first,' said Van Veeteren, wriggling free. 'To be honest, I have some misgivings.'

Ulrike became serious.

'Me too,' she said, and all at once – for a fraction of a second – she looked so nakedly serious that his heart missed a beat.

As if . . . As if death had paid them a brief visit at that late hour, but then decided to leave them in peace for a bit longer.

Nasty, he thought. Who is it, allowing us to lift the veil slightly in this way?

36

Intendent Münster found it difficult to shake off the feeling of déjà vu when he sat down next to Rooth in the pale-yellow conference room in Kaalbringen police station on Tuesday morning.

At first he failed to see why the past seemed to be so tangibly close: to be sure, the town and the premises and the peaceful square outside were the same as nine years ago, but the people involved were almost all new. Neither Rooth nor Probationer Stiller nor the new chief of police had been present last time. Only himself and Inspector Moerk.

Beate Moerk. She was the reason, of course. She was a mother-of-two now and must be getting on for forty, he thought; but even so he could see in her face and her eyes the same things that had affected him so much during the axe-murderer case . . . whatever they were. He noticed that she was avoiding looking at him today: that was no doubt a sensible precaution to take at this early stage of proceedings. Rooth had said that she was a hell of a pretty inspector, and even if Rooth was a pathetic case when it came to love and passion, he nevertheless had eyes in his head.

The sun streamed in through the south-facing window, just

as it had done nine years ago. When he thought a little more about it, he realized that of course it was not only Beate Moerk and this familiar room that was making his sense of time somewhat wonky. The G case had been on the agenda even longer – since fifteen years ago, to be precise! – so the feeling of not really being in the present time was perhaps quite natural, in fact.

And it was Maarten Verlangen who was the catalyst, needless to say. The link with then and now. The remains of the down-and-out private detective had been lying out there in the mushroom woods for several months, rotting away. Then they had been discovered – and it was to find out who had put them there that they were sitting in this room now.

In the first place, that is. Officially. What it also involved was another matter. Synergy effects, perhaps one could say. Or rings in the water, as one might have said in the old days.

But irrespective of what one might choose to call it, Münster thought, two CID officers from Maardam would not have been sent out to investigate what had happened to a drifter like Maarten Verlangen if there had not been more ingredients in the soup than those that were floating around on the surface; that was clear.

And there was no sign of Chief Inspector Van Veeteren or Inspector Kropke in the police station on this warm, late-summer Tuesday, Münster reminded himself. Nor was Chief Inspector Bausen at the helm, but instead a certain Intendent deKlerk. Münster had not yet had time to form an opinion of him, but assumed that he was a competent police officer. There was nothing to suggest otherwise, at least. The chief of police had just hung his jacket over the back of his chair, looked somewhat hesitantly at those present, and clapped his hands.

'Well, nice to see you all again,' he said. 'Shall we get going? God willing we'll be served with coffee an hour from now.'

'*In sha'a Allah*,' said Rooth. 'I'm delighted to hear that we have come to somewhere civilized.'

Remember that you are responsible for your own stupidities, Rooth, Münster thought, taking off his jacket as well.

'As a matter of routine, let me just map out the situation to start with,' said deKlerk, opening a file. 'Our colleagues from Maardam are more familiar with the background of this case than the rest of us, so I trust they will feel free to correct me if I get anything wrong.'

Rooth nodded and Münster took out his notebook.

'Anyway,' said deKlerk, 'at the heart of the matter – or at least, that's the theory on the basis of which we are working – is an old case from 1987: the murder of Barbara Clarissa Henning in Linden. We are assuming it was murder, although the facts have never been established. The victim's husband, Jaan G. Hennan, was charged with her murder but found not guilty by the court on the grounds of insufficient evidence. He collected a very large sum from his wife's insurers, and is assumed to have left the country that same year. In the goings-on surrounding the death of Barbara Hennan we find a private detective by the name of Maarten Verlangen: his exact role is unclear in many respects, but he was employed by fru Hennan to keep an eye on her husband just a few days before she was found dead. Verlangen's evidence at the trial seemed to confirm Hennan's alibi. The view of the police and the prosecution team was that Hennan had employed an accomplice to murder his wife, but nothing was ever discovered to support that view, and Hennan was found not guilty. Any comments so far?'

'None at all,' said Rooth. 'Go on.'

'Thank you. Fifteen years later – last spring, to be more precise – Verlangen's daughter informed the police in Maardam that her father had disappeared, and a few pieces of evidence suggest that he was here in Kaalbringen for some days in the middle of April. The reason why he came up here seems to have been that he had come across something to indicate that Jaan G. Hennan was around. *Nota bene* that Hennan is a free man, but Verlangen claimed – in a telephone call to his daughter and a written note found in his flat – that he had come across evidence linking Hennan to the murder of his wife. What this evidence – or possibly even proof – might be, we have as yet no idea. Chief Inspector Van Veeteren, who was in charge of the investigation in 1987, came up to Kaalbringen at the beginning of May to look for Verlangen – or for traces of him, at least. He made contact with Inspector Moerk, who he knows as a result of the previous investigation, and . . .'

He exchanged looks with Beate Moerk, but as she didn't seem keen to take over the account of what had happened, he continued himself.

'. . . and we consulted all the hotels in the area, but received no positive responses. Now we know that this was because we didn't include the camping site next to Fisher-man's Friend in our original inquiries: Geraldine's Caravan Club. Anyway, to come right up to date – three days ago, last Saturday, Maarten Verlangen was found dead in woods not far from Wilgersee. There is no doubt that he was murdered . . . shot through the head with a large-calibre pistol . . . And it is just as certain that he had been lying there since round about the middle of April. Anyway, that's how things stand. Have you anything to say before we take a look at what yesterday's interviews turned up?'

'Say and say,' muttered Rooth. 'That poor devil was on to something – but I've no idea what it could have been.'

'It might have been pure imagination on Verlangen's part, we mustn't forget that,' said Münster.

'You don't get shot on the basis of pure imagination,' said Rooth.

'You can be if you're unlucky,' said Münster. 'But I agree that the Hennan link seems to be pretty strong.'

'It's been a long time,' said Beate Moerk. 'Since last spring, I mean. If that Hennan character really was here in Kaalbrin-gen then, he's had plenty of time to make himself scarce.'

'No doubt about that,' said Münster. 'He could be in Brazil by now. With a new identity and a new appearance. We shall have to hope that he didn't think that would be necessary – that it was sufficient to get Verlangen out of the way.'

'Shall we assume that he really was here in Kaalbringen in April, at least?' asked deKlerk.

'Assume is a bit strong,' said Rooth. 'But let's play with the thought. It does seem a bit far-fetched to think that Verlangen was wrong about him being here, but was killed by him even so . . . Or at least, I think it seems far-fetched.'

'Absolutely right,' said deKlerk. 'We can more or less exclude any such thought.'

'But if he's living here, he must have changed his name at least,' said Moerk. 'There's no Hennan in the telephone directory, and he's not in the register of taxpayers. Would you recognize him if you saw him?'

Münster had already discussed this question with Rooth, and admitted that he wouldn't be a hundred per cent certain. Especially if Hennan consciously tried to change the way he looked in some way or other.

'We've all seen the photo we have of Hennan from 1987,' he said. 'If he's simply grown older in the normal way, presumably any of us ought to be able to recognize him?'

'But he might be wandering around in net stockings and wearing a wig nowadays,' said Rooth. 'That would make it a bit hard to recognize him.'

'Forgive me,' said Probationer Stiller hesitantly, stretching somewhat. 'We're assuming that Verlangen found Hennan, aren't we? So are you suggesting that he's only started wearing net stockings now this summer?'

Rooth scratched his neck, but said nothing. The chief of police nodded.

'Good point, Stiller,' he said. 'Verlangen must have recognized him. And it's via Verlangen that we'll be able to find our way to Hennan. Isn't that right? The more we can find out about what Verlangen was doing here in Kaalbringen in April, the greater our chances of making progress.'

'Very true,' said Münster. 'But there's one thing we mustn't forget. In no circumstances must we pass this link with the G File to the media. If Hennan really is here – living in Kaal-bringen, that is – he'll obviously do a runner and make himself scarce the moment he sees a word about it in the newspapers. With a bit of luck he won't know that Verlangen has left any trails behind. This is absolutely essential if we're going to have any chance of getting anywhere.'

'Is that clear to everybody?' said deKlerk, looking round the table. 'Absolute silence when it comes to Hennan!'

Stiller and Moerk nodded. Rooth yawned, but when he had closed his mouth again he raised a thumb to indicate that he was in agreement.

'Okay,' said deKlerk. 'The big question of course is what the hell it was that Verlangen had discovered. He claimed that he had found clear proof relevant to that old murder case . . . And as Stiller rightly says, if a worn-out private detective can find that, five excessively talented CID officers ought to be able to do the same! Anyway, what happened yesterday? Shall we take Geraldine's Caravan Club first?'

With the aid of her notes and Probationer Stiller's comments, Beate Moerk spent the next twenty minutes reporting on the meeting with Geraldine Szczok. She left out no details – apart from the possibility that Stiller might become an advisory reader of Szczok's novel – and her description of the burnt-down caravan sent Inspector Rooth through the roof.

'That settles it, then!' he bellowed. 'For Christ's sake! That is the coincidence that makes it crystal clear we no longer need to think in terms of coincidences! That arsehole G is behind all this, and he's here in Kaalbringen – all we need to do now is to go out and bring him in!'

'Calm down, Inspector Hothead!' said Münster. 'But I agree with you in principle. On the one hand all possible leads have been lost in the fire, but on the other hand we don't need to speculate any more. We are dealing with Jaan G. Hennan again.'

This conclusion was met with several seconds of silence around the table, after which the chief of police invited Münster to speak again.

'Horst Zilpen,' he said. 'Did he have anything to add to what his wife said?'

'I don't think so,' said Münster. 'He had chatted now and again to Verlangen, but they didn't discuss anything of consequence. When he asked outright where Verlangen had his home, he didn't receive a clear answer. He said he had the impression that Verlangen was an odd bod.'

'It hadn't even occurred to him to ask why Verlangen was staying at the camp site,' added Rooth. 'He's not exactly a bright spark, this Zilpen bloke – and he had a broken nose: I wouldn't be surprised if he'd been a boxer.'

'What has that got to do with the case?' wondered Moerk, looking surprised.

'Nothing, my lovely,' said Rooth. 'It's just that my brain sometimes works overtime, and it can't help making little observations like that. I can't do anything about it.'

'I see,' said Moerk.

'That's the way he is,' said Münster with a shrug.

'To change the subject,' said Rooth, 'isn't it about coffee time?'

DeKlerk looked at the clock and nodded in agreement. Stiller left the room and returned half a minute later with a coffee tray and a dish of Danish pastries.

'Help yourselves,' said the chief of police. 'It's all from Sylvie's Luxury Bakery just round the corner, as I don't need to explain to those of you who've been here before.'

While they were eating and drinking, deKlerk passed around once more the photographs of Jaan G. Hennan from 1987.

'The annoying thing,' said Moerk, 'is that if we published these pictures we might get a positive response straight away. *I* don't recognize him, but of course that doesn't mean that he isn't living here. Kaalbringen isn't just a tiny village after all. Twenty-two thousand souls or thereabouts . . .'

'Quite a large little village,' said Rooth.

'Three of us who live here don't recognize him, anyway,' said deKlerk. 'But then Stiller has only just moved here . . . I assume you're right, though. There's nothing to stop us asking our nearest and dearest – friends and acquaintances . . . Unofficially. We don't need to say what it's all about, do we? We can just ask them if they recognize the man in the photo.'

He looked at Münster and Rooth, hoping for confirmation. Münster nodded.

'That wouldn't do any harm, as far as I can see. As long as we don't make a big fuss about it.'

'All right,' said Moerk.

The chief of police leafed through his papers again, and nobody seemed to have anything to say.

'I suppose the question is what we ought to be doing with ourselves,' said Rooth eventually. 'Personally, I'd like to become more intimately acquainted with Sylvie over the next few weeks – but perhaps you others might like to have something different to do?'

'There is another unpleasant aspect,' said Münster, ignoring Rooth's comments. 'How are we going to be able to link Hennan with the crime, if we manage to find him? We weren't very successful last time, and it's unlikely to be any easier now.'

DeKlerk looked around the room.

'No,' he said. 'The odds seem to be stacked up against us in many ways. This isn't going to be easy.'

'G is a bastard who never gets caught – I've been aware of that for the past fifteen years,' said Rooth.

'Perhaps you could explain what you mean by that,' said Beate Moerk.

'By all means,' said Rooth. 'Laws don't seem to apply to him. He had already got rid of a wife in the States before that business in Linden. If we don't nail him for the murder of Verlangen, he'll have scored a hat trick. At least. Three murders, but he's as free as a bird. Dammit all!'

'For once you're probably right,' said Münster, looking grim.

Silence ensued while deKlerk leafed through his papers again.

'Is there nothing new from Maardam?' wondered Moerk in the hope of striking a more optimistic tone. 'They were going to talk to his daughter and go through his flat, weren't they?'

'No report as yet,' said the chief of police, stretching the lobe of his ear to twice its normal length. 'But I expect we'll hear from them once they've finished. Anything else?'

He looked around the table.

'One more thing,' said Stiller tentatively. 'We still have to talk to those other two people who were staying at the camp site. It might not get us anywhere, but you never know . . .'

'That's right,' said deKlerk, looking up his notes. 'Willumsen and Holt – those names sound familiar. Anyway, Moerk and Stiller can talk to them this afternoon and hear what they have to say. We mustn't leave anything to chance, of course. We're still waiting for reports from the Forensic Lab and the Forensic Institute, but I don't think we should expect them to come up with anything useful. Four months out in the forest leave their mark – or obliterate all the marks, perhaps I should say. We mustn't throw in the towel, of course, but I have to say that I doubt—'

He was interrupted by fröken Miller, who opened the door and poked in her head with its curly white hair.

'Excuse me, but there's a message from the former chief of police,' she said, trying to remain calm and collected.

'Eh?' said Rooth.

'Bausen?' said Moerk.

'Yes.'

'What does he want?' wondered deKlerk, looking confused.

Fröken Miller poked a little more of her body inside the door and coughed demonstratively into her hand.

'He asked me to tell you that he was expecting a lodger again tonight. And that you were welcome to phone him if you wanted to know more.'

'A lodger?' said Moerk.

'What the hell . . .' said deKlerk. 'Is that what he said?'

'Yes, that's exactly what he said. A lodger. I wrote it down to be on the safe side.'

'Good God,' said Rooth, taking the last remaining Danish pastry. '*In sha'a Allah*, as I've already said – has a government minister been shot, or something of that sort?'

'Thank you, fröken Miller,' said deKlerk. 'We can't complain about being understaffed on this occasion.'

'No,' said Intendent Münster, glancing automatically at Beate Moerk. 'Evidently not. But what the hell are we supposed to be doing?'

'A good question,' said Rooth. 'But I expect we'll find something.'

37

Van Veeteren went for a walk along the beach.

Shadows, he thought. I'm chasing shadows from the past.

Or one, at least. Why does it have to be so essential to come to terms with this sort of thing? he wondered. Why did these question marks insist on being removed, and these stains in the soul on being polished and rubbed out.

Polished *or* rubbed out. There was a difference, of course.

The devil only knows, he thought, lighting a cigarette. Sometimes things persist for no obvious reason. We have that sort of brain.

The sun was still low in the sky – he had woken up early and not wanted to disturb Bausen: just made himself a cup of coffee in the kitchen, then made his way towards the sea. He had come to the beach a couple of minutes before half past seven, bought a bottle of mineral water at the kiosk by the marina, and set off in an easterly direction. An hour out, an hour back, he decided. Movement is the key to clear thinking.

The beach looked just like he had remembered it. Or like he remembered so many other beaches he had walked along during his life. Sea, sky, earth . . . A greyish-white band thirty metres wide running towards the headland just short of

Orfmann's Point. That was what it was called, wasn't it? The restaurant on top of it, Fisherman's Friend, projecting out dramatically over the edge; but the whole cliff and the high coastline beyond was enveloped by morning mist . . . It was more like a dream than reality, as was the next bay on the other side towards Wilgersee. Birds were flying around over the sands and in towards land, a thin white cloud formed a veil around the sun, but the light was strong: he took his sunglasses out of his breast pocket and put them on. There was no doubt that it was going to be a hot day. Another one.

This is my last case, he suddenly thought. Definitely my final case.

In the activity that has dominated my life: chasing murderers.

He knew that this was true. Irrespective of the outcome. Irrespective of whether or not they managed to find G as a result of the faint trail left by Verlangen.

Irrespective of whether or not they achieved anything at all. Facts were facts. This was his last case.

At last, one might say. It felt almost like a sort of relief on a morning like this. He gazed out over the water. Lazy, choppy waves and hardly any wind at all. He recalled having depressing thoughts about this sea on his previous visit. He had gone for a walk along exactly the same stretch of beach, and interpreted the signs: winds blowing in the wrong direction, and lifeless waves. Natural forces reflecting a murder investigation that was getting nowhere, and similar shady goings-on. And doubts. His eternal doubts.

There was uncertainty in his mind now as well. Had he

really done the right thing in coming up here again? It had been easy to make the decision to do so, but it had more to do with emotions than with reason. If such a split was possible in the real world.

Easy to make that decision down in Maardam, that is. Now that he was actually here he was aware of a sort of presumptuousness under his skin, itching away: both Münster and Rooth were already here to investigate the murder of Verlangen, and he knew from the past how capable Beate Moerk was.

So what was he doing here? Should he not have waited until they found traces of G at least? There was in fact nothing he could do that the investigative team couldn't do just as well. Or better, if truth be told.

He had refrained from contacting them yesterday – simply allowed Bausen to inform them of his presence – and he knew that he wouldn't be setting foot inside the police station today either. Unless somebody specifically invited him, that is.

A private detective again, he thought grimly. An old former detective chief inspector who turns up in the backwater after that private dick. Huh. In order to solve the only unresolved case of his career. Was that pathetic, or what?

Perhaps it was. There was definitely an element of that, he could feel it clearly on a morning like this: but what the hell! He couldn't sleep, thanks to that damned Hennan!

And if they really do find him? he suddenly thought. If I actually come face to face with Jaan G. Hennan again? What would happen then? What is there to say that I would actually be victorious this time?

Not a lot, he decided. Apparently not a lot.

He paused and took off his shoes and socks. It's like it was fifteen years ago, he thought. Exactly the same . . . If we find G in Kaalbringen, that means he is guilty of Verlangen's death. I know that. I shall sit there staring into the eyes of a murderer, knowing that I shall have to let him go free again. For the second time. It's a damned awful thought, but there's a lot to support that scenario, isn't there?

He kicked a piece of discarded orange peel into the water. Hell's bells, he thought, I ought to take matters into my own hands.

The thought came to him unbidden. He rejected it. Not this time, he decided. Not again. The moral escape door which involved stepping outside the law in order to ensure that justice is done – he had already opened it once, one single time, and afterwards he realized that it was an exit door one should only allow oneself to use once in a lifetime. If at all.

On that occasion the innocent man under pressure had been called Verhaven.

Now one of the victims was called Verlangen. Almost the same name, but that was a coincidence, of course. Nothing to interpret as a signpost, or an index finger.

He came to the old bunker from the Second World War: half sunk into the sand and half eaten by the teeth of time, it perched on the slope above the sands, gazing out over the eternal sea. He paused, opened the bottle of water and took several large swigs. Checked his watch and decided to continue. As far as the cliff, and perhaps a little bit further. How many times have I walked along beaches like this one? he wondered. If I laid them end to end, how far would they cover?

The next question came totally out of the blue.

How many years have I left to live?

Sixty-five plus what?

The answer was written in some book somewhere, of course – or perhaps in a musical score. In a hundred years from now somebody would be able to write his biography (the one he had never got round to sorting out) and state that when the *Chief Inspector* travelled up to Kaalbringen that autumn in a vain attempt to close down the G File, he had no more than two years left to live.

Or was it two months?

Rubbish, he then thought. Of that day and hour knoweth no man . . . and so on. He started walking again, and made up his mind to settle that question off his own bat.

I shall continue walking for exactly half an hour, he decided. The number of people I pass during that time will be the number of years I have left.

Fair deal.

And when he stopped again after thirty minutes, close to the church in Wilgersee – he could glimpse the pointed spire over the top of the copse of beech trees between the church and the beach – he had not met another living soul.

Not a single one. So that was that then.

'I think I'm on to something,' said Probationer Stiller. 'There's a possibility, at least.'

'Really?' said Beate Moerk.

'This Willumsen. He was living in the caravan next to Verlangen. He seems to have spoken to him quite a lot.'

'Good,' said Moerk. 'What about?'

'Not all that much, in fact – but he had asked about a camera shop.'

'A camera shop?'

'Yes.'

'Verlangen?'

'Yes. He had a camera, and evidently had a roll of film he wanted developing.'

'So Verlangen had been taking photographs, had he?'

'Yes.'

'What of?'

Stiller shrugged.

'I've no idea. He didn't tell Willumsen that. He just wanted to know if there was a camera shop in Kaalbringen . . . But it could have had something to do with G of course, and I thought that if we—'

'Of course,' said Moerk, interrupting him. 'If Verlangen had taken pictures of something, it's pretty obvious what they must have been of. What did Willumsen tell him? Was he able to be of help to Verlangen?'

Stiller nodded.

'Yes, indeed. He referred him to FotoBlix in Hoistraat, and to that new shop in the shopping centre – I don't know what it's called, nor did Willumsen . . .'

'That doesn't matter,' said Moerk. 'Overmaar's or something,

I think. But Verlangen intended to go to one of them and have his photos developed, right?'

'I think so,' said Stiller. 'That's what Willumsen said at least. But in any case, it should be worth following it up, don't you think?'

'Certainly,' said Moerk. 'They might recognize him. It's a pity that developing is done by machines nowadays . . . But it would help if we could find out what Verlangen had taken pictures of.'

'You can say that again,' said Stiller. 'Shall we follow this up straight away, or . . .'

'Immediately,' said Moerk.

'There's one thing I don't understand,' said Inspector Rooth.

'Really?' said Münster.

'All that about proof. The suggestion that Verlangen had discovered some kind of proof about G's guilt. How the hell could that be possible?'

'Go on,' said Münster.

'I mean, it's one thing if he happened to catch sight of G, by pure luck. Coincidence. I can also accept that he decided to start following him – or at least to keep a check on him somehow or other. He must have been a bit odd, this Verlangen character. But how could he possibly have caught on to something linked with a murder committed fifteen years ago? That's what I can't understand.'

Münster thought for a few seconds.

'Nor can I,' he admitted.

'Do you think Verlangen spoke to him?' said Rooth. 'If we assume he did, Hennan might have said something – *happened* to say something – that made Verlangen catch on to something. I suppose that's what might have happened. But there again, why should Hennan let slip something to somebody like Verlangen when he's survived police interrogations and legal proceedings for such a long time? It's beyond comprehension.'

'I know,' said Münster. 'I've thought about that as well. I mean, G was found not guilty. There can't very well have been any reason to start chasing him up simply because somebody happened to see him. It's not illegal to leave the country and be away for a few years.'

'Verlangen was presumably obsessed by him,' said Rooth.

'No doubt. Anyway, you're quite right in this respect. How could Verlangen stumble on something he called proof? It's very odd indeed.'

'Maybe he's the only one who would have thought that,' suggested Rooth. 'That it was so important. An *idée fixe* or something of that sort?'

'But why should he end up getting shot through the head? If it wasn't anything serious?'

'Exactly,' said Rooth. 'It can't have simply been imagination. I just don't get it, as I said.'

'No doubt we'll find out,' said Münster optimistically. 'Anyway, this is Gerckstraat. What number was it?'

Rooth checked his notebook.

'Thirteen,' he said. 'What do you think about this, then?'

'It's bound to be a breakthrough,' said Münster. 'He's

eighty-nine years old and has cataracts, but nevertheless he maintains that he has seen Verlangen in mysterious circumstances. We obviously have to investigate the claim more closely.'

'Obviously,' said Rooth. 'But then we can get a bite to eat.'

Moerk and Stiller had a cup of coffee in the neo-functionalist cafe Kroek in the Passage shopping centre after their visit to the camera shop, which as far as they could make out didn't have a name at all. There was no sign over the entrance in any case.

'What do you think?' asked Stiller.

'I don't know,' said Moerk. 'But if they don't remember him I suppose it doesn't matter if he was there or not. Let's hope he went to FotoBlix instead – it's a bit smaller and more personal.'

'It's not certain that he handed in a film for developing at all,' Stiller pointed out. 'He might have been shot before he got round to it, for instance.'

'That's very possible,' said Moerk with a sigh. 'And the camera was burnt up in the caravan fire. But that's police work for you. Even if only one out of a thousand leads is any good, the other nine-hundred-and-ninety-nine have to be investigated as well.'

'Yes, I've begun to realize that,' said Stiller, and she had the impression that he blushed momentarily. 'But surely it's not necessary to wait until the very end before you find the right one, is it?'

'Not necessarily,' said Moerk, 'although there's nothing to prevent all thousand lottery tickets being losers either.'

'Lousy odds,' said Stiller with a smile.

'The worst in the world,' said Moerk, emptying her cup. 'Shall we carry on?'

'Of course,' said Stiller.

'What on earth are you doing?' wondered Van Veeteren.

'Vajrasana,' replied Bausen, his voice sounding somewhat strained. 'It stretches the whole of your back – a hell of a good exercise. Give me five minutes, and I'll be with you.'

Van Veeteren left him on the floor and went out to sit on the patio. After a while Bausen appeared with two beers.

'Lovely weather again today,' he said, squinting up through the greenery. 'You're an early riser.'

'It's nagging away at me,' said Van Veeteren.

'That case, you mean?'

Van Veeteren nodded and began pouring out his beer.

'I understand. And I suppose it's a bit frustrating, being inactive.'

'Awful,' said Van Veeteren. 'I thought one would learn how to cope with the impatience over the years, but that's obviously not the case.'

Bausen raised his glass and smiled wryly.

'Not without help,' he said.

'Such as?'

'You know that as well as I do. How did you spend this morning?'

Van Veeteren drank half his glass.

'I went for a walk along the beach. To Wilgersee and back.'

'That's one way,' said Bausen. 'Yoga's another . . . It hangs your soul in the right places inside your body, as it were. I'll teach you a few exercises this evening, if you've nothing against it?'

Van Veeteren nodded. They sat in silence for a while.

'Anyway,' said Bausen eventually. 'To tell you the truth, I don't have anything special to do today either. Shall we have a game while we're waiting for them to contact us?'

'By all means,' said Van Veeteren. 'So you think they'll do that?'

'Of course,' said Bausen confidently, getting out the chessboard. 'Let them do the spadework, then we can move in when they get stuck. If you've been waiting for fifteen years, I assume you can hang on for a few more days.'

'Maybe,' said Van Veeteren, beginning to set up the pieces. 'Although there's a bit of guilt to cope with as well.'

'Guilt?'

'Yes. I have a slightly annoying feeling that it ought to have been me lying out there in the mushroom woods with a bullet hole through my skull. Not that poor devil Verlangen.'

Bausen contemplated him thoughtfully for a few seconds.

'I understand what you're saying,' he said. 'But I suggest we ignore that aspect for now. It's your move . . . It would be fun if you did a Scandinavian for a change.'

'A Scandinavian opening?' said Van Veeteren. 'Why not?'

38

'Closed for holidays!' said Stiller. 'Typical!'

Moerk stared at the notice in the window.

'"We'll be open again on Monday",' she read out. 'Yes, that really is typical.'

'What do we do now?' wondered Stiller.

Moerk thought for two seconds.

'The owner's name is Baagermaas or something like that, I seem to recall. It doesn't necessarily follow that he's in Upper Volta just because he's on holiday.'

'Upper Volta?' said Stiller.

'Or Mallorca or the Maldives,' said Moerk. 'We'll look him up in the telephone directory and give him a ring.'

'Okay,' said Stiller, dialling the police station on his mobile.

A minute later he had all the necessary information from fröken Miller, who could also inform him that the name was Maagerbaas, and not the other way round. He keyed in the new number and received a response after one-and-a-half rings.

'Hello.'

'Erwin Maagerbaas?'

'Yes.'

'It's the police. Will you be at home a quarter of an hour from now?'

'What? Er . . . yes, I'll be in. What's it all—'

'Just routine. And your address is Oostwerdingen Allé 32, is that right?'

'Yes . . . Yes, that's right.'

'Thank you, we'll see you shortly then,' said Stiller, concluding the call.

He's starting to grow into his uniform, thought Moerk as she unlocked the car door.

Erwin Maagerbaas didn't look as if he had spent his holidays on Mallorca or in Upper Volta – in a cave in the woods, more likely. His face was greyish white and he seemed to be in a bad way overall when he let them into his flat in Oostwerdingen Allé. The first thing he did was to sneeze three times and explain that he had been ill in bed for several days.

But he said he was on the mend and would no doubt be up to answering a few questions. What was it all about?

Beate Moerk took out the photograph of Verlangen and handed it to him.

'Do you recognize this man?' she asked. 'We have reason to believe he paid a visit to your camera shop.'

Maagerbaas put on a pair of horn-rimmed spectacles and examined the photograph carefully.

'Hmm,' he said. 'It's possible – I think I recognize him but I'm not certain.'

'It's very important for us, as you no doubt understand,' said Stiller.

'I see. Well, I have rather a lot of customers in fact. When would it have been? I've been closed since the middle of August.'

'We know that,' said Moerk. 'This visit took place quite a long time ago. In April.'

'April?' exclaimed Maagerbaas, and started coughing. 'How am I supposed to remember a customer who called in half a year ago? He's not one of my regulars in any case, I'm quite sure of that. What did he want?'

'We presume he simply handed in a roll of film for developing,' said Stiller. 'And then collected it.'

'Why are you looking for him?'

Moerk exchanged glances with her colleague.

'Haven't you read the newspaper?' she asked. 'We asked for information about him last Monday.'

'*De Journaal*?'

'Yes.'

'I've been away for a couple of weeks. I got back yesterday.'

'I see,' said Moerk. 'So you can't say whether this person has been in your shop or not?'

Maagerbaas shrugged and sneezed once again.

'No.'

Stiller cleared his throat.

'Forgive me, but if he did hand in a film for developing in April, it should be possible to check that, surely?'

Maagerbaas took off his glasses, breathed on them a few times and put them back into a brown case.

'Yes,' he said. 'There'll be records in the computer in that case, but—'

'Excellent,' said Moerk. 'Can you come with us, and we'll investigate the matter.'

'Now?' wondered Maagerbaas, looking reluctant.

'This very minute,' said Stiller. 'This is all about a murder, herr Baagermaas – didn't we mention that?'

'Maagerbaas,' said Moerk.

Ten minutes later they were once again at the FotoBlix shop in Hoistraat, but this time inside it. Erwin Maagerbaas switched on the computer and invited them to sit down.

'It's a bit old,' he explained. 'It takes some time to warm up. What was his name?'

It occurred to Beate Moerk that she hadn't thought about this potential problem until now.

'Try Verlangen,' she said.

Maagerbaas waited a bit longer, then keyed in the name.

'Nothing,' he said. 'Sorry.'

'Sommers,' said Stiller. 'Try Henry Sommers.'

Maagerbaas looked at him in surprise for a few seconds, then did as requested.

One chance in a thousand, thought Moerk glumly as he tapped away at the keys. At best.

'Eureka!' said Maagerbaas, coughing up some phlegm. 'Yes, there is a Sommers here. The fifteenth of April, could that fit in?'

Moerk hurried round the desk and took a look at the screen.

'That fits in perfectly,' she said. 'What does this mean? That he's been here and handed in a roll of film?'

'Yes,' said Maagerbaas, studying the information in more detail. 'Handed in, but evidently not . . .'

'Not what?'

'Hmm. He hasn't been to collect the pictures.'

'Not been to collect . . . ?'

It took three seconds before she realized what that implied. Or *could* imply. Stiller was evidently a few tenths of a second quicker on the uptake, for he was the one who exclaimed:

'What the hell are you saying? Hasn't he collected the pictures? Does that mean that . . .'

'. . . that they're still here?' said Moerk, finishing his question for him.

Maagerbaas made quite a show of blowing his nose.

'Presumably, yes. I usually keep them for about a year. Customers sometimes forget them . . . I ring and remind them first, of course . . . Me or my assistant. But that has evidently not helped in this case. And he didn't supply a telephone number.'

'Where?' said Stiller. 'Where do you keep the pictures?'

'Where?' said Maagerbaas. 'Well I assume they'll be in the office somewhere. I have a cupboard where I keep uncollected photographs. Would you like—'

'You bet we would,' said Moerk. 'God almighty . . .'

★

453

'God almighty,' echoed Chief of Police deKlerk just over an hour later. 'Twenty-four pictures taken by the murder victim himself – that surely has to be a breakthrough. But what on earth can we say about them?'

The photographs were spread out on the table in the conference room, and those present had been staring at them for quite a while. Every one of them. Intendent Münster and Inspector Rooth. The chief of police himself. And Moerk and Stiller, who had arrived with the pictures half an hour ago. Every single photograph had been passed round to all present. From hand to hand. Twenty-four of them. Everybody had examined them carefully. Nobody had shouted 'Aha!', and nobody had used the word 'breakthrough' until the chief of police used the word now.

The problem was the motif of the photographs.

They all depicted a house.

The same house.

'In every bloody photo,' to quote Inspector Rooth.

Quite a large single-storey villa, photographed from various angles. Four angles, to be precise. Two from the front, two from the back – most of them from the back. Nineteen of the pictures depicted the rear of the house: a stretch of lawn, two knotty fruit trees (probably apple trees), several small shrubs (probably berberis), and a large terrace with a table and four green chairs. The facade was clad in reddish-brown brick, and the roof was dark-coloured slate. Münster guessed it dated from the 1950s, and nobody objected to that. There were people in some of the pictures: a man and a woman. The man appeared eleven times, the woman eight, and in six of the pictures they were both present. Both of them were wearing the same clothes on each occasion, and it seemed highly likely that all the pictures had been taken on the same day. Within quite a short time as well – an hour, perhaps, judging by the light and the shadows.

As far as the camera was concerned, deKlerk had suggested that it was quite a primitive model. The distance from the two positions at the rear of the house was always the same, about twenty-five metres. The zoom function had not been used, the facial expressions of the man and the woman were difficult to make out, and their facial features in general were not very clear.

As far as one could judge the man seemed to be somewhat older than the woman. He had greyish-white hair and a short beard of the same colour, and seemed to be between sixty and seventy. He was wearing dark trousers and a light-blue shirt with the sleeves rolled up. The woman was wearing jeans and a black, long-sleeved jumper in all the pictures, and she had dark hair tied up in a simple ponytail. In most of the pictures they were on the terrace, standing up or sitting down. The sun was shining, and on the table were coffee cups, a thermos flask, several newspapers and some books. In three of the photos the woman had a cigarette in her hand. The man was wearing glasses in two.

That was all.

'That bloody idiot has taken pictures of a house,' said Rooth. 'Twenty-four times! Brilliant detective work, at least I can give him that eulogy. If he were not dead we ought to reinstate him in the police force immediately.'

'Hmm, I don't know about that,' said deKlerk.

'And we're sure that no one here recognizes it?' asked Münster. 'The house, that is.'

DeKlerk shook his head.

Moerk and Stiller shook their heads.

'Sorry,' said Moerk. 'I don't think so. It seems quite a posh place – but it's not certain that it's in Kaalbringen, is it?'

'Of course the bloody place is in Kaalbringen,' said Rooth. 'Why would Verlangen go to Kaalbringen in order to take pictures of a house in Hamburg? Or in Sebastopol?'

'Yes, yes,' said the chief of police, tugging at his nose. 'Inspector Rooth no doubt has a valid point. But what about the man in the photographs? Could it possibly be Hennan?'

Münster glanced at Rooth before answering.

'Very possibly,' he said. 'Why not? It could be anybody at all, of course, but if there was any point in taking those photographs . . . and this whole business, come to that . . . I'd be prepared to vote for it being Jaan G. Hennan. I've no idea who the woman is, but why not look into the likelihood of it being his new wife?'

'Oh dear,' said Moerk. 'Very bold conclusions, I must say. But okay, if we forget about the possibility of them being wrong, where do they get us? If Hennan really is living in a house in Kaalbringen, surely he has every right to do so?'

'Not if he's shot Verlangen through the head he doesn't,' said Rooth, taking something that looked like a half-eaten bar of chocolate from his jacket pocket. 'If he has, that robs him of the right to choose his own address for at least ten years. But I don't understand . . . These pictures surely can't be the proof he was going on about? Not unless he was completely barmy. Verlangen, that is.'

'It's very possible that he was,' sighed Münster. 'I'm beginning to think he might well have been.'

'He was murdered because he knew something,' said deKlerk.

'Or because somebody thought he knew something,' said Stiller tentatively.

Beate Moerk stood up and walked over to the window. Folded her arms over her chest and looked out over Kleinmarckt.

'That's what we believe, yes,' she said thoughtfully. 'What we convince ourselves is the case, so that the evidence fits in with our theories. But what if it was in fact some other lunatic who shot him? . . . Somebody who has nothing at all to do with Jaan G. Hennan. That's a possibility, in fact.'

Rooth crumpled up the chocolate paper into a ball, took aim and missed the waste-paper basket by one-and-a-half metres.

'That's plan B,' he said. 'You might be right, but surely we should continue with plan A for a bit longer. Shouldn't we?'

Chief of Police deKlerk thought for a moment, then nodded and began collecting together the photographs. Stiller picked up the ball of paper and asked Rooth if he wanted to have another go. Rooth shook his head.

'As I said,' said deKlerk, 'I'm also very sceptical about this leading us anywhere: but we've started and we might just as well finish . . . I suppose.'

'But what should we do?' wondered Stiller, looking round the table. 'What, exactly?'

'Any suggestions?' said deKlerk, also looking round the table at his colleagues.

'There is only one possibility, surely?' said Moerk. 'Identify the house. That must be our first priority.'

'But how?' said deKlerk. 'Should each of us get into our own car and drive around until we find it?'

There followed a few seconds' silence as all present seemed to weigh up that possibility.

'Well,' said Moerk. 'That would probably work in the end – but I reckon there's a faster way of doing it.'

'What is it?' asked Stiller.

'There must be people in this town who are better at identifying houses than we are, don't you think?'

'Presumably, yes,' muttered the chief of police. 'But I think that whatever we do we should avoid appealing for assistance from the general public. We've already agreed on doing that. Or are you thinking of a specific person who might be able to help us?'

'Forgive me,' said Moerk. 'Yes, I did have somebody in mind. He's over seventy years old and has lived here in Kaalbringen all his life. He recognizes every single garden gate and front door.'

'Who could that be?' wondered Probationer Stiller.

'Bausen,' said Beate Moerk, opening the window. 'The former chief of police. I think it's time we let in a breath of fresh air – and interrupted a game of chess.'

39

It was half past six in the evening when Bausen and Van Veeteren scrambled into Bausen's old Citroën, and set off to start looking for houses. A rain shower had just passed over, but the sky was starting to turn clear again, and provided that no more banks of clouds came sneaking in from the south-west they should have a few hours of daylight at their disposal.

Or twilight at least. Bausen did not think there was much point in working in darkness.

'What did I say?' he had let slip as he replaced the receiver after the telephone call from deKlerk. 'We haven't even got as far as move number thirteen!'

Van Veeteren had no comment to make on that. But on the other hand, he did wonder about Bausen's motive in telling the investigation leader when he came round that he was pretty sure he recognized the house from the photographs, but that there were a few other possibilities that he ought to check up on – and then, when they were alone again, saying that in fact he didn't think he had ever seen the house before.

'Why did you lie?' Van Veeteren had asked him.

'There's lying and lying,' Bausen had replied. 'I thought we ought to get out and about, you and I – and surely to God, we're bound to find the right hovel sooner or later.'

'Always assuming it really is in this dump,' Van Veeteren had said.

'Don't be so finicky,' Bausen had said.

He attached the two enlarged photographs to the instrument panel with the aid of a spring clip, and started the engine. Van Veeteren was holding another enlargement in his hands: one of the many pictures of the back of the house and the one in which the man's face was clearest. He had been studying the somewhat blurred features of the man ever since he had first been given it an hour ago, but couldn't make up his mind if it really was Jaan G. Hennan or not.

Maybe, maybe not.

But if I see him in person, he thought, I'll be able to decide in half a second.

'I'd have thought there were two districts for us to choose from,' said Bausen. 'Rikken and Wassingen. You can see that from the quality of the building – it's not exactly a working man's shack.'

'Evidently not,' said Van Veeteren. 'Have you thought about the location of the photographer? I think that ought to tell us something significant.'

Bausen nodded.

'Yes, of course. He seems to have been able to shoot away more or less undisturbed from the back of the house. That could mean that there is a little wood or some sort of natural cover in that direction. The pictures from the front seem to suggest that as well. Anyway, we shall soon see. Keep your eyes skinned, we'll start with Wassingen.'

The residential district of Wassingen was on the south-eastern edge of Kaalbringen – an extensive estate with architect-designed detached houses mainly from the forties and fifties. There were about a hundred in all, with large gardens, and many of them bordering on the deciduous woods that ran around some two-thirds of the area.

Oost Honingerweg ran from east to west through the whole district, with banana-shaped side roads to the north and south, and it took Van Veeteren and Bausen over half an hour to crawl through the whole caboodle. They kept stopping here and there to compare what they saw with Verlangen's photographs, and were twice attacked by an unsupervised male boxer badly in need of a pee (right rear wheel, left front wheel – at least they assumed it was the same dog, but it happened in two different streets); but when they had finished they were able to establish – with a level of probability bordering on certainty – that it was not in Wassingen that the deceased private detective Maarten Ver-langen had stood (sat? lain?) taking photographs five months previously.

'It's only a quarter past seven,' said Bausen, looking at his watch. 'We can cover Rikken as well before it gets dark.'

'And if we don't find the place there either?' wondered Van

Veeteren as he wound down the side window and lit a cigarette. 'What do we do then?'

'We *shall* find it in Rikken,' said Bausen. 'I can feel it.'

Twenty minutes later Van Veeteren could concede that Bausen's optimism had been justified.

He was also able to establish that he was not too old to have palpitations. Bausen switched off the engine and cleared his throat.

'There we have it. No doubt about it, don't you think?'

No, there was no doubt about it. The front of the solidly built brown-brick building was identical to the one in the photograph. Even the low brick wall along the edge of the street. And the garage, which was unclear in the photograph, and the projecting roof over the front door. The two pruned fruit trees at the gable end were now in leaf: in April they were only just in bud, but it was obvious that they were the same trees.

The right house. Definitely. Van Veeteren noticed that his palpitations were followed by a degree of dryness in his mouth, and he wished he'd had a pair of sunglasses with him, not to mention a broad-brimmed hat to pull down over his brow. So that he was ready for anything.

'What's the address?' he asked.

Bausen shook his head.

'We'll have to check the name of the street, I can't remember it. But it's number 14 in any case . . . There doesn't seem to be anybody at home, but you never know, of course.'

'Keep moving,' said Van Veeteren. 'We can't just park here.'

'All right. There's a street sign over there at the corner.'

He started the engine again, and they moved off.

'Wackerstraat,' said Van Veeteren when they came to the junction. 'Wackerstraat 14. Now we know.'

Bausen gestured with his hand.

'The municipal forest borders the garden – that's where Verlangen hid. Just like I did once upon a time . . . Hmm . . . What do we do now?'

Van Veeteren thought for a moment.

'Phone the police,' he said. 'They can find out who lives here. Perhaps they will want to be consulted about the next step as well.'

'You reckon?' said Bausen. 'Ah well, I suppose we have no option but to contact them.'

'No option?' said Van Veeteren. 'What on earth do you mean by that?'

But Bausen did not respond.

'Over to you, Stiller,' said deKlerk. 'You're the one who has dug up the information, so you might as well take us through it. Please forgive the overcrowding, by the way, but there aren't usually nearly as many of us as we are now, and this is . . . as you know . . . the biggest room we have access to.'

The chief of police's comments were justified: despite the fact that it was turned ten o'clock at night all those involved in the investigation had answered the call. The local officers:

Moerk and Stiller. The CID officers brought in from Maardam: Münster and Rooth. The two former chief inspectors: Bausen and Van Veeteren.

And deKlerk himself. Seven in all. As somebody had said the other day: one couldn't complain about the number of staff assigned to this case.

It also occurred to the chief of police that if that down-at-heel private detective was gazing down at them now from his heaven – or peering up from the other place – he really ought to raise an eyebrow as a reaction to the stir his death had brought about. Yes indeed.

He squeezed down onto his chair, and nodded encouragingly at Stiller.

'Okay,' said the probationer. 'What I found out wasn't all that remarkable, in fact. They've been living here for ten years, and all the information I have has come from the tax authorities. Anyway: Christopher and Elizabeth Nolan. Owners of the art gallery and attached shop Winderhuus down in Hamnesplanaden . . . They moved here in 1992, and launched their business the following year. I suppose one could say that they are quite firmly established now. They come from Bristol in England – he's sixty-three, she's fifty-one. As far as I can make out it's fru Nolan who has most to do with Winderhuus: they were quite well off when they came here, and still have a considerable fortune even if the art business has been running at a loss in recent years . . .'

'That's what the tax authorities think, at least,' said Beate Moerk.

'Yes,' said Stiller. 'I've been following up mainly the information I received from them. The Nolans have no children; they bought the house in Wackerstraat in 1995 – they lived in a flat in Romners Park for the first three years. There are no indications of financial irregularities of any kind – on the contrary, they have both declared their considerable wealth every year since they came here . . . Anyway, that's what I've managed to dig up.'

'An art gallery?' muttered Rooth. 'That must be a good place to hide money in.'

'Maybe,' said Münster. 'But Christopher Nolan? I don't know what to think, in fact . . .'

'Harrumph,' said Bausen, looking hard at all present in turn. 'If you'll forgive me for saying so, there's not much point in thinking anything at all so far. Either this bloke is identical with Jaan G. Hennan, or he's identical with Christopher Nolan. Until we've established the facts, we can put all theories to one side. We don't need to start speculating at this stage, do we?'

'You may well be right,' said the chief of police with a slightly strained smile. 'And how should we go about sorting out that little detail? Any suggestions?'

Nobody spoke for several seconds. Then Intendent Münster cleared his throat.

'One possibility is of course to go there and interrogate him. Or talk to him, at least. But I'm not sure if that's the right thing to do in this case.'

'I think it's a bloody daft thing to do,' said Rooth. 'Surely we can't be so naive as to deal with an arsehole like Hennan with all our cards on the table?'

'We don't know that it *is* Hennan,' said Stiller.

'All the more reason for not putting all our cards on the table. Not to start with, at least. My Bible says quite clearly that in a case like this we have to start with a bluff. A premier league, king size bluff.'

'Yes, I'm inclined to agree,' said Inspector Moerk. 'We can't start talking seriously to him until we know for sure whether or not we are dealing with G. It would be plain daft to let slip that we suspect something.'

'I agree,' said Münster. 'He didn't give the impression of having been born yesterday last time. We have to be careful.'

'Does anybody disagree?' asked deKlerk, looking round the table.

Nobody had any comment to make. Van Veeteren exchanged looks with Münster, and seemed to be about to say something, but he changed his mind and took out his cigarette machine instead.

'But we still need to decide what to do next,' said deKlerk. 'Which one of us would be most likely to be able to identify Jaan G. Hennan?'

The question was so rhetorical that Van Veeteren almost dropped his cigarette machine on the floor. Bausen couldn't help laughing.

'For Christ's sake,' he said. 'You seem to have made up your minds to send the happy wanderers out to do the work for you – the amateurs who did their bit long ago. But why not? It obviously makes sense for Van Veeteren to make the first move – you would recognize him, wouldn't you? That's what you said an hour ago, in any case.'

Van Veeteren put the cigarette machine back into his jacket pocket, and clasped his hands on the table in front of him.

'Probably,' he said. 'I'd like to think so, at least. But I also think it's highly likely that Hennan would recognize me. We would need to decide if that was an advantage or a disadvantage.'

'That assumes that you would have to come face to face, doesn't it?' said Beate Moerk.

Van Veeteren frowned.

'Perhaps that wouldn't be necessary,' he conceded. 'But I'm keen to find myself in that situation sooner or later. If it really is him.'

Beate Moerk smiled.

'I think I've understood that,' she said. 'A man's gotta do what a man's gotta do. Right?'

'Hmm,' said the *Chief Inspector*. 'Something along those lines. But how would you go about setting it up in the first place? I have . . . I don't have any great desire to sneak around in that bastard's shadow, hoping that he might turn round and look at me at some point.'

Bausen had been sitting there for a while, scratching the back of his head.

'It doesn't need to be quite as melodramatic as that,' he said. 'We could try this: I can give you a few old paintings, and you can call in at Winderhuus when Mr Nolan is on duty, and try to sell them to him. You could please yourself about whether or not to wear a false beard.'

'As easy as that?' said Van Veeteren.

'As easy as that, yes,' said Bausen.

Perhaps it was due to the late hour, or possibly something else, but three quarters of an hour later nobody had come up with a better solution.

Just around half past one, shortly before he managed to fall asleep, a new thought occurred to Van Veeteren. He didn't like it.

If, it dawned on him, *if* Christopher Nolan was identical with Jaan G. Hennan, that must mean – according to the information that Probationer Stiller had dug up and presented in exemplary fashion – that he had been living in Kaalbringen at the time of the axe-killer case nine years ago.

That was a most unwelcome insight.

I wonder how I would have reacted if I'd known that at the time, Van Veeteren thought. Would it have influenced the outcome of the investigation?

And when he eventually fell asleep he immediately started dreaming about wandering around a large art gallery – disguised with a gigantic white Father Christmas-type beard and intent on cutting out of their frames canvases with the world's most expensive and famous works of art. He recognized *Guernica* and *The Last Supper*, and Van Gogh's *Sunflowers*.

It was pretty unpleasant, but soon became much worse. Both paintings and false beard had evidently been blown away, and instead he was walking along a vast, deserted beach. Apparently on his way to his own death: this was made clear by a series of yellowish-black, rusted signs sunk down into the sand at regular intervals. The distance still to walk shrank rapidly, and no matter how hard he tried, he failed to catch sight of a single person who might be able to help him turn round . . . Not a single one.

When he woke up the next morning he simply could not believe that he had been asleep for seven hours.

Seven minutes, more likely.

40

The following morning, the plan was modified somewhat.

Thanks to her husband (who worked in the art world and regretted that Winderhuus was an awful dump full of amateurish crap), Inspector Moerk was able to inform her colleagues that there was currently a relatively well-attended exhibition on at the gallery (featuring work by local artists – pretty crappy stuff, according to her source).

After a few telephone calls it was agreed that the obvious next step was for Bausen to play the role of somebody with paintings to sell, while Van Veeteren played the rather more discreet part of a straightforward visitor interested in seeing the pictures. If things proceeded as the *Chief Inspector* had foreseen with regard to identifying Christopher Nolan, this approach would give him an excellent opportunity to take a closer look at the man in question. And to hear his voice. Münster and Rooth had been on a reconnaissance expedition and concluded that there was no real distinction – not even a door – between the gallery and the more commercially directed activities, such as the sale of frames and reproductions and picture postcards and goodness only knows what else.

Stiller was first on the scene. He was sitting in a strategically positioned car in the extensive car park by the harbour quite close to Winderhuus, and was able to observe the arrival of fru Nolan, who opened the doors at just a couple of minutes past ten. Stiller's task was to make a phone call and report the exact time of arrival of herr Nolan. According to a theory evolved by Rooth, this was likely to happen around lunchtime – and for once it transpired that the inspector had hit the nail on the head. At exactly half past twelve Christopher Nolan drove up in his Bordeaux-red Rover, parked about ten metres away from Stiller's significantly more modest Fiat, walked over Esplanaden and entered Winderhuus. Apparently in order to relieve his wife, and give her an opportunity to go off and have lunch.

She duly emerged after a few minutes: a slim woman in her fifties, wearing court shoes, a red dress, and with dark hair. Noticeably more modestly dressed than in the photographs, Stiller noted – but the very same woman, no doubt about it. She lit a cigarette, and headed for Fiskartorget. Stiller phoned the police station, where Bausen and Van Veeteren were messing around with a chessboard and four oil paintings depicting the sea.

The call lasted four seconds. A seagull came soaring down and landed on the Fiat's bonnet. The sun was shining.

So, Operation G has started, Stiller thought. He noticed that he was sitting like a coiled spring at the wheel of his car.

'Good afternoon,' said Bausen. 'I don't know if we've met, but my name's Bausen.'

'Nolan. No, I don't think so.'

Bausen put down his unwieldy package and started separating the art works from the blanket he had used to protect them.

'An old aunt of mine died last summer, and I inherited some works of art,' he explained. 'I don't have room for them. I thought you might like to assess them and buy anything you'd like to have.'

'Let's have a look,' said Nolan, assisting with the blanket. 'You never know.'

Bausen placed the paintings carefully along the wall opposite Nolan's desk. It suddenly struck him why he had kept them in a dark room in the cellar – but he stood up and looked pleased with himself even so.

'Well, what do you think?'

'Hmm . . .' said Nolan, stroking his well-groomed beard with his hand. He picked up a pair of spectacles from the table and put them on. The door opened and Van Veeteren came in.

'Where's the exhibition?' he asked.

Nolan glanced up at him over the edge of his glasses.

'Through there. Go on in. There's a leaflet on the table.'

Van Veeteren nodded.

'What time do you close?'

'Six o'clock.'

'Thank you.'

Bausen cleared his throat to regain Nolan's attention.

'They're not bad, are they? And very attractive frames.'

Van Veeteren paused and took a look at Bausen's paintings.

'What a load of crap,' he said.

'What the hell did you say?' demanded Bausen.

Nolan smiled in amusement.

'I must say I'm inclined to agree with you,' he said. 'I think you'll find the exhibition more to your liking.'

'I hope so,' said Van Veeteren, moving on into the rest of the premises.

'That was the most insulting thing I've ever heard,' said Bausen.

'If you'd like a professional opinion, you'd better wait until my wife comes back,' said Nolan. 'She's out having lunch at the moment, but she'll be back in three quarters of an hour or so.'

'Huh,' said Bausen. 'I won't bother. I'll burn them in the garden instead.'

He wrapped the paintings up in the blanket again and stormed out of the Winderhuus Art Gallery in a simulated rage.

'Well?' said Münster.

Van Veeteren made a vague movement of his head and picked a loose thread off the sleeve of his jacket. Three seconds passed.

'Yes,' he said. 'It's him all right.'

There was a deathly silence in the room for several more seconds, then deKlerk exhaled in a long, whistling stream.

'Good,' he said. 'Bloody hell!'

'You're quoting,' said Van Veeteren.

'Eh?'

'Bloody hell! . . . that's what Verlangen wrote before he came here in April.'

'Oh dear!' said the chief of police, looking surprised. 'Maybe that's a bad omen?'

'Bollocks to omens,' said Rooth. 'So we're dealing with Jaan G. Hennan, are we?'

'It looks like it,' said Van Veeteren.

He lit a cigarette, blew out the match, then realized that the rest of them were waiting for him to say something.

'It looks like it,' he said again, slowly. 'But I think how this case is dealt with from now on needs a great deal of thought. Is there . . . is there anything to prevent Bausen and myself sitting in on future discussions for a while?'

DeKlerk rapidly sought the support of his colleagues, and received it.

'Of course we would like you to continue working with us,' he said. 'Naturally. We have a long way to go yet. Anyway . . . we now know that it really was Hennan that Verlangen was interested in here in Kaalbringen, and we've found him. But what else we know . . .'

'. . . is far from easy to understand,' said Beate Moerk, completing the sentence for him. 'He didn't recognize you, I take it?'

Van Veeteren said nothing for a moment or two. Then shook his head.

'I don't think so. I didn't see the slightest trace of anything to suggest that he did. Glasses and a moustache are pretty effective, in fact, as long as you don't go on too long. No, I think we can take it that he didn't recognize me.'

'But he won't forget me so easily,' said Bausen.

'Nobody ever does,' said Moerk with a quick smile. 'Anyway, we can assume that for now at least, Hennan doesn't suspect anything. Is that right?'

Van Veeteren nodded.

'Let's hope not,' said deKlerk. 'But if he is in fact behind the murder of Verlangen, as we are assuming, he must have raised his awareness levels since we found the body. Or at least since they wrote in the newspapers that we had found the body. And let's face it, we haven't come up with much in the way of proof so far. Am I right? Even if we know that he's the one, we haven't exactly managed to pin the crime onto him.'

'No, not exactly,' said Rooth. 'In other words, what do we do now? Personally, I have to say that I get goose pimples as a result of pussyfooting around all the time. Don't you agree that it would be good to have a straightforward, honest house raid, and a hundred-watt lamp shining into the bastard's face? . . . I know that we couldn't put the wind up him last time, but maybe he's grown softer as the years have passed?'

'Do you think so?' said Münster.

'Not really,' said Rooth. 'I'm just sitting here daydreaming, as you doubtless realize.'

'Anyway,' said deKlerk, turning to Bausen and Van Veeteren at the narrow end of the table. 'Perhaps our somewhat more experienced colleagues have a few points of view?'

'Of course,' said Bausen. 'Rooth is right, naturally, and sooner or later we have to put our cards on the table . . . Tell him we know who he is, in other words, and that he's under suspicion. But perhaps it would make sense to lie low and make a few investigations before we go that far – what do you reckon?'

'That seems to me a correct summary of the situation,' said Moerk.

'What investigations?' wondered Stiller.

'That is precisely the question that needs answering,' said Bausen, starting to scratch the back of his neck. 'Perhaps we could approach him via his wife, but that's just a thought that occurred to me and . . . well, I don't know . . .'

He paused, but Münster took up the thought.

'I've also thought about her,' he said. 'Shouldn't we try to extract a bit of information from England as well? If they've been living here for ten years, Hennan must have found her pretty soon after he disappeared from Maardam . . . Within three or four years, in any case. It could be interesting to tell her a bit about his background and see how she reacts. In view of what happened to his previous wives we could congratulate her on still being alive.'

'That sounds fair enough,' said deKlerk. 'The suggestion about extracting information from England, at least. Approaching the wife would be a bit more dodgy, of course.'

'If it's not possible to frighten him, maybe we could frighten her?' suggested Rooth.

'Excuse me,' put in Stiller. 'Are we assuming that fru Nolan doesn't know anything about this Verlangen business?'

Rooth waved his hand, but he had just stuffed two biscuits into his mouth and it was Münster who responded.

'I think so,' he said. 'But if that isn't the case, there's all the more reason to have a chat with her . . . Quite simply to find out just how much she knows. Yes, I agree with Bausen. Our next move ought to be to talk to her, on her own. But God only knows how we can set that up.'

'There's one more thing I'm wondering about,' said Stiller. 'Wasn't there going to be a search of Verlangen's flat in Maardam? Have we had any information about that?'

DeKlerk nodded and produced a sheet of paper.

'Apologies,' he said. 'I forgot about this in all the rush. We had a fax this morning. Negative, unfortunately. Signed by an Inspector Moreno – I assume he is familiar to you?'

'She,' said Rooth. 'The inspector is a she. But she is familiar to us.'

'Really? Anyway, they haven't found anything. And they were very thorough, she writes.'

'That was only to be expected,' said Münster. 'He didn't keep a diary, that's all there is to it. Which is hardly surprising.'

'Thank you,' said Stiller. 'I just wondered.'

'No problem,' said the chief of police, checking his watch. 'Might I suggest that we make a pause now. There are seven of us involved in this business, but I don't think it would do any harm if each one of us spent an hour or two thinking our own thoughts. Stiller and I will get in touch with England, and we'll see if we can get anything of interest from there. I suggest we meet again at four o'clock, is that okay?'

'That's okay,' said Rooth.

'As far as Bausen and Van Veeteren are concerned –'

'– they'll do whatever they want, of course,' said Bausen, rising to his feet.

'You didn't have much to say,' he said when they were seated in the car again.

'I just sat there thinking,' said Van Veeteren. 'And I'm a bit tired. And I didn't sleep very well last night, I'm afraid . . . And there were so many bright sparks involved.'

'That isn't always an advantage.'

'No,' said Van Veeteren. 'Not always.'

'You're sitting there brooding about something.'

'In a way.'

'About what?'

'That suggestion about a hundred-watt lamp. Would he really cope with another session?'

'Hennan?'

'Yes.'

'So you reckon we ought to get tough with him?'

Van Veeteren produced a toothpick from his breast pocket and stared at it in disbelief.

'Where the hell has this come from? I gave them up five years ago.'

'It seems that a lot of things from the past are turning up just now,' said Bausen. 'Should we get tough?' he repeated.

Van Veeteren snapped the toothpick in two and threw the bits out through the window.

'I don't know,' he said. 'I simply can't pass judgement on that.'

'Really? said Bausen. 'As far as I'm concerned there's something else I just can't understand.'

'Hmm?' muttered Van Veeteren. 'What's that?'

'Why the hell did I need to take those damned paintings to the gallery? You could have identified Nolan–Hennan anyhow.'

Van Veeteren eyed him from the side for a few seconds.

'It was your idea to start with,' he said. 'I thought you played your part brilliantly, incidentally. Have you had ambitions to become an actor? I don't think you've mentioned—'

'Shut your gob!' said Bausen, then burst out laughing.

41

It was Münster, deKlerk and Rooth who laid down the guide-lines for the conversation with Elizabeth Nolan – and afterwards, of course, one could wonder if it might have been possible to come up with something better. They worked at it on Friday morning, and quite early on Münster had the feel-ing that something was going wrong. But it would be some time before he realized just how wrong.

It would take far too long.

Intendent Münster was also one of the two police officers who entered the Galleri Winderhuus at half past five on Friday evening and introduced themselves to fru Nolan.

The other was Inspector Moerk – it had been considered appropriate for one of them to be a woman, for some un-stated reason. As far as Münster was concerned, he regarded Beate Moerk as suitable because she was a good police officer, not because she was a woman. But that view was also un-stated.

'Fru Nolan,' said Münster. 'We are from the police and

would like to discuss with you a very delicate matter. My name is Intendent Münster, and this is Inspector Moerk.'

Elizabeth Nolan looked up from the thick art book she had been reading.

'I beg your pardon? I don't think I quite gathered . . . ?'

She looked at them in turn, slightly unsteadily. Stroked to one side a strand of her dark hair.

'The police,' said Moerk. 'We'd like to talk to you.'

'I don't understand . . . Why?'

She had a slight, almost unnoticeable Anglo-Saxon accent. Moerk recalled Bausen and Van Veeteren saying that they hadn't noticed any such thing as far as her husband was concerned.

'Inspector Moerk,' she said, holding out her hand. Nolan shook it hesitantly. Put a bookmark in her book and closed it.

'Is there somewhere we can talk without being disturbed?' Moerk looked around. As far as she could see there were no visitors in the exhibition area; moreover they had been sitting in the car park for ten minutes without seeing anybody enter or leave the building. It seemed that the appeal of the tenth-rate local artists had waned considerably since the exhibition opened a week ago.

Fru Nolan stood up from her chair.

'I'm afraid I don't really understand. What exactly do you want?'

She seemed genuinely surprised, and Münster gestured towards the entrance door.

'Could you perhaps close for the day, so that we won't be disturbed?'

She hesitated. Then she took a couple of steps towards the door before pausing.

'Have you . . . Could I see your ID?'

They handed over their ID cards and she studied them for a few seconds.

'I . . . we're open until six.'

'We know that,' said Münster. 'But perhaps it wouldn't matter much if you were to close half an hour early today. You don't seem to have any customers anyway.'

Nolan shrugged and made some sort of half-hearted gesture with her hands.

'No, the number of visitors to the exhibition has tailed off. But I don't understand why you want to talk to me. Has something happened?'

'If you close the door, we can explain everything in peace and quiet,' said Moerk, resting her hand briefly on Nolan's upper arm. 'You don't need to worry.'

She hesitated briefly again, then nodded and went to lock the door. Münster and Moerk sat down on the two mustard-yellow plastic visitor chairs in front of the desk.

'Fru Nolan,' said Moerk when she had returned and sat down opposite them, 'we're sorry to have to come and disturb you like this, but the way things look we simply don't have any choice.'

'Please tell me what on earth has happened.'

Münster could see that she was expecting to hear about a death, or something equally significant, and perhaps that was understandable.

'All right,' he said. 'The reason we want to talk to you is a bit special, no doubt, but if you answer our questions honestly and frankly, you have nothing to fear.'

'Fear?' exclaimed Nolan. 'Why should I have anything to fear? What do you mean?'

'Let me explain,' said Moerk. 'The fact is, we need some information about your husband. I'm afraid we can't say exactly what lies behind it all, but let me just explain that we are looking for somebody who committed a few serious crimes quite a long time ago . . . Very serious crimes. Your husband is one of a group of eight men, and we know with a hundred per cent certainty that one of the eight is guilty. The one we are looking for. The other seven are totally innocent and have nothing at all to do with it . . .'

'With what?'

'I'm afraid we can't tell you what happened – as I'm sure you understand. And it all took place quite a long time ago, as I said. What we have to do is to find out as much as we can about each one of the group of eight – as discreetly as possible, so that they don't suspect anything. So we shall clear seven candidates – obviously we hope your husband will be one of them, fru Nolan – but this is unfortunately the only method at our disposal. If you knew all the details you would understand our position, but I'm afraid we can't say any more than I've just said. We sometimes need to work with great care and discretion . . . Do you understand the outline of the situation now?'

Elizabeth Nolan stared at them sceptically for a few seconds, then shook her head and dug out a cigarette packet from her handbag, which was lying on the table.

'I need a cigarette.'

'Of course,' said Münster.

'My husband? So it's about my husband, is it?'

'Yes.'

'You want to . . . to clear him?'

'Yes.'

'It's absurd. He would never . . . no. If I answer your questions, will you be able to exclude him? Is that all?'

'That's all,' said Moerk. 'It might well feel like an intrusion into your privacy, of course, but we promise that nothing you say will be repeated outside this room – assuming that your husband isn't the man we're looking for, of course.'

'We also recommend that you don't mention this conversation to him,' said Münster. 'But we'll come back to that.'

Nolan lit her cigarette, inhaled and stretched a little.

'You've taken me very much by surprise,' she said, her voice a little steadier now. 'You must understand that. It feels . . . well, I don't really know how it feels. But I have to trust you, I suppose.'

'You can do that without any problem,' said Münster.

'How long will it take? I have to meet my husband at a restaurant at half past six.'

Moerk looked at her watch.

'We should have plenty of time,' she said. 'It's only twenty to six.'

'Fire away,' said Nolan. 'Let's get it over with.'

Münster nodded and opened his notebook. Moerk took a deep breath and clasped her hands tightly under cover of the desk.

'Christopher Nolan,' said Münster. 'How long have you been married to him?'

'Thirteen years,' said Elizabeth Nolan. 'Since 1989.'

'You were born in England, is that right?'

'Yes.'

'Where exactly?'

'Thorpe. A little village in Cornwall.'

'But you met your husband in Bristol?'

'Yes.'

'Do you have any children?'

'No.'

'Have you been married before?'

'Yes ... Why are you asking about that? I thought you were interested in Christopher, not me.'

'Please don't keep questioning things,' said Moerk. 'That will make things easier. As we're not allowed to reveal the background to you, it may be difficult for you to understand the relevance of all the questions.'

'I don't understand the relevance of any questions at all,' said Nolan, taking a deep drag at her cigarette. 'But all right ... Yes, I was married earlier. It lasted for barely three years. I was young, very young.'

'Where does your husband come from?' asked Moerk.

'He was born in London. Luton, to be exact.'

'What's his job?'

'We run this art business together, as I'm sure you know.'

'Have you been doing that ever since you came to Kaal-bringen?'

'More or less, yes.'

'What did you do in Bristol?'

'I was an art teacher at a college. My husband was a curator at a museum.'

'What was your maiden name?' asked Münster after a short pause.

'Prentice. But I kept my first husband's surname after our divorce. Bowden.'

'So you were called Elizabeth Bowden when you and your current husband got married?'

'Yes.'

'How did it happen?'

'How did what happen?'

'When you met.'

Elizabeth Nolan sighed and looked first at one of them, then the other for a while before making up her mind to answer. Moerk noticed that she was beginning to feel sorry for her.

'It was at a party . . . nothing special. We started seeing each other, and then . . . well . . .'

Moerk nodded encouragingly.

'And this was . . . when exactly?'

She thought for a moment.

'December 1988.'

'And you were both living in Bristol at that time?'

'Yes.'

'Had you lived there long?'

'Which of us are you referring to?'

'Your husband in the first place.'

'I gather he'd been living there for four or five years at

least . . . Yes, since the beginning of the eighties. I don't remember exactly. He was head of one of the departments at the museum.'

'Did you know him before you met at that party?'

She shook her head.

'No. That was the first time I saw him . . . It was a Christmas party at the home of some mutual friends.'

'Had your husband been married before?' asked Münster.

She stubbed out her cigarette and brushed a few flakes of ash from her dress.

'Yes. That's the way it goes nowadays, isn't it? We need to make two attempts in order to learn the ropes . . .' She tried to smile, but it was reluctant to stick. 'He'd been divorced for just over a year when we met.'

'Only a year?'

'Maybe a year and a half.'

'Did he have any children from his previous marriage?'

'No.'

'Have you bumped into his former wife at all?'

'Have I bumped into . . . ? What difference does it make if I've met his ex-wife or not? What are you getting at?'

'Please answer the question,' said Moerk.

Elizabeth Nolan seemed to have something shiny in her eye, and gritted her teeth.

'No, I've never met her . . . I saw her briefly once from a distance. She moved up to Scotland after the divorce. With a new man. I don't understand why you are asking these questions.'

Münster leaned back and exchanged looks with Beate Moerk. She nodded and encouraged him to continue.

'What we are trying to clarify,' said Münster, 'is whether your husband is somebody different from the person he claims to be.'

Elizabeth Nolan's lower jaw dropped.

'Somebody different . . . ?'

'Yes,' said Moerk. 'It might seem quite a shocking thought, but I'm afraid we have to insist on this question. Are you absolutely certain that your husband really is Christopher Nolan, that he was born in London, and that he was working at that museum since the beginning of the eighties?'

Elizabeth Nolan stared at her as if she couldn't believe her ears. Or Inspector Moerk's sanity. She opened and closed her mouth several times without saying anything. In the end she sighed deeply and shook her head vehemently.

'What on earth are you suggesting?' she said. 'Are you saying that Christopher isn't Christopher? I've had about enough of this absurd conversation.'

'Come on now,' said Münster. 'Don't forget the bottom line, fru Nolan! We are trying to eliminate your husband from our list, that's all.'

She blinked in surprise a few times, then gathered herself together. Took another cigarette from the pack and lit it with shaky fingers.

'Forgive me – but it's so absurd . . . So totally absurd.'

'How well acquainted are you with your husband's background?' asked Moerk. 'What he was doing before you met in 1988, and so on?'

'I'm extremely well acquainted with it,' said Elizabeth Nolan. 'We've discussed our previous lives, of course.'

'Of course,' said Münster. 'And no doubt you have met people who could confirm what he has told you – relatives of his, for example?'

Nolan held herself in check and thought for a moment.

'I've met his mother,' she said. 'His father died some time in the mid-seventies, but we visited his mother a few times. At a care home in Islington . . . It was the spring after we'd met, and she died in June. He doesn't have any brothers or sisters.'

Oh yes he has, thought Münster aggressively. He has a sister whom he raped regularly for five years.

'And have you met friends of his who knew him before you got to know him?'

'Of course.'

'Any who you still socialize with?'

'Very occasionally, yes. As you may have noticed, we no longer live in Bristol.'

'Why did you leave England?' asked Moerk.

Nolan drew on her cigarette, and suddenly seemed much calmer.

'Why do you do anything in this life?' she said. 'We were tired of the jobs we were doing, both of us. I had just received a modest inheritance. We decided to make a change, that's all there was to it. Neither of us enjoyed living in Bristol – nor in England, come to that. So yes, we took the plunge. We were both very interested in art – that was what we wanted to devote ourselves to. So we hopped over the Channel, and it became Kaalbringen.'

'Why Kaalbringen, of all places?'

'A good friend of mine had spent a summer here and spoke very positively about it, and, well . . . that was what swung it. We tried living here for a few months and found it suited us. We eventually found a nice house as well . . . and then this place.'

She made a vague gesture, and smiled briefly.

'I understand,' said Münster. 'Does the name Jaan G. Hennan mean anything to you?'

He had signalled to Inspector Moerk before asking that question, and knew that she was just as keen on observing fru Nolan's reaction as he was.

'Hennan?' she said. 'No, I don't think so . . . Who's he?'

Münster swallowed. Nothing, he ascertained. Absolutely nothing to indicate that she was lying, or was put out by the question. He glanced briefly at Inspector Moerk before mentioning the next name.

'What about Verlangen? Maarten Verlangen?'

She shook her head.

'No, I know somebody called Veramten, but not Verlangen.'

'Are you sure?'

She thought for a moment.

'Yes. Can I ask you something?

'Please do,' said Münster.

'What crime is it you suspect this man of having committed? Can you reveal that, at least?'

'Why do you ask that?' wondered Münster.

Fru Nolan looked in two minds for a moment.

'I . . . I don't really know. I suppose I just thought it would be interesting to know.'

'I'm sorry,' said Münster. 'I'm afraid we have to keep that a secret. For now, at least.'

'I understand,' said Nolan.

'Has your husband lived in this country before?' asked Moerk.

'Yes. He lived for a few years near Saaren when he was a boy. Just after the war. But never as far east as this . . . Do you have many questions left? It's turned six now, and I really ought . . .'

'I suppose we can leave it at that,' said Münster.

'Just one more detail before we go our separate ways,' said Moerk. 'We might need to get back to you if we find we need to follow something up, but that's some way ahead. But as we said earlier, we'd be very grateful if you didn't say anything to your husband about this conversation.'

'Obviously, we can't muzzle you,' said Münster. 'We have no right to do that. We reckon that we'll be able to conclude this investigation within the next twelve or fourteen days, and after that it won't matter if you tell him about it. But meanwhile, we'd be grateful – as we've said.'

'I understand,' said Elizabeth Nolan again through gritted teeth. 'This has been extremely unpleasant, but I hope it has been of some use. I won't say anything about it to him.'

'Thank you,' said Münster. 'We won't detain you any longer.'

He closed his notebook, in which he had written no more than a couple of lines, and put it into his jacket pocket. Stood up and shook fru Nolan's hand.

Beate Moerk did the same, and when she turned round briefly on the way out through the door, she noted that fru Nolan was still sitting at her desk with her head in her hands. It was twenty minutes past six, but Elizabeth Nolan didn't seem to be in any great hurry to meet her husband.

The harbour cafe was still open. Münster asked Inspector Moerk if she fancied a beer, and she did.

'Just don't ask me what I think,' he said when he returned from the bar and placed the two glasses on the table. 'Anything else, but not that.'

Moerk looked at him somewhat surprised, and took a drink of beer.

'I can say what I thought, though,' she said.

'By all means,' said Münster.

She paused for a few seconds.

'I would be surprised if she was lying.'

Münster said nothing.

'But on the other hand it would *not* surprise me if Christopher Nolan turned out to be identical with Christopher Nolan.'

Münster leaned back on his chair and stared up at the ceiling.

'Are you suggestion that the *Chief Inspector* was mistaken?'

She paused again before replying.

'I'm only telling you my spontaneous reaction. What do *you* think?'

'That's precisely the question I asked you to avoid,' said Münster, raising his glass to his mouth.

'Oh yes, so it was,' said Moerk. 'Cheers in any case – it's good to see you again.'

42

'Well?' said Van Veeteren. 'What do they have to say?'

Bausen stayed put for a while with his hand on the telephone receiver, gazing out of the window so that Van Veeteren was unable to read his facial expression.

'They're not sure.'

'Not sure?'

'Yes, apparently. Or rather, fru Nolan didn't seem to feel that there was anything amiss. Both Moerk and Münster maintain that she made a very convincing impression. She also provided quite a bit of information – they have sent a request for confirmation over to England.'

Van Veeteren nodded and contemplated the chessboard. They had begun the game in the garden, but moved into the living room at about half past eight when rain drifted in from the north-west. Bausen had prepared a simple ratatouille with basmati rice, and they had more or less finished his very last bottle of St-Emilion '82.

Gruyère cheese with slices of pear for afters.

'Not an enviable position to be in,' said the *Chief Inspector* when Bausen had sat down at the table again. 'Fru Nolan's, that is. It's somewhat paradoxical, in a way.'

'What do you mean?' asked Bausen.

Van Veeteren pulled a face.

'Even if we can't nail him, we can at least smash up his marriage. He has deceived her, and kept her in that state for thirteen years . . . No woman will accept that kind of behaviour. Not in my experience, at least.'

Bausen made no reply, merely sat there in silence, drumming with his index finger on the arm of his chair. Van Veeteren rolled a cigarette and looked at him inquiringly.

'What's the matter?' he said in the end. 'You look worried.'

Bausen leaned forward over the chessboard as if he were about to make a move.

'The chief of police asked me to put a question to you,' he said.

'Really?'

'About Nolan.'

'Well?'

'Hmm. About his identity. Just how convinced are you that he really is Hennan?'

Van Veeteren stiffened. Slowly and lengthily, he could feel that himself.

Like ice forming on a lake in December, he thought. Or when blood coagulates. What the hell is going on? he wondered, and remained sitting there, a cigarette unlit in his mouth, eyeing Bausen over the chessboard. He found it hard to judge which of them was more embarrassed. Several seconds passed, Bausen adjusted some of the chess pieces but didn't make a move. Avoided Van Veeteren's look.

'So that was the cause of the uncertainty, was it?' said Van Veeteren.

Bausen made a vague gesture, but said nothing.

'They doubt whether I'm right, is that it?'

'I'm afraid so.'

'They're questioning my judgement?'

Bausen tried to smile.

'You don't need to—'

He broke off.

'Hell and damnation,' said Van Veeteren, emptying his glass.

This is not the way to consume the final drops of a St-Emilion '82, he thought. It's sacrilege.

'He asked me to put that question to you, in any case,' said Bausen. 'And it's obvious that they want to be quite sure about that point. Absolutely certain . . . Don't take it person-ally – haha.'

'Haha,' agreed Van Veeteren.

Bausen also emptied his glass.

'Apparently she came out with quite a lot of information, fru Nolan. About her own and her husband's past in Eng-land. You might well think that she wouldn't have done that unless—'

'I can see what one might well think, you don't need to fill me in. When do they expect a response from England?'

'In twenty-four hours at the earliest. It'll take a bit of time. It would have been quicker if it had been London, I assume, but it's Bristol.'

'Bristol?'

'Yes.'

'They're supposed to have lived there, are they?'

Bausen nodded.

'Twenty-four hours at least, did you say?'

'Yes, tomorrow evening, with a bit of luck.'

Van Veeteren lit a cigarette and inhaled deeply twice.

'So they think I was mistaken?' he said. 'They don't think I recognize him any more?'

'I don't know what they think,' said Bausen, looking grim.

Van Veeteren picked up a black knight from the chessboard and stared at it. Quite a while passed.

'What does Münster say? He ought to remember what G looks like, for Christ's sake. Why doesn't Münster go and take a good look at him? If they can't make up their minds.'

Bausen said nothing. Just sat there, looking worried.

'One thing has struck me,' he said in the end. 'How the hell would this business hang together if Nolan *isn't* Hennan? I don't understand that.'

Van Veeteren replaced the knight on C6.

'It wouldn't hang together,' he said. 'Although they might think that is what I had in mind when I identified him. That I'd already decided.'

'Could be,' said Bausen. 'Anyway, we'll have to be patient again, I suppose. It's a good job we're not so young and hot-tempered any more.'

Van Veeteren sighed.

'Whose move is it?' he asked. 'I seem to recall it was yours.'

'That's right,' said Bausen, moving a pawn.

★

He woke up at a quarter to six. Spent half an hour trying to go back to sleep, but gave up.

He got up and tiptoed out into the kitchen. Grey dawn was hanging down outside the window: the pane was wet, but it had stopped raining. He didn't doubt for a moment that it would return.

He found the ground coffee and switched on the kettle. Drank a glass of juice while he was waiting. Considered going out to fetch the morning paper, but he wasn't sure that it would have arrived yet, so didn't bother.

Four hours, he thought as he poured water over the powder. Four hours of sleep in his body. That's not nearly enough, for Christ's sake: at my age being awake for four hours a day would be about right.

When he came out into the street he noticed that the weather was clearing up, despite everything, and he ignored his car. The sleepy little seaside town didn't seem to have got out of bed yet, this Saturday morning. So what? he thought: it's only twenty past seven.

He walked along Hoistraat then took the steps down to Fisktorget and the harbour without really being aware of where he was heading: but when he saw the breakwater and the marina, he knew. Of course.

Down on the Esplanade he checked the opening times of Winderhuus: Saturday–Sunday 10–15, it said on a notice attached to the door. He nodded, and continued into the municipal forest.

The meandering path to Rikken for cyclists and pedestrians was just as he remembered it. It dawned on him that quite a lot was as he had remembered it. He cupped his hands and lit the day's first cigarette. Had it something to do with his age, perhaps? That the past could sometimes seem clearer and more tangible than the present and what was happening now?

Rubbish, he decided. I'm completely clear about what is going on in the here and now. But a little historical illumination doesn't do any harm.

He reached Wackerstraat after twenty minutes. Passed by the Nolans' house and noted that there was a small, silver-coloured car standing on the drive. Of East Asian origin, by the look of it . . . Hyundai, or whatever the damned things were called.

He assumed that was the wife's car – they had two, naturally, and Christopher Nolan was the one who drove the considerably more masculine Rover, naturally.

Van Veeteren slowed down until he was barely moving. There was no sign of life from inside the house, and he assumed they were still in bed, the doting pair of art lovers. It wasn't yet eight o'clock, the gallery didn't open until ten, and there was of course no need to get up yet.

Why am I calling him Nolan when I know that his name's Hennan? he thought in annoyance, and stopped at the next crossroads.

And why don't they trust my judgement?

He suddenly felt the anger boiling up inside him.

A reply from England tonight at the earliest!

But probably not until tomorrow morning.

And what sort of a reply would it be? It wasn't especially difficult to predict that. If Hennan had acquired a new name, he would of course have been careful how he went about it. Even an old bookseller going for a morning walk could understand that perfectly well. At a guess there would be somebody called Nolan in Bristol – or would have been – who fitted all the information Münster and Moerk had been served up with. The man was no fool. Far from it.

And what was the investigating team going to do today? Lie in bed and speculate away a whole Saturday?

He remained standing at the crossroads and rolled two new cigarettes. The outline of a plan of action was suddenly beginning to appear in his mind's eye, and just as two joggers dressed in red ran past him in the direction of the woods, he knew what he was going to do.

It wasn't all that complicated, after all. He checked his watch and began walking back quite quickly to Bausen's nest.

His host had got up and begun the morning's yoga exercises. Van Veeteren explained that he had something he needed to do during the morning, but he would be back in time for lunch. Then he ignored Bausen's questions, unpacked all the things he needed, drank another cup of coffee, went to his car and drove off.

At twenty past nine he was back in Rikken. He parked on the other side of Wackerstraat, diagonally opposite number 14. The silver-coloured Japanese car was still there, a light had been switched on in the kitchen, but otherwise everything was as it had been before. Van Veeteren put on his cap and sun glasses. Took out *de Journaal*, adjusted the back of his seat so that he could lie back in comfort, and prepared to wait.

It took just over half an hour. During that time a few people passed by his somewhat battered old Opel, but nobody seemed to pay him any attention. Or to wonder why it was parked precisely there. Van Veeteren had just finished listening to the second movement of Mahler's second symphony when Elizabeth Nolan emerged through the front door and hurried over to her car. Started the engine, backed out and was gone in less than a minute.

Hardly surprising, Van Veeteren thought. The gallery was due to open in five minutes – and even if there were not going to be masses of people tramping restlessly up and down outside, there might just be the odd citizen of Kaalbringen with an interest in culture and nothing better to do on a Saturday morning to look after.

He waited for a while. Then he adjusted his cap and sun glasses and got out of the car.

Christopher Nolan answered the third ring on the bell. He was wrapped up in a yellow bath towel and wearing slippers. Water was dripping off him.

'I was in the shower,' he said. 'What do you want?'

'My apologies,' said Van Veeteren holding out the card. 'I'm looking for this address, but I seem to have got lost. Could you possibly . . . ?'

Nolan dried his hands on the towel, took hold of the card

and tried to read it. Found a pair of glasses on a hall table and tried again.

'Singerstraat? Is that supposed to be here in Rikken?'

'That's what I was told.'

Nolan took off his glasses and frowned.

'Never heard of it. I'm sorry, but I'm afraid you'll have to ask somebody else. But I doubt if it's anywhere around here.'

Van Veeteren nodded, looked concerned and took back the card.

'I'm sorry to have dragged you out of the shower.'

'No problem,' Nolan assured him. 'I'm going straight back in.'

He looked at Van Veeteren for a second, then closed the door.

DeKlerk and Stiller were at their desks in the police station when he entered from Kleinmarkt.

'I heard about your doubts,' he began.

'Doubts?' said deKlerk. 'Hmm, I don't know if one could call them—'

'Call them whatever you like. You seem to doubt my mental faculties in any case. I don't.'

'I don't think . . .' began Stiller.

'We're waiting for a reply from England,' said deKlerk. 'Obviously, we need to be absolutely certain about matters before we go any further.'

He made a half-hearted gesture that presumably meant Van Veeteren was welcome to sit down if he wanted to.

But he didn't.

'I know about that,' he said instead. 'But I think the question ought to be resolved a little more quickly. Here you are, these are his fingerprints.'

He took the little plastic bag with the card from his inside pocket.

'Fingerprints . . . Really?' said deKlerk.

'Hennan's prints are in the register in Maardam,' said Van Veeteren. 'I thought I could let you look after this – it shouldn't take more than a couple of hours, given modern-day technology. I assume you have a computer?'

He could have sworn that deKlerk blushed.

Serves him right, he thought.

'Of course,' said Stiller. 'Obviously, we can fix this straight away. How did you—'

'Never mind that,' said Van Veeteren, interrupting him. 'But don't lose the card – I didn't take a copy. I suggest you contact us at Bausen's place when you get confirmation.'

'Yes . . . Of course,' stammered deKlerk. 'Would you like a—'

'No, thank you.'

He remembered one more thing when he got as far as the doorway. He turned round and stared hard at the chief of police.

'If we get confirmation,' he said. 'If Hennan's and Nolan's fingerprints are the same, I recommend that you arrange to keep watch on them. It would be most annoying if the bird flew the nest just when we have quite a lot of officers on the case.'

DeKlerk nodded. Stiller nodded.

Van Veeteren turned on his heel and left the police station.

Time for a little nap, he thought as he walked across the square. High time.

If I'm wrong, he thought, it'll be best if I never set foot again in this godforsaken dump.

But when he was sitting behind the wheel again, heading back to Bausen's nest, that was not what worried him most. There was something else.

That final eye contact with Christopher Nolan.

That second when they had looked at each other.

It had lasted longer than it should have done.

43

When the telephone call came from Intendent Mulder at the forensic laboratory in Maardam, all five of them were gathered in the conference room.

DeKlerk and Stiller had been at their desks since the day dawned, Münster and Rooth since about eleven o'clock, and Inspector Moerk had turned up at a few minutes to twelve. Now it was ten past. Rooth answered the call and handed the receiver over to the chief of police, who said in noticeably rapid succession 'yes' five times, 'I see' twice, and 'many thanks' once.

Then he hung up and dampened his lips with the tip of his tongue.

'Agreement on eleven points,' he said. 'There is no doubt about it. Christopher Nolan is identical with Jaan G. Hennan.'

'Damn and blast!' said Inspector Rooth. 'That means we can't go home today either.'

There followed a few seconds of silence. Münster tried to exchange glances with Beate Moerk, but could make no eye contact. Stiller bit the tip of his ballpoint pen so hard that it creaked, and the chief of police seemed to be miles away. He started rubbing his right earlobe, but changed over to his left.

'Well, what do we do?' he said when he had finished.

'As he said,' suggested Moerk.

'Who?'

'Van Veeteren, of course. We keep an eye on Nolan. That's the least one can expect.'

Münster stood up.

'I'll go and talk to the chief inspectors,' he said. 'It somehow feels as if we're not going to be able to sort this out without them. Is that how you see it?'

'Fine,' said deKlerk. 'You're probably right. Maybe a bit of an apology wouldn't be out of place as well?'

'I'll decide on how exactly to go about things when I get there,' said Münster. 'But I have to say I find it hard to judge the risk of him running away.'

'What do you mean?' asked Rooth.

'All I mean is that as far as we are aware, Hennan still doesn't know that we know who he is – but as soon as he does realize that, there is of course a risk that he'll do a runner. On the other hand, as it were.'

'But why?' wondered Moerk. 'Why would he run away? We have nothing to charge him with – apart from using a false name, that is.'

'Not a thing,' agreed Rooth. 'We have nothing on him at all. Apart from imagining that he murdered three people. But if we sit in a car outside his house, something should happen sooner or later. There's such a period of stagnation that I'm coming out in spots.'

'Are you suggesting that we ought to provoke him into making a move?' asked deKlerk.

'Provoke and provoke,' muttered Rooth angrily. 'I'm damned if I know. But if Van Veeteren has just served us up with a triple murderer on a plate, it would be a bit of a pain if we allowed him to slip away. That's my own view in any case – and I volunteer to do the first stint.'

He looked around.

'Okay,' said Beate Moerk. 'I'll come with you. How do you judge the risk of him turning violent, by the way? . . . If he notices us sitting there keeping watch on him?'

'He's quite a peaceful type,' said Rooth. 'Apart from the inclination he has to murder people now and then. My advice is that you should take with you your police firearm. You can always sit in the car and polish it to avoid getting bored . . . Personally I intend solving crossword puzzles and filing my nails.'

He made to leave, but deKlerk asked him to wait a moment.

'Just one more question,' he said. 'I don't suppose any of you have discovered anything concerning that crux?'

'What crux?' asked Beate Moerk.

'What it was that Verlangen discovered . . . The proof relevant to that old case. Have any of you got any ideas?'

Nobody had. Not today either.

Bausen and Van Veeteren were sitting on the patio eating onion soup with croutons when Münster arrived.

'Welcome to the jungle, Intendent,' said Bausen. 'Would you like a spot of lunch?'

Münster said he would, and Bausen went into the kitchen to fetch an extra bowl, glass and spoon. He ladled out a serving from the pot standing in the middle of the table, and nodded towards Münster.

'We're drinking a dry white wine with it,' he said. 'Can I pour you a glass?'

He poured one out without waiting for an answer.

'Thank you,' said Münster. 'I have some news – we've heard from Mulder.'

'And?' said Bausen.

'It's true, Nolan is Hennan.'

Until that point Van Veeteren had been deeply involved with the soup, but now he put down his spoon and dried himself thoroughly around his mouth with his table napkin.

'We know that,' he said. 'I thought you said you were coming with news?'

Bausen smiled and looked from one to the other.

'My apologies,' said Münster. 'In any case, we're now a hundred per cent certain. Rooth and Inspector Moerk are in place outside his house. The question is: what the hell should we do next?'

'Haven't you made your minds up about that yet?' wondered Van Veeteren, taking a sip of wine.

'No,' said Münster. 'But I think we should bring him in. Waiting for him to give himself away somehow or other . . . or the idea that we might gain something by hovering in the background . . . No, I don't go along with that.'

Bausen cleared his throat.

'But if you put him under surveillance, he'll soon realize

that you are on his tail, surely?' he said. 'Or are Moerk and Rooth intending to be discreet?'

Münster hesitated.

'I don't know, to be honest,' he said. 'It's a bit unclear, and we didn't discuss that aspect properly. But I don't think Inspector Rooth has any desire to be discreet for very long . . . under any circumstances – it's not really his style.'

Van Veeteren swirled his glass round and thought.

'Ah, well,' he said in the end. 'It's not an easy position to be in. Would you like a bit of advice?'

Münster nodded submissively.

'Keep an eye on him so that he notices what you're doing,' said Van Veeteren. 'Let him get worried. Then bring him in late this evening or tomorrow. And if you would still like my services, I'm prepared to interrogate him forty-eight hours on end.'

Bausen raised an eyebrow.

Münster raised two.

'Good,' he said. 'I'll pass that on to deKlerk.'

He tried to stand up, but Bausen pushed him back down onto his chair.

'Eat up your food first,' he said. 'And that's a fine old chardonnay you're holding in your hand. It's not something you drink standing up.'

'My apologies,' said Intendent Münster again.

It was the first time Beate Moerk had been alone together with Inspector Rooth, and even if what happened at the end of their four-hour stint had never taken place, she would no doubt have remembered him even so.

At least, that is what she thought while it was happening.

'You're married, is that right?' said Rooth even before they had sat down in the car. 'I think that's what Münster said.'

'Yes, I am,' said Moerk. 'How about you?'

'I'm single,' said Rooth. 'Like a crab apple in the taiga. I expect you have children as well?'

'Two,' said Moerk.

'And no plans to get divorced?'

'No.'

'Oh dear,' said Rooth. 'It's not easy for people to be alone.'

Moerk pondered for a moment.

'I thought you said you were going to solve crossword puzzles and clean your fingernails. When do you intend starting on that?'

'Filing,' said Rooth. 'Not cleaning. No, I think we ought to have a philosophical discussion and make plans instead. To start with, at least. What do you say to that?'

'That's fine by me,' said Moerk. 'But start the car now so that we set off before Hennan has had time to do a runner.'

Rooth eyed her ruefully and did as he had been told.

'Can't we talk a bit about the case?' she suggested when they parked directly opposite the Nolans' house in Wackerstraat. 'You reckon this is where we should park, do you?'

Rooth shrugged.

'I don't really know,' he said. 'What do you think?'

'If we want to make sure he notices us, this is the perfect place,' said Moerk, looking at the house. 'If two people spend a whole afternoon in a car on a housing estate like this, then –'

'– they're either the filth or a loving couple,' said Rooth. 'Perhaps we ought to play the roles of a loving couple, so that we don't give ourselves away.'

'You'd better kiss me, then,' said Moerk.

'That's exactly what I mean,' said Rooth.

She glared at him and was tempted to give him a slap, but she held herself in check.

'Cut out that sexist crap,' she said instead. 'You're just making a fool of yourself.'

Rooth looked at her in surprise. Then he scratched himself under his chin.

'Humble apologies,' he said. 'It's just my life as a flirt playing tricks with me. It's always the same when I find myself in the company of a beautiful woman . . . Perhaps we should park just a little bit offside, in fact?'

He started the engine again and backed about ten metres. They still had a good view of the house, but as long as Nolan didn't come out into the garden it was unlikely that he would spot them. Rooth switched off the engine. Moerk checked her watch. It was twenty minutes past two.

'The crux,' said Rooth. 'That bloody crux is incomprehensible. But if we put our clever little heads together, maybe we can solve it?'

Moerk wondered briefly if there was some hidden sexual implication in the putting together of their heads, but when she looked into his honest blue eyes, she decided that was not the case.

'All right,' she said. 'Fire away!'

'Verlangen was an alcoholic,' said Rooth.

'True.'

'Not all that observant, presumably.'

'Presumably not.'

'But nevertheless he claimed that he had found out something crucial in connection with that old murder in Linden.'

'Yes.'

'How the hell could that be possible? What did he mean?'

Moerk thought for a few seconds.

'He must have caught sight of G and recognized him,' she said. 'That's how it must have begun, at least.'

'One would have thought so,' said Rooth.

'Where? Where did he catch sight of him?'

'A good question. Most probably Maardam. G must have been visiting there for some reason or other.'

'In April this year?'

'Or shortly before then.'

'Hmm. And Verlangen happens to see him . . . But that's not enough.'

'In what way isn't it enough?' asked Rooth, adjusting the rear-view mirror so that the pair could have eye contact without putting their necks out of joint.

'There must have been something more. There's no reason why Verlangen should start following Hennan just because he's seen him for the first time in fifteen years. Unless he was away with the fairies . . . Verlangen, that is.'

'You're probably right,' said Rooth. 'Although he didn't discover whatever it was he thought was crucial until he came up here to Kaalbringen. Don't you think?'

'I don't know. Do you think he spoke to him?'

'Where? In Maardam?'

'In both places . . . But he must surely have done so here in Kaalbringen in any case.'

'I'd have thought he spoke to him in Maardam as well,' said Rooth. 'And Hennan could have said something that . . . well, that gave something away. Or made Verlangen wonder, at least.'

Moerk thought for a moment or two.

'But what could he have given away in that case?' she asked. 'The name of his accomplice, perhaps? Because there was an accomplice in that murder, wasn't there?'

'As far as I understand it,' sighed Rooth. 'But we keep coming back to the same question. Why the hell should Hennan be so daft as to give himself away to somebody like Verlangen? No, I think there's something wrong with this line of argument – I've thought so all along.'

'Come up with something that holds water, then,' said Moerk.

'I can't,' admitted Rooth. 'But I've just thought of something else. How do we know that he's at home?'

'Eh?'

'Nolan–Hennan. Perhaps we're keeping watch on an empty house.'

Moerk thought again.

'Stupid,' she said. 'That would be stupid. So what do we do?'

'This,' said Rooth, taking out his mobile phone. 'We telephone him and see if he answers – as easy as that.'

'Brilliant,' said Moerk.

'Brilliance has always been my guiding star,' said Rooth, tapping in the number.

After three rings Christopher Nolan answered, and Rooth hung up.

'Okay,' he said. 'He's in there. At least we know that.'

'He could slip out of the back door,' said Moerk. 'And into the woods.'

Rooth thought for a moment.

'He won't do that,' he said. 'He doesn't even know we're after him. But if you want to sneak around the plot and hide yourself away in the bushes, you're welcome to do so. But if you do, you won't have the pleasure of my company.'

Beate Moerk never had the chance to weigh up the advantages and disadvantages of such a manoeuvre, as at that very moment a silver-coloured Hyundai passed by them and turned into the drive. Fru Nolan got out of the car, took a black briefcase from the back seat and disappeared into the house. Rooth looked at his watch.

'Eleven minutes past three,' he said. 'Elizabeth Nolan comes home after a day at the gallery. You have to agree that it's exciting, being a police officer.'

'Unbearably so,' said Beate Moerk.

It was exactly one hour and two minutes before anything else happened in connection with the Nolans' house in Wackerstraat – but at least, it was just as exciting as the previous incident.

Fru Nolan opened front door, turned to wave goodbye to her husband in the direction of the hall, walked over to her car, sat down in it and drove off in the direction of central Kaalbringen.

'Aha,' said Rooth, who had been dozing off during the last half-hour due to lack of nourishment.

'Hmm,' said Moerk.

She felt incapable of searching in her mind for words any more.

'Off she goes again,' said Rooth, with a yawn. 'Do you know what I'm sitting here and remembering?'

'No,' said Moerk. 'What are you sitting there remembering?'

'Am I not right in thinking that on the way here we drove past a corner shop? Just by the railway . . . I think I'll take a stroll and buy a newspaper and some refreshments. While I'm away maybe you could ring HQ and ask them for instructions as to what we should do next?'

Moerk sat up straight and nodded.

'And ask them if they've got anything to give us to prevent bed sores.'

He got out of the car and started walking back along Wackerstraat. Moerk waited until he was out of sight, then dialled the police station.

It was Probationer Stiller who answered.

'How's it going?' he wondered.

'Going?' said Moerk. 'Nothing at all is happening. Apart

from the fact that fru Nolan has left the house. We have an as yet unconfirmed hypothesis that she's gone shopping.'

'Interesting,' said Stiller. 'Are you bored?'

'A funeral would cheer us up,' said Moerk. 'Have you discussed when we're going to be relieved?'

'Just a moment,' said Stiller, putting his hand over the receiver.

She tried to listen between his fingers, but didn't manage to pick up what was being said.

'Hello,' said Stiller after about fifteen seconds. 'You'll have to stay there for almost another two hours. Münster and I will relieve you at six o'clock.'

'Are you in contact with Van Veeteren and Bausen?' asked Moerk.

'Yes. They also think we should wait until this evening.'

Beate Moerk sighed.

'Okay, let's leave it at that.'

She finished the call and looked again at the house.

Nothing had changed.

Later – much later – when Beate Moerk thought back to what happened between ten to six and five to six, it was always – for whatever reason – the incident with the bag of shopping that first came to mind.

Elizabeth Nolan had just parked at the usual place on the drive. Rooth remarked that Kaalbringen was evidently also blessed by the presence of a Merckx supermarket – as he recognized the logo on the plastic carrier bags that had just been taken off the back seat and placed on the edge of the well-tended lawn – and Moerk had glanced at her watch and established that it was exactly ten minutes to six.

Elizabeth Nolan closed the back door of the car, took hold of the two bulging carrier bags, one in each hand, but when she picked them up, one of the handles broke.

A mountain of shopping spilled out over the grass: Moerk and Rooth could see – rather than hear – the curses she gave vent to. She paused for a second, then carried the unbroken bag into the house and came back out again half a minute later, carrying a brown cardboard box.

As she transferred the goods into the box, Moerk wondered in annoyance why on earth her husband hadn't come out to help her.

A typical layabout husband, she had time to think. He's no doubt sitting in front of the telly, gaping at football!

That was a seriously wrong assumption, as she would soon become aware.

Fru Nolan went back into the house, lugging the heavy cardboard box in her arms. She had considerable difficulty closing the door behind her.

Rooth looked at Moerk. Moerk looked at Rooth. Rooth yawned and looked at his watch.

'Six minutes to go before we're relieved,' he said. 'Do you really not want to come with me for a bite to eat when we've finished?'

Beate Moerk said no for the fifth time, whereupon the door of the Nolans' house opened yet again. Elizabeth Nolan came running out.

Straight out onto the lawn with both hands pressed against her temples and her elbows jutting out. After a few steps she stopped dead. Stood and swayed back and forth for a moment, then fell on her right side and rolled over on her stomach.

Moerk and Rooth reached her at the same time. Together they managed to turn her over: she was groaning faintly, both her eyes and her mouth were half-open, and she seemed barely conscious. Rooth took hold of her chin and shook it gently.

'How are you?' asked Moerk. 'What's happened?'

Nolan became more alert. Stared at them in surprise for a few seconds, then pointed at the house and moved her lips.

'What are you saying?' asked Rooth.

She closed her eyes and took a deep breath. Opened her eyes again.

'The bathroom,' she whispered, in a barely audible voice. 'He's lying in the bath.'

Rooth gaped at her, then he gaped at Beate Moerk.

Then both of them raced into the house.

They found their way immediately. The bathroom in the Nolans' house was at the end of the L-shaped hall, and she had left the door open.

Christopher Nolan was lying in the tub, which was full to the brim. His head was leaning on the rim, and the water was so red that for a split second Moerk had time to think that it looked rather pretty.

'Bloody hell!' said Inspector Rooth. 'Bloody fucking hell!'

'What's going on?' wondered a voice from outside the front door.

It was Münster. Beate Moerk backed quickly out of the bathroom, turned round and met him in the hall.

'What's happened?' asked Münster. 'We've just arrived to relieve you. Fru Nolan seems to be in shock, and—'

'There's no mystery,' said Moerk. 'Hennan has taken his own life. He's lying in there.'

She forced her way past Münster, went out through the door and saw Probationer Stiller squatting down beside fru Nolan, who was still lying stretched out on the lawn.

A faint beam of the setting sun caught her eye, and she felt that she was longing for her children so much that it hurt.

44

During the first three hours that passed after they had heard about the death of Jaan G. Hennan, Van Veeteren uttered at most twenty words: and when it seemed most critical Bausen wondered if he ought to call a doctor.

But he made do with going down to his cellar and fetching a bottle of Château Peripolignac '79. However, not even this most eminent of medicines was enough to revive Van Veeteren's spirits to any noticeable degree.

Not until shortly after ten at night, when at long last they were assembled in the pale-yellow room at the police station, did the *Chief Inspector* seem anywhere near ready to resume contact with the real world. He flopped down at the narrow end of the table, lit a cigarette and glared at the chief of police.

'Let's hear it, then!' he demanded. 'Every damned detail, if you don't mind!'

DeKlerk eyed both him and Bausen somewhat shiftily, hung up his jacket and checked that the cups of coffee and sandwiches had been distributed fairly. Then he cleared his throat and began.

'We couldn't possibly have foreseen this,' he started by

saying. 'But that's the way it is. Christopher Nolan, alias Jaan G. Hennan, committed suicide this afternoon by lying down in the bathtub and cutting his arteries. Both wrists, and a few cuts in his neck also, just to make sure . . .'

'There was more blood in the bath than in his body,' Rooth informed them, taking a bite out of a sandwich. 'The Red Sea in a nutshell.'

'We've just had a call from the pathologist in Oostwerdin-gen,' said deKlerk, ignoring Rooth's comment. 'He confirms that Hennan took a number of sleeping tablets as well – there was a tin on the edge of the bath.'

'What did he use to cut himself with?' asked Bausen.

'A razor blade. That was also lying on the edge of the bath.'

'It all sounds pretty neat and efficient.'

'Very.'

'Have you spoken to his wife.'

DeKlerk shook his head.

'Not yet,' he said. 'She's not feeling too good.'

'Really?' said Bausen.

'She's in shock,' said Beate Moerk. 'We tried to talk to her – we were on the spot after all, Rooth and I – but we couldn't get any sense out of her.'

'Timing?' wondered Van Veeteren.

Rooth wiped his mouth and consulted a sheet of paper.

'She left the house at 16.13,' he said. 'Did a bit of shopping. Bought a few things at Merckx among other items, and was back home by 17.50. Went into the house and found him.'

'Two hours, more or less,' said deKlerk. 'He had plenty of

time. According to the pathologist it took him a quarter of an hour to die.'

'Why did he take sleeping tablets?' wondered Stiller.

'To make it easier, one can assume,' said deKlerk. 'The stuff is called Softal: it's one of those new drugs that won't kill you, no matter how much of it you take . . . But if he took five tablets he must have been pretty far gone when he passed the point of no return. Lengthwise cuts as well, just as it says in the rulebook. And hot water makes the blood flow more easily as well . . .'

'Seneca,' muttered Van Veeteren. 'A well tried and tested method. Any messages? Did he leave a note or anything?'

'Nothing,' said Rooth.

'Nothing at all?'

'Not so much as a word.'

Rooth held out the palms of his hands and tried to look apologetic.

'Anyway,' said deKlerk, taking over again. 'No, this really was a bolt from the blue . . . Fru Nolan is lying asleep in hospital, but we must talk to her tomorrow morning, of course.'

'Didn't you get anything at all out of her?' Bausen wondered, sounding slightly reproachful.

'Very little,' admitted Moerk. 'I was in the car that took her to the hospital, and she really was in another world. No, he didn't leave a single word behind, as Rooth says . . . and fru Nolan didn't notice anything amiss when she was at home for that hour between three and four. At least, she shook her head when I asked about that. She didn't seem to link the suicide with the fact that we had been to the gallery to talk to her . . . Not until shortly after I left her, in any case. Then she looked at me and asked . . .'

'What?' said Rooth. 'What did she ask?'

'She said: "Was he the one, then?" At least, I think that's what she said . . . Her voice was very faint.'

'"Was he the one, then?"' repeated Münster. 'Hmm, I take it you could have said yes . . . that it *was* him.'

Moerk nodded.

'But I didn't say anything,' she said. 'Anyway, I assume we'll have a few things to explain to her tomorrow morning.'

'A few things indeed,' said Van Veeteren. 'By God, yes.'

'You don't say,' said Bausen.

Van Veeteren stubbed out his cigarette but didn't elaborate on his thoughts. If indeed he had any.

'Anyway, we can draw certain conclusions from this,' said the chief of police. 'Don't you think? Nolan . . . Hennan . . . must have realized that we were on to him. Either his wife must have said something, even if we have no evidence for assuming that, or . . . Well, I don't really know.'

'An implication might well have been enough,' said Moerk. 'Something she let slip without having realized it.'

'Very possibly,' said deKlerk. 'And he might have noticed you and Rooth in the car outside as well. Anyway, he realized that the game was up, and decided to give up.'

He looked round in the hope of receiving support for this hypothesis, but only Probationer Stiller condescended to give him a vague nod.

'What you say is right enough,' said Münster after a few seconds of silence. 'It's just . . . just so damned untypical of

G, that's all. Giving up in a situation like this. When we have hardly an ounce of evidence and before we've asked him a single question. You can't help wondering—'

Bausen interrupted him.

'Maybe there were other things on the table as far as he was concerned,' he suggested. 'What if he had been leading a blameless life since that earlier episode, and then he suddenly finds his new identity exposed, the whole of his new existence . . . well, maybe that was simply too much for him? Could that have been possible? Fifteen years are fifteen years, after all.'

'It wouldn't be much fun to have to admit to your wife that you are not the person she thought you were,' said Rooth. 'That you've been in jail and suspected of three murders.'

'That's exactly what I mean,' said Bausen. 'It's not a pleasant situation to be in. We've never actually had him found guilty of anything, but we've kept putting the kibosh on his marriages.'

'He was frightened of being treated roughly, in other words,' said Rooth thoughtfully. 'We can be sure of that. Faint-hearted type.'

The chief of police leafed through his notes.

'As for the question of how he . . . how he caught on to us,' he said hesitantly, 'I suppose we can have different theories about that. He did come eye to eye with Van Veeteren twice, of course . . . Did you get any feeling that he might have realized who you were?'

Van Veeteren clasped his hands behind his neck and closed his eyes for a few seconds before answering.

'I can't judge that,' he said. 'But there's one thing I do know, and that is that during all the years I've spent as a police officer, I have never come across such a pointless and demeaning exit from this life. Never ever.'

'What the hell can one expect from such a king-size prat as G?' asked Rooth. 'Maybe it was typical of him, when all is said and done?'

Nobody seemed to have anything to add to that, and as it was almost eleven o'clock, Chief of Police deKlerk proposed that all present should reconvene to discuss matters further tomorrow afternoon instead.

'What about Elizabeth Nolan?' asked Moerk.

'I'll take care of her,' said deKlerk. 'We're expecting some more information from the pathologist tomorrow. And a response from England, with a bit of luck – although maybe that isn't very important any more. In any case, we must conclude this case in accordance with the rulebook. Tie up all the loose ends. Don't you think?'

'Of course,' said Rooth. 'But on Monday we're going home. I'm missing my pets so much.'

'Have you got pets?' asked Münster. 'I thought you had got rid of that aquarium?'

'Mites and bluebottles,' Inspector Rooth informed him with a smile.

They emerged into the square under a clear and cloudless sky, and he explained to Bausen that he needed to go for a walk.

Bausen looked for a moment as if he were going to object, but then shrugged and clambered into the car.

'See you at breakfast, then,' he said before closing the door. 'Wake me up if you want some good advice.'

'Thank you,' said Van Veeteren. 'I'm going home tomorrow in any case.'

'You can stay for as long as you like.'

'I know. But this business seems to be over now. Go to bed and sleep well.'

Bausen nodded and drove off. Van Veeteren stood and watched the rear lights fade away in the direction of the dairy in Doomstraat. He hesitated for a moment, then set off in the direction of Leisnerparken and the Blue Ship.

I need a beer, he thought.

Maybe two.

It's a damned shame that I don't even have the strength to talk to Bausen.

The Blue Ship was relatively full – he reminded himself that it was Saturday evening after all – but even so he managed to find a table to himself in the small area between the bar and the restaurant itself.

He ordered a dark beer and lit a cigarette, and wondered how many he had smoked since hearing about the death of G that afternoon. It must be more than ten, he thought. That's ridiculous – I shall give up altogether tomorrow.

He was still finding it hard to control all the emotions and thoughts flying around inside him.

Hard to accept the fact.

G was dead.

He had lain down in the bath, cut his wrists and left the stage. Dead!

It was as if . . . He just didn't know what it was as if.

An opponent who no suddenly longer existed?

A chess player who no longer came to the table even though the game was still in progress? Simply because he didn't want to any more.

Bad metaphors, he knew that: but he couldn't find any others to express the strange, sterile irritation he felt.

Was this the last chapter in the G File? How could it be written like this? He had many diffuse images of alternatives, but one thing was clear: none of them was anything like this.

It would have been better if I'd been able to kill him myself, he thought grimly as he sank a deep swig of beer. Then at least I would have had a hand in it.

It was an appalling thought, of course, and said a lot about his true motives; but as usual it was presumably best to simply accept the fact.

Facing up to your own motives is painful – but if you are going to get anywhere, it's the only way! So Mahler had once said – or written – and it was no doubt true. Cheating was easier, and you received no reward for not doing so.

Apart from recognizing your true self.

He drank more beer, and inhaled deeply several times. Spent a few seconds contemplating a man sitting alone at a table opposite him, fast asleep with his chin resting on his chest.

A mercy to pray for in silence? Van Veeteren wondered grimly.

And the vacuum! Jaan G. Hennan had left behind a vacuum, which was also remarkable. Of course it is possible to hate somebody who is dead, he decided, but it feels rather pointless.

It was as if G had somehow avoided his punishment, was it not? Yes, that was what it was all about, of course. In the end – despite the fact that he had lost the game – he had decided his own fate. Instead of granting vengeance to whomever it was due in the name of justice.

In other words, to *Chief Inspector* Van Veeteren.

Damn it all, he thought. If I were religious I could at least try to convince myself that vengeance was the Good Lord's.

He drank the rest of his beer and ordered another one. I don't even know how the murder of Barbara Hennan was achieved, it struck him. He wondered about that for a while. Maybe that was the worst thing of all, when all was said and done? The most humiliating and unacceptable. The fact that G had more or less confessed, but not explained how he had done it. Merely laughed scornfully and died.

Laughed scornfully and died? It sounded like the basis of a book title.

As far as one could ascertain, it seemed that only two people knew the answer to that question. Hennan and Verlangen. Both of them were dead. The game was over, and they had taken the knowledge with them to the grave. Nobody would ever know what had happened to that attractive

American woman that evening in Linden fifteen years ago. That was the fact of the matter.

Or was it? Was there perhaps somebody left who knew? A perpetrator still alive? The accomplice?

God only knows, thought Van Veeteren, and then began to think about what on earth they should say to Elizabeth Nolan when she woke up in her hospital bed.

The truth?

No doubt there were good reasons for keeping it from her. Parts of it, at least. It was easier to cheat a bit, as he had realized already: the truth was one thing, humanitarian action not necessarily the same.

Ah well, he thought. It's not my problem. Every cloud . . .

He drank the second beer and smoked another cigarette. Observed the sleeping man for a while, and felt that he was also beginning to feel so numb that he might well be able to enjoy a few hours' sleep as well. Despite everything.

And with that pious hope in the back of his mind, he left the Blue Ship.

When he got back to Bausen's house it was a quarter to one. Bausen had gone to bed, and Van Veeteren crept into bed with a feeling of shame and a bad conscience with regard to his host.

I must try to make it up to him somehow before I go home tomorrow, he thought. It can't be much fun to be lumbered with somebody like me, day out and day in.

Not much fun at all.

45

Beate Moerk had been looking forward to spending Sunday together with her husband and children, but as early as eight o'clock the chief of police telephoned her and asked her to accompany him to the hospital in order to speak to Elizabeth Nolan.

Moerk realized that what had suddenly become so desirable again was that famous feminine sensitivity, and for a moment she considered telling him to go to hell. But she managed to hold herself in check, and after a spot of arguing agreed on two hours in return for the promise of a whole day off in the coming week.

Franek was standing by the stove, preparing the morning gruel, while the discussions were taking place, and looked slightly worried – not for his own sake, she knew that, but for hers. As she replaced the receiver she wondered if there were other men around like him, or if – as her mother claimed at the time – she had been extremely lucky to find him.

But perhaps it was best to do as he always used to say: don't worry about analysing good things, just hang on to them. That's the most important thing.

'I'll be back before noon,' she promised. 'Then we can go off somewhere.'

'You can tell her that provided she pays well, I'm prepared to exhibit twelve canvases in December,' he said. 'But maybe now isn't the right time for that?'

'Probably not,' said Moerk, giving him a quick kiss.

She hugged the children, then set off on her humanitarian task.

'What's this?' asked Bausen with a frown.

'A small token of my gratitude,' said Van Veeteren. 'An invitation to celebrate Christmas in Maardam – for both you and Mathilde. You said that you generally just sit around on your own and drink Bourgogne . . . The bottle is cognac for you to sip now and then as autumn progresses. Bache-Gabrielsen, a Norwegian product in fact, but every drop is pure gold – I don't know if you're familiar with it?'

'Never heard of it,' he admitted. 'But it's completely unnecessary to—'

'Rubbish. Now I'll just have a sandwich and then leave you and this blasted Hennan business behind.'

Bausen allowed himself a wry grin.

'Ah well, thank you very much,' he said. 'We shall have to see if we live until Christmas, but I promise to drink the Gabrielsen before the call comes in any case . . . I have various other things to empty, come to that.'

'Yes, I've gathered that,' said Van Veeteren. 'How many bottles have you left?'

531

'Somewhere between eleven and twelve hundred,' said Bausen with a sigh. 'I fell behind somewhat while I was stuck in jail, as I've said before. But as long as I stay healthy, no doubt I'll get through them.'

Van Veeteren looked at his watch. It was five past twelve.

'May I borrow your phone and give Ulrike a ring? My mobile seems to have caught some kind of virus.'

'As long as you don't go on for too long,' said Bausen.

Ulrike was out, but he left a message on the answering machine saying he would be home by about five, and he hoped she could cope with the thought of seeing him again.

When he had hung up he hesitated for a few seconds, then dialled the number of the police station.

No reply, so he rang Münster's mobile instead.

'Yes?' said Münster.

'Van Veeteren. I'm about to set off for home. Have you heard anything about Elizabeth Nolan?'

'A little bit,' said Münster. 'She seems to have calmed down somewhat, at least. DeKlerk and Moerk were there and spoke to her for a while, but they decided to interrogate her a bit more thoroughly tomorrow.'

'What did she say?'

'Apparently it was she who asked most of the questions . . . That's not all that surprising, I suppose. I gather they gave her quite vague answers but she was informed that her husband's past was rather different from what she had thought. Even though they didn't go into details.'

'Is she still in hospital?'

'No, I think she went home this morning. Just to be clear, you won't be present at the run-through, am I right?'

'No,' said Van Veeteren, 'I won't be there. I've had enough. But by all means give me a ring when you've tied up all the loose ends.'

'I'll do that,' said Münster. 'It's so damned frustrating that we didn't . . . well, that we didn't manage to sort everything out satisfactorily. I mean, both the murder of Barbara Hennan and that of Verlangen will have to be put on the shelf now. But it's far from clear how—'

'I know,' said Van Veeteren, interrupting him. 'As you rightly say, it's damned frustrating. But give me a ring.'

Münster repeated his promise to do so, and hung up.

Ah well, thought Van Veeteren. That's that, then.

Then he went out into the kitchen and ate a farewell sandwich with Bausen.

He stopped to fill up with petrol on the slip-road leading on to the motorway, and it was while he was standing there staring at the figures flicking past electronically on the pump that he made up his mind to indulge in a little digression.

How had Münster put it? 'She seems to have calmed down somewhat'? That should surely mean that she was strong enough to have a little chat?

If not, he could always leave her in peace, he thought. But despite everything, there were one or two questions it could be interesting to have answered.

A few things that had struck him after he had spoken to Münster on the phone. It wouldn't delay him for more than half an hour, three-quarters at the most; and he was in no hurry.

He had all the time in the world, in fact.

He paid at the kiosk, got back into his car and headed into town.

Those present at the Sunday afternoon run-through of the Hennan–Verlangen case at the police station in Kaalbringen were reduced to a mere quartet. The two former chief inspectors had withdrawn, and Inspector Moerk had been excused by the chief of police, in view of her input at the hospital earlier in the day.

But he was in place. As was Probationer Stiller – who had had his hair cut (how the hell had he managed that? wondered Inspector Rooth, and drew the preliminary conclusion that he must be engaged to a young and shapely hairdresser) – and the two so-called reinforcements from the Maardam CID.

Before deKlerk had a chance to say anything, Rooth set the ball rolling.

'This is our last session, just so that you know that. Tomorrow Münster and I are returning to civilization.'

It was obvious from the chief of police's face that he had some difficulty in linking the two concepts of Rooth and civilization, but he made no reference to that.

'Let's see if we can now sum up the case,' he said instead.

'As far as it's possible to do so, in any case. There are still a lot of things that are not clear, and more work needs doing, but with luck we should be able to sort that out next week. I think we should begin with the information from England. Stiller?'

The probationer looked up from his papers.

'It only arrived half an hour ago,' he said. 'In other words, it took a bit longer than they had promised, and it is very terse . . . They evidently don't have any overlapping systems over there. Maybe we can ask for more information in due course – if we consider it to be necessary in some circumstances.'

'We'll do that as a routine operation,' said deKlerk. 'But what does it say in the information we have got?'

'Hmm,' said Stiller. 'It's a bit surprising, I think. But there really is a married couple in Bristol who correspond very closely to what fru Nolan said. Christopher and Elizabeth, they got married in June 1989. No children. He worked at the Museum of Modern Art, she at some sort of college . . . the School of Advanced Creative Processing, whatever that means. In any case, they left Bristol in 1992, just as she claimed they did . . . That's about all: I don't really know what to say about it.'

Münster spoke up.

'Naturally, Hennan didn't just pluck details out of the air,' he said. 'And of course it's the time before 1989 that really interests us . . . Needless to say a real Christopher Nolan exists. If you want to acquire a new identity, it's always safer to adopt one that already exists – we've known that for ages.

The real Nolan might be dead, or have emigrated to Australia, or God only knows what . . .'

'Yes, of course,' said Stiller. 'I appreciate that. Perhaps this isn't of much use to us, but surely we need to prove – although maybe we've done that already? – to somehow *establish* for certain that the man who died in the bath wasn't in fact called Nolan.'

He looked around, hoping for agreement, and eventually deKlerk nodded vaguely.

'We'll have to check the matter, of course, to be on the safe side. But a fingerprint is a fingerprint after all. Anyway, we'll take that further next week. Any comments?'

Rooth and Münster shook their heads. DeKlerk took out a new sheet of paper.

'The pathologist has sent us a preliminary report,' he said. 'Nothing sensational there either, it seems to me. Just confirmation of what we knew yesterday – or thought we knew. Nolan died of an excessive loss of blood at some time between a quarter past four and five o'clock. Cuts in both wrists and in his neck. Sedated by five 20-milligram Softal tablets that he had received on prescription two years ago. For insomnia . . . Stomach contents: beer, a little whisky, broccoli pie and various other odds and ends – no, I don't think there is anything here of much interest to us.'

'I don't think so either,' said Rooth. 'And I assume we can nail him for the murder of Verlangen without more ado? Without technical proof, I mean. Or are you thinking of driving out there and looking for the weapon?'

'We'll see how things develop,' said deKlerk. 'No doubt the

prosecutor will want to have a say, but I don't foresee any problems.'

'I think it's odd that he didn't write anything,' said Stiller. 'To his wife, for instance.'

Münster nodded.

'Yes,' he said. 'It is a bit odd – but what the devil could he write?'

'Anything at all apart from the truth,' suggested Rooth. 'No, I think that aspect is in the bag. But how did it go at the hospital? Was she told that she'd been married to a triple murderer?'

DeKlerk hesitated for a moment before answering.

'No,' he said. 'We decided to be a bit vague on that point, Inspector Moerk and I. But she knows that there were irregularities.'

'Irregularities!' exclaimed Rooth. 'How about that for a circumlocution? And what does she think, then? That her bloke took his own life without the slightest trace of an explanation? That's hardly something you do because of an *irregularity*!'

'Perhaps not,' admitted deKlerk. 'But I don't think she's had much of a chance to think about it yet, in fact. We'll decide how to proceed tomorrow . . . I assume we shall have to give her the facts no matter what. Sooner or later. Poor woman.'

'There's something here that doesn't fit,' muttered Rooth. 'But never mind, the main thing is that Jaan G. Hennan has passed on into another world . . . even if it is annoying that he slipped out through the back door like this.'

'I agree,' said deKlerk. 'But that's the way it turned out.'

Intendent Münster had been sitting for a while lost in thought, twirling a pencil with his fingers.

'I don't understand why he panicked like that,' he said. 'And how did he discover that we were on to him? As far as we know his wife didn't tell him anything, and Rooth and Moerk could have been on some entirely different mission when they were sitting in the car outside the Nolans' house . . . Yes, I agree with Rooth, I find it difficult to make this add up.'

'Maybe he recognized Van Veeteren,' suggested Rooth. 'That would be one explanation.'

'Very possible,' said Münster.

'And maybe the *Chief Inspector* realized that as well,' said Rooth. 'Think about it, they must have sat staring at each other for hours on end, fifteen years ago . . . And Van Veeteren only needed one look at him to be certain, didn't he? The same could well have applied from Hennan's point of view, surely . . . although I don't suppose it matters much any longer. Is there anything else?'

Chief of Police deKlerk leafed through his papers one more time, then declared that there was nothing else.

Rooth and Münster went back to Hotel See Warf – where they had been staying all the time they had been in Kaalbringen – at twenty minutes past seven on Sunday evening, and just as they were standing in the foyer wondering whether to take the lift up to their rooms or to have a beer in the bar, Münster's mobile rang.

Rooth slipped into the toilet, and when he came out Münster had already finished talking.

'Who was that?' wondered Rooth.

Münster remained standing with his mobile in his hand, looking puzzled.

'Ulrike,' he said. 'It was Ulrike Fremdli, the woman Van Veeteren lives with. She wondered if I knew why he hadn't come home.'

'Eh?' said Rooth. 'Why . . . ?'

'He had said he would be back in Maardam by about five o'clock . . . It's nearly half past seven now, and he's evidently not answering his mobile.'

'Oh dear,' said Rooth. 'Have you met her, this Ulrike Fremdli? I've only heard about her.'

'Yes, I've met her.'

'Is she a good woman?'

'Very good,' said Münster. 'I wonder . . . Ah well, no doubt there's a natural explanation.'

'No doubt,' said Rooth. 'Shall we have a beer, then?'

46

When Van Veeteren pulled up in Wackerstraat and switched off the engine, he suddenly felt doubtful.

He remained in the car for a while, drumming his fingers on the steering wheel and trying to work out what the problem was. Some kind of mysterious intuition, or just another example of his general ambivalence?

He plumped for the latter, and clambered out of the car. Noted that fru Nolan's silver Japanese car was standing on the drive, and that everything looked peaceful. The sun had started to break through the greyish white morning cloud, and a corpulent man in his sixties was busy cutting the grass in the next-door garden. The insistent sound of the lawnmower hung over the whole area like a stubborn virus.

Fru Nolan answered the door after half a minute. She was wearing black jeans, an equally black tunic, and looked at him in a way that suggested she wasn't quite with it.

'Yes?'

'Forgive me for disturbing you. My name is Van Veeteren. I come from Maardam, and I've known your husband for a very long time. Could you perhaps let me have a little bit of your time for a chat?'

She looked him up and down. Ran a hand through her dark hair, which was surprisingly thick in view of the fact that she must be turned fifty, he thought.

'You know what's happened, do you?'

'Yes. You have my sympathy.'

She nodded and allowed him in. He guessed that she had been given some kind of tranquillizer by the hospital: the way she moved and spoke – in a sort of numb, mechanical way – suggested as much.

'After you.'

She ushered him into the living room, and he sat down in a wine-red armchair with yellow antimacassars on the arms.

'What did you say your name was?'

'Van Veeteren.'

She flopped down opposite him on a sofa. Carefully crossed her legs and gritted her teeth so that her mouth became a narrow streak.

'What is it you want? I don't have . . .'

She didn't finish the sentence. Van Veeteren felt another surge of doubt, but resisted it and allowed it to drift away.

'Your husband . . . I understand the police have told you who he really was.'

She made a vague movement of the head, and he was unsure if it was an acknowledgement or a denial.

'The fact that his real name was Jaan G. Hennan, and that he had a past you didn't know about.'

'What exactly do you want?' she asked. 'Are you a police officer as well? I don't think I—'

'I used to be,' interrupted Van Veeteren. 'I had quite a bit to do with your husband in that capacity.'

She frowned.

'I don't really understand.'

'You were interviewed by the police the other day, weren't you? At the gallery.'

'Yes, I was. But what . . . ?'

'What conclusions did you draw from that?'

'Conclusions? Why should I draw any conclusions?'

'But it must have made you think.'

'I suppose it did, yes . . .'

He waited, but she didn't elaborate. Instead she leaned back on the sofa and lit a cigarette.

Just how sedated is she? he wondered. He decided to try a somewhat heavier-handed approach.

'You weren't surprised, were you?'

'By what?'

'The fact that your husband committed suicide.'

'What do you mean . . . ?'

'Or that he had a criminal past?'

She drew on her cigarette, and the way she did so surprised him.

Or rather, the way she sat there, leaning back and observing him. As if his words had simply passed over her head. He repeated the question.

'You knew that your man had another identity besides Christopher Nolan, didn't you? Even before the police told you about it.'

She took a deep breath.

'Of course not. Who are you? I must ask you to leave me in peace now.'

All three sentences in the same breath. Van Veeteren said nothing for a few seconds. She inhaled again, but made no move to stand up or show him out.

'Didn't your husband tell you that I'd been to see him?'

'That you . . . ? Why should you go to see him?'

'Because we had a few things to talk about.'

New pause. He let the seconds pass by.

'I'm sorry, but what did you say your name was?'

'Van Veeteren. Are you sure your husband never mentioned my name these past few days?'

She seemed to be thinking that over.

'Certainly not. He didn't talk about any new acquaintances at all.'

'On the contrary, fru Nolan. I'm a very old acquaintance, I thought I had made that clear.'

She said nothing, but her mouth twitched several times.

'And no doubt they told you at the hospital this morning it is perfectly clear that your husband was called something different fifteen years ago?'

No reaction.

'That he took on the identity of Christopher Nolan in order to shake off his past. The fact that you still seem to doubt that doesn't make a very good impression, fru Hennan.'

He said the name as carefully as . . . as when one moves a harmless knight from a square on the chessboard where it has been standing for fifteen years, and she reacted too late.

Two seconds, that couldn't be blamed on any medicine known to man.

But also a move whose consequences he hadn't foreseen either. Dammit all, he thought.

'Hennan? What did you say . . . ?'

He took out his cigarette machine. Put it on the table in front of him and began filling it with tobacco. Thoughts were buzzing around inside his head now, and he needed something to occupy his hands. Elizabeth Nolan sat there motionless, looking at him.

'You lied to them, didn't you?'

No reply.

'You knew about his background, didn't you?'

She smoked and gazed past him, out through the window. He lit his cigarette and tried quickly to think of what to say next. He realized suddenly that a crucial point was looming.

Crucial? he thought. Could it be . . . ?

'I must ask you to leave me in peace now,' she said again. 'I don't know what you're talking about.'

He ignored her interruption. The noise from the neighbour's lawnmower suddenly ceased, and the silence became as noticeable as a stranglehold.

'You know exactly what happened to Maarten Verlangen as well, don't you?'

The questions were tumbling out more or less automatically now. He realized that her resistance was broken. He could see that by looking at her. She dropped her shoulders and looked him in the eye. Several seconds passed, then she shook her head slowly and sighed deeply.

'All right, Chief Inspector Van Veeteren. Blame yourself.'

She must have had the pistol tucked down between the cushions on the sofa, as he didn't detect it until she was holding it in her hand, pointing it at him from only a metre away.

'It was idiotic of you to come here,' she said.

Something had moved inside Bausen, and at first he didn't realize what it was. Then it dawned on him that it was Van Veeteren's invitation to celebrate Christmas in Maardam.

Him and Mathilde. Together with Van Veeteren and Ulrike. Maybe others as well, he didn't know. And he didn't know why this should be so remarkable: but the somewhat sentimental feeling nagging away inside his skull was incontestable.

Or inside his chest, or wherever. My God, he thought: I'm nearly seventy-four, I should be too old for this sort of thing. But perhaps you get a bit more emotional as you get older.

In the afternoon he spent three-quarters of an hour doing yoga exercises, then he telephoned Mathilde and asked if she'd like to come round for a bite to eat that evening. They hadn't seen each other for a week, and she accepted without further ado. He could hear that she sounded pleased.

He drove down to Fisktorget, bought a kilo of line-caught fish, some mussels and fresh vegetables. Then he drove out to Wassingen to fetch her. Folded up her wheelchair as usual and put it in the boot, and carried her out to the car.

It occurred to him that he hadn't mentioned to Van

Veeteren that she was wheelchair-bound, and wondered why not. Did the fact that he had kept it to himself signify something, and in that case, what?

Ah well, there were three-and-a-half months to go before Christmas. If the trip to Maardam actually did come off, there was plenty of time to sort that detail out on the telephone.

Together, they began preparing the fish. He had made various changes in the kitchen since they met, to make it easier for Mathilde to move around. They each drank a glass of Alsace wine while they were busy with the cooking, and while they were doing so it occurred to him that he was in love with her.

In the autumn of his life he was unable to find any other word for it: but so what? *Love* was as good a word as any other, surely?

He told her as much as well, just as they sat down at the table, and she said that she had come across worse blokes than he was. One or two, at least. He laughed, walked round the table and kissed her.

They had just opened bottle number two when Ulrike Fremdli rang. It was a quarter to nine.

'Bausen?'

'Yes.'

They had spoken two or three times before, but never more than a few words.

This time it was rather more. In view of the reason for the call.

According to what she said, Van Veeteren still hadn't turned up in Maardam. In fact. Despite his promise to be home around five o'clock. And he wasn't answering his mobile. Something must have happened.

'He did mention that there was something wrong with it,' said Bausen.

'His mobile?'

'Yes.'

'What time did he leave Kaalbringen?'

Bausen thought for a moment.

'About half past twelve. Yes, he ought to have been back home ages ago.'

'I don't understand why he hasn't been in touch.'

Nor did Bausen. But he could hear from Ulrike Fremdli's voice that she was more worried than she was trying to seem, and he tried to calm her down by suggesting that there might be something wrong with the car.

He assured her that he would let her know the moment he heard anything – but no doubt it wasn't anything serious.

He said nothing about Christmas – after all, it was only 8 September.

What the hell has happened? he thought when he had replaced the receiver. Has he driven off the road, and is lying helpless in a ditch somewhere?

No, no, he thought as he turned his attention back to Mathilde. We mustn't make things worse than they are.

47

'Very idiotic,' she said again, and once more he noticed how there was an infinitely small twitching of the muscles at the side of her mouth. Butterfly-light stimuli like the puff of a breeze on the surface of a lake.

There was not much more that he noticed. Just a feeling that her judgement was absolutely correct – he really did feel like an idiot – and a certain increasing impression that had to do with his perceptions. Reminiscent of tunnel vision. His surroundings – the furniture, the garish walls covered in paintings, the picture window looking out on the garden and the municipal forest – all seemed to shrink away and dissolve into a vague blur. The only thing that seemed to him to be real, the only thing that was anywhere close to being in focus was the fact that he was sitting in this wine-red armchair opposite this woman dressed in black, pointing her gun steadily at him.

A Pinchmann, if he was not much mistaken, 7.6 millimetres. There was nothing to suggest that Maarten Verlangen had not also become acquainted with it. Nothing at all.

'I understand,' he said.

Which was an obvious lie. She raised an eyebrow and he could see that she also doubted if he understood.

'Let me make one thing quite clear,' she said. 'I know how to use this pistol, and I won't hesitate to use it. If you like I can shoot you in the leg right now, so that you don't need to have any doubt on that score.'

'That won't be necessary,' said Van Veeteren. 'I believe you.'

One corner of her mouth twitched a little more strongly, but no smile came into being.

'Good. You have lived most of your life, after all, and seem to be a sensible man. Until now, that is.'

He made no reply. She appeared to think for a while, then took out a cigarette and lit it using only one hand.

I must talk to her, Van Veeteren thought. Must. Silence is not my ally on this occasion.

'Verlangen?' he said.

'What about him?'

'That private detective. What happened to him?'

She moistened her lips with the tip of her tongue and hesitated for a moment.

'He saw us,' she said.

'In Maardam?'

'Yes. Pure coincidence, but I suppose it had to happen sooner or later.'

'When was that?'

'In March. Somewhere around the middle of the month. We had gone there to look at some pictures left by somebody who had just died.'

'But surely you can't have recognized him? It was—'

'Of course not,' she said, interrupting him and sounding slightly annoyed. 'But he told us about it later. Do you happen to have a mobile phone in your jacket pocket?'

Van Veeteren took it out and put it on the table.

'It's not working.'

She picked it up and studied it for a few seconds, then found the right button and switched it off.

'Just in case,' she said. 'Anyway, you and Verlangen seem to be birds of a feather. He couldn't let sleeping dogs lie.'

'Several of us suffer from that weakness,' admitted Van Veeteren. 'Do you mind if I smoke as well?'

'Not at all. Here, have one of mine so that you don't need to use that nasty little machine.'

He did as he was bidden, and noticed as he lit the cigarette that his hands were less than steady. No wonder, he thought.

'He came up here after you, I take it. Verlangen.'

She nodded.

'Yes. The idiot. He was no doubt egged on by that old detective streak of his, and of course it wasn't especially difficult to track us down once he had got wind of us. Not even for him. He turned up one evening in April, claiming he was some sort of market researcher ... It only took a few minutes for us to realize who he really was.'

'And you shot him?'

She inhaled and paused before answering.

'My husband took care of that. It's a pity he made a mess of hiding the body.'

Van Veeteren pricked up his ears on hearing that last

sentence. The way she said it made it quite clear who had been the driving force in their marriage.

Absolutely clear.

It also made it clear, unfortunately, what kind of an opponent she was. He knew that she wouldn't make any mistakes when it came to hiding his body.

Everything, he thought. I've misjudged everything. For fifteen years.

And now I'm going to get my punishment.

She stubbed out her cigarette and stood up.

'Stand up now, please.'

He raised himself out of the armchair.

'Take off all your clothes apart from your underpants.'

'I haven't carried a gun for five years.'

'Do as I say.'

As he carried out her instructions, she stood two metres away, watching him. Without moving a muscle. He threw his garments over the back of the chair, one after another, but even when he ended up by standing there in nothing but his underpants and his misery she just stood there without so much as a smile.

'All right,' she said. 'You can get dressed again.'

He performed the same procedure in reverse, somewhat long-windedly, then sat down in the armchair again. Without releasing him from her gaze or from the aim of her pistol, she took a small bottle from her handbag, which was lying beside her on the sofa. She also produced a carafe and a glass from a low table at the side of the sofa. She poured out a couple of centimetres – he assumed that it was whisky – and dropped in four or five tablets from the bottle. They started to dissolve immediately in the brown liquid. She stirred the brew with a propelling pencil that she also took from her handbag. It all seemed quite routine, he thought, as if she were performing some mechanical exercise that she had carried out thousands of times before.

My Last Supper, he thought.

'Here you are, drink this,' she said, sliding the glass over to his side of the table.

He stared at the barrel of the pistol. Actually recalled having seen the exit hole of a bullet in the back of the head of a man who had been shot with a Pinchmann. It was rather large, if he remembered rightly.

If I'd been thirty I would no doubt have made a lunge at her now, he thought.

And become no older . . .

He took a deep breath, closed his eyes and emptied the glass. And noted that his guess as to the spirit involved was correct.

Rather a good whisky, in fact. As far as he could judge, the tablets tasted of nothing.

'Good,' he said. 'Possibly a bit on the smoky side.'

She shrugged. They remained sitting there for several minutes without speaking, and the last thing he registered was that the neighbour had started mowing the lawn again.

'I have the feeling we've missed something,' said Rooth.

'You have drunk three beers and a large cognac,' said Münster, signalling to the waiter that they would like the bill. 'That's why you are imagining things.'

'Rubbish,' said Rooth. 'It's been at the back of my mind since yesterday, there's something I ought to have thought of . . . I've had that feeling before, and it's hardly ever been wrong.'

'Do you think you could express yourself a little more clearly?' wondered Münster.

'More clearly? As I said, I don't really know exactly what it's about . . . You sometimes get a little nudge like that which just falls down through your brain and ends up in your subconscious. Does it never happen to you?'

'All the time,' said Münster. 'And it usually stays there as well.'

'Exactly,' said Rooth. 'That's the danger. But in this case I'm determined that it won't do that. I know that I thought: "That was odd", or something along those lines . . . But I haven't had time to think it over properly.'

'No time?' said Münster. 'Surely time's the only thing we've had loads of in this confounded case.'

Rooth nodded, and tried to lick the inside of his cognac glass clean.

'I know,' he said, abandoning his cleansing attempts. 'But it would be a plus if I could pin down this particular detail. There are lots of question marks hovering around, after all.'

Münster said nothing for a while. Looked somewhat listlessly around the soberly furnished hotel dining room, and realized that they were the last customers. It was almost half past eleven, and he began to feel it was time to take the lift up four floors, and go to bed.

The final night in a hotel bed. Great. Over the last few days he had really missed Synn and the children: being away from them for a whole week was simply too long.

Far too long, for Christ's sake. Just a few hours at a time was all he could bear.

But there was something that couldn't be denied in what Rooth was sitting there and going on about. They *had* missed something. Or been deprived of something? he thought. Perhaps that was a better way of putting it. G had been buried in some kind of hidden agenda for fifteen years – not so much his own, but the *Chief Inspector*'s, of course – and now when they had got wind of him again, then been confronted with his suicide, well, it felt as if . . . Hmm, as if what?

As if they had been cheated out of the goodies? Münster wondered. Yes, *deprived* of something.

Namely the satisfaction of arresting him and making him answerable to his crimes. Of ensuring that Jaan G. Hennan was given the punishment he deserved.

A both reasonable and justified reaction, surely? Feeling bad about it all.

But the fact was that they hadn't solved that old murder mystery. Just what had happened when Barbara Hennan ended up at the bottom of the empty pool in Linden – that was a secret G had taken with him to his grave. It could be assumed that he had shot poor Maarten Verlangen; but no matter how you looked at it, the Linden murder was still unsolved. And would presumably remain unsolved. For ever.

All things considered, it was hardly a mystery, Münster tried to convince himself while Rooth sat there looking introverted with his eyes half closed. Hennan had hired an accomplice, they had never found him, and with his employer out of this world the actual killer could feel pretty sure that he would never be found.

No doubt it goes with the territory, Münster decided. Some criminals were never nailed, and some questions were never answered. It was annoying, but something you had to learn to live with.

'I suppose it's just this berk G who's annoying me so damned much,' said Rooth, chiming in with Münster's thoughts. 'Do you know what I'd like to do?'

'No,' said Münster.

'As with Jesus.'

'Eh? Jesus?'

'Yes. Let him be resurrected for a few days. Interrogate him non-stop and then kill him again. Just to torture the bastard. That's what he deserves.'

An interesting Bible interpretation, Münster thought, and couldn't help smiling.

'A good idea,' he said. 'You accept your rock-bottom motives at least – that's good.'

'I'm a pretty rock-bottom type,' sighed Rooth. 'In fact. I know that my chivalrous behaviour can sometimes dazzle people, but to be honest, the fact is . . .'

The waiter arrived with the bill, and Rooth abandoned his confessions. They paid, and left the dining room. In the lift up to their rooms, however, the inspector probed his sub-conscious once again.

'That thing that I don't remember,' he said. 'It must be in connection with when we found him . . . When we went dashing into the Nolans' house.'

'Why?' wondered Münster. 'Why must it have been then?'

'As you said, it's the only time all week that we were in a bit of a hurry.'

Münster thought, but could think of no comment to make.

Instead he yawned, unlocked his door and wished Inspector Rooth sweet dreams.

48

He regained consciousness.

Didn't wake up: the outside world merely shone a thin beam into his brain, no more.

Or perhaps it was not the outside world. Perhaps it was merely reflexes from his own body: fragile, undeveloped signals in the darkness and inertia. His head ached. His tongue was sticking to his gums. The tiredness in his arms and legs was devastating.

He was lying on some kind of hard sofa in a position that was extremely uncomfortable.

On his left side. His hands were tightly bound behind his back. His feet were also tied together. His ankles were rubbing against each other. The rough cover of the sofa smelled of dust, and he felt sick.

Dark. He opened his eyes one millimetre for a fraction of a second, and saw that it was just as black round about him as it was inside him.

He sank back into unconsciousness.

★

Some time later he woke up properly. His tiredness was still like a lead weight on top of him, but she was standing in a light doorway, talking to him.

Saying something to him, giving instructions.

She came up to him and placed something on a table next to his face.

'Coffee.'

That was the first word he was able to understand.

'Sit up now. Drink some coffee.'

He kept opening and closing his eyes. It hurt. He could detect the smell of coffee in his nostrils.

'Sit up.'

It seemed laughably impossible, but the pain in his backside when he tried to obey the order actually woke him up.

'I can't . . .'

His voice broke down, and he tried again.

'I can't drink when my hands are tied behind my back.'

'There's a straw in the cup.'

He leaned forward and drank.

I'm still alive, he thought.

Whatever good that will do me.

He forced his arms to the left and managed to look at his watch.

A quarter past five. In the morning, presumably. A long time must have passed. The room in which he had spent the last sixteen hours seemed to be some sort of lumber-room.

A haven for worn-out furniture, but also a link between the house itself and the garage.

When he had finished drinking, she ordered him to move into the garage. He had to jump with both feet lashed together – awkward to do and difficult to keep his balance. He was forced to lean against furniture and walls. Pains all over his body. I hope she allows me to die with some kind of dignity at least, he thought. All the time a dark curtain was threatening to fall down in front of his eyes. The urge to be sick was keeping him upright.

He caught sight of his own blue Opel. She must have moved them around, he thought. The cars. She must have backed Hennan's Rover and her Japanese car out into the street, and driven his Opel into the garage.

She must have taken the key out of his pocket while he was asleep.

He tried to check if that was the case, but was unable to reach round with his hands tied together. It was obvious in any case that she was leaving nothing to chance.

She never did. He was quite clear about that now.

When it was too late, of course.

Thinking made his headache worse. He took a deep breath with his mouth wide open and looked at his car. Noted that the boot was open.

'In you get.'

He stared at her. Stared at the pistol.

'In there?'

She nodded.

'We shan't be going far.'

'And if I refuse?'

'I'll kill you straight away.'

He thought for a few seconds.

Then he ducked down under the boot lid and crawled inside.

The sofa had been much more comfortable.

All is relative, he thought.

Could death also be relative? Perhaps.

For a few moments he thought about the possibility of escaping. But then he realized how impossible that was. It felt as if he were already buried, lying cooped up in this cramped car boot. The smell of dirt. Of oil and anti-freeze – he recalled having spilled half a litre at some point last winter, and the smell still persisted.

Pitch black and difficult to breathe, pressure on his chest . . . difficulties in moving as well, with his hands tied behind his back. There was no possibility of working them free. And even if there had been, surely it was impossible to open the lid from the inside?

She backed out into the road and stopped. Left the engine running. He heard her open the driver's door and get out. He thought about shouting, but decided against that as well. There would be nobody around at this time in the morning: the chances of anybody passing close enough to hear his feeble voice were as good as zero. He had no desire for his last action in this world to be lying in a car boot crying in vain for help.

He heard another car starting. Realized that she was restoring order. The Rover in the garage, the Japanese sports car on the drive. The intruding Opel removed from the scene.

No, she was leaving nothing to chance.

He tried to change his position, to find a posture that would be a little bit more bearable: but it was a waste of time. Instead he scraped his cheek against something sharp that was jutting out, gave up and began thinking about Erich.

It was remarkable. For some reason he had the impression that his son was watching him just now.

Not Ulrike, not Jess.

Just Erich, nobody else.

It was difficult to judge how long the journey took. The darkness – both inside and outside him – deadened his senses. The pain in his buttocks became more intense, and he doubted if he would be able to stand upright. His shoulders and upper arms seemed to be paralysed, and his head was bursting.

Quarter of an hour, perhaps? He guessed that it was probably no more than that. Not very far out of town, in other words. Ten to fifteen kilometres: the last section was uneven and bumpy – presumably a narrow dirt road through a forest or over a field.

She stopped. He heard the front door open and close again. A minute passed, then she opened the boot lid.

He turned his head and blinked at the light. Scraped his cheek again, on the same place. Varied his gaze several times between the barrel of the pistol and her face.

Speak, he thought. The longer I can manage to talk to her, the longer I have left to live.

'Get out.'

She gestured with the pistol. It took him some time to clamber to his feet. And even longer to straighten his back. He looked around in the faint light of dawn. Trees in all directions, just as he had thought: they had driven along a road that was barely wide enough for a car, with a high strip of grass in the middle of it.

Mainly beech trees, but a few others here and there. Young aspen saplings and small fir trees. Quite well tended: he guessed she had driven westwards, and when he sniffed the air he thought he could detect traces of the sea.

But maybe that was just his imagination. Maybe it was simply that he wanted to feel the presence of the sea at a time like this.

'You're not going to get away with this, you know,' he said.

'Nonsense. You're the one who's not going to get away.'

He could hear that she meant what she said. It occurred to him that he only had a few seconds to live – but then he noticed that she was holding a spade, and he suspected that she had other plans.

'Lie down on your stomach.'

With difficulty he knelt down and then fell forwards.

'Your face touching the ground.'

He did as she said. His back was in agony. But with two swift strokes of a knife she cut through the ropes. Round both his hands and his feet.

This is the moment, he thought. This is my chance to run for it – or would have been if I were thirty years old . . .

But it took quite some time to unwind the ropes and put them on one side, and when he stood up again she was standing only two metres away, and was in full control of the situation.

'Walk.'

She indicated the direction by nodding and gesturing with the pistol. He slowly straightened his back so that he was able to walk, and set off up the steep path.

The vegetation became more dense. There were more twigs and branches everywhere. He began to understand what she had in mind.

He began to understand who she was.

'This will do fine.'

He stopped in the little hollow and looked around. Vision was limited to about ten metres in all directions. Dawn had not yet taken over from night. Not completely. The occasional bird could be heard, but only as an isolated sound in the distance. No wind. A lingering nocturnal chill, and thin streaks of mist that were slowly dispersing. He assumed it was not yet six o'clock, but didn't bother to check. He felt weariness once more taking possession of him.

I'm still drugged, he remembered. Gave a start when she threw the spade down in front of his feet.

'Dig.'

He looked at her.

'What if I refuse?'

I've already said that, he thought. Can't I think of better questions?

'I'll shoot you and do the digging myself.'

'You won't get away with this.'

'I won't get away with it if I allow you to carry on living.'

He thought about that. It wasn't difficult to see her point. Of course she had to kill him.

'What about Linden?' he said. 'I think you owe me an explanation of that.'

She screwed up her eyes and stared at him, raising the gun so that it was pointing at his forehead between his eyes. She stood absolutely still for several seconds, then lowered it a few centimetres.

'Dig.'

He interpreted that as a sort of agreement, and picked up the spade. He looked around for a suitable place.

Suitable? he thought. How do I want to lie?

'Where is east?' he asked.

'Why do you ask?'

'I want to lie with my head in that direction.'

She laughed.

'Over there.'

He nodded. Selected a spot where the ground seemed to be softest. If I have to dig my own grave, he thought, I don't want to have to struggle with a mass of roots and stones. That would be . . . undignified.

'Linden,' he reminded her as he dug into the ground.

She sat down on a fallen tree trunk a couple of metres

away from him and lit a cigarette – just as before using one hand and not releasing him for single second from either her gaze or the pistol.

'What do you want to know?' she asked.

49

Rooth was woken up by church bells.

At least he thought – for one lovely and hope-filled second – that they were church bells. He had been dreaming about his own marriage to a slightly olive-skinned woman by the name of Beatrice – she shared so many traits with his old classmate from grammar school, Belinda Freyer, with whom he had been in love for as long as he could remember – and it was in the middle of the ceremony, in a crammed full church, with jubilant heavenly choirs and a bride dressed in white, that the telephone rang.

He fumbled over the bedside table, switched on a lamp and discovered that it was no more than 6.15.

Who the hell rings at a quarter past six in the morning? he thought.

And what the hell is the significance of dreaming about church bells at that time?

He discovered that the telephone was quite some way away on the narrow desk. He thrust aside the duvet and heaved himself up, and it was just as he heard Münster's voice in the receiver and saw his own chalk-white face in the mirror over the desk – at precisely that very brief split second – that the penny dropped and he identified the missing link that had been hovering somewhere in the back of his mind for several days.

That detail.

Everything went black before his eyes.

'Hang on a moment,' he said to Münster.

He leaned forward, and took a grip on himself.

'What's the matter?'

'I'm sorry,' said Rooth. 'I had a little dizzy fit. I think I jumped up too quickly . . .'

'I understand,' said Münster. 'I know it's damnably early in the morning, but we have a problem.'

'Really?' said Rooth. 'A problem?'

'Van Veeteren hasn't come home to Maardam. It seems . . . well, it seems as if something has happened to him.'

Rooth glared at his face again. It was not a pretty sight, but he couldn't give a toss about that at the moment.

'The *Chief Inspector*?' he said. 'Not come home? What are you saying?'

'Bausen rang a quarter of an hour ago,' Münster said. 'He'd spoken to Ulrike Fremdli down in Maardam . . . No, something has obviously happened. He left here shortly after lunch yesterday: all the hospitals and so on have been checked. But he's . . . well, he's simply disappeared.'

Rooth could feel the synapses groping after one another in his brain. Digging and rummaging away after a link. Van Veeteren had disappeared . . . and he had suddenly realized what it was that he'd seen but hadn't been able to see the significance of . . .

Could it . . . ?

Why should . . . ?

The digging and rummaging came to a halt and uncovered a message.

'Bloody hell!' he said. 'Let me think for a second . . . I think I've hit upon something.'

'Hit upon something?'

Münster sounded doubtful.

'Yes.'

'Out with it then! This is beginning to look like . . . like I don't know what.'

'Come in to me two minutes from now and I'll explain everything,' said Rooth. 'Bloody hell!'

Then he hung up and checked the colour of his face in the mirror one more time.

Then he washed himself very quickly and started to get dressed.

'I feel awful,' said Münster. 'This is ridiculous. I don't know if I'm awake or dreaming.'

'You have your clothes on in any case,' said Rooth. 'We'd better assume that we're both awake.'

'Okay. What was it you'd hit upon?'

Rooth buttoned up his shirt ostentatiously and put on his shoes before answering. Münster watched him impatiently. For a brief bizarre second he considered assisting him, but decided not to.

'Fru Nolan,' said Rooth. 'There's something about Eliza-beth Nolan that doesn't add up.'

'Why?'

'I said there was something nagging away at the back of my mind, and when you rang I realized what it was.'

'When I rang?'

'Precisely then, yes. I jumped up out of bed to answer the phone, and everything went black before my eyes. But I happened to see my face in the mirror. It was white, or a sort of grey.'

'Really?' said Münster. 'And?'

'And then I thought about fru Nolan. When she came run-ning out of the house . . . after she had found her husband dead in the bath. It was Moerk and I who had been sitting outside—'

'Yes, I know that,' said Münster. 'But what didn't add up?'

Rooth cleared his throat.

'The colour,' he said.

'The colour?'

'The colour, yes. She passed out and lay there on the lawn . . . I took a quick look at her before I continued into the house. She was red in the face.'

'Really?'

'Really? Is that all you can come up with? I must say you disappoint me. How can you be red in the face when you've fainted? If all the blood leaves your face, you go pale for God's sake!'

Münster stared at him for three seconds. Rooth stared back.

'So you mean that . . .'

'I mean that she was play-acting. She didn't pass out at all, dammit! There's something dodgy about Elizabeth Nolan, and if Van Veeteren has disappeared now, it could well be that—'

'Good God!' interrupted Münster, taking his mobile out of his pocket. 'That must mean that . . .'

He didn't complete the sentence. Fell silent and rang Bausen's number. Bausen answered after one ring, but Münster had time to wonder why he had chosen Bausen rather than deKlerk.

Perhaps it was simply because that number was still in the phone after the call twenty minutes ago?

Or perhaps there was some other reason.

It didn't take long to fill Bausen in. Münster explained that he and Rooth were about to leave for Wackerstraat, and he asked Bausen to inform deKlerk and Inspector Moerk.

Bausen sounded as flabbergasted as Münster felt.

So they thought Van Veeteren had gone to see Elizabeth Nolan rather than going straight home to Maardam, did they? What did that mean?

Münster replied that he had no idea what it meant, nor what might have happened – but as he said that he felt himself overcome by a sort of icy cold wave so strong that for a moment he wondered if he was having a heart attack.

Then he realized that it must have been something mental

– he wasn't even fifty years old yet – said goodbye to Bausen and hung up.

Rooth was fully dressed by now and ready to leave.

'Tell me what this means,' said Münster. 'If you are right, that is. Does it mean that . . . that Jaan G. Hennan didn't in fact kill himself, or . . . or what the hell are you trying to say?'

'I'm not trying to say anything at all,' said Rooth. 'I'm just trying to get ready to see how things look out there at the Nolans' house. Okay? Are you coming with me, or do you want to go back to bed?'

'All right,' said Münster. 'What are we waiting for?'

50

'I'm beginning to understand that there was a fair amount of planning behind it all.'

She smoked and seemed still to be wondering whether or not to talk to him. Van Veeteren waited.

'A fair amount,' she said in the end.

'More than was necessary in connection with Philomena McNaught?'

She allowed herself a faint smile, and suddenly, thanks to this unpremeditated reaction, he saw her for what she was. In her entirety, inside and out . . . It was as if she had hitherto managed to hide behind her disguise. But now . . . It was remarkable.

Lady Macbeth, he thought. Nice to meet you.

'Dig,' she reminded him. 'If I'm going to explain a few things to you, I expect you to keep working while I do so.'

'Of course.'

He started by measuring out the outlines. Scratched out an oblong shape with the edge of the spade – about two metres by sixty centimetres. He realized it was going to take quite a while. At least twenty minutes, perhaps half an hour.

His allotted time.

Assuming she didn't lose her patience and shoot him sooner than that.

'I'm sorry I needed to kill him,' she said. 'It was your fault – yours and that damned private detective's. But he seemed to weaken somehow.'

Aha, he thought. She feels a need to explain herself.

'Weaken? Hennan?'

'Yes. It happened as he got older.'

He thought for a moment.

'Men grow gentler with age,' he said. 'So do some women, I think. But if there is any of your victims that you don't need to feel sorry for, surely it's your husband?'

She regarded him with an expression he was unable to interpret.

Indifference? Contempt for men in general?

Or was she sitting there and wondering whether to increase the pressure on the trigger slightly? He thought it looked like it. Now, he thought. The time has come.

But nothing happened.

'Don't get any ideas into your head!' she said after a while. 'Don't get any ideas at all. If you start getting awkward I'll shoot you without further ado.'

For a moment he tried to imagine what it would feel like when the bullet entered into him.

Pain. A brief, white-hot pain of course – but where? Where would it begin, where would it spread to, and would he lose consciousness before he was actually dead?

Would it be all over in one second, or five?

He suppressed the thought. No matter what happened, there was no need to experience it twice.

'Linden,' he said again. 'How did you manage that?'

She dropped her cigarette end on the ground and stamped it down into the soft soil. Changed her position on the fallen tree trunk. If I can get close enough to her, he thought, I can attack her with the spade.

One chance in a hundred, but those are the best odds I'm ever going to get.

'She was a whore,' she said. 'Her name was Betty Fremdel – we collected her from Hamburg.'

'Hamburg?'

'Yes. We needed to go abroad, of course, so as to avoid the risk of anybody putting two and two together. We spent several weeks up there before we found her. But there are quite a few of her sort around the Hauptbahnhof . . . Even a few who are not drug addicts – or there were at that time at least. Once we had chosen her, it was easy.'

'What did you tempt her with?'

'Making a film. Pornography, of course. We didn't give her any details, but we paid her well . . . Very well. And discretion was the order of the day, needless to say: she wasn't allowed to tell anybody what it was all about, or where she was going . . . She didn't know herself, naturally. All she knew was that she was going to be away for a few days, making a film.'

She paused and seemed to be thinking it over.

'I collected her up in Oostwerdingen and drove her down to Linden. I was wearing a blonde wig, it never dawned on her how similar we looked . . . I had made a point of dying my hair the same awful reddish tint as hers . . . And I even had a copy of her tattoo done on my arm – no, as I said, it was all pretty straightforward. And we'd waited a month before setting it up as well.'

She fell silent again. Van Veeteren thought over what she had said, but couldn't think of any comment to make.

'She was encouraged to wander around the house for an hour or two and drink a fair amount and leave fingerprints all over the place. Eventually we climbed up into the tower where we were going to take a few pictures . . . we'd set up a camera there. She got undressed and put on the swimming costume. I stood behind the camera and pretended to film her, and as she stood there posing and showing herself off, I gave her a shove. I went down to check that she was dead, then I drove off and kept out of the way. Nobody had any doubt about it being me who was lying there at the bottom of the swimming pool. Did they?'

Van Veeteren stood up straight.

Good God, he thought. So incredibly straightforward. So brilliantly simple. Was it really possible?

'Did they?' she said again.

He realized that it was indeed possible. He recalled that they had tried to get dental records from the USA, but had never received anything. Not as far as he could remember, at least. No, she was right. Nobody had been in any doubt about it being Barbara Hennan lying there in that damned empty swimming pool. Nobody at all.

And that was why he was going to die?

After fifteen years of pondering, he now had the solution to the G File. He had received it from the murderer herself, and the price was going to be his own life.

It was as if there were a sort of justice in that.

Some logic, at least.

'What about the identification?' he asked nevertheless, mainly in order to keep the conversation going.

His final conversation.

'Surely you remember that,' she said. 'I wasn't present personally, but according to my husband everything went according to plan. As everybody suspected him of the murder, the question of the identity of the dead body was never raised. Verlangen swallowed everything – lock, stock and barrel. We had thought that he might be able to help us with the identification, but it wasn't needed. It was enough with Jaan and that awful woman next door.'

'Yes, I remember her,' said Van Veeteren. 'Fru Trotta. But he identified you fifteen years later instead, didn't he? Verlangen, that is.'

She gestured that he should continue digging, and he took hold of the spade once more. He had removed the surface layer now. Dug down a few centimetres and not yet encountered an impossible root or large stone. It will be obvious that this is a grave, he thought. Maybe they will find me one of these days, and move me?

'Yes, he did,' she said. 'It cost him his life and two others besides . . . And she hasn't been resurrected, that prostitute. Can you see any point in him starting rooting around again?'

Van Veeteren had a fleeting memory of something he had discussed with Bausen years ago. During the axe-murderer case nine years ago.

About equations that should be left unsolved.

Chess games that should never be concluded.

Bausen had maintained that there were quite a lot of such phenomena, and that they had to be accepted. He had not been so sure.

And now here he was with the solution to the G File (Equation? Chess game?), and his own death was baked into the answer. Like that of Verlangen and G himself.

Yes, there was a certain logic in it. A necessity in a diabolical pattern.

Or was it a quite trivial pattern? And a quite banal evil? Why exaggerate things?

'I hated him,' he said. 'Your husband, that is. I take it you know that he raped his little sister regularly for five years? He killed a little boy when we were at school as well.'

She didn't react. Not as far as he could tell, at least. And he reminded himself that he was standing there talking to Lady Macbeth. Perhaps she had known about the little sister, perhaps not.

'My husband didn't hate you,' she said after a lengthy silence. 'He was merely contemptuous of you – so am I. You mustn't think that all this talking will do you any good.'

'Did you kill Philomena McNaught as well? Or was it him?'

She suddenly looked scornful. As scornful as a bad actor at an unsuccessful audition.

'Together,' she said. 'We did it together. She was a terrible woman. Dig now, I'm growing tired of waiting.'

He thought for a moment. Then did as he was bidden.

Münster pulled up, switched off the engine and prayed a silent prayer. Glanced at Rooth, who had spent most of the six-minute drive from See Warf to Wackerstraat biting his nails and asking him to drive faster.

Rooth took his fingers out of his mouth and opened the door.

'No messing about,' he said. 'Let's go, for Christ's sake.'

They walked abreast over the flagstones leading to the front door. Münster could detect no sign of life anywhere, just a vague feeling of sickness pulsating inside him. On the outside a pale, early autumn morning: dawn-grey, luke-warm and not a breath of wind.

A morning just like any other. He assumed that some people here and there in this well-heeled part of town must be up and about. It was almost seven o'clock: no doubt some house-owners were in the shower while others were sitting at the breakfast table with the newspaper spread out in front of them, trying to raise enough energy to face up to a new day. Yet another one.

It was difficult to judge the situation inside the Nolans' house, but Rooth placed his finger on the doorbell button and held it there for five seconds – surely that ought to arouse some kind of reaction.

But it didn't. Münster and Rooth stared first at each other, then at the brown-stained wooden door while they waited. But nothing happened.

Rooth tried ringing again.

Marched nervously on the spot as they waited once again.

'Nix,' said Münster. 'Either she's not at home, or she doesn't want to see us. What shall we do?'

Rooth was about to ring yet again, but desisted.

'I don't know,' he said. 'What do you think?'

Münster tried to shrug, but found he was so tense that he couldn't.

'We could check with the neighbours,' he suggested. 'Find out if they've seen anything.'

'What would they have seen?'

'The *Chief Inspector*, of course . . . or his car, at least. Isn't that what we want to know about?'

Rooth suddenly looked dejected.

'Yes, I suppose so. But we don't want to start knocking on doors, for God's sake! I think we should go in.'

'Go in?' said Münster, cautiously trying the door handle. 'It's locked.'

'I didn't necessarily mean through the door,' said Rooth.

'Really?' said Münster, pondering for a couple of seconds. Then he took out his mobile.

'What are you doing?' asked Rooth.

'Ringing deKlerk. I think he ought to have a say in this, in any case.'

Rooth scratched his head as Münster keyed the number.

'Just inform him,' he said as deKlerk answered. 'That will suffice – tell him we're going in. Don't let him start humming and hawing and making a decision, that will only waste time unnecessarily.'

Münster nodded. Rooth started walking round the house, looking for alternative entry points.

51

He dug a few spadefuls in silence. His back ached more with every movement now, but in view of what lay in store he simply ignored it. As long as I'm in pain I'm still alive, he told himself. He had started sweating as well, but didn't want to take off his jacket. A diffuse idea of it being cold down in the ground was in the back of his mind: presumably that was what held him back.

'You needn't have involved Verlangen,' he said. 'It would have worked even so.'

'Rubbish. Jaan had good reason to punish him ... And besides, he was necessary, of course.'

He suspected that she was reluctantly keen to convince him of that. As if she felt a need to justify her actions, despite everything.

'Why?'

'To divert the attention of the police. Jaan G. Hennan had murdered his wife, his wife had suspected something was amiss and turned to a private detective who nevertheless was unable to save her life. That was how you were supposed to see the situation, and that is how you saw it. Was there ever any suspicion that the victim might have been somebody else?'

He didn't reply, but he felt pangs of conscience inside himself. She's right, he thought. That possibility never occurred to us. Not to me nor to anybody else. Only to a drunken private detective fifteen years later. That's the way it was.

Not especially flattering.

It serves me right, he concluded. This finale is an appropriate conclusion to the whole messy business. It ought to start raining as well.

But that was evidently not the forecast for this September morning. Not for the short time he had left, at least. It was almost full daylight now – but no sun, and in no circumstances would it manage to shine into the little clearing before getting on for lunchtime. By then it would all be over and done with.

So just a pale, featureless sky. No wind, no signs. He dug a little deeper without speaking. It occurred to him that he liked the smell of soil, despite everything.

'Who was Liston?' she asked suddenly.

'Liston?'

'Yes. Verlangen went on about somebody called Liston. He was supposed to have received money from my husband.'

Van Veeteren straightened his back and leaned with his elbows on the spade handle.

'I've no idea.'

'Are you sure?'

'My word of honour. How did you meet, by the way?'

'Who?'

'You and Hennan.'

She hesitated for a few seconds, then decided to tell him that as well.

'It was in 1980. A few years before he married Philomena.'

'I see. So that was a bogus marriage from the very start?'

'Bogus marriage?' She burst out laughing. 'Yes, you could certainly call it that. She was an absolute nincompoop – the fact that she actually got married was something she could thank her lucky stars for.'

'You had no moral reservations?'

Her smile was now perfectly natural.

'Morals, *Chief Inspector*. You are using very weighty language indeed. Nobody mourned the death of Philomena McNaught, believe you me. We shortened her suffering in this world by some forty or fifty years . . . And how many mourners do you expect to attend the funeral of Maarten Verlangen?'

He noted that she was addressing him more formally again. He started digging once more, then remembered something else.

'Children,' he said. 'She had a child, that woman you murdered. Did you know that?'

Her smile turned into a grimace.

'Some careless prostitutes have children.'

He got the feeling that he had run out of words. She's not worth it, he thought. Not worth the effort of keeping up this macabre conversation. I mustn't let her think that I regard her with some sort of respect – like an opponent I take my hat off to.

What if she gets away with this? he suddenly thought. With five people's lives on her conscience. Mine as well.

Perhaps there are more? – In England, for instance: they had spent some time there, after all. But he didn't want to ask her about that. Didn't want to say anything else at all. Or to know any more.

Nevertheless, as he carried on digging he tried to assess how probable it was. That she would get away with it. He realized that his analytical capabilities were not at their best in the given circumstances, but the odds seemed to be very much in her favour. Surely that was the case?

Dammit all, he thought. If these were my memoirs, what a dreadful conclusion that would be. The one and only *Chief Inspector* lowers the curtain on his only unsolved case by allowing himself to be killed by Lady Macbeth. It's a good job I shelved my scribbling. A good job that I resigned as a police officer.

But it wasn't his memoirs or his career that this was all about: it was about his life. Nothing else.

Erich? mumbled a voice somewhere inside him. Are you still looking down at me, my son?

He heard no answer, but nevertheless made up his mind how the final scene would appear. There was no reason to delay things any longer. Time had run out. He could feel the sweat pouring down his back.

One chance in a hundred, he had already decided.

At most.

★

'What should we do?' said Bausen. 'I have no doubt about that at all. We must send out an urgent S.O.S. message on every damned radio and television channel you can find, asking for information about Van Veeteren and his car. Without delay! This is not just some sort of coincidence, and if there's anything in what Rooth claims, it could be urgent – absolutely top priority urgent!'

It could also be too late, he thought; but he didn't say that.

'All right,' said deKlerk. 'I'd already intended to do that, of course. But what else should we do, I meant?'

'What else?' muttered Bausen. 'We must help Rooth and Münster. Check with the neighbours to see whether anybody noticed a blue Opel in Wackerstraat yesterday . . . And we can also cross our fingers – and arms and legs and eyes and everything else. Would you like me to come to the station?'

DeKlerk hesitated for half a second.

'Yes, please,' he said. 'That would be best, I suppose.'

Münster and Rooth entered the Nolans' house via a ventilation window at the back.

They then spent five or six minutes wandering aimlessly around from room to room in the vain hope of stumbling upon something that could give an indication of what had happened.

Always assuming that anything at all had happened.

'What are we looking for?' Münster wondered.

'I'm damned if I know,' said Rooth. 'But if you find whatever it is, I'll let you know.'

'Good,' said Münster. 'I have always admired your ability to explain things.'

Rooth didn't respond. Münster looked around the spacious living room. There was no trace of Elizabeth Nolan – not as far as they could see, in any case.

Or rather, nothing that suggested where she might have gone. Naturally there were plenty of conceivable legitimate reasons for her not being at home – they had already ascertained that the two cars, the Rover and the Japanese, were in their usual places in the garage and on the drive: but this was a fact that didn't really throw light on very much. There were buses and trains, for example. Not to mention aeroplanes, if one had reason to travel rather further away. When Münster checked for the third time that fru Nolan was not in her bed, nor hanging in the wardrobe in her bedroom, he began to feel frustrated over the situation.

'We're getting nowhere,' he said to Rooth, who had just come out of the bathroom for the second time. 'We're farting around like a pair of idiots. We're wasting our time here. We must find something more rational to do.'

Rooth shrugged helplessly, and looked out of the window in time to see Beate Moerk and Probationer Stiller getting out of a car.

'Reinforcements,' he said. 'Now there are four of us. Shall we take a neighbour each after all . . . and hope that they haven't already left for work?'

Münster looked at his watch. It was twenty past seven, and he was still feeling sick. It had got worse, in fact.

'All right,' he said. 'I suppose it can't do any harm.'

★

'Coffee?' asked deKlerk.

Bausen shook his head and sat down at the desk opposite his thirty-year-younger successor.

'The S.O.S. messages have been sent out,' said deKlerk. 'They'll be broadcast in news bulletins on the telly and the radio every half hour until—'

'I know,' said Bausen, interrupting him. 'I heard it in the car on the way here. What's happening in Wackerstraat?'

'They're busy interviewing the neighbours. Fru Nolan wasn't at home. That doesn't necessarily imply anything, but for the moment we have no other clues to follow up.'

Bausen nodded dejectedly.

'It's enough, I fear,' he said. 'If we take Rooth's little detail seriously, and assume she in fact only pretended to pass out, well . . . In that case Elizabeth Nolan isn't somebody to take lightly.'

'It's only quite a small detail,' suggested deKlerk.

'Maybe. But that doesn't matter. We have an either-or situation, as they say.'

'Either-or?'

'Yes. If Rooth was right, we mustn't make light of it. She tried to give the impression of being in shock, but in fact she wasn't. That can only mean one thing. The death of her husband was not a surprise to her . . . And the next step isn't difficult to take either.'

'You mean she killed him?' said deKlerk.

'We can take that as a hypothesis. For the moment, at least. And that she presumably had good reasons for doing it . . . And so on. No matter how we think about it, it must all go back to that business fifteen years ago. Don't ask me how. But for heaven's sake, I've got to know Van Veeteren pretty well over the years, and I'll be damned if he's the kind of person who just disappears into thin air for no good reason.'

'What do you think act—' began deKlerk, but was interrupted by the telephone ringing.

He picked up the receiver and listened. Put his hand over the mouthpiece and informed Bausen in a stage whisper:

'A woman with information. In connection with the S.O.S.'

He continued listening, asked a few questions and wrote down notes for a few minutes. Bausen leaned back on his chair and watched him attentively – and as it became clear what the call was all about, he began to feel something loosening up inside him. As if he had been holding his breath all morning.

Or had a firmly clenched fist in the middle of his solar plexus.

At last, he thought. At last something is being resolved in connection with this damned business.

But for God's sake, don't let . . .

He never formulated the thought. He didn't need to.

'I've finished now.'

She stood up from her place on the fallen tree trunk.

'How do you know that?'

He clambered up out of the grave, stretched his back muscles cautiously and took hold tightly of the spade handle with both hands. Was careful to ensure that the blade didn't sink into the ground, but simply rested on a tussock of grass.

'I don't think I want to lie any deeper than that.'

She examined the grave briefly and seemed to be weighing something up. He checked his watch. It was five minutes to seven. The forest had come to life now. He perceived it in a sort of distant and semi-conscious way: by means of sensual impressions that were so subtle, he never registered them singly. Or bothered to register them. Faint noises, faint smells, faint movements.

'Close to heaven,' he said. 'I think I prefer to lie as high as possible. If it were your grave I would dig it a little deeper, of course.'

She had no answer to that. She just gritted her teeth so that her mouth became no more than a thin streak, and raised the gun.

'May I have one final wish?'

'One final wish? Let's hear it then.'

She laughed. A little nervously, despite everything. He cleared his throat and grasped the spade handle even more tightly. Tensed the muscles in his legs and arms.

'A bird. I'd like to see a bird as I die. Can you wait until one appears?'

He looked up at the pale sky above the trees. He heard her producing a sort of noise somewhere between a snort and a laugh.

Then he saw that she was also looking up at the sky.

Now, he thought.

He took a short pace forward and swung the spade.

Heard the shot and felt the pain at the same moment.

A pain so intense that he could never have imagined it. Never.

Then dazzling whiteness.

Then darkness.

52

Fru Laine was a widow, very old and as gnarled as the fruit trees that surrounded her house at the edge of the forest. When she came out onto the steps to greet them, she looked as frail and vulnerable as a spent dandelion – her transparent white hair formed a sort of halo over a face criss-crossed by a century's worth of wrinkles. Within a year or two.

But her bright eyes indicated that there were wrinkles inside her as well, Münster thought – he was the first to shake her hand.

'Well, I'll be blowed,' she chuckled, kicking aside a speckled cat that came to rub up against the visitors. 'I haven't seen as many people as this at once since my ninetieth birthday! If you want coffee you'll have to make it yourselves, as I need to take my morning nap shortly. I've been on the go since six.'

Münster nodded and assured her that wouldn't be necessary. But she was certainly right in that there were several of them. The three cars had arrived at more or less the same time. Bausen and deKlerk from the police station. Himself, Rooth, Stiller and Moerk from Wackerstraat, where they had called off the knocking on doors as soon as they heard about what fru Laine had seen.

Six of them. Yes, she was justified in her comments.

'So you saw that car, did you?' asked deKlerk. 'Where-abouts exactly? I was the one you spoke to on the telephone, incidentally.'

'Down there.'

She pointed with a crooked index finger towards the edge of the forest. Five pairs of police eyes and a pair of former police eyes stared in the direction indicated. The road that meandered down to fru Laine's house from the main road continued in diminished form – barely wide enough to allow the passage of a vehicle in fact – across the meadow and in among the tall, gently swaying aspens and beeches.

'I go for a walk every morning with Ginger Rogers,' she said in a voice loud enough for everybody to hear. 'Every damned morning. To the sea and back – we both need the exercise. Rain or shine.'

'Your dog?' wondered Bausen.

'My dog, yes. I recognize you by the way. She's fourteen years old, and a mixture of just as many different breeds . . . I sometimes have to carry her home – she's lazier than a priest, damn her . . . She's fast asleep now in front of the stove.'

'You heard the S.O.S. on the radio, is that right?' asked Inspector Moerk.

Fru Laine nodded and adjusted her false teeth with her tongue.

'I always listen to the news at half past seven. But you'll have to sort it out yourselves now – it's just a matter of following the road. The car's a couple of hundred metres into the trees. It's blue, as you said.'

Münster shook hands with her again, and thanked her. Fru Laine turned on her heel, went back to the warmth of her stove and closed the door behind her.

Stiller and Moerk were already twenty metres ahead of the others.

It was Stiller and Moerk who first came across the car. They paused and waited for the others to catch up.

'Is that it?' wondered Stiller.

'I think so,' said Moerk. 'A blue Opel, registration number—'

'That's it all right,' said Münster over her shoulder. 'Hell's bells.'

Rooth opened the driver's door and peered in.

'The keys are still in the ignition,' he said. 'Whatever that might mean.'

'Open the bonnet,' said Bausen. 'It might be worth knowing if the engine's still warm.'

Rooth put the keys in his pocket, found the right lever under the instrument panel and pulled at it. Bausen opened the bonnet and stuck in his hand. Münster did the same.

'Not quite cold,' said Bausen. 'So it can't have been standing here all night, in any case. What do you think?'

'A few hours at most,' said Münster. 'But what that implies, I don't know.'

Rooth slammed the door closed.

'Bollocks to implications,' he said. 'Let's talk about what to do next instead.'

Münster looked at the rest of those gathered there. They all seemed to be infected by the same tense unrest, the same suppressed worries that were bubbling away inside himself.

I'll never forget this, he suddenly thought. This damned morning in this damned forest will keep on cropping up in my nightmares for the rest of my life. If this were a film I'd leave the cinema now and go home right away – I don't want to be present when—

DeKlerk cleared his throat and interrupted his train of thought.

'We have to search,' he said, gesturing with his arm. 'If we take this side of the road first . . . fifteen metres in, and, well, let's keep on searching for ten or fifteen minutes. Then the other side, if we don't find . . . anything.'

He looked round at them all, hoping for agreement. He found it at last from Bausen in the form of a nod and a curse.

'All right,' said Rooth. 'Why not? What have we got in the way of weapons? If it turns out that . . .'

The rest of the sentence remained hanging in the cool morning air while each of them produced their service pistol.

'I don't have one,' said Bausen. 'But with all due respect, I don't think that matters.'

'It's up to you to do whatever you think fit,' said deKlerk.

'Shall we get going, or are you going to hang around humming and hawing any longer?' wondered Beate Moerk.

With a certain degree of ceremony they lined up along the narrow road, covering a length of about a hundred metres, and when deKlerk and Münster gave the signal from each end of the line, they set off searching among the trees.

'Make sure you keep in eye contact with the persons nearest you,' said the chief of police, 'and don't fail to shout out if you come across anything.'

Münster looked at his watch, and walked round an uprooted tree.

A quarter past eight. He felt a drop of cold sweat trickling down his brow.

It took less than five minutes, and it was Bausen who found it.

After an overgrown area of aspen and birch shoots he came to a small clearing with rye grass and fescue grass, and was confronted by a sight that made him stop short.

In front of him, only a few metres away, was a grave that had just been dug. There was no doubt about it. The hole was about two metres long and half a metre wide, and lay there like an open wound in the ground. Not especially deep – the dug-up earth was in a neat pile next to one of the long sides of the grave, and the spade was lying in the grass some distance away – but that was not the sight that made Bausen turn away and sick up the simple breakfast he had eaten that morning.

Only one-and-a-half metres away from the spot where he stood was a human head.

A woman's head with dark hair and a wide-open mouth – and equally wide-open eyes, which seemed to be staring at him in a sort of frozen surprise.

And with a sort of totally grotesque smile. Blood and bloody innards had gushed out of the neck to form a dark pool, and he was reminded fleetingly – but just as grotesquely – of a dessert he had eaten with Mathilde at Fisherman's Friend a few weeks ago.

Lemon chocolate sorbet with raspberry dressing.

Maybe that was why he vomited.

The rest of the body was two metres away, next to the spade, and it only took a second for Bausen to realize what must have happened.

How Elizabeth Nolan had been decapitated.

And then he saw Van Veeteren.

He was lying at the opposite end of the clearing. On his left side with his knees drawn up a little and his arms and hands pressed tightly against his chest. A sort of foetal position – he must have been able to move a couple of paces before collapsing, if Bausen understood correctly what had happened. And there was a pistol lying in the grass next to Elizabeth Nolan's outstretched right hand. Yes, the scenario was obvious.

Just as he came to where Van Veeteren was lying, Münster appeared from another direction.

'Good God,' he groaned, staring at Bausen, who was now kneeling by the *Chief Inspector*'s side. 'What on earth . . . ?'

Bausen raised a finger, signalling that Münster should remain silent. He leaned even more closely over the motionless body, feeling cautiously with his hands over neck and head.

Münster closed his eyes and waited. He thought for a moment that the ground was shaking under his feet, but didn't find that in the least surprising.

Not at all.

Good God, he thought. Please make sure that . . .

'He's alive!' Bausen exclaimed. 'Praise be to God, he's alive!'

Münster knelt down beside him. Didn't notice that Beate Moerk and Rooth had just appeared behind him, but did notice that Van Veeteren opened his eyes and that his lips were moving.

'He's trying to say something.'

Bausen took off his jacket and placed it almost tenderly over the *Chief Inspector*. Then he leaned as closely as possible to his face and listened. After a few seconds he straightened his back and looked at Münster.

'What's he saying?'

Bausen frowned.

'If I heard him rightly, he says he met fifteen people on the way back.'

'That he what . . . ?'

'Don't ask me. He was walking on a beach and met those people, he says. Fifteen of them. But never mind that now, ring for an ambulance – I think he's been shot in the chest. And he's been lying here quite a while. Let's hope . . . But there's not much life left in him.'

Münster stood up, but before he even had time to take out his mobile Inspector Moerk was already in touch with the emergency services.

He looked up and thought that the almost white sky felt unusually close.

He rang on her twentieth birthday, and they met a week later. A rainy October evening with smog in the air and yellow leaves on the pavements. They spoke for an hour in a restaurant in the Ku'damm, and when he left she had difficulty in believing that the past hour had been real.

That he was not just a character from some pessimistic saga or a contorted dream, a sort of shadowy figure she wouldn't place any belief in on a bright, sunny day.

Your mother, he had said: I want to talk to you about your mother.

My mother? Mami?

Did you call her Mami?

Mami, yes. Mami went missing. She has always been missing, ever since . . .

Yes, I know, he said. But you don't know what happened when she went missing, do you?

They were drinking red wine. An expensive Italian vintage. They ordered food as well, but she couldn't force it down. Only a few mouthfuls. It was the same with him: she didn't know if he put down his knife and fork in order to demonstrate his solidarity with her; but that didn't matter of course.

Who are you? she asked. Why . . . ?

But he merely shook his head, putting her off.

Then he began to tell the tale. Slowly and elaborately, with long pauses and thoughtful nods. As if he needed to sit there reliving it all while he spoke. As if it had been forgotten for ever and a day.

And then came that evening when she died, he said eventually. You did know she was dead, I assume?

She nodded somewhat vaguely. He clasped his hands and rested his chin on his knuckles.

She died while that film was being shot. Your Mami.

That's what happened.

Film? she thought. So Mami had been a film star, had she?

Fifteen years ago, he said. She was a great actress, but an accident happened. A series of remarkable circumstances resulted in the accident being hushed up.

Hushed up? Why?

What circumstances?

Circumstances, he repeated, taking a sort of ancient cigarette-making machine out of his pocket. He filled it with tobacco and paper and rolled two cigarettes without saying a word. He offered her one. She didn't normally smoke, but she accepted it.

It was a difficult role she had to play, he said. She was a gifted actress, and was just about to break through when the accident happened.

There was something about his eyes when he said that. She didn't realize it at the time, but it dawned on her later. Or perhaps she didn't want to register it when it was happening.

I'm not telling you the whole truth, said those eyes, but I'm giving you a truth that you can live with. You realize that, don't you? *It's not always necessary to question everything. Life is a story.*

She didn't respond.

Fables and stories are our way of achieving an understanding of the world, he explained. *An understanding we can cope with. And if we don't make stories out of our lives, we can sometimes break down on our journey through life. Are you with me?*

He made a strange gesture with his right arm and shoulder. As if he were in pain, or needed to stretch a muscle.

She said she understood, and he observed her seriously and at length. Then he wanted to know about her life now, and what she did. She told him that she was a student. That she had been adopted by new parents when she was six years old, and that she had received a good start in life. That she had been lucky. Despite everything.

She could see that he was encouraged by that – and suddenly a faint voice inside her whispered that . . .

. . . that maybe she wouldn't have been so lucky if Mami hadn't died. And if she hadn't ended up in that home so that Vera and Helmut could come and select just her. It was a remarkable and unpleasant thought, and she pushed it to one side.

Who are you? she asked again. *How come you know all this?*

I'm a good friend, he said. *I was a good friend of your mother's.*

Where is her grave?

There isn't a grave. Her ashes were scattered in the sea, in accordance with her wishes.

There was that look in his eyes again. She asked no more questions.

★

She remained sitting at the table after he had left. Through the rain-drenched window she watched him getting into a car parked outside in the street.

A red car. Brand new, as far as she could judge. A woman was sitting in the driver's seat. She kissed him on the cheek, and he placed his hand briefly on the back of her head.

When they had driven away, she pinched her arm twice.